ELIZABETH IN THE NEW WORLD

Maggie Mooha

www.BOROUGHSPUBLISHINGGROUP.com

ELIZABETH IN THE NEW WORLD
Copyright © 2018 Maggie Mooha

ISBN 978-1-729566-79-4

To Madonna, my sister, my traveling companion, and my friend

ACKNOWLEDGMENTS

When I first began to seriously consider writing about Elizabeth and Darcy entering the world of Fedon's Rebellion, I found the research extremely challenging. It was difficult to find accurate information about the rebellion. In fact, it was difficult finding ANY information about the rebellion. Below is a list of my primary sources.

Fedon's Rebellion 1795–96: Causes and Consequences by Edward L. Cox was used for much of my background material.

Belvidere Estate Fedon's House by Herman G. Hall was a great source of information about Fedon's Rebellion and his home at Belvidere.

Another invaluable source was Chris Buckmire, who led a tour of Grenada from which I learned so much. You may have your own Grenadan adventure by contacting him at christours@hotmail.com.

The Grenada National Museum in St. George's, Grenada, and its staff, were most helpful in my final days of research. On view there are the documents from President MacKenzie to Fedon, and also a portrait of the rebel leader.

Although the characters of Lieutenant Governor Ninian Home and his wife, and the homes they lived in and the route they took in fleeing the rebellion are accurate, I did take some liberties. Governor Home and his wife were actually childless, and she died after only two years in Grenada. Fedon did capture some fifty-one British prisoners and did execute all of them save two when his demands were not met, but there were no women among them. Fedon was a brilliant strategist and may have prevailed if the French had come to his aid. His rebellion lasted over a year.

Also, I needed information about the period and found a great deal of it in *Jane Austen's England—Daily Life in the Georgian and Regency Periods* by Roy and Lesley Adkins.

Another helpful source was the website Jane Austen's World: janeaustensworld.wordpress.com.

Many thanks to Madonna Pence, Lisa Prokop McCallister, and Joan Svoboda Wendt for all their suggestions.

Many thanks also to my editor at Boroughs Publishing Group, who taught me a great deal about getting a book in shape for publishing.

I would also like to recognize Christine King for her photographic skills.

And thank you, Jane Austen, for your amazing characters.

ELIZABETH IN THE NEW WORLD

Joy and Woe are woven fine
Clothing for the Soul Divine
Under every grief and pine
Runs a joy with silken twine.
—William Blake

Chapter 1

From his gaol cell, Wickham tried to recall the exact moment he hatched the plot. Not being a man given to self-examination, nor to reverie even, it wasn't an easy task. His mind kept drifting to the last time he had availed himself of Lydia's youthful charms. As he lay on his side, she'd held his gaze as he traced his fingers along the curve of her hip, then up her inner thigh to…

He needed to think. It had seemed like such a good plan when he'd conceived it, and now it appeared that he would hang for it. Damn that Darcy. He was always the cause of grief. Small comfort that Darcy would not live to see him swing. Small comfort. It was hard for him to believe that only a few days earlier everything was going so well.

As the first fingers of dawn crept through their London garret, Wickham opened his eyes and smiled. He was the happiest of men. It had only been a few days since he had absconded with Lydia. The girl nearly leapt into his arms at seeing him. He knew she would run off with him. He hardly had to convince her of anything. A day later they were here, and she was his.

He knew of Darcy's affection, nay obsession, for Lydia's sister, Elizabeth Bennet. He had delighted at taunting him with it at the major-general's ball. Wickham's own fancies wandered in that direction once. Elizabeth, though, was too, what was the word? Too much trouble. She had a sharp tongue and a lively wit, and what man wanted that? Yes, she was beautiful, but being easily manipulated was so much more appealing. And Lydia had her charms. Besides her youth, she was infinitely malleable. That was a much better quality in a woman than a strong will and a sharp mind.

Wickham knew that Darcy would never, ever, let anyone disgrace the Bennets, although they seemed hell-bent on disgracing themselves more often than not. At first Wickham considered deflowering Elizabeth. That would have been enjoyable, but infinitely too much effort, if Elizabeth had consented to it at all. He would probably have had to marry her, and, although that would have torn at Darcy's heart, he would still have to marry someone who would be more than a match for him. And then there was the matter of fortune.

What really was his objective? Yes, he wanted Darcy to suffer. Yes, he believed afflicting Elizabeth Bennet was the easiest way to inflict that suffering. There was something else, though. Something that was truly the heart of the matter. He needed money. He needed to have the means of a gentleman. He needed Darcy to settle him with an income. The income that he had been so unjustly denied by Mr. Fitzwilliam Darcy.

Elizabeth's sister, Lydia, would do nicely. With only a few weeks in his company, she could perform any act in the repertoire of a two-shilling whore. Her young, nubile body was his to command. He brought her to fits of ecstasy and she him. He had decided in the first week that he should be forced to marry her. Of course, he did have to listen to that constant prattling. That would change, however, when he officially became her lord and master.

Wickham's fellow officers were his willing conspirators. He gathered about him men of his ilk. They could be cajoled. They could be bought. Poor Mr. Bennet and his brother-in-law, what was his name, oh yes, Gardiner, were being sent on a veritable festival of misdirection. They would never find him because they could never bribe his cohorts enough to betray him. What a grand joke.

It was only a matter of time until the scandal was discovered and babbled about everywhere. He wished he could see Darcy's face when he heard of it. Darcy would come after him himself. He would have enough money to buy his friends. Every man had his price. At least a thousand pounds a year would be his.

He rose from his blissful encounter with darling Lydia to pour himself another drink. There was a rough banging at the door. Sure that it was the landlord wanting last week's rent, he opened it before asking who it was and clad only in his undergarments. Lydia squealed. As he turned to look at her, someone pushed him and he wobbled slightly, losing his footing. Two men walked past him.

Much to his chagrin, it was certainly not the landlord. Nor was it Darcy. How did old Mr. Bennet find him? That was not the plan. Darcy was supposed to find him. Darcy alone and Darcy would negotiate with him. That old fool Bennet. He had the instincts of a bloodhound.

He staggered to his feet and turned, and there was Bennet standing there, his daughter, still wrapped in bedsheets, sobbing at his feet. Gardiner was there too. Out of instinct, he turned toward the door. Bennet stepped in his way.

"Scoundrel," he shouted and slapped him roundly in the face. He had not expected that. It was one thing to shout at him. He could endure that. Everyone shouted at him. His regiment commander especially. The slap, though, was another matter.

"Prepare to defend yourself, sir," Wickham said, and lunged toward the sword hanging from its scabbard on the bedpost. As he drew it, Lydia screamed. It was such an ear-piercing scream that he thought every constable in the entire neighborhood would descend upon them. Gardiner, then, attempted to intervene. "Put that thing away," he shouted.

Wickham's head began pounding. *Why does everyone shout under these circumstances?* Even through his alcoholic haze, he knew this would not end well if he pursued it. Still, the man had laid hands on him.

He tried to clear his head. His sword was still in his hand. Gardiner shouted, "For God's sake, man, Bennet is unarmed."

He should have stopped for a moment. Perhaps if his head were clearer, he could think.

But he did not think, and spoke instead. "You decide the time, Bennet, and you choose the weapons. We shall meet upon the field of honor."

***

Darcy's carriage lurched. It broke him out of his reverie. What was he doing? Surely, Wickham would relent at the smell of money. Of course, he would. No shots would be fired. The lanterns clanked against the coach. It was nearly dawn.

The events of the last few weeks had changed his life forever. Elizabeth, his beloved Elizabeth, had refused him. He'd returned to

Hunsford, if not a broken man, at least one who was no fit company for gentle folk. As he dwelt in his misery, a letter arrived. It was from Mr. Bennet. That letter, and how events would unfold this morning, would determine how Darcy's life would reveal itself. *Hope or despair? Happiness or desolation?*

News had come of Wickham's elopement with Lydia, Elizabeth's sister. *She was a silly girl, typical of her breeding and*...He must strike thoughts like that from his mind. Elizabeth was raised in the same family, and she was...she was perfect. Besides, had not his own sister, Georgiana, succumbed to Wickham's charms? He had prevented that tragedy but was not vigilant enough to prevent this one. It was entirely his fault, really. Entirely his fault. He should have realized that the threat was real. Now, he hoped it was not too late.

Now, sitting in his coach, Darcy thought of the countless ways that George Wickham had tried to hurt him. Perhaps he should have given Wickham the allowance his father had recommended lo these many years ago and let him spend it or gamble it away. He would have been rid of him then, once and for all. No, he had chosen to ignore his father's wishes because of Wickham's feckless behavior, and subsequently, Wickham had extracted his revenge at every turn, even involving his own sister, Georgiana. That plot Darcy had foiled. This last one, however, would keep Elizabeth out of reach forever.

George Wickham had run away with Elizabeth's sister, Lydia. They were not married. Although Darcy had offered his services in searching for Lydia, he had arrived in London too late. Elizabeth's father had found the couple in some stinking lair in London, and one thing had led to another. Now Darcy was forced to be a second in a duel. A second for poor Mr. Bennet.

No matter how this turned out, no good could come of it. If Mr. Bennet killed Wickham, Lydia would still be disgraced and have no hope of marrying. That would compromise or ruin her sisters. There would be even more of an impediment to his marrying Elizabeth. Marry her? She had refused him. *Oh, Elizabeth.*

If Mr. Wickham killed Mr. Bennet, which was much more likely, then there would be no hope for Lydia. Wickham would leave her in an instant, and all the Bennet girls would not only be unmarriageable but also eventually without a home, because Mr. Bennet's estate was entailed to Mr. Collins.

There was one way that something positive could come of the entire affair. Darcy could intercept Wickham before the duel and offer him money to marry the simpering Lydia. Once the marriage was accomplished, the duel would be all but forgotten and the Bennet sisters would be saved from disgrace.

Wickham's words, however, rang in his head. Wickham's plan all along was to hurt the Bennets to exact his revenge upon him. He was sure of it. Again, he felt a pang of guilt. Why had he been silent? Had he told of George Wickham's plot to run off with his sister Georgiana and make off with her fortune, the Bennets would have avoided Wickham like the plague. It was spilt milk now. He must think of a way out of this predicament.

Two things that Darcy could rely upon worked in his favor. One was that Wickham was mercenary. The other was that Wickham was a coward. He had no honor. It suddenly became clear to him. He knew what he must do. With his walking stick, he rapped on the carriage ceiling. The driver opened the trap door.

"Sir?" he asked.

"Take me to Regent Street."

***

Darcy arrived at the Gardiners' the following day as the sun's pink and golden rays began to colour the clouds. Although a servant opened the door, Mr. Bennet stood ready in the hall. He looked exceedingly agitated. Darcy made a slight bow.

"Thank goodness you have come, Mr. Darcy," Mr. Bennet said, his voice shaking. "I apologize for involving you, but you are the only gentleman of our acquaintance whom I trust…"

"Anything I can do to alleviate you or your family's suffering," he said gallantly. Mr. Bennet did not smile. He looked as if he would go apoplectic at a moment's notice.

"Did you bring the pistols, Mr. Darcy?" Mr. Bennet asked, his voice quavering.

"Indeed, I did," replied Mr. Darcy. "Have you ever handled a pistol before?"

"No, never," Mr. Bennet squeaked.

Darcy put a comforting hand on Mr. Bennet's arm. "Do not concern yourself, Mr. Bennet. I will teach you what you need to know, but I must speak with you first, as I think we may circumvent these proceedings altogether."

"What are you saying, Mr. Darcy?" Mr. Bennet asked, hope shining in his eyes.

"I do believe that we can make this situation come out to our satisfaction," said Darcy confidently. Mr. Bennet smiled.

"I will rely upon you," he said as they entered the study.

***

"Papa, are you in there? I would like to speak to you before you go," Elizabeth called through the study door.

Mr. Bennet was already at the door, opening it. Elizabeth entered and began to speak but stopped short when she saw Darcy. For a moment, she was speechless.

Mr. Bennet looked from one to the other. It was Darcy who spoke first.

He cleared his throat. "Good morning, Miss Bennet. I am sorry that we are not meeting under happier circumstances. I will take my leave, so that you may speak to your father alone." He made his way toward her to the door.

As if awakened from a dream, she suddenly cried, "No," before he reached the door. He stopped, a surprised look on his face. They both looked at Mr. Bennet.

"Lizzy," Mr. Bennet offered. "I think perhaps you might want to have a word with Mr. Darcy. I will go and have my breakfast." He tried to sound lighthearted, but Elizabeth knew he was hiding his dread from her.

As soon as they were alone, Elizabeth went to the window. She could not look in Darcy's face. She was afraid her countenance would reveal all the tumult of emotions she was feeling.

"Mr. Darcy, why are you here?" she asked finally.

"Your father asked me to be his second in his duel with Mr. Wickham. He felt that I, being a gentleman, would possess the necessary knowledge and..." he groped for the word, "authority, to see that all proceeded fairly with adherence to the rules."

"Rules?" she cried and turned upon him. "Rules. Mr. Darcy, what good can come of this? Can you not do something to stop it? My father—" Her voice broke and she turned away from him once more, burying her face in her handkerchief. "My father is an elderly man, a country gentleman. What does he know of dueling?" The tears welled in her eyes, and then broke free and ran down her cheeks. She wished he would rush to her and throw his arms around her and hold her to his breast. Instead, he stood apart and spoke calmly.

"I do think that some accord can be reached without resorting to violence," he said.

Elizabeth ceased crying at once and turned toward him. "Oh, do you think so?"

"I have made some arrangements." He stopped. She looked at him expectantly. When she saw that he was not forthcoming, she pressed the matter further.

"You are very vexing. You shall not leave this room until you have revealed all your plans to me. My father's life, nay, all our lives, hang in the balance today. If you are to be our savior, you must tell me what you propose to do. If not, I think I shall go mad." Tears sprang to her eyes again, and she turned from him. She was angry at herself for crying so much. *But my dear father, her dear, dear papa.*

Darcy crossed the room and stood so close to Elizabeth that she could hear him breathing. "Miss Bennet. Please. Do not cry. I will tell you," he said softly. His words acted on Elizabeth almost like a caress. She turned to look at him. His dark eyes bored into her. She audibly caught her breath. He offered his hand to her and she obediently took it. He led her to the sofa, where they sat facing each other.

"I was going to reveal all once everything was accomplished. I see now that that is impossible." His intent look suddenly softened into sympathy Did he understand her torment? Perhaps all was not lost between them.

"Please. There is so little time," she said.

"I considered all the facts and was led to one conclusion. Wickham will want money in order to make things right with your sister. I am prepared to offer a generous endowment to him for the rest of his life, and with provisions for your sister and any children they may have."

"Oh, Mr. Darcy. I do not know how any of us will ever repay you."

"Rest assured that I do not do any of this for your family. I do it only for you."

His words struck her like a blow. He does still care for her. *Oh, why does all this have to happen now?* They have no time. She forced herself to think.

"But the duel? Surely Mr. Wickham will have to go through with it. He will be attended, I presume, by at least one man from his regiment. He will have to go through with it to preserve his reputation."

"I expect so," said Darcy. Elizabeth's face fell. Wickham could still kill her beloved papa.

Darcy, gingerly covering her hand with his, continued. "I am his second. It is in my prerogative to finish the duel if your father is unable. I can and will insist on that point. If anything happens to your father, Wickham will have me to deal with, and he knows that I am a very good shot."

He got up to take his leave. "I must be going now. Do not worry. Wickham is a coward. He will not go so far as to fire even one shot. You can rely on it."

Elizabeth looked up into his face and smiled for the first time. He smiled in return.

She was grateful for all he was doing for her, and for her family despite its low connections and its unseemly behavior. Gratitude, however, was not her overwhelming emotion at that moment. She wanted him to take her in his arms. She wanted to kiss him good-bye, again and again. He turned to look at her once more.

She swallowed hard. His eyes. They bore into her like a dagger. It was now or never. What if he were killed? What if he lay in his grave never knowing that she loved him? He was prepared to sacrifice everything for her, his position, his reputation, his wealth, and now he was prepared to sacrifice his life. Could she hold her reputation above that?

He turned away from her and headed to the door. She could not let him go without telling him of her feelings. *What if he was mistaken?* What if Wickham killed her father and killed him too?

As he opened the door and exited, she said in a barely audible tone, "I love you." She waited for the click of the door. It did not come.

The door opened again, and Darcy entered the room once more.

"What did you say?" he asked.

She faltered for a moment, then repeated, "I love you," louder this time. It all happened in an instant. She did not move and yet she was in his arms. He strode across the room with such force that he lifted her off the ground. The touch of his body was intoxicating. Suddenly, a dark cloud crossed his face, and he let her down. He still had not kissed her.

"Perhaps you are only grateful to me," he said, pulling away slightly, but not letting go of her. *Oh no, no, he would know.* She reached up and caressed his cheek.

"How can you doubt me?" she said. "Do you think I do not know my own mind?"

She watched his face. His eyes searched hers as if he would find in them the truth he wanted to know. She touched his face again. He kissed her.

It was not the polite kiss she had seen exchanged so many times among the married people she had known. No, this was something more. His mouth touched hers, parted her lips, embraced her. She felt her body yield to him. He kissed her again and again and then began to kiss her beneath her ear and down her neck. Pulses of a heretofore undiscovered energy radiated from her heart throughout her body. She felt urges from her nether regions that both excited and alarmed her.

When he reached her mouth again, she opened it to his and felt him enter her there with his tongue. She became weak with desire and he held her to him, whispering her name, "Elizabeth."

A knock at the door parted them suddenly. She tried her best to recover herself and called out, "Come in."

By the time the door opened, Darcy had turned from her and was standing at the window, his back to them. Her father entered.

"It is time, Mr. Darcy."

Tears welled in her eyes. She bit her lip to control herself. "Papa," she said, and rushed to embrace him.

"Now, now, Lizzy. Everything will be fine. You will see," he said cajolingly, although Elizabeth could feel the tension in him. Mr.

Bennet planted a kiss on his daughter's cheek. "Be brave. I am counting on you."

"Yes, Papa," she said, using everything in her power to gain control of herself. Her father left the room, and Darcy followed. He turned to look at her, and she tried to speak to him with only a glance: *please come back to me.* The front door closed, and the sound of carriage wheels drifted up from the street below.

***

The secluded glen at Hyde Park had been a favorite of Darcy's. His tastes did not run to London society, but to the green and growing land of Pemberley. When he was forced to be in London, he sought refuge in the parks. This particular place granted the duelists some seclusion from passersby and from the authorities.

As Mr. Bennet and Mr. Darcy approached, they saw Wickham had already arrived with his second. The lad looked about eighteen years of age and was in uniform. Darcy gingerly carried the dueling pistols under his arm. His father had given him the set before he died. He had hoped they would never be used but instilled in young Fitzwilliam the overwhelming importance of honor. As the dewy grass wet their boots, Darcy wondered what price honor would demand today.

Mr. Bennet looked positively grey with anxiety. A small table had been set up to receive the weapons. Wickham's second and a man Darcy could only guess was a physician stood by. Darcy gently laid the cedar box on the table and opened it. The pistols gleamed in the morning light. Wickham smiled.

"Since you are providing the weapons, I have the right to choose first," Wickham said, reaching for the pistol closest to Darcy. Before he laid his hand upon it, Darcy stayed it.

"Could I have a word, Mr. Wickham?" he asked. With that, Darcy looked around. His solicitor should have been here by now with the papers, but was not. No matter. Wickham would have to take him at his word. After all, Darcy's word was not to be taken lightly. The two men adjourned out of earshot.

"Look here, Wickham. My solicitor will be here momentarily. I have papers drawn up and signed by me giving you a generous provision for your lifetime provided you marry Lydia Bennet and take a position with the army elsewhere, out of harm's way, we shall say. There is no need to do further damage by going through with this ridiculous duel. You will have what you want. It is more generous even than my father's 'bequest'," Darcy spoke deliberately, trying to impress Wickham with the finality of his offer. Wickham stood silent.

"I do not see any papers," he said at last, "and time is a-wasting." He grinned again at Darcy and began to walk away.

Darcy raised his voice, "Wickham." Wickham stopped and turned but stood his ground. Darcy had to come to him. "Wickham, you know I am good as my word." Wickham snorted and rolled his eyes. It took everything Darcy had not to thrash him on the spot. Wickham turned his back on Darcy.

"Before you walk away, know this. If any harm comes to Mr. Bennet, you will have me to reckon with." This time, Wickham stopped and returned to Darcy.

"What are you saying?" Wickham asked, the smile finally gone from his face.

"I will finish what Mr. Bennet has started. Since I am his second, you will face me on the field if he cannot carry on."

Wickham's eyes narrowed. "You cannot be serious," he said.

"I am deadly serious. Do not try me."

The smile returned. Wickham finally spoke. "Perhaps you underestimate me. Perhaps I am a man of honor after all and neither your threats nor your money impresses me in the slightest." Wickham turned and walked back toward the table where the pistols lay.

Darcy was in shock. This was the one contingency he had not considered. Had he underestimated Wickham? No, it was impossible. The leopard does not so easily change his spots. *What could he be playing at?* Whatever it was, it was a deadly game. Darcy was forced to follow. Wickham had chosen his pistol and his second was inspecting it as he arrived at the table. Mr. Bennet was wide eyed and trembling. Darcy could hear his every breath.

"I can assure you that both weapons are in the peak of condition," Darcy forced himself to say calmly.

"I can see that, sir. Thank you," said Wickham's second.

Mr. Bennet stood as if paralyzed. Darcy looked at him and then offered him the box with the remaining pistol. "Your weapon, sir,"

Darcy said. He felt as though he were trapped in a flood, unable to gain his footing. Events were taking their own course, and he was powerless to stop them.

In a moment, both Bennet and Wickham were holding their pistols. They were standing back-to-back in the moist air. Mr. Bennett had a resigned look on his face. Wickham, as usual, was smirking.

"With my count, you will both take ten paces and turn. Mr. Wickham, you have the first shot. Do you gentlemen understand?"

With the assent of both, Darcy began the count. He stood with Wickham's second, counting out the last moments of Mr. Bennet's life. As the count proceeded, Darcy noticed Wickham glance toward him.

"Ten," Darcy shouted, and both men leveled their pistols. Wickham looked at Mr. Bennet. To his credit, although shaking, the old man held his pistol out at arm's length and did not waver. Wickham suddenly looked at Darcy and began to laugh. Darcy, confused, turned slightly and noticed his solicitor had arrived and was standing behind him.

With his pistol still pointed at Mr. Bennett, Wickham shouted, "You are right. I have no honor." And, still laughing, he threw the pistol into the air.

Darcy watched every moment of that pistol's slowly revolving descent. It hit the ground, and with a sudden cracking sound, discharged. At first, he was not sure where the shot had landed, until he fell to his knees like a broken marionette and collapsed face first on the ground.

Chapter 2

For a few seconds, everyone was paralyzed. For a moment Wickham could not comprehend what had occurred. He thought he must be running toward the fallen Darcy, but around him time expanded, and his movements felt sluggish and dreamlike. At last he reached the prone and bleeding Darcy. A man sprang forward and rushed to Darcy's side. He turned him over and at that point, everyone heard a horrible, hissing sound. "Get back," he shouted, and every man took a step backward.

The man was a doctor, Dr. Harold Castleden, the physician from Wickham's regiment. His second must have arranged for him to be in attendance. The doctor acted swiftly. Wickham was terrified that those wheezing breaths Darcy was now taking through his chest cavity would be his last. "I need someone to assist me," he commanded. He looked up at Wickham. "You, second lieutenant."

Wickham began to mumble some excuse, but Castleden cut him short. "Now, lieutenant. That is an order." Wickham obeyed wordlessly, even though it occurred to him that it was unlikely that the doctor actually could give him an order. "Pull off his jacket and open his shirt. I need to look at the wound," Castleden barked at Wickham. Darcy lay like a rag doll, but he was still conscious, and Wickham felt his eyes boring a hole into him as he pulled at Darcy's clothing. Darcy winced as Wickham yanked his arm through his jacket and waistcoat. The doctor was looking through his bag and drew out pieces of oil cloth. Disgusted with his clumsy ministrations, he shoved Wickham aside and put the oilcloth over the wound in Darcy's chest. Darcy was breathing shallowly and rapidly. It seemed to Wickham that he was strangling.

"The round punctured his lung," the doctor said to no one in particular. He plugged the hole with gauze and turned Darcy over on his back. Darcy let out a groan. "Sorry, old man," the doctor said. "I need to see if there is an exit wound." Wickham made a move to rise and Castleden held his sleeve. "We are not finished here yet," he said.

There were copious amounts of blood on the ground and on the doctor's coat and sleeves. Wickham rubbed his hands together nervously. It was then he noticed that they were tacky with Darcy's blood. He felt nauseous. "We need to cover this wound but let enough air through so as not to collapse the lung," he told Wickham. He may as well have been speaking Chinese. Wickham had no idea how to proceed. "Here." He held out a piece of oil cloth. "Hold it down here and here, and I will hold down the third side."

Castleden removed the blood-soaked gauze from the wound and applied the oil cloth. As soon as the cloth was stuck to Darcy's chest, his breathing eased. The unfastened side vibrated with each of Darcy's breaths. Wickham fell back onto the grass the minute he heard Darcy take his first easy breath and the realization of what had happened hit him full force. He began to shake, and his stomach churned. It was fortunate that he got to his feet and managed to stagger a few feet away before he vomited. As he stood and recovered himself, he noticed that no one was paying much attention to him anyway.

As Wickham propped his back against a tree, he watched the entire scene as if it were some sort of macabre play. Mr. Bennet stood behind the doctor wringing his hands. *Good*, he thought. *All of this was your fault, stupid old man. You should never have slapped me.*

The rest of the men were loading Darcy into his carriage, and Wickham watched the doctor climb in after him. Thank God someone in his regiment thought to bring a doctor. It was good to have friends who were concerned with your safety. It was fortunate. Suddenly, it occurred to him that he could have been the one lying bleeding in the field.

Wickham finally got to his feet and was leaning against a tree, recovering himself, when someone grabbed him by the shoulder and spun him around. He turned so fast that he lost his footing and fell awkwardly to the ground.

"On your feet, you vile seducer." It was Bennet. Wickham stared up at him in amazement. It was almost funny, really. *Vile seducer indeed?* A smirk must have passed his lips because the next thing he knew, Bennet had hauled him up screaming.

"This amuses you, eh, Wickham? Funny, is it?" Mr. Bennet shouted as he hauled Wickham unsteadily up the trunk of the tree.

"Now, see here, Bennet," Wickham said as he grabbed the tree trunk behind him to steady himself. Mr. Bennett let him go, and then punched him squarely in the nose. Wickham was so surprised and wobbly that the force of the blow knocked him to the ground again. Before he could get to his feet and thrash the living daylights out of Mr. Bennet, two policemen arrived on the scene. After many flying accusations, Wickham found himself in prison, awaiting word of his fate.

***

The carriage arrived at Darcy's house in town. Darcy, through a haze of weakness and pain, could see the dumbfounded servants part at his entrance on a bloodstained litter. Elsie, the chambermaid, fainted dead away, which led to much confusion. Finally, John, Mr. Darcy's man, took charge and got his master safely to his room.

Castleden and John prepared Darcy for bed. John removed his boots and his trousers, but Castleden himself insisted on removing Darcy's shirt. Darcy was surprised when the doctor began to inspect his bloodied shirt, waistcoat, and jacket. He held them up and shook his head over and over. Finally, Darcy spoke to him. His voice was wheezy.

"If I may ask, sir, what is it you are looking for?"

"The piece of material that goes here," he said, putting his finger through the hole the lead ball made in Darcy's shirt. If it is not here, which I believe it is not, it is still in your chest, along with the lead round. If that is so, there is danger of a great infection."

John blanched. "Is there nothing that can be done?"

"I need to return to my surgery for more instruments. When I return, I will have to do some surgery and retrieve the round and the piece of clothing if I can." Darcy moaned from the bed.

"Do what you will, sir. I am in your hands," Darcy said weakly.

"You are not going to leave me, are you, sir?" John asked suddenly.

Castleden turned and smiled. "I believe Mr. Darcy's personal physician has been sent for. But in the meantime, give him water if he asks for it and try to keep him comfortable."

"But, sir, he is still bleeding," John said, shaking his head and staring at Darcy.

"Those liquids flow to clean the wound. There is still blood in them, but no major blood vessels have been breached. So far, he has been lucky. A few more inches and he would have bled to death in the field." Then, realizing that Darcy was still conscious, he added, "Begging your pardon, sir."

With that, the doctor picked up his hat and walked to the door. When he opened it, he had an afterthought and added, "Mr. Darcy should have no visitors. Stay with him." With that, he left.

**

Elizabeth had not left the window since her father left. She had been there for what felt like hours, but she lost track of the time. She could not dismiss from her mind her overwhelming anxiety. *Stupid Lydia. Horrible, evil Wickham.* It made her skin crawl to think that she had once thought so much of him. The sound of carriage wheels on the cobblestones shook her out of her thoughts. She raced from the window to the front door. It opened and in walked her father.

Usually, Elizabeth could control her emotions better than she did at that moment. She threw herself into her father's arms absolutely wracked with sobs. Mr. Bennet neither moved nor spoke. She clung to him and then, gently, he put his arms gingerly around her and patted her back.

"There, there, Lizzy," was all he said. He became suddenly unsteady on his feet. Elizabeth let go and let her Uncle Gardiner do his best to right him and guide him to the drawing room.

Elizabeth's face was creased with concern. As soon as her father sat down, she ran to the kitchen for water, not even thinking to call one of the servants. As she handed him the glass, he drank thirstily, and it suddenly dawned on her that they had not arrived with Mr. Darcy.

"Where is Mr. Darcy, Papa?" she asked. Her father's face was bleak. She looked up for some comfort from her uncle, but he looked no better. "What has happened? Tell me," she said.

Mr. Bennet put his head in his hands and did not speak. Seeing his distress, Uncle Gardiner stepped in. "Come, Lizzy. Leave your father be. I will tell you everything you need to know."

***

"I must go to him," she said, after her uncle finished his account.

"That is impossible, Lizzy. You know that."

"It is impossible for me to see him, but it is possible that he gave his life to save this family from disgrace. I am sorry. I know you mean the best for me, but I must go."

Her uncle attempted to prevail upon her father to insist. At the best of times her papa could sway her or even command obedience. In his present distraught state, she could see he was as firm as field of grass in a windstorm. She, however, was resolute. Uncle Gardiner reluctantly agreed to take her.

They arrived at Mr. Darcy's house in town within an hour. Mrs. Dawson, the housekeeper, greeted them in the foyer and instructed Miss Elizabeth that she was under strict orders from the doctor that Mr. Darcy was to have no visitors. None.

How could she be so close to him and yet have no way of seeing with her own eyes what state he was in? It was more than she could bear. She had to see him. She had to. Almost instantly, she began to conceive of a plan to distract her uncle and perhaps the housekeeper as well.

"Are we to stand in the hall?" she asked as imperiously as she could muster. Mrs. Dawson was taken aback.

"So sorry, miss. I have quite forgotten my duty in all the excitement. Perhaps if you would wait with your uncle in the drawing room, you could have a word with the doctor when he returns. I will bring you some tea." Mrs. Dawson showed them into the drawing room and retreated hastily. Hopefully soon, she could run to Darcy's room unimpeded. They went into a magnificent room, finely appointed with mahogany and exquisite fabrics. She noticed but had no interest in any of it.

They were only a few minutes in the drawing room when the bell sounded again, and Elizabeth heard voices. Before her uncle could speak she was in the front hall. The housekeeper had admitted a man carrying a doctor's bag and wearing a uniform. It must be the doctor who attended at the duel. She waited for no introduction.

"Are you Mr. Darcy's physician?" she asked. Mrs. Dawson jumped slightly at the sound of her voice. Castleden smiled.

"I am, temporarily, I think. I quite expected his physician to be here already. And you are…?"

She didn't know what came over her, but out of her mouth came the words, "Miss Elizabeth Bennet, Mr. Darcy's fiancée." Mrs. Dawson's mouth dropped open.

"Ah," said Castleden, as he began to ascend the stairs.

"I am going with you," Elizabeth announced, and began following him.

Her uncle's voice sounded behind them. "That would be quite inappropriate, I should think," he said firmly. Elizabeth ignored him. She would not be managed.

"On the contrary, Uncle, it is my duty," she said, and she followed Dr. Castleden up the stairs. Her uncle was right, of course. It would be a scandal if news that she had attended Mr. Darcy in his sickroom got out. There would be even more of a scandal when her bold-faced lie that she was his fiancée accompanied that news. None of it mattered. She must see him with her own eyes.

Elizabeth followed Castleden up the stairs and knocked on Mr. Darcy's door. She was aware of her heart beating. Although she so wanted to see him, she couldn't bear the thought of his being wounded or dying. The door opened. It was John. His expression was strained.

"How is the patient?" Castleden asked.

"Oh, I do not know, sir," John said. "I am so glad to see you, sir. Mr. Darcy moans most dreadfully, and I am afraid to touch him."

"Is he conscious?" Castleden asked.

"No, sir."

Elizabeth slowly crept toward the bed as if in a dream. There was a raw, metallic smell in the air, like freshly butchered beef. Darcy lay among the sheets, breathing shallowly, watery blood stains seeping through his bandages and onto the sheet covering his body. She slowly knelt next to his bed.

"Mr. Darcy," she said softly. Then, realizing that she had told everyone of their engagement, repeated, "Fitzwilliam, darling, can you hear me?" Darcy took a long breath and his eyelids fluttered.

Elizabeth instinctively put her hand on his forehead. He turned his head toward her. His eyes opened but rolled in his head before they closed again. He moaned.

"He has been like that since you left, sir," John said, his voice quavering.

"We will have to do surgery at once to remove the round and the bits of clothing that were carried into his chest," the doctor said in an unruffled tone. Elizabeth thought that she might be sick. "I need to get all of it out as quickly as possible. The risk of infection is very great."

As the doctor spoke, he was laying out his instruments on Darcy's dressing table. John looked positively ashen. Castleden looked up at him. "You will assist me," he said. John began to tremble and shake his head violently.

"Oh no, sir. Not I. I get sick at the sight of blood. Oh no, sir," he said, repeating "Oh no, sir" all the way out the door. Castleden looked at Elizabeth.

"I will help you," she said, before he could ask.

"I do not think—"

"Do you have someone else?"

"This is not women's work, Miss Bennet. Surely, Mr. Darcy's doctor has been sent for. He should be here—"

"He should be here when?" she asked stridently. "He could be on another call, or out of the city. He must have been sent for already. Where is he? Where?" She could feel herself becoming hysterical. She dug her fingernails into the palms of her hands and took a deep breath.

Castleden walked over to her and touched her arm. "It is all right. Calm yourself. I will call that fellow downstairs who accompanied you. He may have more of a stomach for this than the poor old butler. Come here," he said, leading her over to the basin filled with water. "Splash some of this water on your face and make a cool cloth for Darcy's head. I will go get..."

"My uncle," she said. "Mr. Gardiner."

"Your uncle," he repeated and left the room.

Castleden was gone and Elizabeth knelt next to Darcy, replacing the cloth on his head with a fresh one. The cool sensation must have roused him, because he slowly opened his eyes and looked at her.

"Oh, Elizabeth," he said in so poignant a fashion that it was all she could do not to weep.

"I am here," she said. "Do not try to talk."

Darcy tried to move but cried out in pain and sank back onto the pillow. "Please, dearest, lie still. You have been badly wounded. Do you remember?" Elizabeth said softly. Darcy looked confused for a moment, like he was concentrating, trying to remember. He turned to her.

"I need to see Wickham, immediately," he said. Elizabeth could scarcely believe her ears. She recoiled from him slightly, and then realized he must be delirious.

"Hush, now," she cooed soothingly. "Try to rest." She brushed his cheek with her fingertips. He only grew more agitated.

"Wickham," he said as forcefully as he could muster. He winced in pain. Elizabeth could feel the tears starting in her eyes and she tried to control them.

Darcy spoke softly and deliberately this time. "Elizabeth, listen to me," he rasped. "You must bring Wickham to me."

"He is in prison," she cried. He closed his eyes at that and gathered himself. He tried to reach for her hand. She grasped his hand in hers and said, "I will do anything you ask, dearest. Please, please try to rest."

"I will rest when I lay eyes on Wickham again," he said. "Tell the magistrate that I am not pressing charges and to release him. Write it down. Write it down and I will sign it. Please."

He was in such pain and so weak that she could only suppress her natural instinct to argue at such a bizarre request, and merely do as he asked. In short order she had taken down what he wished to say, and with shaking hands, held it for him to sign. With that task accomplished, he collapsed again. Elizabeth stayed by his bedside.

The doctor reentered alone, carrying towels and cloths. He set them on the dressing table.

"Your uncle and John are bringing a table in. It will be easier to do the surgery on that," he said. "How is he?"

"He regained consciousness briefly, but ..." She looked down at Darcy's pale countenance. With that, the door opened; the men had arrived to help with the surgery. Two footmen, Uncle Gardiner, and John twisted and scuffled and finally brought the table into the room. Dr. Castleden instructed them to put it next to the window. He covered it with a sheet and then told John, Uncle Gardiner, and the two wide-eyed footmen to lift Mr. Darcy as gently as possible and put him on the table.

"Can you not give him something for the pain?" Elizabeth said, her voice breaking. "Laudanum, or something?"

"There is only laudanum, and it suppresses respiration. He cannot afford that now, not with a wound to the lung," Castleden said perfunctorily while he readied his instruments. They looked like instruments of torture.

As the group moved toward the bed, Uncle Gardiner spoke. "Leave the room, Lizzy. There is no more you can do here."

She opened her mouth to speak, but his expression silenced her. She wordlessly left the room. As she shut the door behind her, she was greeted with the sight of half the staff standing in the hall. "Could someone bring me a chair, please?"

Elsie ran off immediately. Elizabeth had resolved then and there that she would not leave Darcy and would sit here in the hallway until she was allowed to enter his room again. She would send the letter on with Elsie to her father. He would make sure that Wickham was brought here. What purpose could Darcy have in bringing him here and why, in heaven's name, drop the charges against him?

Elizabeth sat down to wait. The letter had been dispatched. Uncle Gardiner, John, and the two footmen were still in the room. She couldn't hear anything except hushed voices. Some part of her wanted to be in there with Darcy and another wanted to run away as far as possible. As she was ruminating on these thoughts, John opened the door. He looked terrible.

"Oh, Miss Bennet," he said, flustered. "I will fetch you some tea." He turned and began walking rapidly down the hallway toward the stairs.

"John, wait. What is going on in there?"

John stopped and grabbed the stair railing for support. He took a deep breath and then began to speak. "Perhaps you should wait in the drawing room downstairs, Miss Bennet," he said. He took another deep breath. "They are beginning the surgery now to extract the round from Mr. Darcy's chest. The footman and your uncle are," he paused for a moment to frame his words, "assisting the doctor."

Elizabeth shot him a quizzical look. "All of them? Assisting him in what way?" That was the last straw. John slid down the wall and sat upon the stair. Elizabeth looked down at him, trembling.

"I would rather not say, miss," he said.

"You had better say," she said a bit too stridently.

He looked up at her. "They are there to hold him down while the doctor probes for the lead ball," he said. "He is conscious, you see, Miss, and the surgeon will have to…" With that he stopped, took another deep breath and stood up. "Come to the drawing room, please, Miss Bennet," he said, not looking at her.

"No," she said softly, and turned back toward Darcy's room.

"I will send up some tea, then," he said and retreated down the stairs.

Elizabeth returned to her post. Her throat felt dry and she felt like running. Running anywhere. *I am a coward.* All of a sudden, a cry accompanied by a gurgling sound pierced the silence. It was Darcy. The surgeon had begun his work. He cried out again, and then, only muffled sounds of someone who is gagged. She was on her feet now, leaning against the door. She could not bear it. She could hear men's voices and scuffling sounds. They must be trying to restrain him while the doctor cut. It was horrible. Tears were flowing down her cheeks unchecked. She clutched her throat. Then, as abruptly as it had begun, the sounds stopped. As she collapsed in her chair, she heard John clattering up the stairway with the tea tray. Quickly, she blotted her face and tried to regain her composure. John would not raise his eyes to her, which was just as well. If she saw any sympathy in them, she would not contain her emotions.

"Your tea, miss," he said, setting the tray on the table.

"Thank you, John," she mumbled. He opened his mouth to say something else but kept silent and began to pour out the tea. The cup and saucer rattled against one another once he handed it to her. Her hands, too, were shaking.

"Have some, miss. It will do you good," he murmured softly. She took a sip, and then another. Her stomach was agitated, but it was surprising how soothing the warm liquid was not only to her body but her state of mind. John retreated again down the stairs.

Since the noises in the room stopped, Elizabeth thought that the worst of the procedure was over. Slowly, she eased open the door and peered inside. The men surrounding the table were so fixated on their work that they did not notice her presence.

Inside, Darcy was unconscious. Castleden, whose back was to her, was working furiously, picking up and laying down one instrument after another. Men surrounded the table, each with their hands upon Darcy's legs, arms, and shoulders. For the moment, he did not struggle against them. At last, Castleden grasped the lead ball with his elongated pincers and drew it, dripping, from Darcy's wound. It clanged into a small basin near the table. Elizabeth closed her eyes momentarily and breathed a sigh of relief. *The worst is over.* Castleden, however, kept on with his work. One more expedition with the pincers and he withdrew a bloody piece of cloth. "Eureka," he said triumphantly, holding it out for all to see. He then dropped it, dripping with blood, into the basin that held the lead round. He then turned to Mr. Gardiner. "How is that iron doing?" he asked. The worst was not over. It had not even begun. Elizabeth felt sick.

She had heard of cauterization, but never thought in her life she would witness it. This was too much. Turning, she closed the door and resumed her seat from outside. Gripping the sides of her chair, she braced herself for the screams she was sure would ensue. The sound of tramping footsteps up the stairs caused her to open her eyes as Darcy's bedroom door burst open and a middle-aged man with a gray mustache entered, shouting.

"Put that thing away," he exclaimed. Elizabeth jumped to her feet and followed them in. No one noticed her.

Castleden, unperturbed, reached for the red-hot device and had it poised above Darcy's prone figure. "And who might you be?" Castleden asked, not looking up.

The man who entered was already removing his jacket and rolling up his sleeves. "I am Dr. Lomax, Mr. Darcy's personal physician. I must ask you to cease and desist."

Castleden stopped with the iron above Darcy's chest. "Mr. Darcy is beginning to regain consciousness and the iron should be applied now," he said, but Lomax was already moving toward him. He shoved Castleden aside and stood over his patient. Castleden continued to mop up blood seeping from the chest wound.

"Cauterizing the wound will cause shock," Lomax said.

"In my experience, it does more good than harm, and it stops the bleeding," Castleden said.

"In your experience," Lomax repeated haughtily. "I am sure, Doctor, that your intentions are good. The battlefield, however, is not the place to remain current with the advances in medicine. I am Mr. Darcy's physician, and," he paused to look Castleden in the eye, "I am here now."

Castleden, with a shrug, took his instrument and plunged it into the water-filled basin at his side. It hissed vehemently. Darcy began to moan. Castleden made a small bow and stepped aside as Dr. Lomax turned to his patient. He began to pack the wound with gauze and bandages. Mr. Gardiner looked up at Castleden for instruction, but he only shook his head. He began to wash the blood from his hands.

Elizabeth stood galvanized at the spot where she had entered. She was torn between an urge to hide her eyes and one to run to Darcy's side. In the end, she stood back in the shadows, watching in horrified wonder.

Her Uncle Gardiner had finished helping Castleden repack his medical bag, and as he turned to leave the room, he spied Elizabeth. The shock of her appearance nearly knocked him backward.

"Lizzy. What in God's name?" was all he could utter. The entire room filled with men turned toward her at once.

"Is he all right? Is he alive?" she asked piteously, still rooted to the spot.

Castleden was the first to move. He walked swiftly forward, took her by the arm, and with one movement turned her around and led her from the room. He tried to lead her down the stairs, but she would have none of it. Disengaging herself, she resumed her seat by the door.

"I will be here if you need me," was all she said.

Chapter 3

Wickham could not believe his good fortune. Less than an hour ago, he was sitting in a damp cell at Margate prison and now he was jostling along in one of Darcy's carriages on his way to the most fashionable district in London. His companions, of course, were glaring at him in angry silence, but no matter. He was out of jail and that was what signified. And Darcy was still alive.

Lydia sat beside him, cowed into silence for once by her father's icy stares. She leaned on his arm, and, even though the events of the day had taken such a dire turn, her touch excited him. He glanced over at her flawless, youthful face and suppressed the urge to caress it with his fingers. He wanted to have her, right there in the coach. He almost laughed to himself at how much his thoughts turned to the activities of his loins. He could attend to those soon. His meeting with Darcy could only mean one thing: His fortunes had changed.

When they arrived at Darcy's house in town, Lydia and her father were installed in the drawing room and Wickham was hurried upstairs by the butler. As he stood outside Darcy's door, he suddenly felt a bit squeamish. What he had seen in the park had been quite enough. After all, he had never been in action or anywhere near a battlefield. His military experience consisted mostly of marching interrupted by brief periods of debauchery. He steeled himself against what he was about to see and tried to keep his wits about him. After all, Darcy was weakened now, and would be in no condition to negotiate.

Wickham opened the door and was assailed by the slightly metallic smell of blood. It made him rather queasy. Darcy was not alone. His solicitor was there. Wickham recognized him from the park that morning. He was shuffling papers by the bedside. Darcy lay unconscious.

"I'm Gerald Meriweather," the solicitor said, "Mr. Darcy's solicitor. He has some documents for you to sign."

Wickham looked over at Darcy's pale face. His breathing was labored, and perspiration beaded on his brow. Wickham wondered if he would last until morning. The air was close and damp, and the room smelled.

"Do we have to do this here?" Wickham inquired.

"Mr. Darcy expressly instructed that he was to be awakened when you arrived," Meriweather said coldly.

The man merely stared at him. He had the look of an undertaker: tall, gaunt, and humorless. Wickham wondered to himself as to how many deathbeds over which the man had presided.

"All right, then," Wickham said. "Let us begin."

Meriweather gently shook Darcy by the shoulder. At first, he did not move, but as the solicitor persisted, he groaned and opened his eyes. They rolled in his head, but soon they affixed themselves on Wickham. His look made Wickham's blood run cold.

Darcy attempted to speak, but his tongue and lips were parched. All he managed to croak out was, "Water." Wickham, in spite of himself, ran to his side and raised a waiting glass to Darcy's lips. He had to prop Darcy up, and hold him in an embrace of sorts. Darcy drank thirstily. Wickham suddenly realized that he felt sorry for what he had set in motion. True, he thought Darcy a haughty and intolerant snob, but at that instant, he remembered them as boyhood playmates and felt heartsick. The moment passed quickly. As soon as Darcy slaked his thirst, he spoke.

"Meriweather, come here," he whispered. The lawyer obliged him and brought his papers with him. He turned his attention to Wickham.

"This is the agreement I so desired you to sign this morning. Sign it now," he said weakly.

"I really should read them and see—"

"Sign it or you will go back to prison and rot there for all I care," Darcy said fiercely. It must have taken most of his strength, for he breathed heavily, and Wickham saw his struggle to keep his eyes open. Meriweather proffered the documents, and Wickham took them. As the solicitor pointed to various lines, Wickham dutifully signed each one. When he was finished, Darcy nodded, unable to speak any more, and again lost consciousness.

"Let us leave him in peace," Meriweather mumbled in Wickham's direction. When they were out in the hallway, Wickham confronted the lawyer.

"I think I am entitled to at least see how I have signed my life away," he said.

Meriweather shrugged and led Wickham to a small sitting room on the second floor. There he handed him the papers one by one for his inspection. As they shuffled their way through the papers, Wickham was increasingly surprised at Darcy's generosity. There would be no charges against him and he would be wealthier than he had hoped. All this for the price of a small wedding. It really was too delicious. Darcy would succeed in expunging the Bennet name, but he would never recover from his wound. He still would never have Elizabeth.

A knock sounded at the door. It was a clergyman. Was he here to anoint the dying Darcy or preside over his wedding? Both perhaps. *We might as well seal the bargain*, Wickham thought. Lydia was waiting in the drawing room with her father and Gardiner. Wickham tried again not to smile. Darcy had done all this for the love of a woman he would never possess. *Poor Darcy. He was such a fool.*

***

When Elizabeth awoke, she was still dressed in her clothes from the previous day. She looked about, and saw the fine drapery, tasteful paintings, and elegant furnishings. Sinking back into the wonderful softness of her pillows and sheets, she remembered that she was still in Mr. Darcy's house. When she rang for the servant, Elsie arrived with clothes that were brought from the Gardiners'. Her first thought, of course, was Darcy. She had to see him before she attended to any of her own needs.

As she rose from the bed, Elsie informed her that her younger sister was married. By the time Elizabeth reached the doorway, Elsie imposed herself between Elizabeth and the threshold. She was under strict orders. She was to keep Elizabeth away from Darcy. He was weak, and she was compromising herself by her inappropriate attentions to him. After all, they were not married. Elizabeth would have none of it. She would see with her own eyes how her beloved had fared through the night.

Elsie was pressing her case all the way to Darcy's room, to no avail. Finally, she said, "I will have to go and fetch Mr. John if you do not listen to me, miss."

"Excellent idea, Elsie," Elizabeth said with a smile. "Please take your time about it."

Elsie's eyes grew wide with shock. She turned and skittered down the stairs. Elizabeth reached Darcy's door. She did not bother to knock but turned the knob and slowly pushed the door open as if she expected an explosion on the other side. Luckily, the room had only two occupants: Darcy lying still as death on the bed and, surprisingly, Dr. Castleden, sleeping in the chair next to him.

Elizabeth crept close to the bedside and stared down at her beloved Darcy. His face was sallow and sunken, almost like a corpse, but he was still breathing in shallow breaths. His lips looked parched and his eyes darted back and forth under the lids. She wondered if he was watching his life pass before him, as many people said happened when one was close to death. No. She had to banish thoughts like that from her brain. He was going to survive this horrendous turn of events. Perhaps, even, he would forgive her for her part in them.

Dr. Castleden awoke with a jerk. He smiled at Elizabeth. "You are nothing if not determined, Miss Bennet," he said calmly.

"How is he, Doctor? Will he live?" she said, her voice breaking with those last words.

"He is young and strong, but I would be happier if the wound were cauterized. He has lost a lot of blood, and there is a great danger of infection." With that he stood up over Darcy and pulled up his eyelids. Darcy's eyes were rolled up in his head. He did not stir.

Elizabeth touched Darcy's forehead. He seemed unusually hot. She looked up with concern at Dr. Castleden.

"It is a fever, surely," Castleden said. "Not uncommon with this sort of wound. Do not worry."

But Elizabeth did worry. She worried a great deal. She looked up at Castleden, who patted her arm reassuringly. "Come now," he said. "Let him sleep."

He took Elizabeth by the elbow and led her toward the door. She suddenly thought of something. "Why are you here, Doctor? I thought Mr. Darcy's physician was taking over the case."

Castleden smiled. "My dear Miss Bennet, if you do not tell anyone I was here, then I will not tell anyone that you were." She smiled wearily at him and realized she had found an ally.

"Go. Go and get some breakfast. I will call you if he regains consciousness."

A hot bath had been prepared in the dressing room and she sank gratefully into it. She was determined now, more than ever before. She would not leave Darcy until he was out of danger, or until... No, she would not consider the alternative. He had saved her sister from ruin, perhaps at the cost of his own life. She would stand by him. She loved him.

Elizabeth would not be kept from Darcy under any circumstances. Her father, her uncle, the doctors, all tried to dissuade her from such a ruinous course, but to no avail. It was worth her reputation, the scandal it was causing Darcy, it was worth everything, to be there when he would open his eyes and call for her. She would be there, and no one could deter her.

Within the day, Dr. Castleden had been discovered and banished by Mr. Darcy's physician, much to Elizabeth's chagrin. She felt that he was Darcy's best hope. With each day that passed, her anxiety increased.

Her ministrations, and those of Darcy's physician, Dr. Lomax, were doing Darcy no good. Every day he worsened. The wound had become red and pus-filled and then the outer layers of it began to turn a sickeningly greenish black color. Dr. Lomax told her it was gangrene, and since there was no limb to amputate, there was no way of ridding Darcy's body of it. He prepared Elizabeth for the worst.

Darcy was becoming increasingly delirious. He ran a high fever and his sickroom smelled of death. Only the doctor and Elizabeth could stomach tending to him. This, of course, meant that she was tending to his every need. If her father knew the extent of her care, he would have had her forcibly removed from the house.

An odd sort of arrangement evolved in the Darcy household. All the servants, even Darcy's manservant, knew that they were not up to the task of tending a dying man, so as Elizabeth's tasks increased to those of a very intimate nature, they did their best to assist without comment or judgment. They treated her as if she were mistress of the house, since none wanted the role of nurse. Occasionally, she forced the issue with John, when Darcy was too heavy for her to turn and bathe. She became intimate with his suffering. She watched him worsen every day, helplessly.

Elizabeth was seated at the dining room table, preparing one of the many useless poultices she had been ordered to prepare by Dr. Lomax, when one of the servants sounded the alarm. Lady Catherine was approaching the door of Darcy's house in town.

Dr. Lomax had just finished his daily visit to Darcy's bedside. It had been four days since the shooting, and Darcy was much worse. The stench of gangrene was in the air. As Dr. Castleden had warned, the wound had festered. Now, the surrounding flesh was dying and so was Darcy. It seemed hopeless. Into this sad state of affairs, Lady Catherine imperiously stepped.

She could hear Dr. Lomax's hurried footsteps coming down the stairs. "Ah, Doctor. What news of my nephew? What is that awful smell?" asked Lady Catherine haughtily. Elizabeth remained motionless in the dining room.

"Perhaps we should talk in here," Dr. Lomax stated gravely. Elizabeth hoped they would not adjourn to the drawing room, or she would not be able to hear further.

"We will speak where we are, thank you. I would like to see my nephew, if you please. Tell him to come down," she said arrogantly.

"I am afraid that is out of the question, Your Ladyship. You see—" Dr. Lomax began.

"Out of the question? Certainly not. Tell Darcy I am here and tell him to come at once," she insisted.

There was silence for a moment, and then Dr. Lomax spoke again. "Your nephew is dying, Madame."

Those words were never spoken to Elizabeth. She abandoned her work and walked to the threshold of the entry hall. Lady Catherine's back was to her and she made no comment. Lady Catherine, her attention focused only on the doctor, breathed in a few times, and closed her eyes. The doctor stared at her for a few minutes.

"Are you quite all right, Your Ladyship?" the doctor asked.

"Quite all right. Quite all right. A cup of tea, perhaps." Dr. Lomax bowed and indicated with his arm that they should enter the drawing room when Elizabeth made her presence known. She stood before Lady Catherine. Lady Catherine drew herself up like a cobra. Elizabeth curtsied, "Lady Catherine—"

"This is outrageous. What are you doing here, Miss Bennet?" She turned from Elizabeth to the doctor. "What is she doing here?"

"Please, Lady Catherine, please come and sit down. I will explain all," said Dr. Lomax. Elizabeth followed them to the drawing room. Dr. Lomax rang for John, who scurried off to bring tea.

When they were all seated, Dr. Lomax continued. "The wound was deep, and we expected some infection. However, it has gone beyond that, I am afraid."

"Is there nothing you can do?" Lady Catherine asked.

"I am afraid not. I have been giving him laudanum for the pain, but I must be judicious in its use. There is someone with him every minute of the day."

"Who, who is with him? Are you with him, Doctor?"

The doctor sighed. "You realize, Your Ladyship, that I cannot restrict my practice to one patient. I cannot be here every minute of every day. I believe the household has taken up the task of caring for Mr. Darcy." Lady Catherine looked pointedly at Elizabeth. No one spoke for what seemed, to Elizabeth, at least an hour or more but was merely a few seconds. Mercifully, John entered with the tea. As he began pouring, Lady Catherine continued.

"John, what are you doing for Mr. Darcy? Who is helping you?"

John looked up at Elizabeth with panic in his eyes. He glanced at the doctor, who averted his eyes.

"Well? Speak up, man. I did not come here to be put off. Speak plainly."

Elizabeth realized in that instant that both John and the doctor were looking directly at her but did not say a word.

"Oh no. This cannot be," she said. "It is too outrageous." Lady Catherine stood, and both men did so with her. "Take me to see him at once," she said. Lady Catherine rushed past Elizabeth, the doctor in tow. Elizabeth followed.

The great lady stood before Darcy's door and covered her nose and mouth with her handkerchief. "Open the door," she commanded, and the doctor obeyed. Darcy was in bed, covered with a sheet. His emaciated body revealed its recent torment. His head wagged back and forth in a feverish delirium. Lady Catherine approached him cautiously. She stood over him and spoke.

"Darcy, Darcy." There was no reaction. Lady Catherine touched his forehead and recoiled. "Have you bled him?" she asked the doctor.

He looked at her with tired eyes. "We do not believe that bleeding a patient does much good anymore."

She looked at him like one would look at the village idiot. "Really?" she asked. "Did you, perhaps, cauterize the wound?"

"No, Your Ladyship. Cauterization causes shock. Modern medical practice dictates—"

Lady Catherine looked as if she had been struck. "You, sir, are incompetent. Her voice rose. "Incompetent." The shouting made Darcy stir.

"Darcy," Lady Catherine said, her voice quivering slightly. "Darcy, how are you feeling?" He gazed at her, uncomprehending, and slid back into unconsciousness. Lady Catherine stood for a moment, looked about the room, and then turned on her heel.

Elizabeth could see the torment in her eyes, even though the great lady did everything in her power to disguise it. That empathy, that softness, hardened as she glared at Elizabeth. "We are not finished, my girl," she said through gritted teeth. With that, she left.

Elizabeth watched as Lady Catherine beat as hasty a retreat as all others who encountered her shattered Darcy. Her stinging words left Elizabeth emotionally drained, but she had not time to think of her own wounded pride and destroyed social position. What did any of it matter if her beloved Darcy was to die? No, she forced herself to think of him, and his needs alone, as she had since this entire unfortunate turn of events began. As her mind cleared of its emotional fog, one word kept repeating itself: "Incompetent." That is what her ladyship called the doctor. Perhaps he was. Perhaps that had been the problem all along. An idea crept its way into her head and bloomed into its full audacity. It would be a bold move, and it might not work, but she had to try. She had to try for all their sakes.

Lady Catherine's coach had no sooner turned the corner than Elizabeth marched into Darcy's sickroom and sacked Dr. Lomax. He sputtered and then tried to stand his ground, but Elizabeth had the conviction of the desperate and would brook no argument. Besides, to whom could he appeal? Darcy was too ill, Georgiana too young and too far away. And as for Lady Catherine, she had nearly sacked him a few minutes before. No, he was defeated. She knew it, and he knew it. He noisily packed his instruments and huffed out the door.

As soon as the door slammed, Elizabeth's doubts returned. What if she had made the wrong decision? There was no going back now. She sent a footman for Dr. Castleden. He was her only hope.

The good doctor arrived within the hour. When Elizabeth opened the door to Darcy's sickroom for him, a waft of sickly stench hit her like an anvil. He didn't first go to Darcy, but to the window, which he opened wide.

"There must be fresh air in here, and immediately," he said. Only then did he turn his attention to Darcy. Elizabeth had catered to Darcy's every personal need but was never in the room when his dressings were changed. Even after all her ministrations and her gradual acclimatization to the sickroom, she still had a primordial fear of looking at his now-festering wound. As Dr. Castleden bent over Darcy, she could hear her heart beating in her ears. This was usually the moment that Dr. Lomax would ask her to leave the room. Not so this time.

"Miss Bennet, come here, please," Dr. Castleden whispered as he began to cut through the bandaging on the weeping injury. "Bring the basin and assist me."

She did as she was bidden, although dread consumed her. Her physical fatigue and emotional exhaustion gave her little to draw on now that she needed strength. The doctor deftly snipped through the gauze and peeled back the layers to reveal a moist, sucking chest wound surrounded by greenish-black necrotic flesh. The stench was overwhelming.

Dr. Castleden did not even cast a glance in Elizabeth's direction. She held the basin, trembling, as he gently removed all the wrapping and bandages from Darcy. The patient, for his part, did not stir. The doctor stood up and took the basin from Elizabeth. "Well, we will let that breathe for a while then, shall we?" he asked cheerfully. She looked at him in astonishment.

"Are you not going to bandage him up again?" she gurgled, trying to control both her emotions and her roiling stomach. She followed him to the small table that was set up near the window for the doctor's use. He laid the basin down, took Elizabeth's hands in his, and looked at her intently.

"Do you trust me, Miss Bennet?" he asked.

"Of course, I do, Doctor," she said instinctively, although she was not sure that she did.

"I will test that trust in the next few days, I am sure," he said, smiling kindly. He gave her hands a squeeze and went over to his bag. There he pulled out a jar filled with tiny, white, wriggling worms. Elizabeth instinctively shut her eyes, and then went to the window for a breath of air. The doctor approached Darcy with his writhing colony.

"Miss Bennet," he said. "I want you to see what I am about to do, and I want you to understand why I do it, because you will be here, and I will not, and you will have to defend me. You are to be both my and Mr. Darcy's champion," he said.

With that, he opened the jar of tiny, wiggling grubs and shook them all over the decaying gash in Darcy's chest. As far as Elizabeth could tell, the air suddenly was sucked out of the room. It was everything she could do to keep her stomach from heaving. Closing her eyes for a moment, she set her jaw and resolved to carry on.

***

The next few days were filled with a mixture of wonder and of horror for Elizabeth Bennet. As soon as she was better from a cup of tea, Dr. Castleden explained his unorthodox treatment.

The doctor had been a physician for many years and had served on many battlefields. He told Elizabeth that, contrary to what common sense would dictate, it was sometimes beneficial for soldiers to be left wounded in the field. Elizabeth became wide-eyed at such a revelation.

"Surely, Doctor, you do not leave men purposely on the battlefield to, perhaps, bleed to death?" she asked, horrified.

"Oh no, certainly not," Dr. Castleden replied, smiling. "I am not implying that at all. It is just that, many times there are so many wounded and some men end up in obscure locations. Sometimes it is a day or two before we find them. In some cases, this is fatal. In others, an odd situation occurs. The men who are wounded and develop gangrene at times are aided by their neglect."

"What do you mean?" Elizabeth asked. She wasn't entirely sure that she wanted to know the answer but was trying to steel herself against whatever the doctor had to say next.

"The men left in the field were many times found covered in maggots."

Elizabeth felt faint again. The picture of Darcy covered with those wriggling worms sprang to her mind's eye.

"The men who were brought to me straight from the field," he paused in his narrative, "were subject to crude field medicine, many amputations. But the men who had been left in the field and survived... Many came in covered with flies and maggots." Elizabeth was trying her best to be objective, to maintain her composure, but her repugnance must have showed on her face. Castleden smiled. "It does sound rather repulsive, I must admit. The odd thing was," he continued, "that the men who were left to the flies and the insects seemed to do better than those who received medical attention immediately."

He looked up at Elizabeth with a kindly smile. Her astonishment shone on her face. "Why did they do better?" she asked.

"Mother Nature has her ways," said Castleden. "The fly larvae have a particular appetite. They feast on all things foul, as you may have noticed. The maggots' appetite seems to be exclusively for the gangrenous flesh and not the healthy. If the soldier's wounds were such that the bleeding had stopped, the flies and their offspring did a much more precise job of removing the dead flesh from the wounds than any human surgeon with his knife could hope to do."

For the first time in days, Elizabeth smiled. "So, Doctor, do you think there is hope? Can these creatures really help poor Mr. Darcy?" Her emotions sought to betray her, but she managed to keep her composure.

"If anything can, they can," he said decisively. "Now it is a matter of how strong our Mr. Darcy is, how deep the infection is in his blood, and how much of a will to live he has. The next few days will be critical. There is a good chance Lady Catherine de Bourgh will return to roust me and then it will be up to you to keep our revolting wormy friends to their task."

"No doubt she seeks to roust me as well," Elizabeth said.

"I have every faith in you, Miss Bennet. But remember, Mr. Darcy is far from well, and anything can happen."

Elizabeth and Dr. Castleden were the only people who would dare to enter Mr. Darcy's room. The stench of the gangrene was intolerable enough, but the sound of flies buzzing day and night was enough to drive one mad. They were everywhere, and Darcy's fevered body writhed with thousands of hungry maggots.

The first few days were nightmarish. Elizabeth got very little sleep even though Dr. Castleden remained by Darcy's bedside as much as possible. He had his own duties with the regiment to perform but returned to the Darcy house often. All of them, Elizabeth especially, needed reassurance that this unorthodox method of ridding Mr. Darcy of gangrene was his only hope of recovery.

It was ten in the morning of the third day since Lady Catherine's visit when the bell rang, and Miss Bennet was requested downstairs. Elizabeth had bathed and was in a fresh frock that morning. To her eye, Darcy actually seemed to be better. He had not spoken or even opened his eyes for days, but the flesh around the wound seemed to be pinker than before, and much of the ghastlier portions of the wound were disappearing rapidly. It was on this morning she first dared to hope for her beloved's recovery.

"Miss Bennet, a visitor for you," Elsie's voice said though Darcy's bedroom door. At first, Elizabeth's blood ran cold. Could Lady Catherine have returned? Then, she thought better of it. *No, if Lady Catherine were here, she would already be in this room, ordering me out of the house.* Elizabeth mopped Darcy's brow with a damp cloth and kissed him lightly on the forehead. "I will return soon, my love," she whispered softly. It was what she always said when she left the room.

When Elizabeth reached the drawing room, she could not have been more surprised. There were Jane and Mr. Bingley. Jane threw herself into her sister's arms. "Oh, Lizzy, how are you?" she asked. Elizabeth embraced her sister and then held her at arm's length. How inscrutable Jane's features could be sometimes. Yet, she could see the concern in her eyes.

"I am fine. Really," she said in a light tone. She could see that her sister was skeptical.

"Really." It wasn't until that moment that she looked over to Mr. Bingley. He was absolutely beaming.

"Oh, Mr. Bingley, how good of you to come and visit your friend," she said. Bingley's face fell.

Jane turned and looked at him, let go of her sister, and took his hand. They approached Elizabeth together.

"We were married, Lizzy. Yesterday. That is what we came to tell you," Jane said softly. Elizabeth could see it now. The two of them were absolutely glowing.

They all hesitated for a moment while the news penetrated her exhausted brain. Finally, Elizabeth broke the spell. She rushed to embrace both of them. "Oh, Jane, Mr. Bingley, I am so happy for you."

"We so wanted you to be there, and Darcy too, but…" Bingley trailed off.

Elizabeth embraced him again. "I quite understand, Mr. Bingley," she said.

"Please, do call me Charles. After all, I am your brother now," said Bingley.

"So you are. So you are," said Elizabeth after a moment. "And you must call me Elizabeth, or Lizzy if you would like." She giggled. It felt so good to laugh again amidst all the pain and sorrow of the past two weeks.

The doors opened, and John came in with tea and cakes. "Oh, where are my manners? Please, do sit down," Elizabeth said, realizing then how much of a mistress of this house she had become. Jane looked up at her in surprise, which immediately turned to concern.

"Has it been terrible for you, Lizzy?" Jane asked. "You look tired. Papa said he has implored you to come home, and you have refused."

Elizabeth took her sister's hand. "If you were in the same circumstance," she questioned, looking over at Bingley, "you would never leave either, would you?"

Jane turned to look at her new husband, and then back at her sister, "But I am married, Lizzy. Whatever will people say?"

If Elizabeth had not been so tired, she would have debated the point, but now, all she could do was sigh. "Have some tea, Jane. And then, Charles, you and I will go see Mr. Darcy."

As Charles Bingley approached Darcy's room, Elizabeth observed him. He had left his new bride downstairs and soldiered forth on his own, but his expression betrayed his revulsion at that obvious odor emanating from the sickroom. He looked over at Elizabeth with a face full of admiration. "My word, have you been by his side through all this?" he asked.

"Indeed. Where else should I have been?" she said and then hesitated. Then, without shame she said, "I love him."

Bingley was silent. Elizabeth opened the door to the sickroom. The buzzing of the flies and the sickening smell hit both of them at once. Bingley reached for his kerchief and covered his mouth and nose. "Good Lord," was all he could say.

Tentatively, he approached Darcy's bedside. Darcy was lying there quietly, his chest bare, his open wound covered in writhing larvae. Bingley stopped, took a few shallow breaths, but to his credit, did not turn away. He sat in the chair next to Darcy's head and spoke to him.

"How are you, old man?" he attempted cheerfully. Darcy did not respond. Bingley looked back at Elizabeth the helplessness showing in his face.

"What can I do?" he asked.

"You have already done it," she said. "You came to see him."

***

To Elizabeth's surprise, Lady Catherine arrived later that afternoon and asked for tea. A feeling of dread overwhelmed her. Would she be ordered out of the house? What means to roust her from Darcy's side did Lady Catherine have at her disposal? Elizabeth was resolved, however. Aside from being physically removed from the premises, she would stay with Darcy.

After preparing herself for the onslaught she was sure was coming, she descended the stairs and entered the room. Silently, she curtsied. All Lady Catherine asked was, "Shall I pour?"

Elizabeth nodded in assent. No shouting ensued. No condemnations. *Whatever could this be about?* Elizabeth was so weary, she bordered on not caring a fig. Still, this change of tack was disturbing.

To Elizabeth's further astonishment, Lady Catherine filled Elizabeth's cup and then proceeded to fill her own.

"Miss Bennet," Lady Catherine began, handing Elizabeth her cup. "I see you are still here."

Elizabeth finally spoke. "Yes, Lady Catherine. I am still here. I will be here until Mr. Darcy is well enough to…" Words momentarily failed her. Lady Catherine waited patiently and did not spring to her usual castigations. Finally, her thoughts coalesced. "Well enough to tell me what *he* wants. Well enough for that, Lady Catherine."

Lady Catherine cleared her throat. "You misunderstand me, my dear. I am concerned for your health. You look so pale. It grieves me that you must shoulder this burden by yourself. It really is…" Elizabeth knew what she wanted to say—*It really is most unsuitable*—but strangely, she did not. "It really is too much for you, I fear. Now, calm yourself, and have some tea."

Elizabeth's surprise at Lady Catherine's suddenly solicitous attitude must have shown in her face. She was sure of it. Elizabeth took the teacup in her hand and drank thirstily. As she took a sip, she grimaced slightly. The tea had a slightly bitter taste that Elizabeth did not recognize. Lady Catherine bit her lip as Elizabeth took another sip and put the cup down. Was the great lady smiling at her? If she was, it was the smile of a fox or a snake.

At that moment, the door panels slid open. It was John. "Miss Elizabeth," John called. "Miss Elizabeth, come quickly. I believe Mr. Darcy is awake."

Elizabeth rose quickly and nearly ran for the stairs. Before she reached them, however, her knees gave way beneath her. The last thing she saw was Lady Catherine standing over her, smiling as she lay in a heap at her feet.

***

Elizabeth awoke from a confusing and disturbing nightmare. Jane was seated next to her, dozing.

"Jane, dear, Jane," Elizabeth said, shaking her arm.

Jane awoke with a start. "Oh, Lizzy, thank the Lord," she exclaimed, and hugged her sister immediately. "We were so awfully worried about you."

Elizabeth looked puzzled. "What happened to me? I cannot seem to recall…" She began searching her mind for the memory of what happened.

"You collapsed at Mr. Darcy's house. Do you remember? Lady Catherine was there. She called on us immediately. Oh, Lizzy, you frightened us so."

Elizabeth closed her eyes, trying to recall the scene. She remembered taking tea with Lady Catherine, but after that, everything was a blur.

"How long have I been here?" she asked. Before Jane could answer, there was a knock at the door.

"May I come in?" It was her father's voice. Elizabeth smiled.

"Come in, Papa, Lizzy's awake," Jane called and jumped up to admit him.

As her father entered, Elizabeth thought that he had aged since she saw him last, which was not so long ago. He must be quite angry with her since she'd refused to come home when he'd demanded it. She could not obey him, though. She could not leave Darcy. *What was happening with Darcy? Who was caring for him?*

Her father reached her bedside. "How are you, my dear? You had all of us quite worried."

"Forgive me, Papa." She was genuinely sorry for the concern she could see in his face.

Her father embraced her at once. "There is nothing to forgive, Lizzy. Now that you are well, I will take you home."

"Oh, no," Elizabeth said at once. "I cannot leave until I am sure that..." She did not even finish her sentence. She turned again to her father and sister. "Please. I need to wash and dress and return to Mr. Darcy. Please, Jane."

Jane and her father looked at one another. Elizabeth recognized that look. They knew their Lizzy. Nothing could stop her once she had made up her mind.

"I will send Clara in to tend to you, but you must eat something before you go, Lizzy. You have been asleep for three days and—"

"Three days," Elizabeth exclaimed. "That cannot be. Oh, my poor Darcy. What has become of him? Who is tending to him? I must go." She sat up quickly and her head was reeling. She closed her eyes and sat back against the pillows.

"First you will eat, and then I will accompany you, Elizabeth," her father said as sternly as he could muster. "I have let this go on long enough."

With that, he took Jane by the hand and left the room. An hour later, he and Elizabeth were on their way to Mr. Darcy's.

When John answered the door, Elizabeth could tell from his expression that something was terribly wrong.

"What has happened?" she cried, pushing past him.

"Elizabeth," her father called after her, for she was already racing up the stairs.

As she pushed the door to his room open, her heart pounded in her breast. What she saw nearly caused it to stop completely. The room where her beloved had lain was empty.

***

What was happening? Rosings? Who was speaking? Darcy tried mightily to stay awake, but speaking was more than he could manage. He wanted to know what was happening to him. *Where was Elizabeth?* He was sure she had been there. *Was I dreaming? Am I dreaming?*

When he next opened his eyes, he was strapped under his arms to a chair and being carried out his front door. *It was night, was it not? Was it?* He next could feel himself rocking and with each movement the pain grew worse. A moan escaped his lips. *Dr. Lomax was speaking, and Dr. Castleden. He should not be moved. Yes, someone said Rosings and Lady Catherine. What was happening?*

From time to time, when he could swim out of unconsciousness to the surface, he could see out of a carriage window. *So, I am on a journey.* When they hit a particularly nasty crag in the road, he let out a cry. At least, he thought he did. He felt oddly disembodied. Then he heard them.

"Really, Your Ladyship," Dr. Lomax pleaded as they made yet another stop in order to minister to him, "the dosages are getting dangerously high. I cannot be responsible for what might happen. The man is weak and—"

"My nephew is not weak," Lady Catherine stated haughtily.

"Your Ladyship, I only meant—"

"Do your duty, Doctor, and I want to hear no more about it," Lady Catherine instructed. Her tone was imperious to be sure, but could he hear fear in it?

He could feel the doctor lifting his head and forcing something between his lips. He knew that taste by now. Laudanum. Before he slipped into another fevered dream, he could hear his aunt's voice carrying in the distance.

Chapter 4

Elizabeth was at a loss. Her return to Longbourn was bittersweet. At first, her mother refused to speak to her, telling her father, in a voice loud enough to wake the dead, that she had brought scandal upon them. Not a word was spoken of Lydia, whose elopement with Wickham had begun the whole unfortunate sequence of events. The fact that Lydia's thoughtless behavior had nearly cost her father his life and the fact that she was now married to the perpetrator of the whole affair did not even occur to her mother. It was as if Mrs. Bennet was a slate in school that could be wiped clean. All it took was a marriage ceremony.

Jane was married now too, and Elizabeth rejoiced in that. Jane and Bingley followed Elizabeth back to the town of Meryton and then took up residence at Netherfield Hall. For that she was grateful. It was wonderful to be near Jane again.

At home, her sister Mary was of a mind like her mother's. All she received from her was short, curt answers to her questions. Mary seemed fated to be a spinster, always with her nose in a book, so it was just as well that she began to agree with her mother. Mary would, very likely, be her mother's companion in her dotage. Elizabeth's sister Kitty, who looked to, of all people, Lydia, for guidance, seemed temporarily cowed by their youngest sister's antics. Although she still seemed to have fascination with officers, her manner was more restrained.

It was Elizabeth, now, who felt she cast a shadow over her family's happiness. Word had reached Meryton of her ministrations to her beloved Darcy, and the town was equally divided on the sisters' suitability for gentle company. Many wished to ingratiate themselves to Jane, and for that they endured Mary and Kitty and even her mother. Elizabeth, had she any interest in local gossip, might have found herself treated with civility, but hardly with affection. The truth was, however, that all she could think of was that she had to see Darcy again.

After her initial shock, Elizabeth saw Lady Catherine's hand in Darcy's disappearance, and perhaps even her collapse. She went over that day in her mind again and again. *Did that tea have a strange taste? Why was Lady Catherine so kind to her on that day when she was so angry with her only a few days before?* On the one hand, Elizabeth could hardly believe that Lady Catherine De Bourgh would stoop to poisoning her with a sleeping draught, but then again, the Borgia family in Italy did far worse. Perhaps she should be grateful that she escaped with her life. She was fairly sure the woman had not been intent on murdering her, just in dislodging her and her family from her nephew.

But what of her beloved Darcy? He had to be either at Pemberley or at Rosings. In all likelihood, Lady Catherine was keeping him under lock and key with her at Rosings if, in fact, he was still alive. Could he be dead and they did not tell her? This not knowing was agony. She went over and over in her mind scenarios in which she arrived at Rosings unannounced and demanded to see Darcy. None of them resulted in her being admitted. More horribly, sometimes, late at night, she would awaken to thoughts that would beleaguer her until dawn. *What if Darcy asked to be removed to his estate to recover? What if he did not want to see me? What if he had found that all this suffering he endured had been caused by his love for me?* Perhaps pain had erased the ardor he had felt for her. She had treated him badly once and in no uncertain terms refused his proposal of marriage. Perhaps, on his sickbed, those memories had returned to him. Coupled with all he had endured since, his heart may have grown cold. Her thoughts turned round and round upon themselves until she felt she could not suffer them more.

It was finally her brother-in-law who inadvertently eased her mind. The family was invited to dine at Netherfield by Jane and her husband. Elizabeth was feeling quite morose, but nonetheless, wanted very much to spend some time with Jane. When they arrived, her mother was in raptures. Two young people, Edward Home and his sister Barbara Ellsworth, were staying with Jane and Charles. They were friends of Mr. Bingley and were spending some time abroad from their home, the island of Grenada in the Caribbean.

Dinner was spent amicably enough. Both young people were of good breeding, but more importantly, friendly and tolerant. Elizabeth watched as her mother fawned over young Edward, pushing him toward Kitty at every opportunity. The young man was tall and quite handsome, with dark brown hair from which frequently a curl would escape to the middle of his forehead, giving him a rakish look. His sister was a handsome young woman in her own right, with blue eyes that crinkled gaily when she laughed, which was often.

When the time came for the men to retire for talk of politics, Edward suggested that instead they play charades all together. It occurred to Elizabeth that Darcy would have been scandalized by such a suggestion, but good-natured Bingley was more than happy to humor his guest.

Edward arranged to be seated next to Elizabeth, and in spite of herself, she was gradually drawn into the fun. In fact, she had almost forgotten how to laugh at silly things.

"You and I shall act the next one together," Edward said.

"If you insist, Mr. Home," she said.

"Oh, I do indeed, Miss Bennet," he rejoined. He drew a paper from the hat and he shared it with her. They were to act out *The Castle of Otranto* by Horace Walpole. Taking her hand, he drew her into a corner and they conspired together.

"I have not the slightest idea what to do," she exclaimed in a whisper.

"I believe I may have an idea," he said. After a few minutes, Bingley began to taunt them, and, laughing, they returned to the floor. Elizabeth and Edward did their utmost to give clue after clue, but alas the only result was hilarity, and no point for their team. As the two of them finished, Edward bowed solemnly after his performance and then deferred to Elizabeth, who curtsied. Laughing, he took her by the hand as they took their seats once more. As the other team prepared to continue, Elizabeth looked down at his hand holding hers. He must have noticed her attention to it and quickly withdrew his hand.

"I do beg your pardon, Miss Bennet," he said apologetically.

"No need," she said, and their eyes met. He was gazing at her most intently. Her mother gave her a knowing look.

"Mr. Home will be my partner next," Kitty said, and stood up in preparation to take her place next to Edward.

"Oh, do sit down, Kitty," said her mother, unceremoniously tugging at her skirt. Kitty sat down immediately, a bewildered expression crossing her face.

Elizabeth turned her head quickly. "No, Kitty is quite right. I have been monopolizing Mr. Home for far too long," she said. She changed places with Kitty, but Edward smiled at her in a most disconcerting manner.

Later that evening, when some of the party were at cards, and some were quietly having coffee, Elizabeth had a moment to take her brother-in-law aside.

"Charles, do you have any news of Mr. Darcy?" she said anxiously.

Bingley, who was in a gay mood, was taken aback. "Darcy? Why no." Elizabeth expected that answer but was disappointed nonetheless.

"You know, Elizabeth, I could ride to Rosings tomorrow and inquire as to his health," Bingley said cheerfully.

"I have to come with you," she said in response.

"Now, dear sister, I do believe that is quite impossible," he began, but she interrupted him.

"It's not impossible. I must—"

Suddenly, Edward was there. "What are you two conspiring about?" he said playfully.

Bingley took the initiative. "I was just telling my dear sister that I was planning a ride to Rosings tomorrow. I believe I can get there and back in a day on horseback and bring her the news she is seeking. That should be all right, do you think, Elizabeth?" he said. His face was so kind and full of concern; Elizabeth nearly lost her composure looking at it. Alas, that did nothing but reinforce her determination.

"Yes, dear brother, I do think that is best," she said. "Jane and I will only accompany you as far as Hunsford and stop with Charlotte and Mr. Collins. We can send one of your footmen ahead to let them know we are coming."

"The Collinses are only just across the park from Rosings, Lizzy," Charles said, exasperatedly. He sighed.

"Exactly," said Elizabeth, smiling. At that, Edward offered his arm and led her to a table where they began a spirited game of piquet.

***

The next morning, Bingley, Edward, Jane, Elizabeth, and Barbara bounced amiably toward their goal. At least, the three of them seemed to. Elizabeth felt, with each passing mile, her agitation was increasing. To add to her discomfort, Charles Bingley took it upon himself to convey the whole, unfortunate chain of events that led to their journey that day. He was careful to emphasize all their concern, rather than betray Elizabeth's part in Darcy's nursing. She was grateful to him for broaching a subject that she could not without betraying the force of her emotions.

"It is all in the hands of Fate now," Bingley said wistfully.

"The Fates have always been kind to me," Edward said, and then added quickly, "and I am sure they will be to your friend as well." He looked pointedly at Elizabeth.

"I pray that it should be so," was all she said.

Edward looked at her face for a moment, and she held his gaze. Elizabeth began to feel uncomfortable at the piercing way he looked at her. It was as if he was seeking something in her countenance that he could not ask her in words. She decided to break the spell.

"Mr. Home, you have told me nothing of yourself," she said. "You and your sister must lead a fascinating life. Have you always lived in Grenada?"

That seemed to be all the encouragement Edward needed to launch into his full life history. He told of his upbringing in England, where he had every advantage, and then how he spent his young manhood on a plantation near Grenville in Grenada. His father, Ninian Home, was now lieutenant governor of the island. His father insisted that he be educated in England, and so he was shipped off to university, where he spent four years of his life. He was older than many of the students there but felt that he fit in quite well. Elizabeth believed him. He had a friendly, open way about him.

"I never knew you attended Cambridge," Bingley said.

"There is much you don't know about me," said Edward. "I believe my father would like me to follow in his footsteps and go into politics, but in politics, one needs a wife."

"I can recommend marriage very highly," said Bingley jovially. He smiled at Jane, who looked up at him adoringly. All this jovial talk, all this passing of the time, made Elizabeth want to scream, but instead, she smiled too. She hoped it did not appear too waxen. *This journey is endless.*

Encouraged by Mr. Home, Bingley began to relate how he met Edward and Barbara. For this small mercy, Elizabeth was grateful. They were carrying the conversation where she could not.

"Do you remember that ball, where was it?" Bingley asked Edward.

"At the Montagu's, I believe." Edward again looked at Elizabeth. She was feigning

attention, was she not? He was looking at her so intently that she could not hold his eye but turned to gaze out the window.

"I believe it was there, Charles, and that your sister Caroline introduced us," chimed Barbara.

The pasture land rolled by, and Elizabeth, twisting her handkerchief in her hand constantly, made every effort to be present.

"I will never forget her face when you told her that you were newly married." Edward turned to his sister jovially. "I do believe she had designs on you and our Charles here."

"Oh, Edward, do be quiet," Barbara said, rather too loudly. That exchange got Elizabeth's attention. She turned from her post of observing the countryside and shot a glance at her own sister. Surely, Edward had embarrassed her. Edward's sister Barbara was one of the women whom Caroline had thought suitable for him, not Jane. Bingley and Edward must have met during that fateful London season in which he entirely ignored Jane. How she had suffered during his absence. Charles's sisters had kept him from even knowing that Jane was in town. All their machinations, although temporarily keeping Jane and him apart, had only clarified for him his abiding love for her. Poor Jane.

Yet, as Elizabeth turned her attention to her sister, Jane sat as placidly as ever and ever so surreptitiously wove her arm into her husband's. Jane, unlike her, was content and sure in her position in her beloved's affections. For a moment, for just a moment, Elizabeth envied her. Barbara, seeking to fill the breach her brother so clumsily made, began to talk of Gerard, her husband.

He was a cacao planter and highly involved with the island's politics. During their present stay, he had been called back early and left her to her brother's care.

"How can you be so long away from Gerard?" Jane asked suddenly.

Barbara began to laugh. "It will be all the sweeter when we are reunited," she said cheerfully. Elizabeth was trying mightily to say something, but the words would not come.

By evening, they were approaching Hunsford. Charlotte must have been waiting at the window, because she was upon them before the carriage had rolled to a stop.

"Oh, I am so happy you are here," she said to Elizabeth, taking her hands. "Do come in out of the night air."

Mister Collins descended the stairs in what Elizabeth thought to be a dramatic entrance. How Charlotte tolerated or even loved the man, she had no idea. It gave her chills thinking that, if she had been less sure of her own mind, and indeed, less willful, he would now be *her* husband. She visibly shuddered.

"Are you cold, Elizabeth?" Charlotte asked, concerned.

Elizabeth was about to deny it but thought better of it. "Perhaps a little."

Presently they were shown into the drawing room. Introductions were being made when there was a frantic banging on the front door. The party turned when a liveried servant stepped in.

"Oh, Mr. Collins, do come at once. Lady Catherine De Bourgh has great need of you." The servant was turning red with urgency.

As Mr. Collins shuffled into his coat he asked, "What has happened?"

"Oh, it's Mr. Darcy, sir. He died tonight."

For a moment, all assembled stood stunned. It was Elizabeth who spoke first. "No," she said. "No, no. It is not possible. He was recovering. He was. I saw him," she sputtered and turned her head away.

Bingley, as if woken from a dream, intervened. "Go, Mr. Collins. Please. You may best bring us news." Mr. Collins was already halfway out the door with the footman.

"No. No, this is some sort of trick of Lady Catherine's. She would do anything not to ally herself and her family with the lowly Bennets. It is a trick, a hoax. I am sure of it." While Elizabeth was speaking, her expression became wilder and more desperate.

She peeked at Edward; he stood there mutely, as if watching a spectacle.

"Miss Bennet," he began. The sound of his voice shocked Elizabeth momentarily. She stood there looking at him. Bingley swallowed hard but did not speak. Edward went on.

"Miss Bennet," Edward began again. "Tomorrow. We will take you to Rosings tomorrow."

"No, I must see him. I must see him now." Elizabeth covered her mouth with her hand. She let her teeth sink into her outstretched finger in an effort to control her emotions. And even as her words echoed in her own ears, she knew it was impossible. Lady Catherine would bar her way. Yet, she must see for herself. She must.

***

All were asleep in the Collins household. Elizabeth waited until the old clock on the mantel chimed midnight. Mr. Collins had not yet returned. She threw on her cloak, opened the door to her room, and swept swiftly down the stairs and into the still night.

The walk across the park had been taken in happier times. A less furtive, sun-drenched, happier time. The time when Charlotte had been newly married. The time she had first met Lady Catherine. Now, as she approached the great house, she was at a loss as to what to do. Where could she gain entrance? Should she announce herself or steal in like a thief in the night?

The opportunity presented itself as she made her way through the manicured garden. The light in the kitchen was still burning, but no voices could be heard. Perhaps some of the household were still awake. Perhaps she could prevail upon one of them. No, that would never do. Their livelihoods were wrapped up in their loyalty to Lady Catherine.

She approached the window stealthily and peered inside. No one stirred. Trying the door, she found it unlocked. Slowly, she opened it and made her way through the kitchen. Peering around the door, she found herself in the passageway that led to the great hall. *No doubt, he is still upstairs. How will I find him? What if I am discovered? It does not matter anymore. It does not matter what I say or what I do, if my Darcy is gone. What do I care for Lady Catherine's opinion of me? What do I care?*

The household was eerily still. Although wrapped in a cloak, Elizabeth shivered. She remembered the look of the house, its plan, from her visit with Charlotte not so long ago. At that time Lady Catherine was of a mind to show her great "condescension" as Mr. Collins would say. Now, she would no doubt have Elizabeth dragged out in chains. With great care, she climbed the staircase in the hall that led to the bedrooms. Some were visible along the landing, while others were accessible only if one turned a corner.

Every door was closed. Elizabeth had no idea how to proceed, or if, in fact, Darcy was there at all. She stood on the landing, angry with herself for not having more of a strategy, when she heard voices. Frightened, she turned one way and then another, trying to decide whether to hide herself or abandon her plan altogether and retreat from whence she came. A door opened, and light spilled into the hallway from one of the rooms hidden from her view. She could hear Lady Catherine's voice.

"You are to stay awake and pray, Mr. Collins. Stay awake and pray," she said. There was a rustling of clothing. Elizabeth could not possibly descend the stairs in time. Turning quickly, she tried the first door in front of her and the knob turned easily. As quietly as she could, she slipped inside the darkened room, leaving the door open ever so slightly. She was terrified that the clicking of the latch would betray her presence.

She peered into the darkened hallway when she heard the rustling of fabric again. The light stopped in front of the door where Elizabeth stood. Inadvertently, she gasped. The rustling stopped.

"Mr. Collins, is that you?" Lady Catherine called. Elizabeth held her breath. All was still. The rustling began again, and the light faded. She could hear a door opening and a latch falling into place. Elizabeth breathed a sigh of relief.

Then, a hand grasped her shoulder.

Elizabeth gasped and the hand on her shoulder moved to her mouth. Someone stifled her cry. Before she could react, she heard a voice.

"Is that you, Miss Bennet? Let me light the lamp." The hand let go of her and Elizabeth gazed into the darkness, trying to discern who it was. It sounded like a young woman.

Finally, the lamp was lit, and Elizabeth could see. It was, indeed, a young woman. For a moment, they both stood staring at one another and then the girl spoke again.

"I am Georgiana, Mr. Darcy's sister," she said. Elizabeth couldn't account for it, but tears filled her eyes. "You must be Elizabeth Bennet. My brother told me so much about you."

The strain of her secret entrance into the house, the news of Darcy's demise, the narrow miss with Lady Catherine, and now meeting Darcy's sister in such a way all fell upon Elizabeth at once. She put her hand to her mouth and stifled a sob. The tears that had filled her eyes started to pour out unceremoniously.

"Oh," Georgiana said and ran to her side. Taking her by the arm, she led her to one of the armless chairs that flanked each side of the room. Wordlessly, Georgiana brought Elizabeth a handkerchief and she took it gratefully. Elizabeth did not know what to say to this poor girl who had lost her brother in such a manner. She was overcome with guilt and sorrow.

"I am so sorry," was all Elizabeth could manage through her tears. She was trying mightily to regain control over herself.

"I feel quite lost now," Georgiana said. "I still cannot believe it. I saw him, and yet I cannot believe it." Georgiana looked at her companion in such a sympathetic way that it took all of Elizabeth's strength not to break down completely. She tried to breathe slowly. "I will get you some water," Georgiana said.

It struck Elizabeth that people often suggested a drink of something or other when others were overcome with emotion. She wondered at it. Latching on to that thought distracted her enough that she began to regain her composure.

"Thank you so much for not betraying me to your aunt," Elizabeth said as she sipped from the glass. "As you have guessed, I am Elizabeth Bennet."

"I am happy to finally meet you." Georgiana smiled weakly. Elizabeth's heart went out to her. "My brother spoke of you often. I feel that I know you already, somehow. You have come to see him, have you not?" Elizabeth nodded mutely. "I will pave the way for you then. I do believe my aunt has retired, so we have only Mr. Collins and perhaps my brother's man, John, to deal with, but I'm sure he will want to help." Georgiana rose and took a candle from the sideboard. She lit it over the lamp.

Before they reached the door to her room, Elizabeth touched her arm. "I cannot tell you how sorry I am that all this has come to pass. I feel that it is my fault." Georgiana shook her head.

"No one is to blame, except perhaps George Wickham," she said bluntly. Elizabeth felt a wave of relief wash over her. She did not expect such a sweet and forgiving nature from one so young. She squeezed Georgiana's arm, and the young girl disappeared down the hall.

Elizabeth waited, and Georgiana returned with John. Elizabeth joined them in the hallway.

"I am so glad you have come, miss. He would have desired it, I am sure," John said. The candlelight fell upon his features. He looked more tired and worn than Elizabeth had ever seen him.

"We should not talk here," Georgiana whispered. "My aunt's chamber is very near." She took Elizabeth's sleeve and the three of them crossed the landing to the farthest bedchamber. The door was open slightly, and Elizabeth could see a light within.

John leaned in toward her and whispered, "Mr. Collins is asleep again. If you are quiet, he will not wake. Trust me." Elizabeth did not want to share her last moments with her beloved Darcy with Mr. Collins, but it could not be helped. As they approached the door, Georgiana squeezed her hand.

"I will come back for you soon," she said, and she and John withdrew.

Darcy lay upon his bed, a solitary lamp burning in the corner. The window was open, and the cool night air filled the chamber. There was no fire. Mr. Collins snored.

Elizabeth approached the bed where her beloved lay, his hands clasped across his chest. As she gazed at his peaceful face, she could only think of what could have been between them. She could only think that she would have to live forever on one embrace and one kiss, one passionate kiss.

He lay so still, so pale. She knelt next to the bed and touched his sleeve gently. He remained unmoving. Running the back of her fingers along his jawline, she thought that perhaps he still lived, that maybe the warmth of life still filled his shattered body. He felt cold to the touch. As cold as the room in which she now stood. She could observe no movement, no fever, only peace. He was gone. She now knew it as a fact. She had seen it with her own eyes.

Could she survive Darcy's loss? She was overcome with guilt. It was all her fault. He should have followed his first instincts and run from her. She spoke softly to him, telling him so. Telling him but understanding that he could never hear her voice again.

"Miss Elizabeth, what are you doing here?"

Elizabeth was startled almost to the point of faintness. She jolted backward, and then regained her composure. Mr. Collins was awake.

"I had to see for myself," she said as he stood, mouth agape, staring at her.

"I will see you out. I will see you out, now," he whispered, if whispers could be a shout.

There was no reason to stay any longer. Elizabeth touched Darcy's hand, and Mr. Collins snatched it away. She knew then that she was on the verge of madness. It was almost as if she felt warmth there in Darcy's touch, but she knew it could not be. Her mind was playing tricks on her.

Before five minutes had passed, Mr. Collins had deposited Elizabeth unceremoniously outside the kitchen door. "We shall never speak of this," he muttered as he closed the kitchen door and bolted it from within. *Georgiana will arrive to find me gone.*

As she entered the dark night, the full import of what she had seen washed over her in a great wave of desperation and torment. She managed to walk almost halfway to the parsonage, tears streaming down her face, when she collapsed unseen in a copse where she began to wail in earnest. No one but the moon to hear her, she unleashed the floodgates of her grief.

***

When she awakened the next morning, she tried to remember where she was and realized that she was at the parsonage. She remembered then her undertaking of the night before. No one had seen her leave for Rosings and none had seen her return. For that, she was grateful.

The summer weather was heavy with moisture and she rose to wash. Pouring the water in the basin, she disrobed and sponged herself. As she wrung the last droplets from the sponge, she realized that she felt nothing. No sorrow, no pain, nothing. Yesterday, her heart had been wrung out, the last drops of feeling dripping onto cool grass. She wondered if she would ever feel anything again.

As she entered the breakfast room, Jane jolted upright from her seat and ran to her.

"Oh, my poor Lizzy," was all she could say, and took her sister's arm. *I must look a fright*, but she had no care for her looks. She could see Jane and Charles exchange looks, and then Charles spoke.

"I will do my best to gain you admittance to Rosings," he said soothingly. "I will do my best."

"That will not be necessary," Elizabeth said flatly. They looked at each other again. "You needn't worry, Jane. I have accepted the news. I have accepted it." She looked down at her hands folded in her lap and knew she could not sit at that table for a moment longer. She rose and, passing Edward and Barbara without speaking, returned to her room.

***

"Give me a moment with him, Mr. Collins."

"Yes, m'lady. As you wish, and may I say—"

"You may not."

Darcy heard the voices again. It was not Elizabeth this time. He knew he had heard her recently. *Where had she gone?* What was happening to him? Was he dreaming?

"Oh, Darcy." A plaintive wail reached his ears. It sounded like his Aunt Catherine. He had never heard her voice in such a manner. Never so full of sentiment. Dry, paper-like fingers lightly touched his hand.

"I will miss you... I will miss you, dear boy."

Weeping. It was the sound of weeping. Aunt Catherine weeping? That seemed impossible. He tried mightily to speak, to move, but somehow seemed locked within his own body.

I am here. He must make her understand. Try as he might, he could not make himself known to her. *What sort of hell is this?*

Hell. That was it. Perhaps he was dead, and he was in hell. So, hell is not what they told him when he was a boy learning his catechism. It was not filled with tortured souls burning in never-ending fire. It was this. It was darkness. It was isolation. It was being on the verge of life, but not of it. He was so confused.

For a time, he heard nothing. He knew not whether he was asleep or awake. Then, *what was that sound? Pounding. Nails into wood.* His mind raced. *What could it be?* No, he was not dead. He was alive, and in darkness. He could hear but could not speak. He could think but could not move. The pounding again. That infernal pounding.

A man whistling while he worked. Whistling a dirge. And then, he understood. Someone was hammering nails into a coffin. His coffin. They were burying him alive.

Chapter 5

As Elizabeth entered the carriage that was to take her back to Meryton and home, Charlotte emerged from her garden with a single rose. "For your journey," she said. "Do come back and see me, please, Elizabeth." Charlotte smiled weakly and Elizabeth took her hand. She nodded mutely, and Bingley helped her into the coach.

They rode for a time in awkward silence, each looking at the other and then out of the window of the coach as if something outside would break the discomfiture. Talking of weather was out of the question, even though the day, which to Elizabeth's mind should have been raining and overcast, was stubbornly fair and sunny. She was pensive and took to biting her lower lip every time she could feel the tears well up in her anew. Finally, Jane looked at her and began, "I wonder what delights Mother will have in store when we return with Edward and Barbara."

"We will not be able to stay long, you know," Edward informed her. "Preparations need to be made to return to Grenada."

This last statement seemed to lift Elizabeth out of her lethargy. "But surely you are not leaving so soon?"

"I am afraid so. Father is expecting us back and we must leave before the storm season begins."

"Oh," Elizabeth murmured. It seemed to her that this was to be her time of loss. *How odd.* The idea of their leaving caused another pang in her heart. A few weeks ago, she did not know their names, and now Edward and Barbara seemed almost like saviors to her. Was it their tales of faraway lands? Was it their unprejudiced acceptance of her and her family even though they were of more Charles Bingley's social class than her own? Perhaps it was all these things, but most of all, Edward made her laugh. Laughter was such a gift to her in this season of sorrow. She dared not think of it too much, but the tears were already starting unbidden from her eyes. Barbara looked at Jane, and then at her brother. A determined look came over her face, and she suddenly smiled.

"I do think that we have made the best of acquaintances, do you not, brother?" she said to Edward.

"Oh, indeed," Edward replied. "The best of friends, really."

"Yes, indeed we have, but we have had far too short a time to cement our friendship, so I believe it is only fair that Elizabeth accompany us and visit with us in St. George's. Father and Mother would be delighted, and I do so hate to say good-bye to you, Elizabeth."

Momentarily, Elizabeth forgot her sorrow in the shock of this new proposal. "Really," she began. "I could not—"

"But why not?" Edward asked. Jane looked in stunned surprise at her husband, who was smiling for the first time in days.

"Yes, my dear, why not?" said Bingley, looking at Jane for approval. "That is, if our dear sister is amenable." He looked over at Elizabeth. This was all too much. She looked from one face to another, all leaning eagerly toward her.

"If I may, I would like to have a moment to think, surely," she said, and Barbara laughed. At that Elizabeth laughed also, and Bingley and Jane joined in. Jane took her sister's hand and then addressed Barbara.

"Do tell us about your life in the islands," she said, and Barbara and Edward began their tale of life in a Caribbean colony, of sugar cane, of cacao, and of the French.

***

Darcy waited. He waited for the sound of dirt shoveled onto his coffin. He could not tell if it was day or night, or how much time had passed. A cold panic overtook him, and he cursed himself for being a coward. *Aside from burning alive, I cannot think of a more hideous death,* he thought to himself. His body, although not willing to shout, or move, or even weep, still felt the pain of his injury. It also, unmercifully, could hear all that was going on around him. *In my weakened state, it will not take me long to die,* was his most comforting thought. He had been abandoned by all, even his beloved

Elizabeth. Of course, it was not her fault. She thought he was dead. Everyone knew he was dead.

He must have slept for a time, because he was suddenly aware again and felt himself being jostled. Was this all a dream? Perhaps he was still in a coach with his Aunt Catherine. Was he ever in that coach? No matter. He was moving. He could feel it. After a time, he stopped, and could hear someone talking.

"Gah, I don't half like dead 'uns." It was a boy's voice.

"Mind yer tongue, Rupert," a man said. "This 'ere's Mr. Darcy and 'e's to be given the respect 'e's due. Besides, you don't want 'im comin' back to haunt ye now, do ye?"

"Ye don't think 'e'd come back, do ye?"

"Not less 'e's been mighty 'ard done by, I reckon, so mind your manners in 'is presence, that's all I'm sayin'," the man said. "Now, sit ye down 'ere, and I'll fetch ye come supper."

Things were becoming clearer. With all his concentration, he tried moving his hand. He tried again. Nothing. His breath was coming in short, painful bursts, but he was breathing. He was aware of that now. He was so thirsty. *I am still on this side of the soil. There is still hope.* He tried to speak but could not.

Time passed. He could smell something. Food. His senses were becoming clearer. He tried to remember the last time he ate anything. There were sounds all around him: horses, wheels crunching through gravel, shouts.

Then he heard the boy's voice again. What was his name? Rupert? "I am an official mourner, that's what I am."

Something was said that was too far away.

He could hear more voices. Children. Children were talking. He must be dreaming again, but no, he could hear everything. Darcy began to concentrate. *I must move. I must speak. I must let them know I am here and I am alive, before it is too late.*

Rupert's voice again. "Well, I can tell ye somethin'. This ain't no ordinary coach. Is an 'earse." He was accompanying Darcy's hearse. It penetrated his confused brain. He was being transported to Pemberley. *Thank God. My aunt did not decide to bury me at Rosings. There will not be six feet of earth thrown on top of my breathing body. At least, not yet. I must stay awake, move my hands, pound on the coffin lid.*

"What's an 'earse?"

"It's a hearse. It is a coach for dead people."

This one holds a live man, boys. A live man. I must have air.

"You mean there is someone dead in there?"

"That's what I'm sayin'," said Rupert.

"We don't believe you, do we, Kenny?"

"No, we don't."

The conversation ceased. Darcy was gasping for air. Concentrating. Concentrating on moving his hands, on finding his voice. *Don't leave, boys. I am here.*

"I can prove it. Want t'see? That is, unless you're scared," said Rupert.

"We are not scared," the boys practically shouted.

"Father told us to wait over there." It was a small child. *No, do not go.*

"He won't be back for a while. Show us, if you dare," he teased.

"Well, then," Rupert said. "Let's get to it. Come on, if ye want t'see."

Darcy could hear his own heartbeat. He could barely breathe. Try as he might, he could not call out.

Darcy could feel movement. He was being slightly jostled again.

"They didn't nail it in with too many nails," said Rupert. "Lucky for you."

"Aye, lucky."

"Are ye ready now?" Rupert asked.

"'Ow long's he been dead?"

"Only a day or two," said Rupert. "Shouldn't be too 'orrible."

Darcy could hear the scraping sounds of something metal being shoved between planks of wood. The nails screeched and creaked as they set loose from their housing.

With the whiff of fresh air filling the compartment, Darcy took a deep breath and opened his eyes. Two boys were holding the coffin lid open and staring down at him. Darcy turned his head and looked directly at them. He opened his mouth to speak, but the boys screamed and slammed the coffin lid shut.

Darcy found that he could move. He could finally move. He pushed at the coffin lid and it gave way slightly. He could breathe again. He could move again. The nightmare was over.

He could hear children shouting, "It's a ghost. It's a ghost."

Darcy waited, filling his lungs with the fresh night air. He was horribly thirsty, and his mouth and throat were parched. A few minutes passed, and he again heard the man's voice he heard before.

"Now, see there. All's quiet. No one there that can 'arm ye'," he said. Darcy found himself moaning. The lid of the coffin bounced up slightly and slammed shut. For a moment all was still. Darcy used all his strength to push the coffin lid again.

"See, Mr. Croft," the boy said, whining.

"That ain't no ghost, my lad. That man is alive," Croft told him. Darcy could feel the wagon shift with the man's weight and the coffin lid opened. He looked at Croft, who was staring silently at him. Darcy reached up and clutched at Croft's lapels. He pulled Croft close enough so that he could hear his words. "Water," he whispered.

Chapter 6

"It is all settled, then." Barbara beamed. Elizabeth's mother was in raptures. For the last few days, Elizabeth had to listen to how wonderful it was that her daughter would be the guest of Lieutenant Governor Home of the British colony of Grenada. Of course, Jane had done better with Bingley at five thousand a year. Still, one should not scoff at political connections either. Edward seemed a fine young man, and he was definitely interested in Elizabeth despite what her mother perceived as her obvious shortcomings in temperament. And the scandal. Attending Mr. Darcy alone all that time with no marriage to follow. Surely, no one this side of the Atlantic would look in her direction now. An island home for Elizabeth was just the thing. And her well-to-do sister-in-law Barbara. Of course, she wasn't quite her sister-in-law yet, but that was only a matter of time to be sure. What a delightful young woman. Perhaps the Bennet family could put the last few months permanently behind them.

Her mother always did this sort of thing. Went on and on, extrapolating the most extraordinary fantasies from the most ordinary of facts. She also seemed to have no sensitivity whatsoever for Elizabeth's feelings.

Kitty and Mary persisted in their sullen silence during all the packing and preparations. Mary, she observed, continued her vexing behavior of keeping her nose in a book, only to lift it out occasionally to pronounce everyone silly. Kitty merely pouted. Elizabeth knew her mother was equally anxious to marry off her younger daughters but seemed slightly cowed by what Lydia's antics had brought down upon them. As an added precaution that history would not repeat itself too soon, her mother had forbidden Kitty her visits into town to meet officers.

Jane spent much of the next few days helping Elizabeth prepare for her journey. In quiet moments, Elizabeth wondered at how all of this had come about. She did turn things over and over in her mind. Why should she not go? That seemed to be the chief argument for the journey. What remained for her here? Her family was here at Longbourn, of course, but how much longer would they have their home? Their father was in good health now, but he was aging as they all were. What prospects had she here? None to speak of. The story of her nursing Darcy was all about the neighborhood and doing her and none of them any good. Such a scandal. None of that meant anything, though. None of it meant anything to her, that is. It was the rest of her family who must bear the brunt of any condemnation. No, it was better for her and for everyone that she should go.

It was decided that Elizabeth should depart from Netherfield and that Bingley would accompany her to Portsmouth. Edward and Barbara had gone ahead to make arrangements for themselves and their guest.

Her last night at home was a restless one. The family had long ago gone to bed, and the house was quiet. She heard the clock in the hall chiming eleven and then twelve. Finally abandoning her attempt at sleep, she crept downstairs to her father's study, hoping that a book of some sort might help her spend the hours until morning. As she reached the bottom of the stairs, she noticed that the lamp was lit. On reaching the open door, she saw her father with a book in his hand, but his eyes looking somewhere into the distance. He started when he saw her.

"Oh, I am sorry, Papa, I did not mean to startle you," she said.

"Come in, Lizzy. Come in," he beckoned. She crossed the room and sat at his feet. "You cannot sleep, eh? Neither can I."

"No. Sleep will not come tonight." Elizabeth would not look into his eyes, nor could she bring herself to say what she wanted to say.

He swallowed with difficulty and began looking off into the distance again. Elizabeth suspected that he was trying to control his emotions. She, on the other hand, was far less successful at keeping herself in check.

"Oh, Papa, I will miss you," she said. She squeezed his hand and leaned her face against his knee, not daring to look at him.

"I cannot help thinking," he said softly, "that this entire situation is my fault."

That statement snapped Elizabeth from her emotional quagmire. "How on earth is any of this your fault?" Before he could assemble an answer, she continued, "If it is anyone's fault, it is Lydia's…and Wickham's." She stood now and leaned on one of the bookcases with her back to him. Her eyes were filling with tears again, but she would not have it. The time for weeping was done.

"Dear Lizzy," her father said softly. "I will miss you very much…very much. You will come back to me, will you not? Someday?"

Elizabeth turned, and her father embraced her. She let her head fall upon his shoulder and he patted her back as he had done when she was little.

"Now, now," he said. "Go to bed. You will need all your strength tomorrow for your mother's good-bye." He was chuckling when she pulled back and looked into his face. She kissed him on the cheek without a word and returned to her room and slept soundly until the morning.

***

Darcy, for his part, was unsure of what had happened, which was probably just as well. He was weak from lack of food and water, and his mind was still muddled from whatever sort of waking sleep he had been in, but his wound was healing. On the morning of the third day, Darcy awoke fully alert for the first time since his ordeal began. He looked about the simple room in which he was housed. There was a pitcher of water and a glass beside his bed, curtains at the window, and a soft breeze blowing. He could hear voices inside the house and coming from the garden. He tried to sit up, but the pain was too great.

"Hello," he called, "hello?" Darcy recognized one of the voices from his ordeal. Croft burst into the room.

"Oh, thank God, sir," he said, and rushed over to Darcy's side. Darcy looked at him uncomprehendingly.

"Where am I?"

"You're at the doctor's house here in Bixley, sir. I'll go fetch the doctor." With that, he left the room.

The doctor told him that he should not be moved for at least a week, perhaps two. He was not out of danger yet, and the laudanum had nearly finished what the pistol ball had started. Not wanting to tire him, the doctor soon left Darcy alone to rest and to ruminate on what could possibly have transpired since he last saw the light of day.

***

The departure from Netherfield was even more painful to Elizabeth than the departure from Longbourn. Of all her family, Jane was dearest to her, her companion and confidante. One thing that gave Elizabeth comfort was the knowledge that her sister had a fine husband, and one who adored her. She deserved to be adored for she was the kindest person Elizabeth had ever known. It distressed her so to see how Jane would turn suddenly and wipe a tear from her eye, trying to be brave in the shadow of their separation. Truth be told, Elizabeth would have preferred to bury herself at Longbourn in her father's library, at least for a time. She felt so weary. The events of the last several weeks had nearly broken her spirit. She dared not think of Darcy today. *Brave and cheerful, that is what I will be*, thought Elizabeth. *For everyone's sake. Even mine.*

The carriage was waiting to take Elizabeth to Portsmouth. Charles Bingley would accompany her and see to it that she was safely delivered into the hands of her new friends, Barbara and Edward.

"Oh, you will come back soon, won't you, Lizzy?" asked Jane as she pressed her sister close.

"Or perhaps you and Charles may take an ocean voyage," said Elizabeth brightly. She continued the embrace so as not to have to look into her sister's eyes.

At last they parted, and Elizabeth entered the carriage. She waved cheerfully to her sister's diminishing form as the carriage pulled away from Netherfield. Finally, she looked up at her brother-in-law. *He is wearing his cheerful countenance just for me.*

"You know, Lizzy, you could always change your mind," he said. She was taken aback. From whence did that thought arise? "Jane will miss you so. You could come and live with us. It would be ever so jolly."

A picture of herself playing pique with Charles's sisters suddenly burst into her mind. Looking into their haughty faces year after year was not the future she envisioned for herself. No, however painful the parting, this solution was better for everyone. It would be a new world for Elizabeth Bennet.

"You are very kind, Charles, but I think this is best," she said. His face fell momentarily, and he patted her hand.

"You are quite independent, sister," he said. "I have always admired that about you."

What an awfully kind thing to say. Jane would be fine and have a happy life. It was a comfort to be sure. Although no one said it, Elizabeth was nearly sure that she was never coming back.

***

Buried alive. The thought of it made Darcy shudder. If the garbled story Croft related was in any way true, his aunt had a great deal to answer for. What business did she have in taking him from his house in town and away from his beloved Elizabeth? He had felt Elizabeth's presence, he was sure of that, and remembered snatches of her sympathetic face above his and her cool hand upon his forehead. Croft, of course, could neither confirm or deny Elizabeth's presence at his bedside, but Darcy remembered it. At least, he thought he remembered it. His memory was muddy. Much of what was said or done, he remembered not at all. One thing he did remember: fear. Fear and dread.

Poor Elizabeth. She thought he was dead. His first order of business was to get word to her. He would send Croft. His aunt could wait, but Pemberley? No, he must send news to Pemberley that they could expect their master to return. He could feel his strength returning bit by bit, and he would soon be able to travel home. Home. They must be wondering what became of Croft and his "body." He shuddered to think of it. He had heard of corpses unearthed years later with their skeletal hands poised above their chests, the insides of their coffin lids scratched to pieces. No, he must not give in to dark thoughts. He was very much alive and would remain that way. Elizabeth would soon be his. All was right with the world.

A boy of about eight years old padded into Darcy's room on the third day of his convalescence so Darcy could thank him. The young boy arrived, hat in hand, and walked to his master's bedside.

"What's your name, boy?" Darcy asked.

"Rupert, sir."

"So, I have you to thank for my life," Darcy said. Rupert smiled, but said nothing. "Would you like to come work for me at my estate in Pemberley?" Darcy asked.

Rupert's eyes widened. "Do you think I could, sir?" he asked.

"I do indeed," Darcy said, "but I have one more undertaking for you to complete. I am sending you to the town of Meryton. I have a letter for someone there that you need to deliver."

***

My dearest Elizabeth,

I hardly know where to begin. My mind has been muddled since I awoke from what I must term as a most horrible nightmare. I can remember voices and yours most definitely, my dearest one. I feel that I am recovering steadily, but slowly, and the doctors say I soon will reach my former vigor. We will then make our plans for our future together. Send word to me that you have received my letter. I am in a small village called Bixley in the house of a Dr. Soames on The Green. My intent is to return to Pemberley as quickly as circumstances permit. Send word at once so that we may arrange a place to reunite. As you can see, I must be recovering as I grow impatient. I await word of you and look forward to the time we will be together again. There is an important question I must ask you forthwith.

Ever yours,

F. Darcy

As he looked over the letter, he was astonished at how feeble his handwriting looked, like that of an old man. He did have to write in his own hand, so she would believe this astonishing news. Mr. Fitzwilliam Darcy had risen from the dead.

Chapter 7

Darcy's letter to Elizabeth was too important to entrust to a small boy, so Darcy insisted that Croft accompany him to Meryton. Another messenger was dispatched with a letter in Darcy's own hand to Pemberley. With all his duties seen to and a letter on its way to Elizabeth, Darcy began to regain his strength. The country air, the commonsense ministrations of the doctor, and simple fare helped Darcy immensely. And to complete his recovery, Elizabeth would be walking through the door of this cottage in a day or two.

By the time Lady Catherine arrived with Georgiana at the small hamlet of Bixley, Darcy was sitting up in his bed, and the doctor was in attendance. When the knock came at the door, Darcy asked, "Elizabeth?"

"Certainly not," came the arrogant answer. Darcy sighed. The doctor tucked the blankets around Darcy's chest and legs and answered the door. Lady Catherine entered with Georgiana at her heels. She overtook her aunt and rushed to her brother's bedside.

Darcy held her face in his hands and kissed her forehead. Both were speechless. Into the void swept Lady Catherine, who gently dislodged Georgiana and peered into Darcy's face.

"I cannot believe it," she stated. "It is not possible." She laid her hand upon his forehead. "The warmth of life," she said, almost wistfully, then resumed her commanding air. "Bring me a chair, Doctor, and then you may go. I have brought my own physician," she said, and sat next to Darcy. "Georgiana, wait outside, if you please. I need to have a word with Darcy," she commanded. Darcy smiled at his sister and nodded. Georgiana temporarily withdrew.

Then, an odd thing happened. Lady Catherine de Bourgh suddenly turned her face from Darcy, and he saw that she brought her handkerchief up to her eyes. *Could she actually be moved by finding me alive?* He could feel himself smiling and then abruptly stopped. She would be mortified that he had noticed, so he, always the gentleman, pretended that he saw nothing. Then a thought entered his mind of something half remembered. *Had she wept for me once?*

Dr. Lomax entered the room and bowed solemnly to his retreating colleague but said nothing. When the country doctor had left, Lady Catherine continued.

"You will be wanting an apology, I suppose," she said to Darcy. He merely blinked at her, uncomprehending. She continued, "For nearly burying you...prematurely."

Darcy tried to speak but could think of nothing. The doctor came to his bedside and gave him a cursory examination.

"Well, Doctor," her ladyship said, "apologize to Darcy."

The doctor seemed taken aback and looked at her uncomprehendingly. "I beg your pardon, Your Ladyship. I was under the impression I was here to examine Mr. Darcy and—" he began.

Lady Catherine would not be put off. "Was it not you who gave Darcy so much laudanum that it induced such a deep sleep as to feign death?" When there was no immediate reply, she continued, "And was it not you who determined that Mr. Darcy was indeed dead and that we should bury him forthwith? Is that not true?"

Dr. Lomax looked at Darcy and his face contorted. Darcy knew full well that the doctor was only following his aunt's orders, and if too much laudanum was given, it was surely not the doctor to blame. The doctor's expression, however, was priceless and Darcy began to chuckle and then to laugh out loud.

"My word," Lady Catherine said impatiently. "The man is hysterical." This made Darcy laugh even harder, which brought on a spate of coughing.

"Please, Your Ladyship," Dr. Lomax said. "We must leave Mr. Darcy to rest now. Please."

"Very well," Lady Catherine acquiesced. The doctor plied Darcy with water and her ladyship rose. Before she reached the door, she turned back to Darcy.

"It is good to have you back among us," she said. "I have made arrangement to return you to Rosings so that you may recover." Before Darcy could object, she turned and left the room.

Dr. Lomax stayed and examined Darcy. His wound was finally healing. Healthy pink tissue was forming a rather formidable scar on his left side.

"I have to admit I was wrong," Dr. Lomax said as he buttoned Darcy's shirt and laid him back down on the bed. "I do believe those revolting maggots did you a service, Mr. Darcy, and you fell into good hands here as well. And…" The doctor stepped back and hesitated. "And I do apologize for nearly killing you. You see, when we were transporting you, Lady Catherine was insistent upon—"

Darcy held up his hand. "Say no more," he said. "I have survived despite all good intentions." The doctor seemed embarrassed by his remark, which was not Darcy's intent. He snuffled about a bit and took his leave.

***

"What do you mean, you have sent word to Longbourn already?" Lady Catherine asked.

They had stopped again on the road to give Darcy time to rest. He thought that he was ready to travel again, but the journey was proving difficult. He was glad that his aunt insisted on bringing him to Rosings. He could not remain forever in Bixley, and the journey to Derbyshire and his beloved Pemberley would have been too taxing. Unfortunately, this particular expedition was fraught with argument. Poor Georgiana could do nothing to mitigate it.

"I have every intention of marrying Elizabeth," Darcy said firmly. "There is nothing you can say or do to dissuade me."

"So unsuitable," Lady Catherine mumbled under her breath, but did not pursue the subject. "We shall talk of this later," she said resignedly.

"Later, nothing will have changed," Darcy remarked, and settled himself back into the seat and closed his eyes.

"Humph," was the last thing he heard when sleep overtook him.

Chapter 8

Before this moment, Elizabeth had thought herself well traveled. Well traveled indeed. She had been as far as Derbyshire, which at the time seemed such a distance, but now she was to embark on an ocean voyage. The ship creaked and groaned and swayed from side to side while still in port. Her meager luggage had been stowed. Barbara Ellsworth chattered on about a new tropical wardrobe for her. Edward was very solicitous, always, in her presence.

She leaned against the rail and turned from time to time to watch the sailors going about their duties. What a life it must be to be on the sea. She was trying mightily to be happy and content, but thoughts always returned to her of Darcy. What time she wasted being angry with him, not trusting him. Whatever was she thinking? And now, it was because of her and her family that he lay in the dark, never…

She was shaken from her gloomy thoughts by Mrs. Ellsworth, who joined her at the railing. "We are about to get under way," she said to her friend. Seeing Elizabeth's sorrowful aspect, Barbara attempted to distract her. "Are you feeling well?" she asked. "I hope you are not having a bout of seasickness. Many are afflicted with it, especially at the beginning of a voyage."

"Oh, no, I am quite well in that respect," Elizabeth replied.

She was not in a mood for trivial repartee, but Barbara persisted. "Edward, I'm afraid, is already quite green. It is always so for him at the outset of a voyage."

Elizabeth was diverted from herself at last. "Is there anything we can do for Mr. Home?" she asked.

"Oh, do call him Edward and call me Barbara. We are fast friends now; I do feel it."

"Then you must call me Elizabeth." She paused and then reiterated her question. "Is there something we can do for poor Edward?"

"I will look in on him later, but I believe he would like to be left to himself for a while," Barbara replied. "He usually finds a place on deck where he can be relatively alone and breathe the fresh air. Poor lamb. He will not be quite himself for a few days."

There was an unexpected lurch and a flurry of movement among the seamen. They could hear the captain barking orders and Elizabeth watched swarthy and barefooted sailors scurry up the rigging.

"Our voyage has begun," Barbara said, smiling as she gazed aloft. In spite of herself, Elizabeth felt a twinge of excitement at the new adventure before her. She was suddenly overwhelmed with gratitude for her new friends, Barbara Ellsworth and Edward Home. "Come, Elizabeth. Let us go below and I will show you where you will sleep. Later, we have been invited to share our first meal aboard with the captain. Won't that be nice?" With that she took Elizabeth by the arm and led her to the hatchway.

Elizabeth saw nothing of Edward at the captain's table, nor later that evening. Barbara was good company, however, and lively. They were invited for cards after dinner, and the evening proceeded pleasantly. England had faded into the distance, and with so many new sights and sounds for Elizabeth to absorb, she had little time to brood except in the evening when she was alone. As she readied herself for bed, she thought again of Darcy. She thought of how she felt in his arms, the touch of his lips on hers, the fury of his passion. She swallowed hard and breathed in the salt air. She would not give in to melancholy. That part of her life had ended before it had begun. Now it was time to start a new life.

On deck the next morning, Elizabeth walked arm and arm with Barbara. There were small groups of passengers on the deck taking the air. Sailors were tending to their duties, and Elizabeth was surprised at how adept with a needle some of the men were. She remarked about it to Barbara.

"Of course, my dear Elizabeth, there is no one on a ship to do womanly chores, so the men must tend to them. I have seen it many times."

"How lucky you are to be able to travel so much," Elizabeth mused. "This is my first and perhaps only voyage out of England."

"I am sure there will be many more," Barbara said. With that they had nearly collided with a group of plainly dressed folk at the aft railing. These passengers had not been at the captain's table the night before. Barbara gave them a stern look and rushed Elizabeth past them.

"Who are those people?" asked Elizabeth.

"They are abolitionists," Barbara replied. "They mean to ruin us and all we have built in Grenada."

Elizabeth turned and looked over her shoulder at them. "Surely not," she said. Then turning to Barbara, "Abolitionists. Certainly, they can pose no threat to you."

Barbara stopped walking and looked Elizabeth in the face. "You do realize that we own a large estate in Grenada and that my father is the lieutenant governor there."

"Yes, of course," Elizabeth said, feeling vaguely as if she had just been insulted or treated like a dunce.

"All of our servants, the workers on our sugar plantation, the workers on my husband's plantation, and those on many of our friends' plantations are all negro slaves."

Elizabeth did not know what to say. She had never considered slavery before. The thought of slaves and slavery never entered her mind. It never occurred to her that Edward, Barbara, their father, in fact all the English people with whom she was most likely to come in contact, all had slaves. She turned again to look at the abolitionists standing at the rail. None were observing her.

The captain saw them looking toward the group of plain-dressed folk, and as he passed he uttered, "Quakers."

Perceiving her discomfort, Barbara softened her tone. "I am sorry, Elizabeth, but I just find these people so vexing. They come from their comfortable lives in England and sow discontent among the free blacks and the slaves and endanger our entire way of life, all the while sipping tea and eating cakes made with our sugar."

Elizabeth again said nothing but resolved to have a conversation with these people whose cause she so little understood.

***

An agonizing five days had passed since Darcy's letter to Elizabeth. There had been no word and his messengers had not returned. He gathered enough strength now to move about his bedroom, but little else. *Still, I could be lying with my ancestors in a tomb at this very moment and no one would have been the wiser.* He shuddered to think of it. At last, on the morning of the fifth day, Rupert and Croft returned. Darcy, who was sitting near a window, could see the back garden. What went on at the front of the house was a mystery to him, but all the comings and goings of the gardeners, the servants, the scullery maids, the delivery men from the village, he was privy to. In that way, he saw the two return. Ringing for Andrew, a footman of Lady Catherine's who was now his personal valet, Darcy summoned the two travelers. With them arrived Lady Catherine.

Before they could utter a word, Lady Catherine began. "Well, speak up, man, do you have a message for Mr. Darcy from..." She hesitated. "Miss Bennet?"

"No message, m'lady," Rupert announced. For that, he received a cuff from Croft.

"The young lady has left the country, m'lady," said Croft. "'Er father informed me and the boy. She's gone on a voyage. That's what 'e said." Rupert nodded.

"The letter?" Lady Catherine began.

"Delivered it," said Rupert, ducking and stepping away from Croft. When a blow was not forthcoming, he continued, "Gave it to Mr. Bennet, we did. 'E's sending it on to Miss Bennet, he said. Don't know if 'e will, though."

"Whatever do you mean?" Darcy interrupted. All eyes went to him, as if they had only just noticed that he was in the room. His weakened state made him easy to ignore. This frustrated him to no end.

Rupert looked at Croft. "Well, speak up, boy. You've gone this far."

"Don't think 'e believed us. Thought we were lyin' or up to somethin' 'e did." Croft nodded in assent.

"Did Mr. Bennet send a reply?" Darcy asked.

"No, sir," said Croft. He shifted his weight back and forth, hat in hand.

"But..." Rupert began, but a look from Croft silenced him. Darcy would not have it.

"But what?" asked Darcy.

"But Mr. Bennet said 'e'd go and see for 'imself. 'E said 'e might go to Bixley to see you."

Darcy looked up at his aunt. Her face was the mask he knew too well. She would not show what emotions were churning behind that countenance. He could guess, though.

"Thank you, Croft, Rupert. You can go now," Darcy said disconsolately, averting his eyes from theirs and his aunt's. "Go to the kitchen and get something to eat," he added. They left immediately, but his aunt stood firm.

"What do you know of this?" he asked gruffly.

"Do not speak to me in that tone, Darcy," she retorted haughtily. "I know only what you know."

"Who could she possibly know that would take her on a voyage? Who is with her? It is not possible. Not two weeks ago she was at my bedside day and night."

She turned and gave him a surprised look. Lady Catherine laughed. "Whatever makes you think that?" she asked. Darcy was astounded. "You were very feverish and under the influence of laudanum. I assure you that Miss Bennet was nowhere to be found after that unfortunate duel. She turned tail and ran, as you would expect from someone of her station. I have washed my hands of the Bennets, and it would benefit you immensely if you would do the same." She turned from him, but before she reached the door, a thought occurred to him.

"Is this 'voyage' she has undertaken your doing?" he asked bluntly.

"You credit me with too much deviousness," she said.

"You have not answered me," he persisted.

"No, I have nothing to do with it. You have my word." She caught his eye and looked at him pointedly.

"Leave me," he stated abruptly.

"As you wish." And with that, she left him to his misery.

It was then that Darcy rang for John. He would send a message to Mr. Bennet forthwith, inviting him to Rosings. There must be an explanation for this unfortunate turn of events.

***

"You see many had negro slaves on their estates, here," Jonas said. Elizabeth smiled slightly, and he amended his statement. "Not *here*, of course, but back there in England."

Elizabeth stood by the rail listening to her new friends, Jonas and Priscilla Starling. They were an older couple, more akin to her parents than to her. They dressed plainly and spoke plainly. The Starlings explained to her that they considered themselves belonging to a community they referred to as "friends." Many of their fellow believers had emigrated from England to America where they found more tolerance for their beliefs. There was a city in America, in fact, that they referred to as "The City of Brotherly Love" where many Quakers now lived. Elizabeth found them easy to talk to and their views enlightened rather than threatening. Whenever Barbara retreated to her cabin, Elizabeth sought their company. Edward still remained below.

"You are familiar, are you not, with the Somersett case of '72? We were watching that quite closely. That was before your time, Miss Bennet, but we remember it well. Under English common law, there can be no slave in England."

"I hadn't realized that there ever were slaves in England," Elizabeth said.

"Oh, there were slaves. They were primarily domestic servants, unpaid and with no hope of emancipation. They did a different sort of work than those in the Caribbean who toil in sugar or cacao plantations like the ones belonging to your friends, or those producing cotton in America. Still, these English slaves were chattel. They were owned by their masters."

Elizabeth found all this information both intriguing and disturbing. Her thoughts had never before turned to slavery or the lot of slaves. Listening to the Starlings made her feel as though the inequality between herself and Mr. Darcy was not as formidable as she or, more to the point, as he, once imagined. There, she had done it. She had brought Darcy to mind again after resolving to occupy her thoughts elsewhere. Her new-found friends noticed her mood.

"Is something troubling you, my dear?" Priscilla Starling asked her.

Elizabeth so wanted to unburden herself to these two sympathetic souls, but it was too soon in their friendship for such intimacy. She merely shook her head. "No, not really. I was just thinking of home," she said wistfully.

The two of them turned in tandem toward the east. Mr. Starling spoke first. "I fear we shall never see home again. We are emigrating, you see, to America, the New World, you know." He was smiling, but his eyes betrayed melancholy.

"Are you not stopping in Grenada, then?" Elizabeth asked, surprised. This was not what Barbara had told her.

"Oh, no," said Priscilla cheerfully. "We are stopping only a short time in Grenville and will change ships. Our final destination is New York. From there we will travel overland to Philadelphia. Our son is there, with his wife and children."

She didn't know why, but that news somehow cheered Elizabeth. These two kind and forthright people were not fleeing their homeland to live in a strange, new land. They were traveling to be with family, and to have a new beginning. It suddenly occurred to Elizabeth that perhaps Kitty or Mary, or even her parents, might someday join her in Grenada. By then, she might be married and have children of her own. Married to someone she was fond of, perhaps, not someone she loved, as she had loved Darcy.

"I am so glad," Elizabeth switched focus away from Darcy. She needed to immerse herself in what was happening now, at this moment. Dwelling in the past would do her no good. "Now that I am separated from them, I realize how much I do miss my family."

"There, there now," Priscilla continued. "You have good friends here on this ship and are a very personable young woman. You will make friends, and perhaps, find a husband in the New World."

With that, Elizabeth blushed. Not the maidenly blush of old days, but a rush of heat that returned her to Darcy and all that could have been. She managed a smile, and then excused herself. She needed to be alone with her thoughts, and perhaps even to surrender herself to grief once more.

***

He needed time to think, and what had been great anticipation was now turned to enormous disappointment. Darcy spent the day trying to recall exactly what had happened to him from the time he was shot until the time he'd awakened at his house in town. Elizabeth was there when he was first brought home. He remembered that clearly. She had helped him send for Wickham. After that, his memory was unreliable. There was a great deal of pain, he remembered that. Pain and feverish dreams.

There were obscure memories, seeming to him to come in tiny segments, of Elizabeth's voice, her face, the touch of her hand. It could not all be a dream, could it? His memory was patchy, to be sure, but did he hallucinate Elizabeth's presence at his bedside? Elizabeth was not one to turn and run, either. Of that, he was equally sure. She spoke her mind to him without hesitation and pounced on him like a lioness when she thought he had destroyed the happiness of her sister. No, his aunt's story could not be true, or at least not wholly true. *Was she deliberately deceiving me? Damn and blast this stupid wound.* All the trauma of the past few weeks had taken its toll on him, and he was still as helpless as a babe.

In his weakened state, Darcy still needed vast amounts of rest, so that his thoughts were often overtaken by sleep. Vivid dreams assailed him. A dream that recurred over and over was one in which Elizabeth was walking toward him, her hand outstretched. He went to take it and bring it to his lips, but instead she lay it upon his chest. When he looked down at it, he noticed he was completely naked, his member rampant. In shock at this discovery, he dared not look her in the face, and then he would awaken covered in sweat, his nether regions on fire.

***

"A Mr. Bennet to see you, sir," Davis announced. It had been more than a week since he had arrived at Rosings, and only a few days since Rupert and Croft had brought their news. Darcy put all his hopes in Mr. Bennet. He would know the whereabouts of his daughter and the circumstances of her disappearance. Also, he had no reason to hide the truth. The man had traveled over two counties to reach him. *Perhaps he has even brought a message from her. No, that was too much to hope.* Hope, however, was keeping him alive. If nothing else, Darcy was sure of that. He must have paused for a moment to cogitate all these thoughts because Davis broke in, "Shall I send him in, sir?"

"Oh, by all means, Davis. At once. At once." Darcy arranged himself in his armchair. The plumping of pillows and the fussing and prodding by all manner of well-meaning persons, relatives, servants, physicians, and the like, was driving him mad. The one thing he really needed was news of his Elizabeth, and here it was. As Mr. Bennet entered the room, Darcy tried to stand, but his legs thought otherwise. He plopped backward in a most humiliating manner, but Mr. Bennet, who rushed in all in a flurry, did not seem to notice. The elderly gentleman stopped short and gazed at Darcy.

"I had to see with my own eyes, Mr. Darcy, I do hope you forgive me," Mr. Bennet began, all out of breath. He made no motion to sit down but stared at Darcy in a most discomfiting manner.

"Do have a seat, sir," Darcy said, trying to break the spell.

"Oh, yes, yes," Mr. Bennet replied, trying to reach behind him for the chair without taking his eyes off Darcy.

"I will not disappear, sir," Darcy said amiably. Mr. Bennet turned this way and that and finally sat down. "Davis, do bring us some tea, or perhaps some sherry, Mr. Bennet?"

"No, no, tea it is. I fear my heart would not stand anything stronger."

At that Darcy realized what the man must have been going through. Mr. Bennet must have blamed himself for Darcy's death. Many others had suffered during these unhappy circumstances. *Poor Mr. Bennet.* Darcy could feel himself developing an affection for the man.

"I am very glad you came to see me, Mr. Bennet," he said. Mr. Bennet exhaled rather loudly and smiled for the first time. "Do you have news to bring me of your daughter, Elizabeth?" Perhaps he should have made small talk a while longer, asked if he had traveled to Bixley first perhaps, or had Croft delivered his invitation, but he had no stomach for that. He had to have news. *Where is Elizabeth?*

"Oh, that is why I came to see you, Mr. Darcy," he said. He looked away from Darcy's face and began wringing his hands. Then, he stood up and began pacing the room in small circles.

"Speak up, man. Where is she?" Darcy demanded, and suddenly his heart sank. Something had happened to her. His mind instantly ran to the direst of possibilities.

Mr. Bennet suddenly turned to him and handed him back his letter. Darcy stared at it in his hand and looked at Mr. Bennet with wide eyes.

"So, she has not seen it," he said glumly. At that, Davis opened the door and arrived with a tray of tea. Darcy bit his lip and motioned with his head to lay it down on the side table. Davis said nothing, discharged his duty, and left without a word.

Darcy took a few gulps of air and spoke as calmly as he could manage. "Please, Mr. Bennet, sit down. Tell me what has happened to Elizabeth."

Mr. Bennet sat down and looked directly at Darcy. "She has left the country."

"Yes, Mr. Bennet, I know that," Darcy said impatiently. Mr. Bennet opened his eyes wide in surprise. "What I do not understand is where she has gone, why she has gone, and with whom she has gone. That is what you must tell me."

Mr. Bennet nodded and then looked imploringly over at the tea. Darcy followed his gaze.

"Do forgive me, Mr. Bennet, in the excitement I have forgotten my manners. Will you pour?" Darcy listened patiently as Mr. Bennet related his tale. He tried mightily not to interrupt but had so many questions as to Bingley's relationship with the visitors from Grenada, and of course, of Edward Home.

"This Edward fellow—" Darcy began.

"Oh, a fine fellow, he," Mr. Bennet said enthusiastically. "Affable, friendly, given to jollity and humor. A fine fellow indeed. He rather reminds me of my son-in-law, Charles Bingley. Perhaps not as reserved as Mr. Bingley. I find him to be more…"

As Mr. Bennet paused to think of yet another complimentary attribute for Mr. Edward Home, Darcy's mood turned sour. It sounded to him as though Edward was everything that he was not. Now, Elizabeth was to spend an entire ocean voyage with him, and then a lengthy tropical visit.

"Charming. That's the word. Charming," said Mr. Bennet with a self-satisfied look.

The entire situation was beginning to take on a desperate aspect for Mr. Darcy. Elizabeth had no idea he was alive, and was now in the clutches of this charming, affable…fine fellow.

"Oh, and he is quite good-looking too," added Mr. Bennet as he took a bite of a cucumber sandwich. "I remember when we were playing a game of charades, and Lizzy and Mr. Home were partners—"

"Stop," shouted Darcy suddenly. Mr. Bennet's teacup clattered into the saucer. The alarmed look on Mr. Bennet's face caused Darcy to take a deep breath and a calmer tone. "What I meant to say was, let us change the subject. I need your help, Mr. Bennet. I need to get a message to your daughter somehow. She must know that I am alive."

Mr. Bennet seemed flustered for a moment. Then he reached his hand out to Mr. Darcy. "I will take the letter back with me and have it sent on to Elizabeth."

Darcy, realizing the letter was still in his hand, extended it to Mr. Bennet and then pulled it back.

"You have an address for her already then, in Grenada?" He looked at Mr. Bennet and observed his expression. "Yes, yes, of course you do. How silly of me. In that case," continued Darcy, "you merely have to give it to me, and I can have the letter sent on from here."

Mr. Bennet began examining his shoes, and then looked up without looking Darcy in the eye. Finally, he said, "I never thought to bring it."

A great deal of frustration and anger began to well up in Darcy at that moment, but when Mr. Bennet raised his head to look at him, the sorrow in his eyes gave Darcy pause. The poor man had been through so much, and now his daughter was beyond his protection. Neither man spoke for a moment.

"Perhaps," said Darcy at last. "Perhaps you can do a favor for me, Mr. Bennet."

"Oh, anything, sir. I am at your service."

"Perhaps you can deliver a message for me to my friend Charles Bingley. If we all put our heads together, perhaps we can sort this matter out to everyone's satisfaction."

With that, Darcy put the letter in his waistcoat next to his heart.

***

After seven days at sea, Edward finally emerged from his cabin. Although his aspect was pallid, he seemed in good spirits. Elizabeth realized that she was glad to see him. The machinations of keeping Barbara ignorant of her friendship with the Starlings was proving tiresome. She longed to bring them together so that they could talk to one another and reach some understanding, but broaching the subject proved difficult. Barbara was adamant. The Starlings and their ilk were the enemy, and that was that. Edward's appearance was a welcome diversion.

"I am so sorry, Miss Bennet," was the first thing he said to her. "Sea voyages do not agree with me at first. I am afraid I have been an abominable host. I hope that you and Barbara have entertained yourselves in my absence."

"We have missed you, Mr. Home, but illness is nothing to apologize for. Barbara and I have found many things to divert us, not the least of which are dinners and card games with the captain," said Elizabeth in a jocular tone. He still did not look well.

Barbara approached them, smiling. "I see you have recovered yourself, brother. Elizabeth and I have missed your company."

"So Miss Bennet has told me," he replied.

"You must call me Elizabeth. Barbara and I decided."

"Elizabeth, then," he said. "And you must call me Edward." The wind was brisk, and the ship was making good headway. There was a certain degree of choppiness, however, and Elizabeth was concerned for her companion.

"Shall we walk about the deck, Mr. Home?" She had reverted to the formal address until she observed him looking at her askance, "I mean, Edward."

"Yes, perhaps that is best. Some fresh air might do me a world of good," he said and offered Elizabeth his arm. Barbara smiled. Elizabeth noticed her companion's satisfied expression, and it crossed her mind that Barbara was engaging in some subtle matchmaking. It was too soon to think of such things, to be sure. Her heart still ached for Darcy.

The next few weeks flew by quickly for Elizabeth. Edward had gained his sea legs and Elizabeth had a routine that suited her. She spent the morning with Edward and Barbara, and after luncheon, when they retreated to their respective cabins for a rest, she sought out her Quaker friends. Their philosophy made more and more sense to Elizabeth. It also surprised her that she had never thought about it before. The religion in which she was raised was a given, inviolate, and therefore she never questioned its precepts. She attended services with her parents and her sisters, read the Bible from time to time when her father suggested a passage, but in general, she did not philosophize. Her new reality, however, demanded it. She was about to enter a world in which many of the people around her were slaves. They were born into slavery and had little, if any, chance of escaping save through death. It embarrassed her to think that she felt her own social condition was hopeless at times, when it was so much better than that of a slave. Perspective, that was what she was gaining. Perhaps travel did broaden the mind. She would regret the landing in Grenada when she would bid adieu to the Starlings. Nevertheless, there would be a host of new experiences awaiting her there. Without Darcy.

***

Even in his weakened state, the time passed slowly for Darcy. He had heard nothing from anyone of his acquaintance, save a letter from his sister. A week or more had passed since his visit with Mr. Bennet. Surely, he had contacted Charles Bingley as he was asked. Darcy had put a great deal of faith in Mr. Bennet and his ability to mobilize the forces he needed to contact Elizabeth, and soon, to retrieve her from Grenada.

With each passing day, he felt a little stronger. He had mentioned his return to Pemberley almost daily to his aunt, but it fell on deaf ears. Citing the pretext of his delicate health, she had made him more or less her prisoner. Of course, he could not say so, but he felt it nonetheless. It was now nearly three weeks since his miraculous resurrection. It crossed his mind more than once that perhaps he should have returned to his house in town for his recovery. Ah well. It was too late now.

Since the doctor recommended it, Darcy was given to leaving the windows and door to his room open to catch the breeze. He was dozing in his chair one afternoon when he heard a disturbance on the stair.

"M'lady is not at home, sir," said Davis.

"No matter." It was Bingley's voice. "I am here to see Mr. Darcy."

"But, sir," Davis said rather loudly. "Mr. Darcy is not to be disturbed. Lady

Catherine has given strict orders—"

At this point, Bingley called out in a loud voice, "Darcy. Darcy, are you here?" Darcy could hear their footsteps ascending the stairs, and Davis's protests. "I say, are you here?"

"In here, Bingley," Darcy called. In seconds through his doorway marched a smiling and triumphant Bingley. The smile faded quickly from Bingley's face when he laid eyes on his friend. Crossing the room in strides, he grasped Darcy's hand and squeezed. Both men struggled to maintain decorum.

"Thank God," Bingley said at last. "Thank God." For some moments he was unable to utter anything further but kept a firm grasp on his friend.

"It is good to see you, Bingley. Very good," said Darcy. The breathless Davis, who had been standing by helplessly, was finally noticed by Darcy.

"Davis, bring Mr. Bingley and me some tea, there's a good man," he said.

"But, sir, Lady Catherine, has expressly…" Davis began, but was silenced by a look from Darcy.

"Tea, Davis. Now," he repeated, and Davis left the room.

"Do sit down, my good fellow," said Darcy. "Stay with me a while."

"I am unsure of how much time I have," Bingley said gleefully. "I observed your aunt leaving just now and made a mad dash for it." Darcy looked at his friend as if he had gone mad.

"Why on earth did you do that?" Darcy asked.

Bingley cocked one eyebrow.

"My father-in-law alerted me as to your situation, so Jane and I paid a visit to the Collins's. We have been there for days trying to gain admittance. Your aunt would not have it."

Darcy turned and looked at his friend incredulously, then sighed. "I had no idea. I apologize for my aunt's rudeness."

"To be honest, she was not exactly rude, merely adamant," said Charles, laughing.

"It is fortunate then that my aunt is out and about visiting her tenants and dispensing either her rewards or punishments. Usually this activity takes the better part of the morning, and most of the afternoon," said Darcy absently.

"Yes, we learned as much from Mr. Collins. He aided us in our daring plan to see you without realizing it. He does go on and on about Lady Catherine."

"Charles," Darcy interrupted. "I need to return to Pemberley. Today, if possible." Bingley looked at him incredulously.

"Are you sure? Do you think you are strong enough?"

"It will take less strength to leave here than to stay," said Darcy. "Come, help me." It was then that Bingley noticed the cane next to Darcy's chair. He handed it to his friend without a word. Darcy struggled to his feet and then hobbled to the bell. Within a few moments, John appeared.

"Pack my things, John, I am leaving for Pemberley," he said sternly. As soon as John turned to see to his duty, Darcy gave Bingley a wide smile.

"Bingley, help me to the desk, there. I must write a letter to my aunt. She must hear the news from me personally." While Charles supervised John's preparations, Darcy began to write.

My dear Aunt Catherine,

I am leaving for Pemberley today. I feel that I am strong enough to travel, and with the help of my good friends, the Bingleys, will make a slow journey back to my estate. I have neglected things too long and must return post-haste. Forgive me for making such an abrupt decision, but I feared that your concern would delay me, and I must resume my duties as master of Pemberley as soon as I am able. Thank you for your kindness and care.

I remain your loving nephew and obedient servant,

Fitzwilliam Darcy

Darcy thought the tone of his letter conciliatory, but his mention of the Bingleys was a definite jibe. In this subtle way, he let her know that he was aware of her machinations. The tone of the letter, however, was not hostile. He realized that she did care for him in her way. *Why are family relations so complicated?*

He lay the note down on the writing table as all preparations were finished. Charles bounded out of the room to arrange the carriage, and before the sun had risen to its apex, they were on the road to Pemberley.

When they were well on their way, Darcy asked after Elizabeth. "It is quite a tale and I will relate all of it if you feel you are strong enough," said Jane softly in reply.

"I am quite all right," said Darcy, trying to contain his emotion. "Your father has told me most of the story, but I think, perhaps, that Elizabeth might have been more candid with you. I do not wish to pry, of course, but I am most anxious to acquire as much knowledge of her as I can."

Jane spent the better part of an hour relating all that had happened from the arrival of Barbara Ellsworth and Edward Home to the present moment. Darcy sat staring in disbelief.

"Surely something can be done to bring her back," he said finally.

"She felt leaving was for the best. Poor Elizabeth. She was overcome with grief and quite ruined here," Jane rejoined.

"Ruined?" exclaimed Darcy. "In what way, ruined?"

"My dear fellow, she never left your bedside for a moment, even though you were not married. No one could persuade her to leave. No one," said Bingley.

He knew it. Of course, she wouldn't leave him. "Ruined, by God. That is unjust and unfair," Darcy said. He curled his hand into a fist and brought it to his lips.

"I believe we can send letters to her with any ships that are leaving for Grenada, Barbados, or the Grenadines and hope for the best," Bingley suggested.

"That will do for now," Darcy said resignedly. "It will have to do until I can go after her. I will send a man to every port to find which ship is leaving the soonest for Grenada. She will not be there a month and I will fetch her back."

Jane smiled, but Bingley looked concerned. "You are barely fit to travel to Pemberley, surely you will not attempt an ocean voyage."

Darcy sighed. "No, I am not foolish enough for that. I will regain my strength, and then I will pursue her. There is nothing on earth that will stop me."

"There's a good fellow," Bingley exclaimed. Both Jane and Darcy looked at him in disbelief. Darcy was not used to such a display of enthusiasm from his friend. Simultaneously, they both laughed.

"Would it not be wiser to wait and see if Elizabeth returns?" Jane suggested.

Darcy smiled indulgently but held firm. "I do not trust the post to bring her news of me, and begging your pardon, Charles, I do not trust your friend Edward in her company."

Bingley raised his eyebrows and blinked. "Surely, Darcy, you do not cast aspersions on the character of my friend."

"You too noticed Edward's interest in Elizabeth. I am sure his intentions are honorable, but…" Jane interjected calmly.

"But those honorable intentions do not serve me well, do they?"

Bingley smiled ruefully and shook his head.

"No," continued Darcy. "I will not wait for word. I will follow her."

"Perhaps you are right," Bingley said. "And if your mind is set upon an ocean voyage, you should set yourself a bar, and once you reach it, you will know you are able to travel."

Darcy considered this proposal for a moment. He did not enjoy being told what to do, and that was all he had been enduring for these past weeks. About to argue with Bingley, he abruptly said, "When I can ride again. If I can ride, I can sit in a boat."

The journey to Pemberley was slow, difficult, and took several days, but eventually Darcy could see his beloved home in the distance and soon would be installed as master once again. Word spread quickly of his return, and many of his tenants lined the road to Pemberley to glimpse him through the coach window. He was, indeed, alive, and he had returned.

It was gratifying to sleep in his own bed, have his own people about him, and view his own property from his own window. He felt that he had been away for a year, when, in fact, it was merely three fortnights. How much had happened in that short time. He had been nearly mortally wounded and almost buried alive. He had declared his love for Elizabeth and now she was out of his reach and thought he was dead. One positive development was that his friend Charles Bingley was married to sweet Jane and was quite happy and at his service. As the events of the past few weeks worked their way through his consciousness, his resolve to follow Elizabeth only became stronger. She would be his, and no one on earth could stop him, unless... unless he were to arrive too late and find her married already. How long would it take him to regain his strength, book his passage, and find her again? He rang for his servant. "Bring me some broth," he said. "Beef broth." Although he had no appetite, he resolved to build up his body beginning that day.

Chapter 9

The ship nearly encircled the south of the island before depositing its cargo and passengers in St. George's. There was a definite change from the choppy, white caps of the Atlantic to the smooth glassiness of the Caribbean Sea. The sea in the Caribbean was a blue that Elizabeth had never seen before. It was some kind of green and blue mixture that was translucent to the bottom of the ocean. The island itself was green and lush, the way Ireland had been described to her, but with vegetation she had only seen pictures of in her father's books. Tall, lanky palm trees dotted the coast and swayed in the breeze as if dancing for the sheer joy of living in such a beautiful place.

St. George's was a lovely horseshoe harbor dotted with red-tiled roofs and buildings of bright white and pastel colors. Above all, on a steep hill on the north shore of the lagoon, sat Fort George overlooking the harbor. With all this exotic beauty before her, she suddenly missed her family, and Longbourn and rainy afternoons when her father bade her to put another coal on the fire. She was shaken from her reverie by her companions, who excitedly pointed out places as familiar to them as Meryton was to her.

Elizabeth had never witnessed such a look of relief on anyone's face as she observed on Edward's as he stepped on solid ground. It nearly made her laugh, but she quickly reminded herself that he had suffered on this voyage and restrained herself. She bid a tearful good-bye to the Starlings, much to the surprise of Barbara, who was unaware of their association. Barbara, to her credit, held her tongue.

A group of dark-skinned, liveried servants were at the port to greet them and see to all the necessities of their luggage. An open-air carriage awaited, and soon the small party and their entourage wound its way through the streets. And such streets: they seemed to rise straight up from the shoreline, the area was so mountainous.

Such a novelty of sights and smells assailed Elizabeth as they drove by. The town itself could almost be taken whole into England, or perhaps France, and no one would have been the wiser, so similar was the architecture to that of home. Edward, on one of his more salient days, informed her that the ship carrying them also carried ballast of granite blocks from Wales and cobble stones from the quarries of England that were used to build the towns of St. George's, Grenville, and Gouyave. On their return voyages, ships were laden with sugar and cacao for English tables.

The architecture was familiar in some ways; the people, however, were a different matter entirely. From the conversations with the Starlings and the Homes, Elizabeth expected well-to-do white people and shabbily dressed, poor slaves. What greeted her eyes was something else entirely. Many of the negro people she observed were dressed as finely, or possibly more so, than she and her hosts were. She observed them riding carriages similar to the one in which she was presently ensconced and walked about freely, laughing and talking, entering shops and sitting and dining in open-air restaurants. Contrarily, there were many white persons as ragged and threadbare as any cockney street urchin in London. She resolved later to mention these surprising contrasts to Edward or Barbara.

The sounds and smells were also different from home. The cool sea breeze permeated everything and brought to her the smell of spices, grilled meat, and exotic fruits. Of course, odors familiar to anyone who stopped long in London were also present, but that was a fact of all cities. This place was new and exciting. The abundance of sunshine was an added treat. She closed her eyes momentarily and reveled in it.

"I hope that the sun is not too strong for you, Elizabeth," Barbara said, interrupting her thoughts.

"Oh no, on the contrary. I am enjoying it immensely," she said, opening her eyes.

Edward smiled. "Really, you must be careful here. An hour in it can cause a most painful burn to the skin, and too much exposure makes one as brown as the natives." He chuckled.

Soon they passed through an iron gate and wound down a drive that led to a large, white, two-story house covered on four sides by large verandas. Blooming pink and orange bougainvillea climbed over the white walls of the compound. A large lawn stretched out in front of the house planted with exotic species Elizabeth had never seen before. When they reached the front door, the servants who had been traveling with them set out footstools for them to disembark, and the front door swung open as if by magic. An older, coloured gentleman greeted them.

"Oronoko," called Edward as he stepped from the carriage.

"So good to see you back, Mister Edward, Mrs. Barbara," he said. "Mrs. Home is in the morning room waiting to see you." Barbara disembarked first, and before Elizabeth set foot out of the carriage, she was already in the house. Elizabeth could imagine how eager was she to see her mother and perhaps her waiting husband.

"Oronoko, this is Miss Bennet. She will be staying with us. Send Poppy up to the bedroom facing the harbor and have her prepare it for our guest," Edward ordered.

"Right away, sir," he said. Relieving them of their parasols, he disappeared into the house. Elizabeth accompanied Edward to the morning room.

"Oh, my dears, my dears," Mrs. Home said, embracing her children. "I'm so happy to see you. Did you have a pleasant voyage?" She looked pointedly at Edward. "I know you did not, dear Edward. We will have Cozzie make your favorite goat stew. That will help put back some of what you have lost." She laughed and then turned to Elizabeth. "And you, my dear, welcome to Grenada."

This warm greeting from Edward's mother was exactly what Elizabeth needed. Her first words weren't "And who is this?" or "Oh, you brought a guest" but "Welcome."

"I am so glad to finally meet you, Mrs. Home. Barbara and Edward have told me so much about you and your lives here. I am Elizabeth Bennet."

"We are happy you are here, Miss Bennet," replied Mrs. Home. With that, the tea arrived. Elizabeth realized she was quite hungry. Sandwiches and cakes were plentiful, and Edward began to make up for lost meals aboard ship. Soon they were all happily chatting.

"It is so wonderful to have a new face here," said Mrs. Home finally. "Have you ever heard of 'island fever,' Elizabeth? It afflicts those of us trapped on a small rock for too long."

"England is an island, Mother," Edward teased. He winked at Elizabeth.

"Do not be impertinent, Edward, you know what I mean." She smiled at her son's banter. "I promised everyone that we would have a garden party when you returned. How nice that you also brought someone new for everyone to meet. Your father will be so glad to see you all."

"Where is Father?" asked Barbara.

"There is some trouble with the French and the free coloreds these days," she said. "He is at a meeting in town. It is the French, if you ask me, spreading discontent. All that talk of *liberte*, *egalite*...and, oh I don't remember."

"*Fraternite*," said Edward. "Leave it to the French. Sour grapes, I think. They would like nothing better than control of this island again."

"Your father will see that it does not happen, mark my words," said Mrs. Home firmly.

All this talk of politics intrigued Elizabeth. The French, free blacks, *liberte*. This was not what was talked of at home. The weather, that was talked of at home. Not women including themselves in political talk. It was the governor's family, though. Everything was different here. Her thoughts must have shown on her face, because Barbara spoke.

"Poor Elizabeth. You have only just arrived and already you are treated to the intrigues of Grenada's politics. Come, I will show you to your room. I have a dress that I think you might like. It will be a bit cooler than the one you have on at present." With that, Barbara whisked Elizabeth off.

When they arrived at her room, they found a young dark-skinned woman there, her hair tied in a red kerchief, unpacking Elizabeth's things. The room was bright and airy, with a diaphanous canopy over the bed.

"What is that?" asked Elizabeth as soon as they entered the room.

"That is a net that protects one from the insects at night," Barbara said. "They are used in India as well." Elizabeth crossed the room to examine it.

"Poppy. What are you doing here?" said Barbara in surprise. Elizabeth turned to look at her.

Poppy seemed equally surprised and smiled. "I am here stowing the young miss's clothes," she replied. Elizabeth had never heard an accent like that before today. It was lilting and bubbly; English on a tropical island.

"And who told you to do that, may I ask?" Barbara asked in a tone Elizabeth found oddly strident.

"Mister Edward," Poppy replied.

The strangest look crossed Barbara's face, and Elizabeth took note of it. Was she concerned, or even appalled? Before Elizabeth could remark, Edward appeared at the doorway. "Oh, I see you are getting settled in. Good. And I see you have met Poppy. She will be your personal servant while you are with us."

This time Elizabeth was sure. It was alarm on Barbara's face. "May I speak to you for a moment?" Barbara asked her brother. The smile faded momentarily from his face, and he stepped back into the hall. They shut the door behind them and Elizabeth was left alone with Poppy.

"Hello, Poppy, I am Miss Bennet," said Elizabeth by way of introduction. Elizabeth extended her hand to Poppy, who looked at it as if she had never seen a hand before. Poppy then looked up at her and smiled. She grasped the ends of Elizabeth's fingers and then holding them, curtseyed. "I'm Poppy, miss. I am your slave," she said.

"Oh dear," said Elizabeth.

"Somethin' wrong, miss?" Poppy said, rising and resuming her work.

"No, no, of course not," Elizabeth replied, but it was far from the truth. All of it was wrong. Barbara, Edward, their mother, all *seemed* like kind people, generous people, and yet, here was another human being they were holding in bondage. Poppy herself seemed cheerful enough, but she suddenly remembered what the Starlings had told her. They warned her to be careful that she not try to justify slavery to herself. That was what happened to English people when they were exposed to it long enough. It began to seem normal to them. It began to seem right.

"May I help you with these things?" Elizabeth asked, not knowing what else to say.

Poppy's eyes grew wide. "Oh no, miss." She turned and smiled at Elizabeth. "You've never been to the islands before, have you, miss?"

"No, never," said Elizabeth, grateful to talk of small things. "I have never been out of England before."

"Is Grenada different 'dan Englan'?" Poppy asked, still working.

"Oh, very," said Elizabeth. "In England the summer weather is cool and rainy, and the winter is cold and wet. Sometimes we even have to have a fire in summer."

"I don't tink I be likin' dat too much," said Poppy cheerfully. "And what da' people like in Englan'? Are they all as kind as you?" She said it in such a matter-of-fact tone that Elizabeth was touched. She was about to protest the remark but thought better of it. She thought she would answer Poppy's question instead. She was about to say that there were many different kinds of people in England, but when she compared England to here, all of them seemed fairly alike. "The people are similar to me and to the Homes family."

"All the same, 'den. All white," she stated.

"All that I have ever seen." She'd never thought of it before, how homogeneous her native land was. Darcy again sprang to mind and then Lady Catherine. Her ladyship did not think they were all alike, to be sure. How odd it was to be in this place. All the things that seemed so inviolate now were beginning to seem fluid.

"Who are de slave, den?" Poppy asked.

"Oh," said Elizabeth in alarm. "There are no slaves. Slavery has been outlawed on English soil."

Poppy abruptly turned to her. "Is it true, miss? Der are no slaves der? Oh, but no black people, either, I t'ink." Elizabeth pondered a moment. She remembered the Starlings talking about the Somerset case that had led to the emancipation of slaves and indentured servants in England.

"No, that is not entirely true. There are a few and it was decided that, according to English common law, they could not be held as slaves. I am almost sure of it."

Poppy looked at Elizabeth with wonder. It was some time before she spoke. "I t'ink I get used to de col' and de rain if I be free," she said. There was a knock at the door. It was Edward.

"Well, then, it is settled," he said cheerfully, but Elizabeth saw his eyes shift from one of them to the other. "Poppy stays with you.

Barbara will be in shortly, Elizabeth. I believe she has some clothes you might like. This weather can be uncomfortable in heavy garments. Well, then…" Edward said, looking around. He was suddenly awkward, shifting from one foot to the other and not looking Elizabeth in the eye. "I will be off then. Until dinner," he continued self-consciously, and was gone.

*** *

The Bingleys took their leave of Darcy a few days later. He was able to move about a bit more now, albeit with cane in hand, and there was no sign of Lady Catherine on the horizon. In any case, he was master of his house, and although he tired easily, he felt able to take the reins of his duties for short periods of time. He so wanted to be able to be on horseback and see for himself how things were faring, but he dared not, not yet. Although impatient, and those nearest to him were bearing the brunt of his impatience, he knew full well that any overexertion would set his timetable back, and he could not afford that, not in the least. Elizabeth was nearly two months gone, and he still was not ready to travel. Although the doctors claimed otherwise, he began to think that too much rest was not helping him regain his strength at all.

One morning, after he was helped to dress, he sat by the window looking out over the gardens. From his vantage point, he could see the gardeners working among hedges. With the men were two small boys, apprentices of some sort most likely. For a time, they attended to the task set for them, but after a while, as small boys do, they began to tease one another, and soon were chasing each other and playing. Darcy, watching them, remembered when he and Wickham were two boys, much like these two, but not set to work, but free to play and amuse themselves to their hearts' content. Darcy's musings were interrupted by the appearance of the older boy, running full tilt toward the pond at the edge of the garden. Darcy threw open the window, and from there he could hear the boy shouting. The younger boy was nowhere to be seen. Could he have fallen into the water? Darcy looked about, but not one of the gardeners seemed to be within earshot. There was only one thing to be done.

Darcy flung off his coat and, as fast as he could manage, made his way down the stairs and out of the house through the kitchen, much to the shock of the cook and her staff. "A boy... in the pond," he shouted as he exited the kitchen. The staff looked on in amazement, and by the time the full import of his words sank into their astonished brains, Darcy had flung aside his cane, and, holding his side, ran to the pond where the older boy, up to his knees, was shouting and pointing. Darcy pulled off his boots and threw himself into the water, swimming to...he could not tell where. The shock of the cold water took his breath away, and he nearly blacked out himself. As he swam deeper, he heard nothing, but suddenly saw a small splash. Diving toward it, he bumped headlong into a struggling child, who clutched at Darcy's neck. Darcy went down, the child clinging and flailing. As he struggled to disentangle himself and bring both of them to the surface, he thought of the irony of the situation. Perhaps it would all end here, at the bottom of a pond on his own beloved Pemberley.

Thinking quickly, he disengaged the child's arms from his neck and spun him around in the water. With one arm hooked under the boy's armpits, he pulled with the other and kicked his way to the surface. Gulping air, he shouted at the lad to keep still. The boy, obedience overcoming panic, went limp in his arms. Darcy struck out for the nearby shore. Soon his feet felt the bottom, and he set the boy upright on his feet. By this time, the shore was crowded with the entire kitchen and gardening staff. The small lad slopped through the few feet of water into the waiting arms of his brother. Before Darcy knew what was happening, two gardeners hoisted him onto the shore, where he immediately sat down to catch his breath. His side ached, but he was surprised find that he not only was still alive, but quite elated. In the next moment, he realized that he was sitting on his bottom in the mud, soaking wet and shivering, boots off, waistcoat off, with his entire kitchen and gardening staff staring.

He could see John running toward him from the house. How grateful he was at that moment that he had not sent him back to his house in town. "For God's sake, pull the master from the mud," he shouted before he even reached the assemblage. Everything had happened so fast, and everyone was so stunned, that no one, including Darcy, had had time to think. Two strong arms on either side of him pulled him to his feet. Then suddenly a cheer went up. Darcy found his feet and walked slowly up the bank. He realized he was very cold. John, ever to his aid, removed his jacket and put it around Darcy's shoulders. Then, through the crowd of admiring faces, two boys were shoved in front of him. One of the gardeners said, "Speak up, boy. Say thank ye to the master for saving yer life."

The younger boy, the one who had nearly drowned, was looking at his sodden shoes and from the movement of his shoulders, Darcy could see, was sobbing. Darcy put his hand on the boy's head. "There, there," he said. The boy suddenly threw himself at Darcy and grasped both his legs in an embrace that nearly knocked him down. "It is all right," was all Darcy could think to say. He looked up at the boy's brother, who was rubbing at his eyes as well. "Take him back to his mother now," he said simply, and the older boy nodded, disengaged his still-weeping brother, and made his way through the crowd of onlookers. As soon as they were through the crowd, Darcy saw them running across the lawn, back to the village, he suspected. He suddenly felt very tired.

Leaning on John, the crowd parted to let him through. John spoke to them, "Have you all no duties to perform?" and they scattered like chickens, all save the cook.

"Would you like some breakfast, sir?" she asked.

He looked up into her face, seeing a kindness in her eyes that quite moved him. "Yes, indeed I would. Eggs," he said. "Eggs and bacon. I seem to have worked up an appetite."

From that day forward, Darcy's recovery began to accelerate. Ignoring the doctor's orders, he started each day walking the grounds with the aid of his cane, then worked on the books in his study. He took a short rest before luncheon and then took more exercise. Again, in the afternoon, he needed to sleep, but each day, those times of sleep grew shorter. Nearly a week after he'd saved the boy from drowning, he ordered his carriage. It was time to see for himself how work was going on the estate. Soon, he would be able to ride, and soon, he would start out after his beloved Elizabeth.

***

Life in St. George's was something so new to Elizabeth that sometimes she was unable to comprehend it all. Her introduction to society by way of small dinner parties for select guests had been quite a success. Many complemented her on her wit and bearing, some commented on what they considered her rather radical views, which she tempered according to her audience. In some ways, the normal rules of society were more relaxed than they were at home. Perhaps it was the phenomenon of the "second sons of second sons" that she heard people speak of. Many of the plantation owners here, and many who went to the newly formed United States, were living with the same dilemma as she. The rules of inheritance in England were such that only a single male heir received property, and those sons of noble families not born first were destined to live on an allowance (a generous one, to be sure) but not as master of their fathers' estates. These "second sons" sometimes went abroad to seek their fortunes, and many made them as planters or other types of landowners all over the British Empire. So too, it was with the people she met here on Grenada. They were creating new fortunes and new estates in the New World. Elizabeth admired that on one hand; it showed initiative and ambition. On the other hand, they built their fortune on the indentured servitude and slavery of others, and the more she witnessed it, the more abominable it had become to her. It was all she could do to hold her tongue sometimes. Hold it she did, though, as she was beholden to the governor and his family for her existence here. The only person she seemed to be able to discuss her views with was Edward. He seemed not to condescend to her, but to genuinely listen and appreciate what she had to say, although he disagreed with it, sometimes vehemently. Still, he was the one person to whom she could vent the entire range of her feelings and opinions and that made things bearable, and even enjoyable for her.

The other source of great joy for Elizabeth was her servant, Poppy. Although Elizabeth knew intellectually that Poppy was a slave, she felt about her the way she felt about the servants in her own modest home at Longbourn. Since Elizabeth was not born on the island, she realized that she did not grow up with a preconceived notion of what her hosts viewed as the natural inferiority of the negro race. Yes, the color of their skin, the shape of their noses and lips, the texture of their hair was very different from the people to whom Elizabeth was exposed all her life, but for the life of her, she could not see a fundamental difference in temperament, ability, spirituality, or the elemental, emotional, or physical needs of the Grenadian slaves when compared to the English. Elizabeth, although she could not as yet articulate it in so many words, felt a nagging sense of a fundamental injustice in this society. More so, however, she was developing a real affection for Poppy, who rapidly was replacing Jane as her confidante. This was the primary reason why, during the long, hot afternoons when the rest of the family were resting, Elizabeth began reading lessons with Poppy.

It was appalling to Elizabeth that slaves were not encouraged to read and to better themselves. Of course, it was obvious to her why they were kept in ignorance. She could see it in the emerging strata of free blacks who owned property, ran estates and businesses and, in rare cases, even had slaves of their own. The English, especially, found this class threatening. The more knowledge these people acquired, the more discontented they became. She had heard many an argument from white slave owners that their slaves were infinitely better off here than they were in Africa. Since she had never been to Africa, and neither had they, that argument seemed specious at best.

Then, there were the French. Mrs. Home was correct that the French Revolution and its doctrines of equality and brotherhood for the oppressed was spreading rapidly in the islands, chiefly among the free blacks and certainly the disenfranchised French. They had lost control of Grenada to the British and were treated as second-class citizens. There was much discontent here that troubled the Home household, and therefore spilled over onto her and her visit here. But in the afternoons, when everything was peaceful, Poppy and Elizabeth sat down to read.

"I t'ink I got it now," Poppy said in her lilting voice.

"Try it, then, and I will listen," Elizabeth encouraged.

Poppy began haltingly to read from a primer Elizabeth surreptitiously absconded with from the Homes' library. It was engraved by an unsteady, small hand with the word "Barbara." Now, Poppy made her first tentative steps into the world of literacy. For Elizabeth, it was extremely gratifying.

The lesson proceeded, and Poppy proved to be an apt pupil. Elizabeth suspected that her fluency increased due to the fact that she took what she learned each week and then taught it to the other slaves in the quarters. It was the first time in Elizabeth's life she felt as if she were doing something worthwhile. How her hosts would feel about it if they knew, she shuddered to think.

Her hosts also provided a lovely diary for her when she asked for it. Instead of a journal of her day's activities, it was filled with rudimentary sentences and simple arithmetic problems.

"Here," said Elizabeth. "This is how you write your name … P-O-P-P-Y." First Elizabeth printed it, and then Poppy followed. She had learned the alphabet quickly, but now the next order of business was words and sentences.

"Can you write for me where you from?" Poppy asked.

"I can," Elizabeth said, "but would you not prefer to write where you are from?"

"No, miss," Poppy said adamantly. "When I learn 'nough, I will write your maman and tell her what a good teacher you are, Miss 'Lizbet."

Elizabeth dutifully printed out, "Longbourn," "Meryton," and "England" and then wondered if she would ever see those places again.

The quickness of Poppy's mind impressed Elizabeth greatly. In different circumstances, she could see her sister Mary and Poppy becoming friends as Poppy's appetite for the written word and her desire to educate herself seemed virtually insatiable. Elizabeth's only fear was that, while she was having her long discussions with Edward, she would slip and say something of her education of Poppy. Perchance she was misjudging Edward and he would come around to her way of thinking once he saw what an apt pupil Poppy had become. More likely, though, the lessons would be forced to stop, and she would create a strain between herself and her most generous hosts. No, for now, Poppy's education was better kept a secret.

***

Dearest Lizzy,

I have such wonderful news. Perhaps you know of it already, but since the post overseas is so unreliable, I will reiterate the news myself. Mr. Darcy is alive, Lizzy. He is alive. Apparently, the doctor gave him too much laudanum on his journey to Rosings, and it put him in such a state as he appeared dead. Oh, Lizzy, he is most anxious to see you again and has assured Charles and me of his continued deep affection for you. One of the first things he did upon awakening from his deep slumber was to send word to you that he was still among the living. The letter, unfortunately, arrived a day after you set sail and there was no way to get word to you. Papa immediately set out to verify the authenticity of the letter and he met with Mr. Darcy himself. We have enclosed his letter along with ours, so you may at least see his hand, and know that all is well. Perhaps soon you will be on your way home to us. Perhaps even in the company of Mr. Darcy. Oh, Lizzy, I wish that were so. I do so miss your company.

One concern is preying on my mind, though, and on that point, I would like to reassure you. When you left, you were absolutely sure of Mr. Darcy's demise and therefore a free agent. Have you developed an attachment for someone else, Lizzy, Edward perhaps? If that is so, and there is already an engagement, no one would blame you for that or begrudge you your happiness. I do not believe Mr. Darcy has entertained this idea, however, but I am sure he would resign himself in time. He loves you so, Lizzy, and would only want your happiness, of that I am convinced.

All in the family are well. We hear little from Lydia, as she is such a poor correspondent. I know Wickham has been sent away but know not if he is to be reassigned to France or perhaps somewhere else. I am afraid this marriage may be a harsh introduction to adulthood for our Lydia, and I think of her often. Kitty and Mary are still safely at home, and Kitty has become quite calm—and dare I say, demure?—without Lydia's influence. Mama and Papa are much the same, although I do think Papa misses you. I go often to visit, which results in effusive welcomes for my Charles, as you can imagine.

I do hope this reaches you, my dear sister, and it finds you well. I remain forever

Your loving sister,

Jane

Thus, the news of Mr. Darcy's miraculous resurrection was dispatched again to Elizabeth. Tucked inside was Darcy's letter that he still held in his possession, restored to him by Mr. Bennet. Darcy sealed both letters and dispatched them before the Bingleys left Pemberley. With them, he sent a prayer that neither pirates, nor storms, nor the French would interfere in their delivery. Once the rider had left his estate for the post, he began another letter. In these uncertain times, it was good to have something in reserve.

Chapter 10

It was decided, much by Edward's insistence, that Elizabeth's official introduction to Grenadian society should be a large garden party hosted by the lieutenant governor and his family. That society, of course, consisted of British citizens or the descendants of same, and excluded the French and the free black population. Elizabeth was grateful for the efforts made on her behalf by the governor and his family. She rarely saw the governor, but Edward, Barbara, Gerard, and Mrs. Home saw to it that she was entertained. The evenings, however, were hard for her. She found herself sinking into melancholy, and to combat it, she often softly knocked on the window of the slave quarters to give reading lessons to Poppy. She was a clever pupil, and Elizabeth marveled at how she could work from dawn to dusk and still embrace her studies with such enthusiasm.

The day of the garden party arrived, as did the governor's guests. Many were in open carriages and chaises, the women carrying parasols to protect themselves from the relentless tropical sun. Elizabeth found herself relieved that the style of dresses, a light muslin with a high waist, was all the rage here in the islands. She felt sorry for the gentlemen, who seemed quite flushed and warm in their jackets and waistcoats.

Dancing was arranged, and Edward asked her immediately. Elizabeth enjoyed dancing, but one of the quadrilles played later in the evening was exactly the one played at the ball Mr. Bingley first held at Netherfield, and all her memories of that day—her encounters with Mr. Darcy, her subsequent misjudging of him, and all that followed—came flooding back to her. At that point, she was dancing with another partner, a Mr. Hamilton, and quickly excused herself. She escaped to the garden and disappeared among the gigantic leaves and made her way toward the pond. There, sitting on an alabaster bench near the water, sure that she was alone and unobserved, she gave way to tears.

A few moments later, she felt a hand upon her shoulder and she bolted upright.

"I am so sorry," said Edward, quickly removing his hand.

She quickly relaxed and hastily dried her tears. "I am afraid I am not good company tonight," she said, gathering herself.

"No, sit, please," he reassured her. "It is I who should be apologizing to you. I came upon you secretly, but you see, I have been observing you all evening, Elizabeth. I cannot help myself. You have bewitched me."

Such a confession would normally have appalled Elizabeth, or even filled her with suspicion or scorn, but somehow, when she looked up into Edward's face, it gave her an odd sort of comfort. There was no guile in his expression, only sympathy.

"Oh, Edward," she said, "it is too soon..." She wanted to continue but could not think of what to say. Since she did not get up to escape from him, Edward persisted.

"I am a clumsy ass, am I not?" he said, and that made Elizabeth laugh through her tears.

"No, you certainly are not. I am glad you came out here after me. I should not dwell on what cannot be changed. It is unlike me, really, to...to...wallow in self-pity."

"You are too hard on yourself," Edward said softly. "You need to grieve, and I am only thinking of myself and what I want. My affection for you must take into account what is best for you, is that not so?"

Elizabeth was surprised by the frankness of his conversation, but then again, he had always been honest with her. Perhaps it was a trait of those living in this strange, new land.

"When you are ready to begin again, please tell me. There is something that I want to ask you." With that, he took her hand and kissed it, then in a real gesture of intimacy, turned it over and kissed the palm. The feeling sent shivers up Elizabeth's spine. She tried to suppress her physical reaction to his touch but could not. She suddenly felt deeply disloyal to Darcy, her body at war with her heart. The situation was intolerable. She stood up.

"Mr. Home," she said. He took her hand again, but this time held it lightly. She reverted to her formal address of him as a shield against further familiarity.

"I am sorry, Elizabeth," he said. "I do understand. Really."

How odd, she thought. To come this far in such a short time. Her parents rarely called each other by their first names. She suddenly felt exhausted...confused and exhausted.

"Would you mind if I retired?" she asked him. "Please make my excuses to your mother and sister and the other guests."

"I will," he said.

She turned to look at him as she reentered the house. "Thank you, Edward."

Later, in her room as she gazed at the shining leaves and pungent flowers billowing their perfume into the air, all illuminated in the silver light of the moon, she thought of their encounter. Perhaps he was in love with her. How would she feel to be Mrs. Edward Home?

***

A rider arrived at Pemberley early, a few weeks after Mr. Darcy's rescue of the gardener's boy. He requested an interview with Mr. Darcy, who was now walking about unassisted. Darcy opened the door to the drawing room and there stood Dr. Castleden, the doctor who had saved his life not so many weeks before. Darcy greeted him warmly.

"So good of you to come," Darcy said.

"I see you are making a speedy recovery, sir. I am glad," Castleden said. "If you would not mind, Mr. Darcy, I would like to examine you to see how your wound is healing."

"I expected as much," Darcy replied. "Let us have some luncheon first and I will tell you what I am proposing."

During their meal, Darcy told Castleden of his nearly premature burial and of his plans to follow Elizabeth to Grenada. He trusted no doctor more than Castleden and wanted his opinion.

"Your body and your mind have received a great trauma, Mr. Darcy. I have seen it many times with soldiers on the continent. Sometimes their bodies heal before their minds do. How have you been sleeping?"

This was a question Darcy had not been prepared for. He had difficulty sleeping some nights, awakening calling out or screaming. John was now installed in the room next to his because of these night terrors. When Darcy did not answer immediately, Castleden spoke, "I surmised as much."

"Whether I sleep well or not is beside the point," Darcy said testily. "Can I travel? Am I well enough for an ocean voyage?"

"I will determine that after my examination," Castleden replied evenly. After luncheon, Darcy submitted to being poked and prodded by the doctor.

"I would recommend another month's rest before you set out."

Darcy jumped up impatiently and turned away from the doctor. He winced.

"Sudden movements, such as those, can injure you again. Just because the outer wound has closed does not mean that all is well inside."

This was not what Darcy wanted to hear. "So you think I should loll about in bed, and be pushed about the garden in a chair?" he asked impatiently.

Castleden laughed. "Certainly not. I will advise you as I advise the soldiers I treat. Eat well, but not to excess. Stay away from strong spirits. Walk as much as possible. Take in fresh air. By February, you could join the Royal Navy if you had a mind to."

Darcy turned and looked at him. "And if I ignore your advice?"

"You could injure yourself permanently and spend the rest of your days being pushed about in a chair. It is up to you."

When Darcy sat alone that night by the fire, his thoughts were filled with Elizabeth. Surely, she would have received his letters by now. At least one, surely. She would be waiting for him. He would write to her again and tell her to expect him by March. He closed his eyes and felt her supple body yield against his. It was too long to wait, but he would wait.

***

When Wickham arrived in St. Lucia, he was in an ebullient mood. Except for the erasure of all his debts and a sizable allowance from Darcy, matrimony had not agreed with him in the slightest. Bad luck that he had ever cast a glance at any of the Bennet girls, and worse luck that Darcy had taken such a fancy to Elizabeth. He could have enjoyed himself with Lydia and never looked back if she had not had such powerful friends. Ah well, there was the money to think of anyway. If Darcy had not been indisposed, he would probably have interfered with this escape to the tropics. As it was, Lydia was back with her mother, her honor restored, and he had his freedom, at least temporarily. He could be lolling about in a blockade ship off the coast of France. Instead, as he stood at attention on deck, he could see over his commander's shoulder the white sand beaches, the red roofed houses, and the waving palm trees of his new, momentary home. He wondered if the luscious brown girls swam out to meet the ships as he heard they did in Tahiti. Perhaps he could be sent to Tahiti next. Life was good.

***

Elizabeth had been away from home for four months now. She began to adjust to the rhythm of life on the islands. What she could not understand was why no letters from home had arrived. She asked Edward about it one morning, and he began to enumerate on his fingers all the fates that could have befallen her letters, not the least of which were pirates. There never was a day in which something did not surprise or even astound her. Pirates, indeed. He suggested that in her next letter home, she should prevail upon her family to send letters through the fleet. If they were addressed in care of the lieutenant governor, they would have a greater chance of reaching her. His Majesty's naval ships, after all, possessed cannons, which were sometimes discouraging to pirates.

In these many ways, her reality was being inexorably altered, and this was due entirely to the Home family. She was becoming part of them and they of her. She moved with a certain independence that she could only dream of in Meryton. Day trips into St. George's became routine for her. As did her keeping company with Edward.

It was during one of these short trips into town that Elizabeth first heard of Julien Fedon. Barbara was busy with her own household and Edward was sent to investigate some irrigation problem on the plantation. It was Governor Home who suggested that Elizabeth take Poppy and a driver and go explore St. George's. What a wondrous place this was. This independence of movement unheard of at home. She thanked the governor and took advantage of the offer.

The shops in town were full of goods from home as well as local treasures. The people, though, were what fascinated Elizabeth the most. She knew from her hosts that the island was placed under British protection in 1783, but that many of the displaced French residents were still there, having nowhere else to go as their homeland was wracked by revolution. There were also free blacks and mulattos who owned property and, at times, were better off financially than their supplanted French counterparts. Yet, there were slaves here as well.

Elizabeth was in a shop, looking over some island-made goods that she was considering sending home to her sisters, when a young French woman accosted her. She was dressed well, in the empire fashion. Her head was covered with black curls, and she had the most flawless olive skin Elizabeth had ever seen. She introduced herself, which was not the manner of the English, certainly.

"I beg your pardon, but are you new to St. George's?" she asked in French.

"I am sorry. Do I know you?" Elizabeth asked in English.

"Ah, you are English, of course. I should have guessed. I am Juliette Benoir," she said in heavily accented English and extended her hand to Elizabeth.

This was most extraordinary. Here was a French woman, speaking to her without an introduction, while their two countries were on the brink of war. Elizabeth stood stock still for a few moments, collecting her thoughts. Finally, she grasped Juliette's hand.

"Elizabeth Bennet," she said, and waited for her companion to continue.

"Would you like to have a coffee with me?" Juliette asked.

"I... I...do not know if I should," Elizabeth blurted.

"Oh, I mean you no 'arm," continued Juliette in her lovely French accent. "It is just that I am so bored, and would love someone new to talk to, but if you prefer not..."

Elizabeth smiled. She liked Juliette, despite, or perhaps, because of her unconventional ways. "Thank you, I will," she said, and the two women left for Juliette's favorite cafe.

Poppy and Elizabeth's driver followed meekly along, though Poppy was making faces at Elizabeth, probably trying to tell her of the inappropriateness of her meeting. Poor Poppy had no idea that when confronted with something her mistress was told not to do, it inflamed her will all the more to do it. Life was fast becoming a real adventure for Elizabeth, and days like this one took her out of herself and her brooding thoughts completely. Her companion was engaging, and the slight hint of doing something wrong gave the act of having a coffee at a cafe a hint of salacious danger.

"We lost all our possessions and nearly our lives in Santa Domingue last year," Juliette continued. "The slaves, inspired by our own revolution, rose up and deposed French rule. Ironic, is it not?" she asked, laughing.

"You lost everything?" Elizabeth asked. It hardly seemed possible. Juliette hardly had the look of someone who had fallen on hard times.

"Our house, our plantation, our livestock, this is all we lost," said Juliette. "Papa was fortunate that he sent gold out of the country, to Austria or some-sing, I don't remember. He would like to rebuild again, this time in West Africa." Juliette sighed as if she had just said the most common thing in the world. West Africa.

Elizabeth was astounded. Who would think to begin again in such a place? "Will you not go home to France?"

Juliette laughed a bubbly, tinkling laugh. "Certainly not. I do not feel French, really. I have never seen France. Have you been zer'?" She smiled at her companion.

"No," said Elizabeth. "This is the first place I have traveled in the world." *Here is someone without a country,* Elizabeth thought. *French, but not French.* Perhaps she soon would be English, but not English. Certainly, her children may be.

"Perhaps you are thinking of settling 'ere," Juliette said, rather as a question.

"I really do not know. I have only just arrived."

"I think it is not a good idea, *n'est-ce pas*? There will be a revolution here soon too, I am thinking," Juliette said matter-of-factly.

"A revolution? Why ever would you say that?" Elizabeth asked, alarmed.

"Ah, one hears zees t'ings. There are many angry French here on the island, and many successful mulattos, and many ill-treated slaves. There is Julien Fedon, who owns Belvidere Estate. He is quite a follower of the revolution in France."

"Julien Fedon?"

"His father was French and his mother from 'ere, or one of 'za nearby islands. He is not accepted by British society, but zen so few of us are." She looked at Elizabeth slyly. Was she making light of the situation? Elizabeth was not sure. Juliette continued, "And he sees his people in oppression. He has money and land, but not…equality of life. The British even required him to produce evidence that his wife was not born a slave. Can you imagine? There has been talk in the north…"

Elizabeth was becoming more and more uncomfortable with the conversation. "What have you heard?"

"The ideas of revolution have spread from America to France and back again to za New World. There are many 'ere who would like to be accepted as men, and why not? What does za color of one's skin have to do with any'sing?"

This young woman was quite right, of course. What did the color of one's skin mean, really? Or where one was born, or to what family one was born, or who had money and who did not? *Oh dear. I am becoming quite French.*

"Perhaps even the French government will attempt to retake zee island, who knows?" Juliette said lightly, as if she were commenting on the weather.

With that their conversation drifted to more mundane topics: the tropical weather, island food, the scant knowledge of the latest fashion. After a time, an open chaise pulled up and an older European gentleman got out.

"Juliette, where have you been? I have been looking everywhere. Your mother was quite worried," he spoke in French. Juliette's father, Elizabeth surmised.

"Papa, zis is my friend, Elizabeth," Juliette said, in English. "She has just arrived in the islands."

"Welcome to our part of the world," said Juliette's father. "Oh, there is your mother. Come, we need to depart. *Enchanté*, mademoiselle." He took Elizabeth's hand, and kissed it. He then turned and helped another woman into the coach. She had arrived from one of the shops across the street. Her skin was the color of ebony. Juliette took Elizabeth by the hand and introduced her in French, "Maman, this is my friend, Elizabeth."

The woman extended her hand from the carriage and clasped Elizabeth's. "*Enchanté*," she said.

Elizabeth replied, "*Enchanté.*" *Yes,* she thought, *I am becoming quite French.*

***

"So, you have met Juliette," Edward said matter-of-factly. Was there no end to the surprises in store for Elizabeth? How on earth did he know Juliette?

Edward laughed when he saw Elizabeth's expression. "Do not tell my father, but I consort with the French," he said, whispering in Elizabeth's ear and then grinning at her.

Elizabeth's astonishment left her speechless. "You are surprised, I can tell," he said, almost laughing. She knew he loved throwing her off balance.

They were sitting alone in the music room after dinner and were supposed to be playing piqué, but Edward was not concentrating and seemed more interested in courting "his beloved." He thought of her as such and told her as much, repeatedly. She was growing very fond of him, she had to admit.

"You always astonish me," Elizabeth said when she could finally think of something to say. "I thought the French were…"

"*Persona non grata?*" he suggested.

"I assumed that, since your father is the governor and the French are no longer in control here, and from your family's conversations that—"

"I am not so closed-minded as all that," he said. "I occasionally attend social gatherings that include people my father would find…how can I put it…unsuitable." He smiled again. The golden evening light was falling on his face. She realized that he was very handsome.

To distract herself from such thoughts, Elizabeth stood and walked over to the window. She was constantly enthralled by the brilliant sunsets here in the islands, the pink and billowing sea clouds that gathered in the west like towering, airborne mountains. Even in the midst of this astounding conversation, she could not take her eyes off it.

Edward stole up behind her so close that she could feel the warmth of his body. Without so much as a "by your leave," he encircled her waist with his arms. She did not draw back from him but turned and looked into his face. Without waiting for permission or words of any kind, he leaned forward to kiss her. She reacted quickly, holding her finger to his lips.

"Edward, I—" she began. He did not wait for her to finish. He took the opportunity to kiss her finger. It made her smile. She took it away.

"You know how I feel," he interrupted. "I am trying to be a patient man."

She had to smile. "Yes, I believe you are," she said. She paused, as if weighing the next words she was going to say. "I am very fond of you, Edward, but—" she began.

"No, stop," he rushed in, the smile never leaving his face. "I know how this sentence ends, and I will not hear it. Let us take a walk in the garden," he said, and slipped her arm into his. She did not resist.

"Tell me more about the French," she said, as they entered the fragrance of the tropical evening. The frogs were just beginning to sing.

***

The sun had barely risen when Darcy walked out to the stables. The servants, of course, were already up and about tending to their chores. Archie, the stable boy, saw his master coming. He was carrying water to the stalls. He put the buckets down and touched the brim of his hat as Darcy approached.

"Mornin', sir," he said under his breath.

"Good morning, Archie. Do you think you could saddle Marigold for me this morning?"

"Aye, sir," he replied, and smiled. Darcy was deliberately trying to be kinder, or at least less imperious, than he had been before his injury. It seemed to him that the servants were more cheerful as a result. It might be just his imagination.

There was nothing else to say as Archie went about his business. Darcy was a trifle agitated. He had to admit to himself that he was not sure he was ready for his first time back on horseback, and frankly, for the mission that he had set for himself afterward.

During his long convalescence, he had not heard a word from Elizabeth. Surely one of his letters had reached her by now. Perhaps she was already on her way back to him. Then again, she may still think that he was dead. Perhaps she had already formed another attachment. His mind almost always went in that direction, and he struggled not to think of it. He had a vision of himself arriving at St. George's and seeking her out, only to find her married to another man. No, surely nothing of the sort could have happened so quickly. She loved him. She had said so. She risked her reputation and her future to tend to him all the time he was at death's door. Elizabeth would be loyal to him, surely. Of course she would.

"Sir. Sir." Archie's voice came through the fog of his convoluted thoughts. "Marigold is ready now."

"Yes, of course. Thank you, Archie," he said as he stepped up and swung himself into the saddle.

"I want to thank you, sir," Archie mumbled into his chest.

"For what?" Darcy asked, wincing a bit at the pull he felt in his chest as he mounted the gentle Marigold.

"For saving my brother, sir. You remember, sir? From the pond?"

Great heavens, this was the lad whom he'd seen from the window. There had been so much hubbub at the time, he'd barely glanced at the faces of the boys involved. He recovered himself quickly. "Yes, of course, Archie. How is your brother?"

"He is well, sir. Thanks to you, sir."

"Thanks to you too, Archie. If you had not called out when you did, all would have been lost."

Archie lifted his head to stare at his master, admiration shining in his face. Darcy was quite touched by that look, but never one to betray his emotions, he looked away and pulled the reins. Marigold trotted happily from the stable out into the field beyond. He felt as if he was taking the first full breath of fresh air he had had in months. He had to admit that, with every bounce in the saddle, he could feel some twinge of discomfort from his wound, but it surely was not pain. No, the pain was gone, and he could ride. Perhaps the mild Marigold might be convinced of a trot.

***

Dear Jane,

So many things have happened and things here are so strange and wondrous I do not know where to begin. I am sorry that I have been such a poor correspondent, and, although I know you must have written, I have not received even one letter from home. I suppose the post is not as reliable crossing an ocean as it is traveling from Meryton to London. I do hope this letter reaches you. I must tell you all that has been happening with my dear friends, the Home family, and of all the sights and sounds of Grenada.

I will begin by telling you that I think of Mr. Darcy every day. I cannot help it, Jane. With all the kindness I have received and all the fascinating places that I have visited I still find myself dwelling on what might have been. I still love him, Jane. I cannot help myself. I wish you and I could sit, our heads together in the drawing room at home, and you could advise me. How I need your counsel and advice, dear sister. If you do receive this letter, please tell me what I should do. Many have said that "time heals all wounds," but I do not think there is enough time in my lifetime to mend the wound left by my dear one's death.

Barbara and her mother have taken me under their wings and have done their utmost to assuage my grief. Barbara is with child and will enter her confinement soon. We are all overjoyed at the prospect of a new member of the Home family. I have been recruited to assist with preparing clothes for the infant. My needlework is steadily improving, I must say. Edward is a constant joy and an easy companion. I do believe he has set his cap for me, but I do not love him, although I value him as a friend. How lucky you are, sister, to have married for love. I, alas, will not. Sometimes I convince myself that I shall not marry at all, but I know that is impractical. Could you imagine if Mama heard me say such a thing? I dare not think of it. Perhaps, after a suitable time of mourning, if Edward remains constant, I will consent to marry him. He has as much as asked me already. Fortunately, he is the soul of patience, which is a gift to me. He also can make me laugh. I do treasure him.

Now, Jane, I will take you on a wondrous journey into life here in Grenada. There are so many various and different people here. There are the English, of course, who are the planters and, shall I say, governors of the island. Then there are the French, who are dispossessed and quite hostile much of the time to us, the English. There are also free Black men, who have property and even have servants of their own. Finally, there are the slaves. Slaves. People held in bondage. I even have a slave of my own, Poppy. She is very like a lady's maid, but somehow different. She cannot escape her station by any means and is not free to move about as she wills. She is not even allowed an education, but I have intervened in that regard. I am teaching her to read, Jane. I quite enjoy it, but I feel that our hosts would be very displeased and even angry with me if they were ever to find out.

I met a young woman here called Juliette. She has a black Grenadian mother and a French father. You may wonder how I should ever be acquainted with such a person. She merely introduced herself to me in a shop. Can you believe it? We had coffee together and she told me of her life here. I was surprised to find that Edward was acquainted with her and he subsequently accompanied me to a ball held in the French quarter of the city. Oh, Jane, there is such a myriad of different people there. Free Black planters and their wives, French merchants, and couples who were like Juliette's parents, one of Africa and one of Europe. I believe that I must have stood stock still in astonishment more than once during the evening. Edward seemed to enjoy my amazement as much as he enjoyed the ball. His father would have been scandalized to know that we were fraternizing with the enemy, so to speak, but they did not seem like the enemy to me, Jane. I do not know what is happening to me and to my way of thinking. Everything I learned as a child seems not to fit with what I am experiencing now.

The person who impressed me the most, though, was a fellow called Julien Fedon. He is a mulatto landowner of some wealth and reputation. He seemed fascinating and dangerous at the same time. He is quite a believer in the French revolutionary motto, "Liberte, Egalite, Fraternite" and proved it by having quite a long conversation about politics with me, of all people. How many times have we been banished to another room with the rest of the women while the men discuss politics over coffee and cigars? That night, Jane, I felt that someone valued my opinion. Oh, what is happening to me? I fear my Darcy would not know what to make of me now.

See, there? I have thought of him again. I find myself measuring my thoughts and actions against his approval or disapproval. All of it is fiction, since I will never see him again this side of Paradise.

There is a knock at the door and I must close. Do not forget me, dear Jane. Give my love to Papa, Mama, Kitty, Mary, Lydia when you hear from her, and of course, my dear brother, Charles. I nearly forgot. When you write to me again, please post the letter in care of Lt. Governor Home and send it through official post. It will have much more chance of reaching me, I am told.

Your loving sister,
Elizabeth

Elizabeth slipped the letter into an envelope and was dripping sealing wax onto the flap when she called for Barbara to enter.

"The post leaves the island tomorrow," Barbara said in reply to a question Elizabeth had yet to ask. "I will put it in Father's correspondence. Come, now, Elizabeth, there are some people downstairs I would like you to meet."

***

That evening, Elizabeth noticed that Edward was absent after dinner. Their guests had gone, and Lt. Governor Home and Gerard had excused themselves to work on papers that were leaving for England in the morning. Elizabeth's letter was among them.

"Where is Edward?" Elizabeth asked, looking up from her book. Barbara and her mother exchanged a look. Maybe she just imagined it.

Barbara sounded guarded. "Perhaps he has taken a walk about the grounds. He does that sometimes."

"Oh, well then, I shall go and find him," Elizabeth said.

Before she even had a chance to close the book she was reading, both Barbara and her mother said, "No," emphatically and in unison. Then they exchanged that glance again.

"Have I said something wrong?" asked Elizabeth. Barbara's mother looked absolutely stricken, but Barbara spoke up promptly. She sighed.

"No, Elizabeth. I believe he might have gone into town, to one of the taverns he frequents. He has such an odd assortment of friends." She and her mother exchanged glances again. "I hope you do not disapprove too much."

How odd. Why would she disapprove at all? She had already been to a ball with Edward's "odd friends." Of course, neither Barbara nor her mother knew that. Elizabeth smiled.

"It is not for me to approve or disapprove, really," she said. Barbara stood, walked to the settee, sat next to Elizabeth and took her hand, all in one fell swoop.

"Oh, we do so want you to like Edward," she said imploringly. Elizabeth looked from one to the other and suddenly burst out laughing.

"You two have no worries on that account. I do like Edward, very much."

Mrs. Home visibly relaxed. "So, you will not be going out to find him, then?"

"Honestly, Mother," Barbara retorted. "She is not about to go into town after him, is she?" Now she was laughing. "Let us play some cards, shall we? I feel lucky tonight."

Elizabeth noticed Mrs. Home's sigh and look again at her daughter. It was such a strange look.

***

Darcy was perusing his wardrobe and deciding what he needed for a long ocean voyage. The weather was chilly, so he would need some warm clothes for at least a few weeks on board. What does one wear in the tropics? How warm was it there? He had traveled with his father as a youth to France, Germany, and even Italy. Perhaps he should dress for Italy. It was warm there. John was sorting things out. The two men were getting in each other's way when the butler entered through the open door.

"Lady Catherine de Bourgh," he announced.

"Oh, great heavens," Darcy exclaimed, with not a small amount of irritation. "I believe you will have to carry on without me, John."

"I will do my best, sir," John replied.

How did news travel this fast? thought Darcy. *How did she know I was planning to leave soon for the islands?*

"Aunt," he said, bowing and taking her hand.

"Nephew," she said haughtily. "You are looking well."

"I have been taking exercise," he said.

"You must stop that at once," she commanded. "You will injure yourself."

"Nonsense," he said heartily. "Will you have some tea?" Without waiting for an answer, he rang for the servant. "Tea for her ladyship and myself."

"I will have a great deal more than tea. I have come for an extended visit," she announced.

Now he did not feel as robust as he did two minutes ago. Of course, she would not come all this way and not stay for a time. Why did she not send word first? He turned and looked at her and he knew. She suspected that he would be leaving to follow Elizabeth, and she was here to stop him. It would not do.

"I am afraid that I cannot stop and entertain you, dear aunt. Today I leave for Portsmouth."

"Oh?" she replied feigning ignorance. It was not very convincing. She noticed him observing her. "I am not in error then. I surmised as much."

Darcy readied himself for a lengthy and exhausting argument. Instead, his aunt surprised him yet again.

"I hope you do not mind," she said, "but I took the liberty of sending one of my servants to Portsmouth to obtain the schedule of ships leaving for St. George's, Grenada. I assume that is where you are going?"

With that she handed a bewildered Darcy a paper on which were copied ships' names and ports of call. He stared at it in stunned silence. Receiving no verbal reply, Lady Catherine continued. "As you can see, a ship for Grenada sails at the end of the month. I have already booked passage for you; therefore, you are in no hurry. We have sufficient time for an extended visit."

Darcy eyed her suspiciously.

"I know you do not consider it to be so, but I do feel somewhat responsible for at least some of your troubles of late," she said. Darcy knew, for her, those were difficult words to speak. She continued, "I also have come to realize that you know your own mind and that I should cease interfering in your choice of a wife."

This really is remarkable. Darcy could scarcely believe it. Still, it was possible that she finally acquiesced to his wishes. It was his duty to give her the benefit of the doubt. Yet all he could do was stand there, speechless. Ruffling herself up like a self-satisfied brood hen, she sat down.

"Now, Darcy, where is that tea?"

***

The family was off to another political dinner, and Elizabeth decided to invent a headache. She did enjoy socializing with the friends and political allies of her hosts, but some of the newness of her situation was wearing off, and so was her enthusiasm for yet another evening of talk of a possible French invasion. It had been over a week since she was able to have a reading lesson with Poppy, and it was long overdue. Tonight, they would embark on another chapter of Barbara's primer.

After the family left, Elizabeth set out for the slave quarters. Many of them were outside tending fires and cooking. She had become familiar to them, so they merely nodded and went about the business of caring for their own families. She came upon Poppy's window and knocked three times. It had become their signal. Elizabeth waited near the red, carpeting blooms of the flamboyant tree. It was named aptly. Sometimes, she wished she could climb up into its branches and cover herself in its red and fiery blossoms. For now, she would content herself with standing beneath it.

When Poppy did not arrive promptly, Elizabeth returned to the window. This time, she peeped in. The room was empty. No wonder Poppy did not answer. As she turned away again, she nearly collided with Poppy. "Oh, Miss 'Lizbet, whachu doin' here?" she asked hesitantly.

It was a strange greeting for her usually enthusiastic pupil. "I thought we could read tonight. I've escaped from my social engagement, you see," Elizabeth said brightly.

Poppy looked agitated, which was not her usual manner. "I don' know if we should, Miss 'Lizbet. I t'ink they gettin' suspicious up in the house about it." Poppy was looking around as if she expected a tiger to jump out of the bushes. Elizabeth was surprised at her obvious agitation.

"Really?" Elizabeth asked. "I do not want to cause you any trouble, Poppy. I do not think there is any cause for concern, though. The family is all in town tonight."

With that, Poppy seemed visibly to relax. "*All* of dem in town?"

"Yes, Poppy. I am the only one here."

"And you right sure?"

"Yes, Poppy, quite sure."

"All right, den, I get me a lamp and we go under de tree."

Thus, among the fallen scarlet blossoms, an evening of *Tom Thumb* began, but seeds of doubt also began to sprout in Elizabeth's mind.

***

It was nearly a month later that Darcy began his journey to Portsmouth. His aunt's visit would have been unbearable but for the fact that Georgiana played the part of mediator between them. When his cousin Anne arrived, Darcy felt as though he could have jumped out of his skin with impatience. Anne's visit was as contrived as his aunt's to his way of thinking. Lady Catherine made no secret of her wish that Darcy should marry his cousin and Lady Catherine's daughter, Anne. He endured the visit, but it made no difference whatsoever to his plans. As he bade good-bye to all of them he felt nothing but relief, save Georgiana. It was now that his life could begin again. The visit did one thing for him, however; the extra time at home helped him regain the strength that he needed for his journey.

As it happened, Darcy decided to stop at Netherfield on his way to Portsmouth. He had been so anxious to see his friends that he arrived a day early. Jane and Charles were enjoying coffee after dinner when Barnes announced him.

"Mr. Darcy," he intoned and a moment later, Darcy was shaking Charles's hand.

"You look much better than when I saw you last, my friend," Charles said, smiling.

"I should hope so," Darcy said.

Darcy then greeted Jane and managed a few more pleasantries before he could contain himself no longer.

"Have you heard from your sister Elizabeth?" he finally blurted out to Jane.

Jane smiled serenely. "As it happens..." she said, and from the mantelpiece, she produced Elizabeth's letter.

Both Charles and Jane withdrew to the settee and let Darcy read. Finally, he looked up at them. "She has not received my letters," he said at last.

"Nor ours. She has received nothing. I cannot imagine what could have happened," Jane said miserably.

Darcy said nothing for a moment and sat thinking. "It is possible that the first letters were lost or misdirected, but that subsequent missives were delivered, is it not? That is possible, is it not?"

Both Charles and Jane admitted it was possible. "In fact," Darcy continued, "she might have received one of my letters the day after she posted this one." He waved the letter in his hand. Again, he paused as in deep thought. Jane and Bingley looked at one another, and then again at Darcy. He was grasping at straws. He gazed down again at the letter.

When he looked up at them again, his entire manner changed. "This Edward fellow," he demanded. "How could she possibly—" He stopped again.

"She has no idea what has happened, my good fellow," Bingley put forward cautiously. "She thought, we all thought, you were dead. Elizabeth was inconsolable, Darcy. At the time, Edward and Barbara were a godsend."

Darcy looked up at both of them miserably. "No one is to blame for any of this," Darcy said. "If you are not too tired, please sit with me. I will tell you my plans. I am more convinced than ever that I have made the correct decision. And, Bingley, you could offer a fellow a drink." He smiled weakly at his friend and his kind and lovely wife and began to sketch out his proposal for retrieving his beloved Elizabeth.

***

It took more than two days to travel from Netherfield to Portsmouth, and during that time Darcy had more than enough time to ruminate on his situation. He turned over and over in his head the shooting and his subsequent convalescence, much of which he remembered only vaguely or in disjointed images that he did not wholly trust. Most of his time, though, was spent on turning the words in Elizabeth's letter over and over in his mind: "I really do treasure him." That's what she'd said of Edward Home. Perhaps all this effort on his part was in vain. Perhaps he would arrive in St. George's only to be greeted by a married Elizabeth. She said she still loved him, but she might marry Edward out of necessity. After all, where would a woman be if she were unmarried? Elizabeth would have no money of her own after her father's demise—no money and no property. She would have no place, really. He knew she was intelligent and level-headed. She would weigh her options and choose. What did she have to come home to in England? Her reputation was in tatters due to her refusal to leave his side. Now, she would have a chance to build a life of her own in a faraway place, with a man who, perhaps, loves her. *What happened to my letters and to her family's letters? Why can this carriage not go any faster?*

Darcy arrived in Portsmouth with three days to spare before his voyage. He sent John ahead to the port to see about his accommodations on the ship and to attend to his luggage. The time spent with his aunt was almost unbearable. He could not settle his mind to anything but seeing Elizabeth again. Lady Catherine, for her part, seemed positively serene. It was gratifying to Darcy that she finally accepted the inevitable.

When John returned to Darcy's hotel, his face was ashen. Darcy could see that he was the bearer of bad tidings.

"Well, man, what is it? Is everything arranged?"

"Most assuredly not, sir," was John's rapid and squeaky answer.

"What? Why not? Out with it." Darcy was shouting. John cringed.

"The ship, the *Lady Gay*, has sailed without you, sir," John said meekly, waiting for another outburst.

"What do you mean? How could that have happened?" Darcy took two large strides and was across the room, his face scarcely two inches from John's. He took John by the lapels of his coat, then seeing the terror in John's eyes, released him immediately. He turned away.

"I do beg your pardon, John. That was uncalled for. Tell me…tell me what happened."

Darcy took a seat and motioned for John to do the same. He took one some distance from Darcy.

"According to the log, sir, you were never booked on the *Lady Gay*. They, the booking agents at the port, never heard of you."

How could I have been so stupid? Of course, they had never heard of him. Lady Catherine had set the entire chain of events in motion to delay him even more. She would not prevail, however. He was there in Portsmouth. He could book passage on another ship. It was a mere distraction, nothing more.

"I am sure something can be done. I will book passage on another ship," Darcy said calmly. John looked more miserable than ever.

"You cannot, sir," he said softly. "There will not be another passenger ship going to Grenada until April."

The rage began to rise in Darcy again, but he held it in check. There was no useful purpose in getting angry now. Now was the time to solve problems. He closed his eyes in thought.

"Jamaica, then," he said. "I will book to Jamaica and take a smaller boat to Grenada. How difficult could that be?"

"I thought of that, sir, begging your pardon. No passenger ships are on their way to Jamaica now, sir. They have had trouble with pirates. All ships are delayed until further notice."

"Good God," Darcy said in exasperation. "No post, no ships—"

John interrupted him. "I didn't say there were no ships, sir. Just no passenger ships, you see."

Darcy looked confused. "Whatever do you mean?"

"You see, sir, there are navy ships heading to the Caribbean and sir, and there is a cargo ship, *The Marlin*, leaving day after tomorrow for Grenada."

A cargo ship. Darcy pictured himself sleeping on bags of rice or bolts of fabric headed to his countrymen in the colonies. Before his flight of fancy proceeded any further, John spoke again.

"I did not think you would consider traveling on a cargo ship, sir."

"So you did not enquire, I suppose," Darcy said, exasperated. He stood up and ran his fingers through his hair.

"Actually, I did, sir," John said.

"You did? Good man. What did they say?"

"They will not take any passengers, sir."

Darcy's face fell. "But, begging your pardon, sir, they are looking for crew."

Darcy looked up at him in disbelief. What was the man proposing? He said nothing, so John continued.

"If you want me to, sir, I will sign aboard the ship and carry a message for you to Miss Bennet."

Darcy smiled. John was a good man, to be sure. "I could not ask you to do that, John." John, for his part, looked noticeably relieved. "We will have to think of something else."

Chapter 11

"We goin' to Paraclete, Miss 'Lizbet." Poppy practically bounced in as she brought Elizabeth's breakfast. She set the tray on the small table, and Elizabeth blinked.

"Is the rest of the family not having breakfast downstairs?" Elizabeth asked.

"No, miss, dey not. Dey up and about, getting ready to leave. We goin' to Paraclete."

By this time Elizabeth was tucking into her toast and pouring herself a cup of tea. "What is a Paraclete, may I ask?"

Poppy laughed her bubbly laugh. "It our home away from here," she said, "in the mountain where it cool and breezy. St. George's get too hot now, don' you tink?"

Elizabeth did think it was hot, but she just expected everything to be warm and humid and slow moving. It never occurred to her that that there might be an escape.

"You like it der, Miss 'Lizbet. Don' you worry."

"Oh, I am not worried. I know you will take good care of me. It must take a few days to get there."

"Oh no. Don' take no time t'all," Poppy said as she carefully packed Elizabeth's things.

"We along de Gran' Etang Road, tru de fores', y'see. Maybe one day, we 'dere safe and soun'."

"I will go and pack some books to take then, after I dress. We will continue our lessons in the mountains."

Poppy smiled. "Good t'inkin'."

Poppy was right. It only took a day to drive the mountainous track through the island, and they reached Paraclete a few hours before nightfall. Barbara and Gerard decided to stay in St. George's as Barbara was nearing her time, but the governor, his wife, Elizabeth, and Edward retreated to the cool of the mountains.

Here the vegetation was unrelentingly green, displacing the ever-flowering trees and shrubs near the coast. The cool, fresh mountain air greeted them at their arrival. The late afternoon sun illuminated the row of palms that lined the entrance to the estate, and here, as elsewhere, the road wound up the cultivated expanses to the plantation buildings at the top of the hill.

Elizabeth, for her part, found life in Grenada peaceful on one hand and disturbing on the other. She had received no letters from home yet, even though she had been gone nearly six months. She mentioned that perhaps it was time for her to consider travelling home, and the governor's family did everything in their power to dissuade her. This trip to the country estate seemed part of the plan. Although not sinister in nature, Elizabeth felt as though the family was pushing her and Edward together, hoping that Edward and she would soon come to an arrangement.

Technically, she was still in mourning, although no one could outwardly tell. Did she even have a right to mourn Mr. Darcy? After all, he was not her husband, nor were they even engaged, although she claimed that to be true, and believed it personally to be so.

However, since she'd arrived in Grenada, she had been to numerous social functions, never in black, and even out and about in town with Poppy. No one knew of her entanglement at home besides Barbara, Gerard, Edward, and the governor and his wife. Still, every day she mourned Darcy. In her mind, she saw him still as he was the day she'd declared her love for him. She saw the passion burning in his dark eyes, and at night, as the tropical breezes blew through her window, she felt the press of his body against hers. Would she feel that way again? Would she ever feel that way with Edward? At the moment, it was a moot point. Edward had not asked her to marry him, and she really had no decision to make. Yet…yet she felt it was imminent.

After a restful night and a day of unpacking, dinner was early that evening as the governor was to meet with Alexander Campbell, another prominent planter on the island, later in the evening. News had reached them of a rebellion in nearby Jamaica, and tension was mounting in Grenada as well. As they sat down to dinner, and as the soup was being served, Mrs. Home addressed her husband.

"Mr. Home, is it true that there is talk of a slave rebellion here on Grenada?"

Her husband seemed taken aback by such a direct question. "And where have you heard such rumors, Mrs. Home?" he asked.

"I hear things, Father," interrupted Edward. "They are dealing with an uprising of Maroons on Jamaica, and there is talk of a coalition of the French and the free Blacks here," he said, looking over his spoon at his father.

"Rubbish," Governor Home retorted. "White men and mulattos fighting together? Whoever heard of such a thing? And why would free Black men join together with slaves? Rubbish."

"You do not know the French, then, or their allies," Edward rejoined.

"And I suppose you do," said his father. "I think, perhaps, you know them better than you should."

Elizabeth could see this conversation taking a dangerous turn and tried to redirect it. She was, in fact, worried about the idea of a rebellion. What would it mean for her and for all of them? Would they be safe? Perhaps she had better return home. At least there, the worst danger was from wagging tongues, not torches and machetes.

"Are you not preparing for a rebellion then?" asked Elizabeth.

"There you are, Father. That is a valid question. We should strengthen the garrison at least."

"Are you governor? Have I been relieved? I am telling you all, there is no danger of a slave rebellion. I am meeting with Mr. Campbell this evening and he will apprise me of the situation here in the north. There are almost two hundred regular infantry on the island and more than five hundred militiamen. Even if they were so foolish as to start an uprising, it could be easily put down."

"And how many mulattos, French, and more to the point, slaves are there on the island? Four thousand? Five thousand?" Edward persisted.

His panicked talk was at odds with his manner, Elizabeth thought. He calmly ate his soup with hearty appetite, while building a case for them all being overrun and killed. For a moment, she saw a bit of Wickham in him. She banished the thought from her mind. She was being unfair.

"They are slaves and they are rabble—disorganized rabble. You are worrying for nothing. If anything, the French may have designs on retaking the island, and that is why I need to meet with Mr. Campbell tonight," his father said, and began to eat his soup. This ended the conversation for the time being, but Elizabeth felt uneasy. She glanced at Edward, and he smiled at her. She would talk to him later.

After dinner, Edward suggested a walk in the garden. The sun was beginning to set and dipped below the mountain peaks. He took her hand and led her to a meadow just outside the grounds. As the sun set and the darkness grew, thousands of tiny blinking lights appeared. Soon, the whole meadow was alive with tiny yellow lights. For the moment, all talk of rebellion, a French invasion, and all the problems of mortal men seemed to have ceased. Nature, in its eternity, was putting on a display.

"What are they?" Elizabeth asked.

"We call them fireflies. Wait, I will catch one for you." With that he ran off into the darkness. Elizabeth closed her eyes for a moment and breathed in the moist, cool, tropical air. The buzzing of insects and the soft, creaking sound of the frogs enveloped her senses. Soon, Edward returned. Opening his hand, he revealed small insects with glowing bellies. The lights blinked on and off. He closed his hand suddenly so that they would not fly off.

"You can touch them. They will not hurt you," Edward said. He opened his fist again and Elizabeth grasped one of the insects. It flashed on and off in her fingers. She smiled.

"I thought they would be warm, like a fire," she said, amused. "They are rather like glow worms back home."

She let go of the insect and it fluttered away. For a long time, they stood silently together and watched the quiet spectacle of light.

Edward was the first to speak. "This could be your home, Elizabeth," he said, his voice as soft as the darkness. "I love you. Be my wife."

***

Darcy did not sleep at all that night. He would have to go home in defeat to Pemberley after all that had transpired. Between the rumblings of war with the French and the damnable pirates, he was trapped here in England. He knew that every day cost him dearly.

Elizabeth did not know he was alive, and that Edward person had—how did she put it?—"set his cap for her." It was unbearable.

Even though John had volunteered to sign aboard the *Marlin* for his sake, he could not let him do so. He admired the gesture, but what were John's chances of success? Would they even take him? How determined would he be once he arrived? A thousand things could go wrong. No, he had to go himself, but how?

The answer was staring him in the face just as surely as the moonlight fell upon him now. It was a thought so foreign to his birth and place in society that he deemed it unthinkable, and yet he was considering it. It was the one thing that was impossible for him to do, yet the only thing he could do if he wanted to see Elizabeth again.

He would have to debase himself and sign aboard the ship as a common seaman. That seemed to be the only answer, but it was an intolerable one. How could he grovel among the common folk, not even the middle classes, but the working classes? If anyone in his circle ever heard of such a thing, they would—

Suddenly, it came to his mind, the words he'd used to propose to Elizabeth: "Could you expect me to rejoice in the inferiority of your connections? To congratulate myself on the hope of relations, whose condition in life is so decidedly beneath my own?" He had let her know that she was decidedly beneath him. How could he have said those things? Of course, she told him that he was the last man on earth that she could be prevailed upon to marry. It almost made him laugh. What would she think of him now, contemplating signing on as a common seaman? Even her mother would not address someone in so lowly an estate, and here he was, thinking of demeaning himself in this manner. Could he do it for her? Could he?

***

Darcy had stood in line at the quay with many other men, hoping and then not hoping, for a chance to sign onto the *Marlin*. Over and over he told himself that she was the only vessel bound for the Caribbean for quite some time, and this would be his only chance for months in catching up with Elizabeth. He looked about him and tried to imitate what the other fellows were doing. This was abominable. More than once, he nearly turned heel and retreated, but thoughts of his beloved drove him onward.

"You look a bit of a dandy," Hackett said as he eyed Darcy. With a canvas bag thrown over his shoulder containing an extra shirt, a pair of breeches, some underclothes, and a few necessities as well as a few shillings, Darcy thought he looked like a penniless tar. Apparently, he did not. "What's your name, then?"

Of all the things Darcy prepared himself for, he forgot what name he would take to travel incognito. He could not very well tell this first mate that his name was Fitzwilliam Darcy, now could he? "Well?" Hackett said, looking impatient.

"William," Darcy said. It was close enough to his own Christian name and common enough, he supposed.

"William what?" asked Hackett, looking impatient.

"…Bennet," he said finally. His Aunt Catherine would be apoplectic at that choice. Of course, she would be beside herself at this entire situation.

"Have ye sailed before, Bennet?" Hackett asked. Darcy decided that honesty would do for this question.

"Only as a passenger, sir," he answered. He wondered what Hackett would think of his tour of the continent when he was a lad of eighteen, traveling with every comfort.

"Passenger, eh? Well, Squire," said Hackett sarcastically, "this ain't no pleasure cruise."

The men listening to this exchange laughed at the jest. Darcy shifted in his spot uncomfortably.

"Can ye handle a weapon?" Hackett asked.

"I am quite competent with a sword and rapier," Darcy replied. He saw Hackett smirk. "We'll have you prove that, then, shall we?" he said. This interview was not going well. Darcy began to think that Hackett meant to make sport of him and let him go. Instead, he threw Darcy a cutlass, which he caught and assumed a fighting stance. Hackett drew a similar weapon from his belt and lunged at Darcy. He had never handled a weapon of this kind before but had fenced enough that its shorter blade did not interfere with his skill.

There was a short skirmish, and by some act of providence, Darcy's defense turned into a rout. Before he knew it, Hackett was weaponless on the ground, with Darcy's boot on his chest. This drew similar merriment from the men at hand, but this time, not at Darcy's expense. The look on Hackett's face, however, told him that he might have rather overplayed his hand. He removed his boot and handed the cutlass back to Hackett.

"Think yer a smart one, don't ye, Bennet?" Hackett snarled.

"I think we could use a man like that, Mr. Hackett," came a voice from the mainmast. From the look of him, it was the captain.

Hackett began to splutter. "Captain Ambrose, sir. Just testin' out the men's skills, cap'n," he said, sending a cold sneer Darcy's way.

"Yes, I see," said Captain Ambrose.

"Never been to sea before, though," Hackett said.

"I suppose we can teach you all you need to know easily enough. Don't get seasick, do you?" the captain asked.

"I do not think so, sir," Darcy said. He kept his eyes lowered and his hat in his hand. This entire encounter was not very pleasant. Still, this was the only ship bound for Grenada for two months. He had to be on it.

"Well, ye look hearty enough…a bit thin," the captain commented. He stood up and looked Darcy over. "I will expect you to fulfill your duties for the entire voyage, down to the Windward Islands and back again. It will be hard work, harder than you're used to I'll be bound, but if you're willing…"

"Oh, I am willing, sir," Darcy said.

"Can you write then, Will? Make your mark?" asked the captain.

"Oh, I can write, sir, and do figures," Darcy said.

"Well, Hackett," he said, turning to his first mate, "we might find some use for this one other than the rigging from time to time then," the captain said. He looked at Hackett and raised his eyebrows.

"All right then, Squire," Hackett said, sighing. "Go make your mark."

He pointed toward another sailor at a table near the mainmast. A piece of parchment titled "Ship's Company—*Marlin*" was shoved toward Darcy. As he dipped the quill into the ink pot, he hesitated.

"Here, sign or make your mark," said a rough-looking character.

Darcy took the pen, signed "William Bennet," and handed the pen back to the sailor. There was no turning back now. He was a crew member of the good ship *Marlin*.

Darcy was not the only seaman signed aboard that day, although it appeared he was the cleanest and the least experienced. An old hand called Foster was assigned to "see to him" and thus he acquired his hammock and his small space below decks to stow his belongings. Foster was a burly man, with a weathered face and graying hair. He had an air of patience about him that Darcy appreciated, for he felt completely out of his element.

"So, what do they call yer?" Foster asked when they were belowdecks.

"William, Will, if you like," Darcy said. He looked at his hammock dubiously. "The first mate calls me 'Squire'."

Foster laughed. "Ye 'ave the look of a squire about ye. Never slept in one of these, then, have yer?" Foster asked, a smirk on his face.

"Never," Darcy said, swinging the hammock gingerly.

"Ye will tonight, if ye can get into it. Come now, we'll go topside and ye follow me. We'll be setting sail soon. Hope you can climb. Better stow those fancy shoes ye got there. Won't need 'em aloft." They climbed the ladder that led to the deck.

Great heavens, thought Darcy. *Aloft.* Of course, he would have to climb up into the ship's rigging and set sails. He never was particularly fond of heights. He could remember as a boy having Wickham tease him because he was so nervous swinging his leg over the banister on the grand staircase at Pemberley. Perhaps this was not a very good idea.

"What sort of jobs are there belowdecks, do you think?" Darcy asked Foster as they climbed the ladder to the deck.

"We'll get you started on stowin' the cargo, then later you can 'elp with the cookin' and then the washin' up. Tomorrow, I'll take ye aloft," he said, pointing upward. Darcy looked up to where Foster had indicated. The mast seemed to recede forever into the blue beyond. He had to forcibly remind himself of his love for Elizabeth to keep from running down the gangplank, back into his carriage, and speeding back to Pemberley.

***

Wickham sat huddled belowdecks with his fellow soldiers waiting to disembark at Fort Royal. There were rumblings of discontent all over the Caribbean due to the French and their idiotic democratic leanings. Since he had nothing better to do, he began listening to the talk among the sailors and marines. They were mentioning some

Windward Island, Grenada. Why did that sound familiar? Perhaps Lydia mentioned it in one of her letters. Yes, that was it. He groped around in the inside pocket of his uniform and withdrew his wife's letter.

Dearest, dearest Wickie,

I miss you so much, my darling. I am again at Longbourn and am so bored I could scream. I had so much fun with you, my dearest, and now I am at my mother's home again being treated like a child. I cannot bear it. We hardly ever go out anywhere, and Jane asks us to dinner at Netherfield only once per month.

I blame all of this on my sister Elizabeth. If she had not disgraced us with that Mr. Darcy, your former friend, we would be much more accepted in society. I hope Lizzy is having a terrible time on that island of hers, Grenada. She gets to have all the fun when she is to blame for all our suffering...

There it was, Grenada. So, Elizabeth was there. She might be right in the thick of it soon enough. He folded the letter and put it safely away. He could not bear to read about Darcy's resurrection again, or Jane's marriage. There was a twinge of regret every time he thought of Darcy. He may have thought himself ill-used by his boyhood friend, but he certainly did not want to be the instrument of his death. So far, he had not been the instrument of anyone's death. No glorious battles for him, at least not so far. The situation in France worsened every day, and it was only a matter of time until he was sent there, unless, of course, he could make himself indispensable here, out of harm's way. Of course, they might see battle yet. The very fact that he was on this vessel portended trouble. At least he was not at home playing the doting husband. That became rather odious quickly enough.

As they disembarked at Fort Royal, he was cheered by the colour and liveliness of his surroundings. He stood at attention in the courtyard of the fort, listening to his commanding officer. "Men," he began, "our orders are clear. We are here to defend this island against the enemy we have fought so long against: the French, gentlemen, we are to protect this island from the French."

Wickham's heart sank. *All the way across the blasted ocean, and here they are again, the French.*

***

Elizabeth was expecting this question almost from the time she had first laid eyes on Edward. Over the past few months, she had been mulling over what she would say to him when the time came. She wanted to marry for love. She wanted Mr. Darcy. How foolish of her to think in this way. In her heart of hearts, she knew that her life was here. There was an inevitability in her relationship to Edward. She could feel it. When he touched her cheek and asked her again, she found her voice and assented. She would be Mrs. Edward Home.

Elizabeth, at that moment, was hoping for a long engagement and hinted at it right away. Edward said he understood, but she felt he did not. Young men were so impatient. She, for her part, needed time. She did not love Edward but supposed that would come. He loved her. He was adamant on that point. There in the soft darkness of the mountain meadow, she let him kiss her. It was nothing like the ardent embrace of Mr. Darcy, but gentle and tender. Edward was a good man with prospects. What more did she want?

They came inside and told his mother first. She clapped her hands, her eyes dancing, and embraced Elizabeth immediately.

"Oh, I am so happy, so happy," she kept saying over and over again. "I must dash off a letter to Barbara and tell her the news. She will be so pleased." His mother flounced out of the room, leaving them alone once more. Edward took her hand.

"I will make you happy, Elizabeth, I promise," he said, turning her toward him.

"I know you will, Edward. It is just..." She trailed off. How could she tell him that her heart burned for another?

"I cannot compete with a ghost, Elizabeth," he said, interrupting her. She let her hand drop from his.

"I know that," she said. He was perceptive. And what she appreciated even more, honest with her. She would be so with him. "And I cannot help how I feel."

"I will not mention it again," he said as he took her hand again and kissed the palm.

He really is the soul of patience, she thought. She knew then that she could learn to love him. *I can make a success of this marriage.* Most people she knew married for social standing, for security, for companionship. Many of those were happier in their later years than those who had married for love. Certainly, her parents were an example of ardent lovers whose flame burned out quickly. Maybe this was a better way. It had to be. She wished that Jane were here. She would know what to say and what to do.

"I do not know why you want to marry me, Edward. I am wondering if I will make you happy," she said. "It is not too late to change your mind, you know."

Edward smiled and took her in his arms. "You have already made me the happiest man on earth, Elizabeth Bennet. You will see, we will have a wonderful life together. Reverend Abernathy will be here in a fortnight, and we can be married then."

"A fortnight?" Elizabeth exclaimed. "I thought you had agreed to wait for a time."

"I am," Edward said, smiling wickedly. "I am waiting a fortnight." Her heart clenched.

She smiled at him, and then closed her eyes to think. Even the most serious of situations, he was always there to lighten it. She thought of the circumstances in which she'd left home and how impossible it would be for her to return. She thought of Edward's devotion to her and of his family's acceptance and even embrace of her. Why was she waiting? Would she love her Darcy less a month from now or a year from now? A husband, and perhaps soon, children of her own may one day fill the hole in her heart. No amount of waiting would do that.

This time, it was Elizabeth who embraced him. As she pulled away from him and saw the moonlight shining on his expectant countenance, she made a decision. "All right, Edward. We will marry in a fortnight."

***

The rest of that first day, Darcy worked stowing long, rectangular wooden crates and blocks of granite below decks. The work was hard and unrelenting. He thought to himself more than once how grateful he was to Castleden and his sterling advice. He felt strong enough to complete his task, although the work was considerably more taxing that anything he had experienced before.

All proceeded as planned until late afternoon. Darcy was slower than his compatriots, so he and Foster were the last in the hold. They were carrying one of the final wooden crates to its resting place when Darcy's grip slipped, and the crate crashed to floor. The force of the mishap split the side.

"Oy, now look what ye've done," Foster said, for the first time betraying any impatience.

"I do beg your pardon," Darcy said, and then realized how superior he sounded. He corrected himself. "I am sorry," he added.

"'Tis no matter. Keep movin'.'"

Darcy bent to pick up the side of the crate and, as he raised it, peered inside. It was filled with muskets.

"There are guns in here," he exclaimed to Foster. He glanced up at Darcy and gave him a hard look.

"Hush, now. Ain't none of our concern," Foster retorted.

"But—"

"Do yerself a favor, Squire, and forget what ye saw." They worked together in silence for the remainder of watch. Darcy did not mention the guns again.

Darcy's dinner of hard tack and salt beef was disgusting, but he was famished and ate all of it. Foster told him they'd get a ration of cheese later in the week. This was greeted by sounds of approval from the other men.

"Enjoy yer bread there, Squire," Foster said as Darcy tucked in. "It ain't weevily yet."

The thought of worms crawling through his dinner would have made Darcy sick on any other occasion, but hunger gave him immunity in this instance.

"Why are we stowing rock in the hold?" Darcy asked when he'd finished his repast and he and Foster were outside of earshot of the other men.

"Ballast," he said. "We'll be loading sugar cane and cacao when we get there, but the ship can't be top heavy. Needs somethin' to keep it steady in the water." That made sense. "They use these here stones for buildings and making the streets over there."

"And those wooden crates?" Darcy asked, bringing the subject up again.

Foster put his finger to his lips, indicating silence. "Yer din' see nothin' and neither did I, if yer as smart as I think ye are," Foster said. Darcy knew the conversation was over. He was prepared to follow Foster's lead for the time being.

Darcy's first attempt at the hammock proved unsuccessful, but again, observation and determination won the day. He slept the sleep of the dead.

Whenever Darcy had been a passenger on a sailing vessel, he'd never really noticed the crew. The sea vistas, the conversation, the games of whist below deck, even the books he brought along for the voyage, all held his attention more than what was actually happening aboard ship. During those times, it seemed to him as if the ship were running of its own accord. He never gave a thought to what the crew was doing.

Now, he was painfully aware of what was expected of the crew. Foster had mercifully taken him under his wing, so on that February morning, as the tide went out, the good ship *Marlin* went out with her. Darcy, stripped of his boots and stockings, was climbing the rigging to set the sails. He tried to listen to Foster shouting in the wind, but all he could think of was the sound his back would make when he fell to his death on the deck. Through sheer determination and keen observation of Foster, he managed to hold his position and do his part in setting the mainsail. He was never so happy as he was the moment his feet touched the deck again.

"Not too shabby," Foster said cheerily. "Time for porridge for our watch. Come along, then." Darcy wished he had his boots. His feet were cold. It was still winter. Here was another reason to wish for a speedy voyage to warmer climes.

For most of the first week, Darcy was so exhausted at the end of each day, he did not give a thought to Elizabeth, his abandonment of his rightful position, or the weapons he found stored in the hold. When they were a week out of port, he climbed into his hammock, and for the first time, did not fall asleep immediately. He was getting used to the system of bells and watches and of not sleeping for more than four or five hours at a time. The fear of falling to his death from the rigging was slowly easing. He could hear Foster snoring in the bunk above him.

What had he done? Here he was in the foul-smelling hold of a ship among men who would not even hold his glance in former times and feeling their inferior in skill and adaptability. It was stinking there in the forecastle. *Why did the common folk never wash?* he thought to himself. *No, that was unkind.* They had no one to carry water or heat it, or even a farthing to buy soap. Why had he not considered any of this before? What would Elizabeth think if she saw him now? How inferior were his connections to hers now? Sleep was beginning to overtake him. He was grateful. It struck him how idle he had been, even with the responsibilities of Pemberley. There was a great comfort in working to exhaustion. It gave one very little time to think.

***

"We should celebrate your betrothal," Edward's mother said at breakfast. "Let us invite the Campbells, the Bellinghams, the Hathaways—"

"The entire district, Mother," Edward said, teasing. Mrs. Home stared at him, her lips set in a tight line.

"My only son is getting married, and I want everyone to celebrate. Am I wrong?" she asked. Elizabeth recognized the feigned hurt feelings from her experiences with her own mother. She attempted to smooth the way.

"Certainly not," Elizabeth told her. "I do wish Barbara were here, though."

"I do not know why your father insisted on coming here at this particular time, Edward. His reasons are so opaque to me." Mrs. Home fretted.

"I think he wants to keep an eye on the French, but he really should be watching Julien Fedon," said Edward pointedly.

"I wish you would not mention his name," Mrs. Home said. "He and the rest of those coloureds and French are constantly getting above their station. It is most vexing."

"I am sure Father is quite displeased by it all too, mother," Edward said.

"Indeed," Mrs. Home said with an air of revulsion in her voice. "I am going to insist that your father pursue an appointment in Scotland. I do so miss our home at Paxton house. We did decorate it so beautifully, and there it sits, abandoned."

"It is not abandoned, Mother, and judging from Father's mood, I would avoid asking him about Scotland for the foreseeable future. In any case, we have an engagement dinner to plan, do we not?" he asked, smiling.

"Does nothing ever worry you, Edward?" his mother asked.

"I worried about only one thing," he said, looking at Elizabeth, "but my Elizabeth has assuaged all my fears."

"I am glad, Edward," said Elizabeth.

"It is all settled, then. We will have a grand dinner in both your honors in three days' time," Mrs. Home said.

"And next week," said Elizabeth, "we will be married."

Mrs. Home ran and embraced her future daughter-in-law.

That night, as Elizabeth lay in bed, the tropical breezes wafting through her window, she thought not of her impending marriage, but of the man she loved who would never be hers.

***

By the time a fortnight had passed, Darcy was rather adept at setting sails. He was scrambling up the rigging with all the other men without even a thought to the distance between him and the deck below. As the weather turned warmer, the men went about bare-chested. One morning, Darcy too removed his shirt.

"Oy, Squire, what 'appened to ye?" said Foster, pointing to the large scar on Darcy's left side.

"Shot," Darcy said matter-of-factly, digging into his porridge. It was amazing how much constant activity and hunger could improve the taste of food.

The men on their watch gathered around. "Tell us the tale, then, Squire," said Pigeon. It was an unfortunate name that stuck to the young man. He really did resemble a pigeon with a smallish head and a slightly protruding stomach.

Darcy began to invent a story that closely resembled the one that actually took place, only in this one, he was reaching beyond his station for a young woman of means and was shot for his trouble by her brother. He had lost his position in the household as a gentleman's gentleman and ran away to sea.

"Well," said Foster, slapping him on the back, "when we get into port, we'll show you 'undreds of brown beauties to take your mind off yer troubles." The men laughed. Suddenly, Hackett appeared, and the merriment ceased.

"Clear this away then and get to work," he sneered. "I see someone tried to kill you once already, Squire," he said, indicating Darcy's scar.

"He did not succeed, though, did he?" Darcy replied, standing up to face him. He knew immediately it was the wrong thing to say. He disliked being bullied by this pompous poseur, but again, he forgot his station. His station.

"What's that now?" Hackett asked, inches from Darcy's face.

"Nothing, sir," Darcy said, swallowing his pride. It was at these moments that he detested his decision to lower himself beneath his rightful place in the world. Who did this Hackett think he was, addressing him, Fitzwilliam Darcy, in this manner? It took all his self-discipline not to thrash the man.

"Get aloft then and take in the tops'ls," he shouted at all of them. A moment later, they were scrambling up the rigging.

There was something grand about being atop the yardarm, looking out at nothing but sea and sky. What started out as something Darcy dreaded had now become something that he enjoyed and even anticipated with a certain zest. How things had changed in only two weeks. He did his best to put Hackett and the lowly station in which he found himself out of his mind. Here, atop the rigging, he was a free man. He began to understand why men ran off to sea.

When he arrived back on the deck, Captain Ambrose was waiting for him. "Will," he said. The captain was the only one aboard who didn't call him Squire. "I would like to see you below." When they arrived at the captain's quarters, Captain Ambrose pushed a large ledger in front of him. "You said you could do figures," he said.

"Yes, sir," Darcy answered. "I used to keep the books at the estate on which I worked."

The captain smiled. "It is grand to hear you talk, Will. Not too many men come to sea with an education and refinement."

"No, sir," Darcy said, returning his attention to the ledger. Under different circumstances, the captain and he could have been friends. No, that was not quite right. The captain was of the wrong social class to associate with someone like Darcy. How odd the world was. The tables had completely turned.

"Take a look at these figures and see what you think," said the captain. "I will return soon." With that he left. Darcy took his pencil in hand and began trying to balance the books.

***

The night of the dinner party had arrived. Mrs. Home had the already opulent dining room festooned with flowers. Everything looked lovely. Elizabeth, with Poppy's help, had bathed and dressed hours earlier than she needed to. Even though there was a heaviness in her heart, she tried to think of all the good that would come of her marriage to Edward. There was no use thinking about the past.

Poppy had disappeared about an hour after her duties with Elizabeth were done and was nowhere to be found. *She must be employed somewhere else on the grounds.* Elizabeth knew not where for she had checked everywhere she could think that Poppy would be.

Thoughts came unbidden into Elizabeth's brain as she tried to calm herself and prepare for the evening's festivities. She could not get Darcy out of her mind, and it would spoil everything if she could not manage to quiet her thoughts. She tried reading. It was no use. She penned a letter to Jane, then one to her father, but again, she began thinking of all that she had lost. Finally, she came upon an idea. She would go check the slave quarters again and, if she was lucky, give Poppy a reading lesson. She hoped against hope that Poppy was there, and not assigned to some duty or other.

By now the sun had begun to set. The guests would be there in an hour. They would have just enough time to read another story, and Elizabeth was convinced that it would be just the right pursuit to consume her nervous energy.

There was activity everywhere in the house. Elizabeth peeked into the kitchen where steam was rising in clouds above dishes and all the servants were mopping their brows and scurrying to and fro. The dining room looked exquisite with last-minute preparations being accomplished by more servants. The governor was finally home and ready to celebrate the betrothal of his only son.

Elizabeth clutched her small tome, *The Adventures of Tom Thumb and Other Stories*, and made her way out to the slave quarters. It was unlikely that Poppy would be there, but Elizabeth needed a task to pacify her mind.

As she approached the quarters, she thought that she heard voices. She and Poppy had already developed a system here at Paraclete in order to remain undiscovered in their pursuits. They set a time when they would meet, and Elizabeth would arrive at the quarters. She would listen for any sounds before knocking. If she heard voices or activity, she would come to the window, carefully, and see who was about. If Poppy was alone, she would knock, and gain admittance. But this time Poppy was not expecting her. She probably would not even be there.

The voices inside the slave quarters sounded strange. *Who is there now?* Elizabeth crouched by the window and looked in. From her vantage point, she could see two figures prone on Poppy's bed. At first, because of the gathering darkness, she could not quite make out what was transpiring before her eyes. Then, she saw naked flesh. Her first instinct was to look away, but the scene facing her was so compelling that she could not tear her eyes away.

The body lying on the bed was glistening and brown and definitely a woman. Her face was obscured by a crate with an oil lamp that sat next to the bed. She was rocking in rhythm with the body on top of her, naked and white, and definitely a man. Her legs were wrapped around his exposed buttocks, and he was pumping into her furiously. His face was buried into her neck and the two of them were gasping and moaning. She clutched at his back and gripped his shoulder blades. Her pelvis rose up rhythmically to meet his every thrust. She let go of his back and grasped his buttocks as if to push him into her more intensely. The more the thrusting went on, the more passionate their moans became. Finally, she grasped him more tightly and he thrust again and collapsed on top of her. They were both breathing heavily.

Elizabeth was transfixed. Her mind was racing. What was it that she just witnessed and why did it have such a strange effect on her? Her nether regions were so stimulated that she was tempted to touch them to gain relief. Her underclothes were soaked with moisture.

Then, the man raised his face from where it had been hidden in the crook of the woman's neck. He pushed himself up on his elbows and with one hand squeezed the woman's breast. He shook his head and laughed. He then rolled off her and stood up, his manhood exposed. By now, they were in near darkness. He struck a match on the small crate near the bed and lit the oil lamp. Elizabeth could finally make out his identity.

She gasped and dipped her head beneath the window to keep from being discovered. She covered her mouth to keep from crying out. It was Edward. Edward had taken one of his slaves as his mistress.

"Did you hear something?" he asked the woman on the bed.

"No, Mister Edward, I don' hear a ting." It was Poppy's voice.

All in a rush, everything made sense. The look on Barbara's face when she'd first arrived, and Edward suggested that Poppy be her lady's maid. Poppy's nervousness when she thought that the family might still be in the house when she came to the quarters to teach Poppy to read. Barbara and her mother's anxiety that she not look for Edward when he disappeared of an evening. This "arrangement" had been going on for some time. Everyone knew about it. Everyone except her. No wonder his mother and Barbara were so pleased that Edward was to marry.

She could hear shuffling and movement inside Poppy's room. As quietly as she could, she slipped away and escaped to the house. She was disgusted and heartsick and, most outrageously, engaged to be married to this man. What was she to do now?

Chapter 12

Half an hour later, she was standing next to Edward, greeting their guests. He descended suddenly from upstairs when the first guests arrived, and Elizabeth had had no time to confront him, not that she had any idea of what to say to him. She kept on looking at him while they were in the receiving line. He looked immaculate and smelled of rosewater. Could she have imagined the entire experience? No. Up until that moment, she had no idea of what happened between a man and a woman. Her mother had told her nothing, and she'd had no time to ask her sister, not that Jane could have brought herself to tell her anything.

Dinner was opulent and beautiful. Elizabeth had to force herself to eat something even though her stomach was churning, and she felt heartsick and tense. Every time she looked at Edward, being so pleasant and charming, she had to use every bit of discipline at her disposal not to begin screaming uncontrollably. Finally, the ordeal ended. What should have been a joyous occasion, a new beginning for her, tasted in her mouth of ashes.

After the guests left, Elizabeth excused herself and retreated to her room before Edward could speak to her alone. She had no idea what to say to him and needed time alone to think. As she entered her room, she stopped short. Of course, Poppy was there, laying out her nightclothes. She was there to help Elizabeth get ready for bed, as she always was, but tonight everything had changed. Elizabeth steeled herself and resolved to act as normal as possible so that Poppy would leave promptly, and she would be alone with her thoughts.

"Good evening, Poppy," she choked out.

Poppy, whose back was turned, jumped at the sound of her voice and twirled around.

"I'm his property, Miss 'Lizbet'. Dat's the only reason," she said suddenly, her eyes wide. Elizabeth froze. *Poppy had seen her at the window.*

"I am sure I don't know what you mean," Elizabeth began, turning her back on Poppy as she felt her eyes brim with tears.

"Yes, you do, miss. I saw you. You came to teach me, and dis' what you saw," Poppy said softly. Elizabeth could feel her approaching, but dared not turn around, as she quickly wiped away a tear that had fallen.

When Elizabeth did not respond, Poppy continued, "It mean notin' to him, Miss 'Lizbet'.

He love you. I could see." The more she talked, the worse Elizabeth felt. She wanted to stop her, but she made herself listen to all Poppy had to say. When there was still no response from Elizabeth, Poppy tried her last argument.

"He don' even rec'nize his pikny," she said.

"'Pickny'," Elizabeth asked, turning around. "What's that?"

"His chilren', miss," Poppy said.

Elizabeth clutched the bedpost to steady herself and sat down. Everything around her seemed to be in flames. Children. Of course, what could one expect? If he had been visiting Poppy's bed often enough, there would be consequences, surely.

Elizabeth took a deep breath, and then asked, "How many children do you and Edward have?"

"Three," Poppy said. "Dey slaves. Mr. Edward don' wan' rec'nize 'dem as his own, but no udder man come near me b'cuz o' Mr. Edward. Dey his chil'ren."

Elizabeth felt sick. How could he? How could he make advances to her while he was the father of three children with another woman? This was unforgivable.

"I'm so sorry, Miss 'Lizbet,'" Poppy near cried. Elizabeth looked up and surprised herself by taking Poppy by the hand. It occurred to her at that moment that both of them had been treated shabbily by Edward. She, through an accident of birth, could do something about it whereas Poppy could not.

"This is disgraceful," Elizabeth stated.

"I know I did wrong," Poppy muttered. Elizabeth rose and embraced Poppy.

"Not you. Certainly not you," she said vehemently. "You had no choice in the matter. I am angry with Edward. There will be no wedding next week. No wedding," she continued, immersed in her own thoughts. She sat down again. There was a knock at the door.

"Elizabeth," Edward called. "Are you awake? May I come in?"

Elizabeth swallowed hard. "Yes, Edward, come in," she replied. He opened the door. As he walked in, Elizabeth observed his manner. He was calm, cheerful, and casual. He looked only at her.

"That will be all, Poppy," he said, never giving her a glance.

"Yes, sir," Poppy responded, and left the room. Edward extended both his hands to Elizabeth.

"I can hardly wait until next Saturday, my love," he said. She rose to meet him. "Mother has made arrangements for Reverend Abernathy to officiate. By this time next week..." He smiled at her slyly.

She had no idea what sort of expression was on her face, but she could barely contain her revulsion. She dropped his hands and stared at him, unblinking.

He looked at her curiously. "Is something the matter, Elizabeth? Did something happen at dinner that escaped my attention?" he asked. Elizabeth took her time. She stepped away from him, putting some distance between them. He walked toward her, and she held out her hand to dissuade him.

"Keep your distance," she stated coldly.

"Whatever is the matter?" he asked, with a little more heat in his voice than she had ever heard before. She was breathing hard. Finally, she asked, "How old are your children?"

Edward's head jerked back as if he'd been struck. His eyes darted back and forth and then became two slits. His stance hardened.

"What has Poppy been telling you?" he asked curtly.

"I saw with my own eyes," Elizabeth replied, "at the slave quarters this evening."

"You saw some mulatto children, what does it matter?" he questioned. She knew he was attempting to ascertain exactly what she knew.

"Oh no, Edward. I saw far more than that," she said, feeling her emotions getting the better of her. She would not cry. She would not. "I did not tell you, Edward, because I assumed you would disapprove. I have been teaching Poppy to read. We had a signal to make sure all was safe for our lessons. I was at the window of the slave quarters this evening. I was at the window and saw you there…with Poppy." Those last few words she choked out and then turned away from him to hide her face.

For once, Edward was silent. He made no attempt to approach her.

"You do not understand," he muttered.

"I understand that you let your children live in slavery," she said, turning toward him. He looked miserable.

"Slaves are property, Elizabeth. They are not like you and me," he explained. "They are naturally inferior." Elizabeth thought of Poppy's reading lessons and her eagerness to learn. She knew people here kept slaves, but more and more it railed against everything she held dear.

"But not so inferior that you could not keep one of them as your mistress," she replied.

"I wish you would stop looking at me that way," Edward rejoined, a little too loudly. "I am not any different from any other man. We have…compelling needs…"

It almost made her laugh. Great heavens, he was different from Mr. Darcy. She wanted to slap him. When she took a step toward him, her intent must have shown in her face because he stepped back from her.

"There will be no marriage, Edward. I want you to book passage for me back to England as soon as possible."

He shook his head and turned to the door. After he opened it, he looked back at her and said, "We will discuss this in the morning when your head is clearer."

Before she could reply, he shut the door.

***

Six bells had come and gone, and Darcy was still working on the books. The captain opened the cabin door and peered over Darcy's shoulder.

"What have you found?" he asked. Darcy turned to look at him and then back at the books.

"Try as I might, sir, I cannot get these books to balance," he said. "I am sorry."

"Don't be," said the captain. "I thought as much. I have suspected for a long time that someone has been pilfering, and you have only confirmed my suspicions. Do you have any idea how it is being done?"

"I do not know exactly, sir, but I suspect that the cargo is being rerouted before it ever gets on the ship. It could be someone ashore who is stealing it, or the very people you are receiving the cargo from, hoping to blame you for the loss," Darcy suggested.

"If it is either of those two scenarios," said Captain Ambrose, "I will never prove it."

"There is one other possibility," said Darcy. "The man on board who is in charge of loading the cargo could be misdirecting it." Darcy knew he was implicating Hackett but had the discretion not to say so in so many words.

The captain merely harrumphed in Darcy's direction and then dismissed him. As Darcy ascended the ladder onto the deck and breathed in the warm, tropical air, he felt suddenly free. If he were back at Pemberley, these types of worries would be his. For now, all he had to do was mend sails, clean out the mess, polish the brass, and tend to the rigging…and stay out of Hackett's way.

***

Elizabeth had already changed into her nightclothes when Poppy burst into her room. She ran about pulling open dresser drawers and opening cupboards, emptying them of their contents. "We have to go. We have to run," she kept saying, and Elizabeth tried to elicit some sort of response from her.

Edward burst into her room and took hold of her. "You must dress quickly, Elizabeth. Father has informed me that the English in Grenville have been attacked by a mob of coloureds and many of our people have been killed."

"What?" Elizabeth asked incredulous. "What is happening?" By this time, Governor Home was at the top of the stairs. The governor paused for a moment, his features working. He looked from Edward to Elizabeth and back again. He was more agitated than Elizabeth had ever seen him before.

"Do not panic, but it appears that the French have landed in Gouyave. I have sent a message to President McKenzie in St. George's to that effect. They will be waiting for us on the Grand Etang Road, so we will travel by horseback north and take a boat to St. George's," he said curtly. He was trying to retain his composure, but Elizabeth could see the anxiety in his face. Mrs. Home came running from her room, her arms full of clothing and boxes.

"I do not know what to bring. I cannot think of what to pack," she kept repeating. Her husband stopped her.

"Tell the kitchen staff to put up provisions for two days for at least five people. As for you," he said to his son, "and you too, Elizabeth, take only the clothing and necessities you will need for two days. Wear something suitable for riding. We have very little time." With that, he ran downstairs again. Edward looked absolutely panicked.

"We should do as your father says," Elizabeth said. "Get a few things. Poppy will help me. We will all rendezvous downstairs." She felt oddly calm, even though disaster was breaking all around them.

Lt. Governor Home reached the bottom of the stairs when his trusted servant, Oronoko, brought him further news. Elizabeth heard their voices and walked to the open door of her room. She could hear Oronoko. The French had not landed. It was, in fact, an uprising.

"I must get word to President McKenzie," he said as he followed Oronoko toward his study. "Oronoko, see to it that the family is prepared. You will stay behind with the servants," he continued. "See to it that the house is secured." Elizabeth could hear the servant's steps rattling toward her and returned to her preparations.

Elizabeth finished her arrangements well ahead of the rest of the family due to Poppy's help. She entered the upstairs hallway and could hear Edward in his room opening and slamming bureau drawers and those of the armoire. She hesitated, then walked to his doorway. Clothes were strewn on the bed. One of the manservants was hastily packing for him. Edward turned toward her just as he secreted a small pistol in his waistcoat. Governor Home called from the foyer, and she hastily descended the stairs.

Because she had many things with which to occupy her mind, she had not yet time to think of the horrors that might befall them. Now, standing at the staircase, she thought of them. A cold fear gripped her for the first time. She turned first one way and then another, as if her body searched for a way to run from this disaster, while her mind told her there was nothing she could do except what she was told. She swallowed hard and gathered herself. Clutching her small bag containing her meager belongings, she quickly, but steadily, exited the front door. Within minutes, the family with a few servants, including Poppy and her children, were en route on horseback north to the sea.

The ride through St. John's Parish had been hard and fraught with peril in the darkness. Still, they reached La Fortune in St. Patrick's at dawn and embarked on a small sloop bound for St. George's. It was not until they were safely at sea for a few hours that Mrs. Home recovered herself enough to mention to Elizabeth that this would postpone Edward's and her wedding day. Elizabeth did not correct her. She need not know of what had transpired between Edward and her and the ruination of their plans. They were fleeing for their lives.

Elizabeth was forward in the packet boat that now contained her, the governor, Mrs. Home, Edward, their servants, and many of the guests she had met the night before. Reverend McMahon and Mr. Campbell were on board a second craft with lesser dignitaries and all and sundry other English refugees.

The news at the dock had not been heartening. Many English were killed at Gouyave by an uprising led by none other than Julien Fedon. She'd had a conversation with him only a month or two ago, and now they were enemies. Perhaps he would be the instrument of her death. After all that she had endured the last few months, Elizabeth wondered if she cared at all about her imminent demise. Her "nearly" mother-in-law thought of her as a tower of strength, but the truth was, it was easy for her to be strong. When one has no hope, one has no fear either. She knew that whatever strength she had, it would be tested in the events that were inexorably unfolding.

Edward approached her as soon as they were under way. "Forgive me, Elizabeth. Forgive me," he said.

"I am not the one from whom you should beg pardon. Ask forgiveness of the mother of your children. It is she whom you have ill-used and then cast off," she replied, and turned from him.

He turned from her silently and then turned back. "You see," he said, "the slaves have now shown you their true colours." There was so much, yet at the same time, nothing that she could say to that. She watched him walk away from her and join his mother. They would discuss all these things when there was time. If there was time.

Aboard the sloop, she was afforded some time to herself and time to think. The plans her mother had so hoped she would fulfill were now dashed. There were things she could forgive in a husband, especially one that she was fond of but did not love, but Edward's actions were beyond the pale. It was not merely infidelity on his part, because as yet, she had no right to demand that of him. Nor was it that he had acted immorally or dishonorably, not gentlemanly at all. That was part of it but did not quite reach the heart of her revulsion. She closed her eyes and tried mightily to sort through her feelings, and then she came upon it. It was his abuse of power. That was it. He had power over Poppy and he took advantage of it, many times, to satisfy his lust at her expense. She raised her head and looked at him across the small sloop. His back was to her as he stood by the railing. How easily she had been misled by him and his charming ways. Now she thought of Wickham and how he had so easily misled her. Was she so susceptible to the winning ways of charming and devious men? Then she thought again of Mr. Darcy. He was none of those things, neither charming nor affable in his ways, yet he had possessed all the attributes Edward lacked: integrity, morality, steadfastness, loyalty, and above all, honor. He took all of those things to his grave. Why did this always seem to be so? Those with the finer qualities died young and those who were devious and deceitful lived on.

Now she would have to return to her family at Longbourn, even though she had little to return to in England. Perhaps she could be the maiden aunt, helping her sisters with their children. Charles had already invited her. Or alternatively, she could live out her life in quiet seclusion with her mother and sister Mary and her father, until his death evicted her from her home. Jane would take her in, bless her. Poor Jane. Poor Jane and poor Elizabeth. She was thus engaged in self-pity when, as they approached Gouyave, she could make out two more sailing ships heading straight for them.

"Those are French privateers, I am sure of it," she heard the governor say to the captain.

"Look," he continued, pointing toward the shore. Gouyave was flying the French flag and armed men in canoes were patrolling the shore.

"Sir, please," the captain entreated. "We are quite safe. Get below. Please."

The governor would not hear of it. He insisted that the sloop pull ashore. Elizabeth could see that they were in a quandary. Either they would be captured by the privateers or captured by rebels ashore. As they approached, the governor exclaimed, "Look. There is Oronoko. There on the road. He has horses and is beckoning us to him."

This was good news. The captain, however, was still arguing for continuing their journey to St. George's, assuring the governor that his ship could outrun anything they were presently encountering. Nonetheless, at Mr. Home's insistence, Elizabeth, Mrs. Home, Edward, and the others followed the governor into canoes that rapidly pulled ashore. She could hear him talking to his wife. "We will ride north again. Our good Oronoko has saved us."

As soon as they reached the shore, however, they were seized by their own servants and those with them. The men grabbed the arms of the nearest English and began shoving them toward a waiting donkey cart. None of the women aboard had been handled roughly before and many were going to pieces. Elizabeth was not one of them. She would not be cowed by violence. She was determined, although she could feel her heart beating rapidly.

There were scuffles and shouts and screams coming from every direction. Some of the men were resisting capture. One or two broke free and ran for the forest, pursued by rebels wielding knives and machetes. As she was being pushed along, Elizabeth scanned the crowd looking for Edward and Mr. Home.

Oronoko and other rebels seized Governor Home as soon as he came ashore. They began dragging him toward a waiting donkey cart. Elizabeth could hear his commands and then his pleas as they pulled him along. Then Edward, drawing the pistol Elizabeth had seen him secreting in his waistcoat, took aim and shot the man holding his father. The pistol gave a loud report and the young mulatto holding the governor's arm spun around with a surprised look on his face and with a gurgling cry, crumpled to the ground. All the women began screaming. Ninian Home, briefly freed of his captor by his son's impulsive action, ran for his horse. Several rebels fell upon Edward. The governor's escape was short-lived. Oronoko had eyes only for his former master, and before he could mount, greeted Mr. Home with a pistol to the temple. The governor froze on the spot. The escape had been foiled. Edward, his gun now in a rebel's hands, was struggling face down on the ground. Many of the rebels were shouting. Some were ready to hang him on the spot.

Oronoko, however, intervened. Governor Home and Edward were bound and jostled into a line with the other men. The women, by now, had been loaded into carts. The entire ensemble then began to move. To where, Elizabeth did not know.

***

So far, there had been no French and no rebels to occupy Wickham's time, so he turned his attention to other pursuits, primarily the amply stocked brothels outside of Fort Royal. His duties were light, and he therefore resorted to his two most accomplished vices: gambling and womanizing. No other letter arrived from his wife, so she was pleasantly of little concern.

Therefore, it was a great inconvenience when, a week after their arrival, word came from Grenada of a slave rebellion. The troops were apprised of the situation. Governor Home, his family and guests, and other planters from the north of the island had been taken captive. Many in Grenville had been killed on the first night of the uprising. The response from the English had been swift. The stage was now set. Each side would wait for the other to blink.

Wickham found, for the first time, that he was actually concerned that his sister-in-law might be in danger. Actually, she might have been killed or... One heard tales of what was done to women captured in war.

Fort Royal was to be left with only a minimum detachment and the rest of them were to set off for Grenville by morning. This would be his first experience of combat, and Wickham did not find himself relishing it as much as he did when it was a mere idea and not impending reality. He was again belowdecks with his fellows cleaning pistols and sharpening swords.

"You'll have your first taste of it by morning," said Cummings. He had a bushy black mustache that made him look more like a Russian hussar than a member of the Royal forces.

"Have you seen much fighting?" Wickham asked.

"Enough," said Cummings. He then twisted his head to one side and pulled down his collar. There was a large scar running from the back of his ear and disappearing into his clothing. "Got this from a frog on the continent. He didn't fare as well," he added, smiling.

This encounter would involve bloodshed. It made Wickham fairly faint, but he tried not to show it. His friend noticed the pretense. "Everyone is a bit nervous at first," he said. "Later, you'll get used to it." He smiled again. Wickham had a taste for many things, but he doubted that killing, or worse, being killed, would be one of them. He returned to cleaning his pistol and ruminating about what awaited them at dawn.

***

His watch finished, Darcy was slowly descending the ladder to the forecastle where his hammock awaited him. He was bone tired. The duties aboard ship had wrought many changes in him, not the least of them physical. His wound had ceased to trouble him, to his surprise. The exercise, the sea air, and even the simple rations had all contributed to his health and well-being. When he saw himself reflected in the water barrel, he was amazed. His skin was browned by the sun and he was well-muscled and lean. He could feel himself gaining in strength every day. That was why, when Hackett ambushed him from behind in the darkness of the forecastle, he reacted swiftly and soon broke Hackett's chokehold. He shoved Hackett against the bulkhead.

"What is the matter with you? Have you gone mad?" Darcy shouted.

"You and your fancy words, Squire. Thought you'd use a few of them to turn the captain against me, eh?" he asked. It was then that Darcy saw the glint of a knife blade.

Darcy looked around quickly. Hackett had planned his attack well. Usually there were men around, but they were totally alone. He had to think fast. "You will never get away with killing me," was all he could think of to say.

"I didn't kill you. You fell overboard," Hackett sneered and lunged at Darcy. Those hours of fencing lessons stood Darcy in good stead. He feinted to the right, and Hackett missed his mark.

"You can't dance around me forever, Squire," Hackett said, and lunged again. This time, Darcy caught his arm and twisted it behind his back. Hackett let out a yowl that sent men running from above decks. By the time they reached the two struggling men, Darcy had pinned Hackett to the deck and broken his arm.

The men formed a circle around the two combatants to hopefully see more of a fight, but Captain Ambrose emerged from his cabin and was on the scene in an instant. "What is going on here?" he demanded. The men parted to let him through. Darcy was rising off his prone opponent, and Hackett had rolled over and was clutching his arm in agony.

"'E attacked me, sir," Hackett gasped. "Look, 'e's broken me arm."

Darcy looked up at Captain Ambrose. He said nothing. "What do you say, Will?"

"I would rather not," he said.

"You had better say," the captain demanded. Darcy was looking about at the rest of the men. The captain looked from him to the others.

"All right, you swabs, get back to your duties," he commanded, and the men obeyed. Foster lagged behind.

"Get Hackett to the surgeon, Foster," said Captain Ambrose. "I will see you in my quarters immediately too, Bennet."

Foster hoisted Hackett to his feet, none too gently. He was moaning and cradling his arm.

"Go on, now, ye great git," Foster said to Hackett.

"Watch yer tongue, you—" Hackett began, but being hauled up unceremoniously by the none-too-gentle Foster silenced him temporarily. Before Darcy could adjourn aft to the captain's quarters, a cry went out from the crow's nest.

"Ship ahoy," he called. The captain was on deck almost instantly. Darcy followed.

"Can you make out the flag?" he called up to the crow's nest.

"It's the Union Jack, sir," he called back. Captain Ambrose looked visibly relieved. Darcy knew that the nearer they came to Nassau, the closer they came to the pirates who plied these waters. It was the best of news not to see the Jolly Roger.

"It's a Royal Navy ship, sir. They want us to heave to," came the call from the crow's nest.

The captain began shouting orders and Darcy hopped to with all the others. They drove their ship toward the navy vessel until they were within shouting distance of one another.

"Lower my gig," the captain ordered. And with that, Captain Ambrose went for a parlay with the captain of the H.M.S. *Resolute*.

At six bells, the crew was assembled on deck. Captain Ambrose addressed them. "Men, in another three weeks, we are putting in at Grenville, in Grenada. The captain of the *Resolute* has informed me that there has been an uprising there. Seems some mulattos and the blasted French have overrun the island. Even took the governor prisoner. There's been quite a bit of bloodshed. We'll be in the thick of it, I'll wager."

Good God. A revolution. Darcy was nearly crawling out of his skin. *The governor is captive. Where is Elizabeth? Is she a captive as well? Is she dead?* His brain was swimming.

"We will be in Grenville only long enough to unload our cargo, but you men may be called upon to defend this ship against the rebels and the French. Are you with me?" A cheer went up.

"I knew I could count on you men. An extra ration of grog all 'round," continued Captain Ambrose. "Crew dismissed."

Those on mess duty ran to get the kegs open, as those on watch climbed the rigging to set the sails. Darcy, who should have been lining up for his grog or retreating to the forecastle for his sleep, turned and began to follow the captain. Foster, who was watching him, ran up behind him and grabbed him by the arm.

"'Ey, now. What're you about?" Foster said in Darcy's ear.

"I need to see the captain," Darcy said urgently.

"You ain't gonna tip 'im you know about them guns, are ye now?" Foster asked.

"Of course I am. These men could be training to use those guns once we reach the island," Darcy said, a little too loudly, apparently.

"Hush, now. Ye'll get us both clapped in irons," Foster said, and tightening his grip on Darcy, led him to the rail. "Ye saw that Royal Navy ship, din' ye?"

"Of course."

"Ambrose got his orders, ye can be sure. 'E's 'ad 'is orders from the beginnin'. Them guns is headed for the army, not for the likes of us," Foster said. "Better men 'n you and me have got it all planned. There ain't nothin' you can do."

Better men, thought Darcy. He had seen those "better men." Men who, by an accident of birth or a paid commission, were given the responsibility of life-and-death decisions. Men like he was only a few weeks ago.

"Are you sure they are going to the army?" Darcy asked.

"I'd bet me life on it," Foster answered. "They just need to make sure they get into the right 'ands now. That's in Grenville. Now, come along and get some sleep. Ye never know what else they got in mind for the likes of us."

Darcy reluctantly followed Foster belowdecks. He swung himself into his hammock, and despite his troubled mind, sleep soon overcame him.

***

The road from Gouyave to Fedon's plantation in the mountains was in rebels' hands, so that within a day Lieutenant Governor Home and his party were summarily unloaded at the foot of Fedon's camp at Belvidere in the interior of the island. Elizabeth and the other women were unloaded like cattle for their trek on foot into the mountains. The men were to follow soon after.

Many of the women were weeping, but Elizabeth was numb. So many things had happened in such a short span of time that she remained focused only on each moment as it occurred. It was just as well.

As they trekked, Elizabeth could see that Fedon's camp was well situated for defensive purposes. It was high in the mountains and accessible by only one road that she could see and nearly impenetrable jungle. The journey there was exhausting. There was no water, no food, and the insects were Elizabeth's idea of hell's torment.

When they arrived, there were primitive barracks for them, a coffee boucan, a two-story building with a foundation used for drying coffee. Still, Elizabeth was glad of a roof and walls as it had begun to rain. The prisoners were all housed together. All their servants had disappeared, save Poppy.

"Where is Janard and Wilard and Cozzie?" Mrs. Home asked when they were finally able to sit on some filthy pallets in their new quarters.

"Dey gone off wid da revolution. They following Oronoko," Poppy answered as if the question had been addressed to her.

"Do not be ridiculous," Mrs. Home said imperiously. "I never gave them permission." Then she looked at Elizabeth and Poppy, who were staring back at her incredulously, and Mrs. Home burst into tears. Elizabeth went to comfort her.

Soon, provisions were brought for the captives. "I go get you and Missus some plantains," Poppy said.

"I will go with you, Poppy," she said, grateful for a moment or two away from the distraught Mrs. Home. As soon as they were out of earshot, Elizabeth asked, "Poppy, why are you still here? Why have you not gone off with the others? Is this not your chance to be free?"

Poppy looked shocked. "I not leave you," Poppy said. "You help me learn to read. I help you however I can now." With that, she turned and gathered food for herself and Mrs. Home. Elizabeth wondered if she'd ever had a friend such as this in England. Charlotte, perhaps? She tried to imagine Charlotte in this situation. It was almost comical to think of it. Now, though, food and water were all she could think of. Not home, not Darcy, not Edward.

There was little to sleep upon and only the most primitive sanitation. Still, there was a roof over their heads, and so far, there was no violence in the camp. Guards were posted near the doors and windows, but by now, everyone was too tired to think of escape. The married couples stayed together, and all the other prisoners segregated themselves into men's and women's sections. There were nearly fifty of them altogether. After Elizabeth finished eating, she and some of the other women were commandeered to do the washing up. They did so outside. The building they were housed in opened to a dirt courtyard of sorts, bordered by trees. Elizabeth could see in the distance some outbuildings and what looked like a larger house. This must be Fedon's estate. He had told her of it once.

When they were outside, a tub was provided, and Elizabeth and two other women were set before it with piles of dirty bowls and spoons. Elizabeth had washed dishes before, but even she had servants. Now, she was the servant. Some of the slave and mulatto women who had just been liberated by the rebellion gathered round them to jeer and poke fun. They shouted at them in patois and French. One of the English women began to cry.

"Ignore them," Elizabeth said. "They want you to cry. Do not give them the satisfaction." She said these words with such conviction that one woman stopped crying and set her mouth hard. Soon, the three of them were finished.

By now, night had fallen, and a fire was built in front of the boucan. The flames illuminated the building, and Elizabeth could see guards near every window and door. To keep the prisoners contained, the shutters and doors of the building were closed. It was nearly pitch dark when Elizabeth and the other women returned. She heard Poppy's voice in the blackness and felt someone touch her arm and then take her hand. Poppy led her a few steps and they lay down on the hay that had been spread there for them. Elizabeth was so exhausted that, despite the shocks of the last day, she fell instantly asleep.

The next morning, they were awakened by shouting. Some men had flung open the door and dragged the governor and several other men outside into the light. Elizabeth rose immediately and ran to the window to see what was transpiring. There was Julien Fedon himself, flanked by armed black and mulatto men, talking with Governor Home. The group left together and walked through the trees toward the large house. Mrs. Home began to panic.

"They will kill him. I know it. What shall we do? What shall we do?" She began to cry. Her fears, however, were assuaged an hour later when the governor returned with a large piece of paper that he brought back to the barracks. A small table was set up in the clearing and the prisoners were told to line up. The governor addressed them.

"I have been informed," he said in a steady voice, "that our captor, Monsieur Julien Fedon, has issued an ultimatum to President Kenneth McKenzie, who is in command of the island during my absence. The ultimatum is this: any attack on his headquarters by any British forces will result in the death of all of us."

An audible gasp escaped from those assembled. Elizabeth looked at Poppy and said, "You should not stay with us. Go with your own people. You will be safe there. There is nothing you can do for us anymore."

Poppy looked at her and opened her mouth to say something, but no words were forthcoming. She squeezed Elizabeth's hand, and she left, melting into the crowd of insurrectionists that surrounded them.

"I have here," the governor continued, "a statement to that effect that we are all to sign. It says 'Julien Fedon, leader of the French Revolutionary Republic of Grenada, makes a positive declaration to kill all prisoners captured in the insurrection if there is any attack upon the Belvidere Estate.'" With that, the governor sat at the small table in the courtyard and all prisoners lined up to sign his statement. Most did so with shaking hands. It felt to Elizabeth like signing her own death warrant.

Chapter 13

For a time, things settled into a routine at The Camp of Equality, which was Fedon's name for the prisoners' camp near the Belvidere Estate. The prisoners were allowed to wash themselves and clean their clothes, although most of them had never done any menial work in their lives. After the first few days, a fence was built around the open clearing in front of the boucans, creating a kind of courtyard. In a way, Elizabeth was grateful for it as it allowed them to come outside into the sunshine. Now, the men and women were only allowed to see each other out of doors in the courtyard that remained open to all during the day. From time to time, Elizabeth noticed Poppy at the perimeter of their enclosure.

It was outside on one of these occasions when a young Frenchman, Maurice Viel, appeared. Elizabeth was scrubbing some of the men's clothing in a washtub. She found it oddly satisfying, and it relieved the combination of boredom, fear, and suffering that she had endured every day since they had been caught up in the rebellion. One of her compatriots, who was doing the rinsing and wringing out, said something amusing and Elizabeth raised her head to laugh. It was then she noticed him.

"Mademoiselle. You. Hallo," Viel called in her direction.

"I think that 'hero of the revolution' wants to talk to you," the young woman said sneeringly. She recognized Maurice as he had recognized her. She must have seen him at one of those French gatherings that she and Edward had attended without his father's knowledge and certainly without his approval. Now, he had a tattered look. His dark hair was unkempt, and he was unshaven. His clothes were wrinkled and dirty.

Walking over to the fence, she addressed him. "Do I know you, sir?" she asked.

"I do not know, but I sink so," he said in his best English.

"Have you come to liberate us?" she asked sarcastically.

"If it were in my power, I would," he said, smiling. "Are they treating you well?"

"If I were a horse, I would be perfectly content," Elizabeth said. He looked at her for a moment, and then laughed.

"You are not afraid of me, zen?" he asked.

"I do not know. Should I be?" she asked him.

"You are answering a question with a question. It is not fair," he said. Someone called to him in French. He turned and answered, and then turned back to her.

"I must go now, but I will return," he said, smiling charmingly.

"Unfortunately, I will be here," she said as she watched him leave. Life was odd. It was almost as if they were at a ball or a dinner party exchanging pleasantries. Instead, he was her captor and she his prisoner. He could do anything he liked to her or her companions and there would be no recourse. She could be awaiting death at his hands. Or could it be that he could help her escape? She was sure there would be a price for that...a price she was not willing to pay.

***

As Wickham's ship approached the harbor in Grenville, all on deck watched the fires of the burning city. The captain had sent an advance of a few sailors and marines ahead to shore to see where a good landing spot might be found. It would not do to be set upon by rebels as soon as they came into port, or worse yet, sunk before they even got to shore.

As it was, the British still held the harbor and the men disembarked without incident. The rebels held the interior of the city, and Wickham and his fellows were deployed in haste directly into the fighting. It occurred to Wickham that he could meet his end here, cut to pieces by Caribbean islanders wielding machetes. They were told that there were no large guns to bear upon the rebel stronghold, so fighting would be house to house, which was unnerving.

Upon landing, a musket was thrust into Wickham's hand as it was with all his fellow soldiers. They were unceremoniously loaded into wagons at the port and jostled into the interior of the city. They could have been in any small city in England or France save for the oppressive heat, smell of fire close by, and the rubble caused by warfare.

Unloaded in a nondescript lane, they were ordered to march in formation down the street. They made perfect targets to Wickham's way of thinking. The first musket ball that whizzed by Wickham's head so frightened him that he began to laugh uncontrollably. The soldiers by his side were falling like flies, so Wickham, recovering himself, roared out, "Take cover," and the rest of them scattered to hide behind carts, barrels, and any sort of barrier or debris the street would offer. From his relatively safe position, Wickham could gather himself and assess the situation.

He could see repeated musket flashes from a second-story window across the street. Carefully loading his musket with powder and shot, he waited for an eruption of fire, poked his head up above the overturned cart behind which he was hiding, and fired into the open window. He heard a cry and the firing ceased.

At that point, a crowd of rebels burst from doorways and windows and rushed down the street toward the British. No one was giving them orders. Wickham waited until he could wait no longer and called out, "Don't fire until you see the whites of their eyes." He didn't know where he had heard that phrase, but it seemed appropriate now. "Affix bayonets," he added. It seemed sensible considering that the rabble running toward them were armed with pikes and machetes.

All along the street, musket fire began sounding in a wave. His fellow soldiers were bringing fire to bear as the crowd approached them. Suddenly, the horde was upon him. He stood and fired and then, in a fit of uncharacteristic courage, he charged, bayonet forward, as he had been trained to do. A Negro, his eyes aflame with blood lust, flew at him, machete raised. Wickham aimed for the man's chest, and as he propelled himself toward him, Wickham caught him with his bayonet in the throat. There was a fountain of blood and the man doubled over, clutching his neck without a sound. Wickham stood stock still for several seconds, the fury of the battle waging around him. He had never killed a man before. He was knocked from his trance by a cry of "Look out," and reacted instantly. As he turned, he stabbed another attacker in the stomach.

Finding the crowd of attackers had moved down the street, he had the presence of mind to reload his musket. Then, charging down the street after his men, he saw that the rebels, who once seemed so overpowering, were scattering. He took aim at a retreating figure and fired. The man's hands flew in the air and with a cry, he fell on his face. The rest had disappeared, retreating, no doubt, to reassemble for another day.

Many of the men with whom he had marched down the street were lying dead or wounded. His captain was among them, shot in the head. Wickham suddenly realized that he was covered with blood, and as his breathing slowed, he felt a sharp pain in his shoulder. Looking back over his right shoulder, he saw that his uniform had been sliced through and he was bleeding copiously. He suddenly felt unsteady on his feet.

"'Ere now, sir," he heard someone say, and felt an arm come up around his chest, to steady him. "Let's get you out of 'ere."

Reinforcements had come, and he was helped into a wagon that held the other wounded. That was the last thing he remembered until he woke the next morning in a bed in a large, airy room. The place must have been a warehouse of some kind before the hostilities. It had a high ceiling of unfinished wood dotted with several skylights that illuminated the dust and particles in the air. There were rows of cots containing moaning and wounded men, Wickham among them. When he opened his eyes, light was streaming through the windows. The atmosphere was damp and sticky. He felt enormously thirsty.

"Water," he said. One of the men caring for the sick and wounded heard him and brought him a cup. It was one of his compatriots from the street the day before.

"Glad to see yer awake, sir," he said. "I'll tell the general yer up." With that the orderly jumped up and ran to the door of the large room. He closed his eyes momentarily. *Oh no. A general. That cannot bode well.*

"Wickham, wake up." He debated feigning sleep as the owner of the voice did not sound pleased. It occurred to Wickham that he had commandeered his unit of soldiers and led a charge under no one's direction but his own. They had broken ranks, scattered, and fought like…fought like…well, Americans.

"Wickham," said the voice of authority. Wickham opened one eye in a squint.

"Sir?" he said unsteadily. His shoulder burned like a hot poker.

"Can you sit up, man?" he asked. "I am General Lindsey." Wickham hoisted himself on his elbows, wincing at the pain in his shoulder. When he was in an upright position, the general addressed him further.

"Giving orders yesterday?" he said, rather as a question than a statement.

"Sir?" Wickham asked, delaying the inevitable.

"Odd that Captain Carlisle would have entrusted such a young and inexperienced officer with command duties. Still, you saved the day, Wickham. Total rout of the enemy. Those blackguards didn't stand a chance, no indeed," the general continued, his mustache twitching with merriment. He moved to slap Wickham on the shoulder. Wickham winced before the blow, and the general desisted.

"Should be a field promotion in it for you, Wickham. Well done," he said and extended his hand. Wickham took it.

"Thank you, sir," Wickham said simply.

"No, thank you, Wickham. Need more men like you. Well done," he snuffled and was gone.

Wickham lay back on his cot rather pleased with himself. *I routed the enemy single-handed and will probably get a medal.* Besides, the wound in his shoulder should keep him out of harm's way for, well, for as long as he could wince whenever anyone in authority approached. As thoughts of this kind went through his head, he sobered. He had killed men yesterday. They were the enemy and did not look at all like him, but they were men nonetheless and he'd taken their lives. He wondered if his comrade aboard ship was right. He wondered if he would get used to killing. A great weight seemed to press upon him and he lay back down on his cot and closed his eyes. *Best to think pleasanter thoughts.* With that, he fell asleep.

***

The amount of physical labor demanded of the female prisoners was far above what was usually demanded of Elizabeth in the course of her former life, so that when sunset came, she sank onto her sleeping pallet in a dreamless and exhausted sleep. It had been three days since Maurice Viel had seen and spoken with her, but it was his hand that clapped itself over her mouth, and his body that fell on top of hers in the middle of the moonless night. She could feel the cold, steel blade against her throat.

"Do not cry out, mademoiselle," he whispered as she awoke with a start to this weight that shook her from sleep. At first, Elizabeth had no idea what was happening, and when the realization came, her mind began to race. She was afraid, but oddly, not panicked. She nodded her head, and he removed his hand. He settled himself on top of her, spreading her legs to make room for his own between them. She did not resist...yet.

"You see," he whispered, "I have come to visit you again."

"We have hardly been introduced, sir," she said formally, and he stifled a laugh.

"Oh, you English," he said quietly in her ear, "you do have the most astounding manners." His left hand began to travel. He clasped her breast and squeezed it and then moved down the outside of her hips and then, feeling for the hem of her skirt, began running up the inside of her legs. His hardness was discernible through his breeches and he stopped his journey up her legs to unfasten his buttons.

"Wait," she whispered, and oddly, he stopped momentarily. She heard him laughing in her ear.

"Perhaps I will wait, but I will not stop," he said, and pulled up to look her in the face.

She mustered all her courage and said, "Would you take me against my will?" she asked.

"I do not believe it is against your will. You would like to live, so you will submit," he said. "Now, hush. You will wake the others, and I do not wish to hurt you." As he said that, his right hand left his breeches and clasped itself around her throat. He maneuvered his index finger up to her lips to silence her. All this time, her mind was racing. It was now or never. Her hands were free.

She had never touched a man in a way that was intimate, but she could feel his hardness pressing against her. His buttons were undone and his member rampant. Pushing down her distaste, she smiled at him in the darkness and forced herself to relax under him.

"I will not resist," she said. "I have never been with a man before. Let me touch you."

"Ah, *une vierge*," he whispered, and took her hand, guiding it to his manhood. Gritting her teeth, she took it in her hand and then, with all her strength she squeezed it, trying to crush it in her fist.

He cried out and she let go and rolled out from under him. She began screaming then, and all the women awoke and also began crying out. Before long, the door to the boucan slid open and men with torches and lanterns came in to see what the disturbance was about. Viel had escaped, undoubtedly limping through the window from whence he came.

"What is the matter 'ere?" cried one of the men, his dark, glistening skin illuminated by the torchlight.

Elizabeth stepped forward. "It was…" she began, but with her mind still working rapidly, she knew that the truth would just give these men ideas to try similar escapades from which she had just escaped. "It was a great fat rat," she said. "I felt it come over me," she continued.

There was a brief moment of silence all around, and then the man with the torch began to laugh, and with that, all assembled laughed with him. The women were, of course, relieved and at the same time terrified.

"Go to sleep, silly women," said the leader, and the men left, the stable door shutting after them. Elizabeth could hear a great deal of rustling in the room as women felt about in the dark for rats in their hay mats. The full import of what happened began to seep into Elizabeth's consciousness. She sat in a corner, her knees drawn up, and began to shake uncontrollably. The tears sprang to her eyes, and she tried in vain to stifle them. It was then someone touched her arm and she jumped as if someone had burned her.

"I am sorry," said the voice in the darkness. "I did not mean to startle you." It was one of the prisoners, Sally. She was an indentured servant in one of the plantations that were raided by Fedon and his men. It was under her tutelage that Elizabeth made herself so indispensable when wash day came.

"It…it…it is all right," Elizabeth finally choked out, trembling. Sally came and sat against the wall next to her shivering companion and put her arm around Elizabeth's shoulders. That act of tenderness released a floodgate. For several minutes, all Elizabeth could do was weep and Sally held her until she was able to draw a few calm breaths.

"He tried to force himself on you," Sally said. Elizabeth started. "I heard the whole thing. You do not sleep far from me." The thought of someone witnessing her disgrace was more than Elizabeth could bear. She wrested herself from Sally's embrace and, moving to the bucket that they kept as a chamber pot, vomited.

"I will get you some water," Sally said, and in a few moments, reappeared with a dipper that Elizabeth accepted gratefully. The sat together again.

"It happened to me too," Sally said. "Not here. In the house where I worked. And not a revolutionary either. It was the master of the house."

What sort of place is this? Elizabeth thought to herself. It seemed that, the farther from home people were, the less they remembered what it was like to be civilized. Or perhaps she was just naive. Maybe things like this went on all around her back in Meryton and she just never knew.

"I wanted to help you, but I was too frightened. I am sorry."

Elizabeth could finally speak. "There was nothing you could do. He had a knife."

"A knife?" Sally exclaimed a little too loudly. There were murmurs from the women near them. "How did you ever escape?"

How could Elizabeth tell her? It was too humiliating. "I need to wash," she said suddenly, and the two of them sought out the water bucket.

***

It seemed to Darcy that every day dragged into the next. The wind was blowing a steady gale to speed them along, but every time the captain ordered the crew to reduce sail, he wanted to countermand the order. As Mr. Darcy of Pemberley, he probably could have. As Will Bennet, lowly seaman, he had no power whatsoever. It made him angry and irritable, two traits he could ill afford to show aboard ship. He struggled every day now, as a wild horse with a bit in its teeth, against his natural tendency toward imperiousness. He had lowered himself of his own free will, and now he would have to deal with his helplessness. His situation with Hackett grew worse by the day. Now, with Hackett's arm immobilized, he had a constant reminder of his defeat at Darcy's hands. He did everything in his power to get Darcy to rise to his bait so that he could mete out some sort of punishment. Darcy, however, was the soul of willpower and more than once sacrificed his dignity to avoid further conflict.

At last the day came when, from the crow's nest, the cry of "land ho" went up. Darcy was on watch and felt his heart leap. This endless voyage was now coming to a close. They were ordered to full sail, and from the rigging, Darcy could see two islands, one to the north and one to the south. Foster was on the yardarm with him, and he asked him, "Are one of those islands Grenada?"

"No, Squire, the one to starboard is St. Lucia and the one to port is Barbados. Ye can't see Grenada just yet. We'll be comin' up on it soon if I'm any judge of the wind."

First, though, they passed St. Vincent and the Grenadines. They belonged to the British, and like the others they had passed were lush and green and beautiful. The water turned an azure colour now, and the beaches were covered in sand the colour of sugar. The sailors talked excitedly about their docking in Grenville. They seemed to be oblivious to the conflict raging there and were talking of shore leave filled with brown girls and drink. It was all wasted on Darcy. All he could think of was Elizabeth. What was her fate?

It was nightfall by the time Grenville came into view. At first, Darcy thought the city was brilliantly lit, but then realized that parts of it were on fire. An unexpected cold fear came over him. There was a good chance they would be fired upon or have to fight hand-to-hand. Within a few minutes, the entire ship was silent, gazing at the flaming city. The laughter and anticipation of the previous hours evaporated. The captain called the off-duty watch on deck to join the others. Most of the crew was already assembled.

"Men," he began, "it is time you know what cargo we are really carrying. It is muskets and ammunition for the British forces at Fort George's. Because of the slave rebellion, we are ordered to unload our cargo here. I need four volunteers to take the dinghy ashore and let the British forces know that we are coming. I need not tell you that we cannot afford to have our cargo fall into the wrong hands."

"I will volunteer, sir," Darcy said at once.

"I should go," Hackett said immediately afterward. The captain looked at the two of them, and they at each other. It seemed an unlikely match. "I am the first mate, sir. They will be expecting someone of rank, sir," he added. The captain seemed skeptical, but neither Darcy nor Hackett backed down.

"Your arm, Hackett," continued the captain.

"It's healing nicely, sir," he said, removing the sling from his shoulder and bending his arm back and forth from the elbow.

"Very well, then," he said. "Two more."

"I'll go," said Foster. "I'm as good as any man aboard at sailing that dinghy."

"I'll volunteer," said Kipper. Darcy smiled at the name. The young man acquired that name on board since the sailor who occupied his hammock while he was on watch had difficulty rousing him. He liked his "kip" or nap, as it were.

"All right, men, ready the dinghy for launch," ordered the captain. "It's better if we send you off under cover of darkness."

As they readied the dinghy, a sailor came to them with cutlasses and pistols. "Cap'n said you might be needin' these," he said. "Good adventure now," he added, smiling. Of course, this type of adventure might lead to disaster. When they were all aboard and lowered away, Hackett spoke, "You men will have to row. Me arm, you know."

They all peered at each other in the darkness. "I thought you said it was all right," Kipper said.

"Shut 'cher gob and row," Hackett ordered. He slipped the bill of lading from the captain into the inner pocket of his tattered waistcoat. The three of them turned their backs into it and when they were about five hundred yards from the ship, they raised the sail.

They kept far enough off shore so that the white sail would not be spotted in the moonlight and furled it when they were close in and rowed the rest of the way. As they approached the dock, they could hear the sounds of men talking. They were nearly upon them when they recognized the language. It was English.

"Ahoy, there," Hackett called out. Darcy could hear the sound of running feet and make out figures on the pier. Lanterns were swung about, illuminating the faces of the men who came to greet them.

"State your business," one of them called out. He had a military air about him and before long the four of them could see he was a British officer, a marine, in fact. "We are of the merchantman *Marlin*," Hackett announced. "We need to speak with your commanding officer."

With the mention of the *Marlin*, the officer invited the four of them to follow him. After they secured the dinghy, they made their way down the pier into the streets. They were all but deserted except for some British soldiers patrolling or keeping watch.

"We have secured this section of the city, near the docks," the marine said. "It was a hard fight, though. We lost quite a few men."

"We could see fires from the ship," Foster said.

"Many parts of the city are still under siege. These blighters seem to get stronger every day. Word is they captured loads of arms and supplies from plantations nearby. Their forces are growing every day."

"What do you know of the governor and his party?" Darcy asked. Hackett and the others gave him a quizzical look.

"Can't say," said the marine. "Probably up at Belvidere."

"Belvidere? What is that?" Darcy inquired.

"It's the rebel stronghold up in the mountains on the other side of the island," he said.

***

They made their way to the counting house by the docks, which the marine had told them had been commandeered by the British as a makeshift headquarters. There was no fort on that side of the island. Hackett, of course, led the party, and they were escorted into the commander's office. The officer was standing with his back turned, gazing out the window onto the black water below.

"First mate and men to see you from the *Marlin*, sir," the lieutenant informed.

"Ah, good," said a familiar voice. When the officer turned around, Darcy nearly reeled from surprise. *Wickham. Damn my eyes. What is he doing here?* The man was the bane of his existence.

"You have the weapons, then?" Wickham asked, not even noticing Darcy. At first, he was surprised that he was not immediately recognized, and then realized that his appearance was much changed since Wickham had seen him last. Besides, he was the last man on earth he would be expecting with this lot.

"Yes, sir. Captain wanted to make sure that the port was secure, sir," Hackett said.

"Go back to your captain and have him anchor off the Telescope Point, and we will send boats out to you. All will be in readiness when you arrive. Send my respects to your captain. I will meet with him at three bells. You had better be off in deeper water by morning," he said very competently.

This was a Wickham whom Darcy had never seen before: expert, able, authoritative, and—dare he think it?—responsible. He must speak with him. Perhaps he had news of Elizabeth.

"Well, then, off with you," Wickham said, and they were summarily dismissed. Wickham still did not recognize Darcy. As soon as they were outside the door, Hackett said, "You men go back to the ship. I will coordinate delivery from here."

That seemed odd, but since Hackett was senior officer, none of them said a word. "Go on, then," he said. As soon as they were outside the building, Darcy turned to the other two. "Can you wait at the dinghy for me?" he asked them.

Foster gave him a quizzical look. "We can do that. Where'll you be, then?" he asked.

"I think I had better keep an eye on Hackett. Wait at the dock for word. I should not be too long," Darcy said. Foster gave Darcy a knowing look but said nothing. He then clapped his wide hand on Kipper's shoulder and led him back to the pier. Darcy could hear Kipper asking questions as they disappeared out of earshot.

Darcy returned to the counting house and spied Hackett skulking down the hallway and out into the street. He kept his distance but followed him. Hackett seemed to be purposely avoiding any British military stationed in the port area, and soon Darcy found himself in the darkened streets of the burned-out and abandoned section of the city that separated the British-held positions from those sections he assumed were held by the rebels. Once or twice, Darcy would dislodge a stone or scrape along a stray board he could not see in the dark and make a sound, but since neither he nor Hackett had any lanterns, when Hackett turned and peered into the darkness, Darcy kept his cover.

Hackett turned a corner, and Darcy, a good distance away, saw him suddenly surrounded by figures. A doorway opened, and the light spilled out from one of the buildings. Darcy could see barefooted black men whom he thought must be rebels and white men he could only assume were French. They had weapons drawn, but Hackett drew from his waistcoat the bill of lading from Captain Ambrose that he should have given to Wickham. *Perhaps Wickham is not as competent as I thought.* He asked them for no documents.

This was the list of the ship's cargo and it was being waylaid by Hackett. He was selling arms to the rebels. Of course, Hackett could not have possibly foreseen this rebellion, but must have planned to sell these arms to the French and then desert the ship. Even Hackett did not know until now with whom he was dealing.

Darcy was privy to the ship's books; he realized that Hackett may have been successful, but for his own greed. His colossal mistake was that he could not resist selling some of the muskets and pistols for some quick money before they left Portsmouth. If those discrepancies on the books had never reached his attention, Darcy, and more importantly the captain, would have been none the wiser and Hackett's scheme might have worked.

Darcy felt his way back through the abandoned streets as soon as Hackett was safely inside with the revolutionaries. He had to warn Wickham. In no time, he was back at the counting house. The marine who had walked them from the dock recognized him and he made his way without interruption to Wickham's headquarters. His orderly announced him.

"Mr. William Bennet of the merchantman *Marlin*," he said. Wickham was at his desk poring over some papers, but Darcy instantly recognized the ruse. Wickham would utilize the same ploy as a boy to confound his tutors. He would be playing with some toy or doing a puzzle and when the teacher walked in, he would cover his desk with books and papers and pretend to study. Darcy had no doubt that a bottle of brandy was within reach under his desk.

"Bennet, you say," he replied jovially. "I have a wife from a family of that name. Perhaps you are a relation," he said, smiling condescendingly at Darcy.

"Perhaps I am closer to your relation than you think," Darcy stated. Wickham reacted as if he were struck. He staggered back, his eyes wide with incomprehension. Wickham came slowly around his desk and walked up to within a few inches of Darcy. He stared at him as if he were the eighth wonder of the world.

Darcy knew he was quite a sight. He was brown and weather-beaten in breeches with no stockings, and a billowing shirt open to his waist. Wickham stared at him for a several long moments, and said in a very meek voice, "Darcy?"

This really was too enjoyable. Wickham had gotten the better of him so many times through such duplicity that this revelation was to be savored.

"Yes, it is I, Fitzwilliam Darcy," he said with a smirk. Wickham backed up slowly and, feeling his way, sat down on the edge of his desk.

"By God, Darcy," he said, gulping for air. "You... You..." He pointed at Darcy's clothes and was shaking his head.

"I will tell you the tale at a later time, but now, I need your help, or all is lost for you, for me, and for all the English on the island." Then Darcy told him of Hackett's duplicity, and how they must act quickly, or a shipment of arms would land in rebel hands. Wickham sent for an orderly. "Where can we unload the arms we are carrying while avoiding the harbor?" Darcy asked.

Wickham smoothed the chart and pointed. "Here," he said. "Soubise Point. Do not sail there, however. The sail might be spotted. Take any small boats you have with oars. I will have men, also in small boats, there to meet your crew."

Again, Darcy was surprised by Wickham's efficiency. Darcy paused for a moment and then asked, "Have you heard any news of Elizabeth Bennet?"

Wickham looked up at him. Ordinarily, Darcy expected that he would resort to withholding information just to torture him. Surely, he could see that now they were on the same side, fighting for their lives. It was not time for petty grudges.

Surprisingly, Wickham rose to the occasion. "No, nothing specific. I assume she was in the governor's party at Paraclete, his country estate. They were captured trying to escape. Julien Fedon, the leader of this rebellion, has all of them captive. God knows what is happening with them, especially the women," Wickham said. Darcy closed his eyes and took a deep breath.

"What can be done?" he asked.

"We have received orders to attack the stronghold at Fedon's in three days. We are only waiting for some Spanish reinforcements from Trinidad," Wickham continued.

Darcy's darkened countenance brightened briefly. "That is good news, then. There is hope."

Wickham did not reply, but the look on his face betrayed his skepticism. He returned to his study of the charts. Darcy noticed immediately. "Tell me, Wickham. For God's sake, man, tell me." He took hold of Wickham's uniform and shook him.

"All right," Wickham shouted, and pushed himself away. "Fedon threatened to kill all the prisoners if his stronghold was attacked. The president, who is in temporary command of the island in the governor's stead, broke off negotiations."

"Do you think this Fedon fellow is capable of killing innocent civilians?"

"In a rebellion such as this," Wickham said, "there are no innocent civilians."

Darcy abruptly turned his back on Wickham and was breathing hard. In his heart of hearts, he knew as much. He had to think. At least he had three days' time. Three days in which to find a way to rescue Elizabeth. At the same time, who knew what horrors she was enduring in the meantime?

Darcy gathered himself and turned to look at Wickham. He was bent over his desk, spreading charts and maps of the island. "I have been in command of this sector for only two days," he admitted. "We need to find a way to land those weapons so that we may use them to mount a rescue."

Those words acted on Darcy like a tonic. He turned back to the table and fixed his eyes upon the charts.

"Let us see what we can do," Darcy suggested.

Chapter 14

Wickham captained one of the several jollyboats from Grenville port to meet the *Marlin*. By that time, Darcy, Foster, and Kipper had returned and explained to Captain Ambrose how Hackett had attempted to sell the cargo to conspirators on shore. The captain did not seem surprised by the news.

"You were right about him all along, Will. I don't expect I'll ever see him again. We'll proceed to the port at Grenville so as not to arouse their suspicions for a time, although they will watch in vain for this cargo," said the captain. "Can't imagine what they'll do to Hackett when they discover what has happened."

"I can imagine it," said Wickham with a shudder. He was standing on deck supervising the loading of muskets.

Wickham, with his small fleet of boats, sailed to the south to unload their cargo contrary to the rebels' expectation. The *Marlin* upped anchor and sailed round the point.

***

Captain Ambrose sat in Wickham's office, twenty-four hours after the midnight delivery of arms, finalizing the documents he was to bring back with him to the government. With the first mate gone, Darcy stood in his stead.

"Your arrival, Captain, was very timely," Wickham said pompously. "We are to mount an attack in two days on the rebel stronghold."

Although he had no idea of what he would do next, Darcy knew at that moment that his adventure aboard the *Marlin* was over. His first impulse was to resign on the spot, but that would involve a myriad of explanations. No, he would be patient. If he had learned nothing else from this entire ordeal, it was patience.

"I wish you every success, sir," Captain Ambrose said, rising, "but my duty is to commerce. I must depart with my ship immediately if we are to return to England with something besides an empty hold."

Wickham had explained to him that the load of sugar that the *Marlin* was supposed to take back to England had long since been tossed into the bay by the rebels. They were to go home empty-handed unless the captain could find a cargo at St. Lucia or Martinique. In any case, they were due to begin their return voyage immediately. The two of them shook hands, and the captain left Wickham's office.

When they arrived at the dock, Foster, Kipper, and three other crewmen were there to meet them to take them back aboard.

Before the captain stepped into the waiting craft, Darcy stepped forward.

"This is where I say good-bye to you, sir," he said, extending his hand.

"What?" exclaimed Captain Ambrose. "Bennet, what is this? Are you mad?"

"I very well may be, sir, but I am staying here nonetheless," he continued.

"You have a promising career in the merchant marine ahead of you, man. Would you throw it all away? I could use a man like you," he continued.

"Thank you, sir," said Darcy, "but there is a higher duty that I need to perform here, and there is nothing you can say that can dissuade me."

"A higher duty? Whatever do you mean?" asked the captain impatiently.

"It is personal, sir. I would rather not say."

A short silence ensued and then the captain made another attempt. "I will withhold your wages."

Darcy smiled. "That is nothing to me, sir."

The captain looked at him as if he could not believe what he had just heard and shook his head. "What will you do?" he asked.

"I will go and fight the rebels, sir," Darcy answered.

"I'd like to go with 'im, sir, with your permission," said Foster suddenly. This was something Darcy never expected.

The captain looked from one man to another. "Are the rest of you going soldiering too?" he asked. They all shook their heads. "Well, then, let us get aboard. Time's a-wasting."

The rest of the crew clambered aboard the dinghy. Darcy and Foster turned to leave. The captain called after them.

"You, men, come here a moment," he said. Darcy and Foster turned and walked back to their commanding officer. He was reaching into his pockets for something.

"Here," he said to Darcy, and placed two coins in his hand and two in Foster's. "I believe I owe you that," he said and turned on his heel and boarded the dinghy, not looking back.

As soon as they had shoved off, Darcy and Foster looked at the coins each of them held. The captain had paid their wages for half the voyage.

"Well, I'll be," Foster said, smiling. It was a surprise to Darcy as well, but not as much as Foster leaving the ship.

"Why are you here?" Darcy said, looking at him incredulously as they began walking off the dock toward town.

"Well, Squire, I thought that maybe I should keep an eye on you," Foster said, smiling. "I worry about 'cher," he added.

"I am glad of your company," Darcy said. "But you may live to regret throwing your lot in with me."

***

The prisoners watched, as the days progressed, more and more men of every color and stripe joined Fedon at his camp. Many of them brought with them food and arms they had raided from nearby plantations and paraded by the prisoners for them to see. No more prisoners joined them, so Elizabeth assumed that any other English the rebels had come upon had been killed where they stood.

Mrs. Home could not elicit much more than a few words from Elizabeth for the next few days. Her answers to every question was monosyllabic. She had no choice but to continue with the chores they had set for her. While she worked, she could see the governor and his wife visiting each other in the yard during the daylight hours.

It was during one of these visits that Edward approached her. Now wary of every sound and movement, she turned suddenly at his approach. When she saw it was him, she felt overwhelming rage. She had a sudden compulsion to strike him, although she restrained herself. He looked thin and disheveled. Her anger faded as she observed his hangdog expression. For a moment, she almost had sympathy for him, but then her ordeal and Poppy's sprang to her mind.

"Mr. Home."

"Please, Elizabeth. Can we talk, just a little?" He waited for her answer, but she had already turned from him and resumed her washing.

"There is nothing to say that has not been said, Edward."

He shifted his position to face her, but she would not look up at him. "Please, Elizabeth. Please. We all may die soon, and I know that you can never love me, but please, please forgive me."

Abandoning her task momentarily, she looked up at him. "I have forgiven you, Edward," she said, and his face brightened momentarily, but then she continued. "I have forgiven you for my own sake, but I can never excuse you. What you have done is inexcusable, even more so because you do not even recognize it as wrong." And reading his perplexed expression she added, "Do you?"

"Elizabeth," he began, "you do not understand."

"We have had this conversation before, Mr. Home. I understand more than you know." Looking into his eyes, she repeated, "More than you will ever know. Now, leave me."

He gave her a look that was hard for her to interpret. Was it anger? Defeat? Whatever it was, she felt hardened against him. He turned from her without a word.

***

For the next few days, Edward made no move to approach her again. For that, she was grateful. She had nothing left to say to him, or anyone, for that matter. After she had finished her chores, Elizabeth was sitting alone, brooding near the fence, when she heard a familiar voice. "Oh, Miss 'Lizbet, I am glad as can be to see you." Elizabeth turned and there was Poppy, smiling at her. Elizabeth smiled back in spite of herself.

"Are dey treatin' you bad, Miss 'Lizbet?" she asked. Elizabeth burst into tears. She was so ashamed and yet she had to tell someone what had happened to her. Poppy took her hand through the fence and Elizabeth spilled out all that was in her heart. Poppy just stood there shaking her head.

"Mr. Fedon, he give an order that no mens are to be molestin' no womens prisoners," she said. "I heard him wit' my own ears. I find that Viel man and I slit his throat, I will," Poppy said fiercely.

"Oh please, Poppy, no," cried Elizabeth. "There has been enough bloodshed already. Besides, what's done is done. I am ruined...more ruined than I ever thought I could ever be."

"I don' know about bein' ruin', but you da kindes' English woman I know, and dat should be good 'nuf," she said definitively.

Elizabeth was much touched by this declaration, and for a moment, stopped dwelling on what had befallen her. "Beside," Poppy continued, "I have somethin' importan' to tell all of you. Mr. Fedon and da res' say the English are comin'. De army. Dey comin' soon. You know he say if de English army come, he gon' to kill the prisoner. All the English, he gonna kill."

Elizabeth thought to herself that whatever shame she had to live with, she would not have to live with it for very long.

"You should tell all dem what I tol' you," Poppy said. "Maybe when it starts, dey'll be ready and can fight back."

"Fight back with what?" Elizabeth asked. "We have nothing."

"Den maybe you can run," Poppy said. "Please, when de time come, please run." She squeezed Elizabeth's hand and disappeared into the forest.

***

Foster, Darcy, and Wickham sat in one of the few operating "inns" left in the city. Of course, Wickham had found it. If there was drink, gambling, and women to be had, Wickham would find it. It was his contention that, if they were going to be going into battle soon, they should have at least a night in town. Darcy, with Foster in tow, and at loose ends, had no objection to some sort of repast. They had to eat, after all. After a meal of foods that Darcy had never tasted before—plantains, goat, and God knows what else—he felt satisfied and he had his pay. They had drunk some of the local beverage, rum, and it made Darcy light-headed. This altered state had loosened his tongue, and poor Foster sat, his mouth agape, as Darcy told his tale.

"Well, Squire, you are leagues above us both," he said finally.

"Two months ago, I would have felt so," he said, "but today, I owe my life to you several times over, Foster, and that is the truth of it."

"And you two know each other, then?" Foster asked.

Wickham laughed. "We grew up together. Who knows, perhaps we will be brothers-in-law before long."

Ordinarily, Darcy would have bristled at such an insensitive comment, but tonight, he felt full of optimism and alcohol. The raid on Fedon's camp was forty-eight hours in the future, Darcy was free of his obligation to the *Marlin*, and soon he would have his Elizabeth back again. That was the thought he would keep in his mind, not the myriad of less optimistic thoughts that were more realistic, such as he was too late, and Elizabeth was dead, or she was in the grasp of men who... He really could not let himself entertain the possibility that his beloved was in the clutches of rebel gangs who, like pirates, would molest any captured women at will. No, tonight, all was well and soon he would hold Elizabeth in his arms again.

Wickham took advantage of Darcy's state of mind. Tonight, he let Wickham refill his glass without resistance. Soon the trio was joined by some ladies of the evening, glad to find Englishmen who seemed to have money to spend.

Wickham and Foster were determined to avail themselves of the carnal delights offered in Grenville, but Darcy would have none of it. At first, their presence was resisted by Darcy, but as the evening wore on, and the drink flowed freely, his resistance weakened. Darcy marveled how Wickham seemed never to be intoxicated. He certainly knew how to enjoy himself with the ladies and they flocked to him.

How he managed to return to the quarters Wickham provided was not entirely clear to him, but he awoke the next morning in a simply appointed but clean room in the counting house. His head was splitting. There was a basin and a looking glass above it in his room, and after he had dragged himself from bed, he looked in it. The man he saw was unrecognizable. His face was nearly as brown as the native Grenadians, his eyes bloodshot, his hair tangled, and stubble covered his face. His shirt was open and dirty. He was grateful that a pitcher of water and a glass was next to his bed and he drank thirstily. This improved his physical as well as his mental state immensely. Taking a few deep breaths, he opened the door to his room and saw that he was on the upper floor of the counting house, on an indoor balcony that ran three quarters of the way around the upper floor. These rooms had been offices of the mercantile marine, no doubt, and now served as either quarters or offices of the Royal Army. Darcy recognized Wickham's door, and knocked.

"Enter," Wickham said firmly. There he was, clean shaven, immaculately dressed, and surrounded by other officers and men. They all looked up at Darcy with surprise, and a few, with undisguised disgust. He remembered many a time when just such an expression was on his face.

"Oh, there you are, D—" Wickham began, then catching himself said, "Bennet. Let me call for my orderly. He will set you to rights and you can join us." Some of the officers looked at Wickham in surprise. Darcy retreated through the door, and within a few minutes, an orderly appeared and took him for a bath, a shave, and some fresh clothing. Although he could not even look at breakfast, a pot of tea with plenty of sugar alleviated his headache. When he felt able, he returned to Wickham's office. He was alone.

"I do beg your pardon for my behavior of last evening," Darcy said at once. Wickham smirked.

"Nothing to apologize for, old chap," he said breezily. "You have now been initiated into the life of a fighting man. Eat, drink, and be merry, for tomorrow we die, eh?" he added.

Darcy had no reply to Wickham's frivolity, so he asked, "What is the plan for tomorrow?"

Wickham displayed the charts and showed Darcy the plan of attack. They would come up the river below the Concord Falls. Another squadron would land at Grand Roy and attack from the north.

"How well do you know the country there?" Darcy asked.

"Therein lies the rub, old boy," Wickham said. "All of our best scouts joined the rebellion and what you see here," he said, indicating the charts, "is all we have."

"How in God's name are you going to surprise them, then?" Darcy asked a little too loudly. His head was throbbing again.

"I am afraid we will not," said Wickham.

"And the prisoners?" asked Darcy.

"I have orders to attack tomorrow without regard to rescuing the prisoners. They are as good as dead, Darcy. You know that."

Darcy put his head in his hands and sat down heavily. He would not accept that. He had come too far.

"I was as good as dead, too, Wickham," he said, standing and looking Wickham in the eye. He turned toward the window and closed his eyes to think. Suddenly, he turned to Wickham again.

"What if Foster and I start out today? Provide us with horses and we will scout for you. When you arrive, we will have all the information you need to—"

"Darcy, do you have any idea how outnumbered we are? There are, perhaps, five hundred to a thousand British soldiers and marines on the island. Fedon has twice that, at least. I am attacking tomorrow because I have orders to attack tomorrow. I predict that we will retreat before we get halfway to Belvidere."

"All the more reason for me to try alone," Darcy said. Wickham shook his head.

"If that is what you want, Darcy, you may try. I will give the order, but I do not think that it will do you, Miss Bennet, or any of us any good. The odds are too great." He looked at Darcy, and then, to Darcy's surprise, extended his hand.

"Godspeed," he said.

***

Elizabeth, who kept a watchful eye on all those who occupied the other side of the fence from where she was held, saw nothing of Viel after his attack on her. She was relieved and, at the same time, wary. She had also not seen Fedon for several days; he usually came by to see how the prisoners were faring. It occurred to her that he was the only one standing between the women hostages and the men who watched them.

She did not imagine that Maurice Viel would take his defeat at the hands of an English woman with the good graces of a gentleman. She was also sure that he did not want any of his fellow revolutionaries, whether freeman or slave, white or black, to know what he'd attempted or that he had been foiled. Perhaps she was safe from him. In some ways she was grateful for the never-ending and exhausting toil she and her fellow prisoners were subject to every day. The fatigue at least allowed her to sleep at night, but never the way she had done before. Wariness and anxiety were now her constant companions. Poppy had told her that Fedon was very clear in his instructions to his troops. No one was to molest any of the women prisoners or he would be flogged in public. The numbers of rebels, however, grew day by day, and men greatly outnumbered women, especially available women.

Governor Home told Elizabeth and his wife that he was not at all optimistic of their fate. To Elizabeth, he had the look of a dead man already, and his wife, who needed comfort, could get nothing from him. The news he brought them from the men's quarters provided no solace. A few of the men plotted an escape one night but were lost in the jungle highlands that surrounded the camp and by morning were dragged back in chains. They heard that Fedon was disposed to hang them as an example, but relented, keeping them in irons and chained to a tree like dogs. Elizabeth could see them from the courtyard. There was nothing she could do to help. There was nothing she could do to help herself either.

As the camp became more crowded, the rebels became more restive. Men would call out to Elizabeth and the other women cooking or washing in the courtyard and make obscene gestures at them and laugh. Some would shake the fence and shout things in French. Elizabeth's French was that confined to the schoolroom, so she did not understand most of what they said, but her imagination filled in what her schoolroom lacked. She spent her days in anxiety and fear.

Although there were many rumors that the English were planning an attack on Fedon's stronghold, as each day passed nothing happened. The thick vegetation and mountainous terrain were Fedon's greatest defense, but nonetheless, Elizabeth observed men who were set to work on barricades around the perimeter of the camp in preparation for the inevitable. The tension in the camp was palpable on both sides of the prisoners' fence.

The morning began as any other. Elizabeth and her fellow female prisoners were in the courtyard washing clothes when she heard a crack from the wooden fence and a roar of men's voices. Then she saw them, streaming into the compound, the women running and being felled like hunted animals. The man at the apex of the attack was none other than Maurice Viel.

The male prisoners were herded into the boucan by machete- and pike-wielding rebels, who beat and slashed any of them who resisted. A few of the men lay on the ground bleeding, but Elizabeth had little time to notice or to care.

She also began to run, when many arms grabbed hold of her and her feet went out from under her. She was on the ground then and used her fists and legs to defend herself. Soon, though, her arms were pinned behind her and many hands were pawing her body. She was on her belly, her face pushed roughly into the dirt and held there while she felt hands work their way under her skirt, and clutch at her inner thighs. Then, probing fingers worked their way through her underclothes and touched her in the most intimate of places. She was screaming helplessly.

Then she saw Poppy near the fence. She stood stock still, but instead of rushing to help Elizabeth, she ran in the other direction.

Elizabeth twisted and screamed, but the men were relentless. She began to feel herself separating from her own body, as if she were bearing witness to what they were doing to her and not actually there at all. She squeezed her eyes closed. How many minutes had passed she did not know.

Elizabeth, her dress torn to pieces, was still struggling against her attackers when she heard the sound of horses neighing and men shouting. Suddenly, all of them released her and she rolled on her back in time to see none other than Fedon himself slashing away at his own men with a whip. He drove his horse into the crowd and it reared up over the prone bodies all around. He and his mounted followers began shouting and liberally applying their whips and clubs. Her attackers were trying to shield themselves from Fedon's wrath, raising their arms to protect their faces and scattering like so many vile insects. Soon, the courtyard was empty except for the English women in various states of undress, clutching at their clothing. Some were still screaming, many were sobbing. Elizabeth got to her feet and tried to cover herself as best she could.

Fedon, scanning the scene, looked at her for a few moments as if puzzling about something, then he turned his attention to the matter at hand. "Count the prisoners," he ordered. "Some of the women may have been carried off. Anyone caught with an English woman will be hanged." He repeated his orders in English and in French. Later, when Elizabeth was thinking of what had transpired that day, she thought of those orders as a gift to all of them, to assuage their fears. Men had odd rules in wartime. Today, Fedon had rescued all of them from rape and murder, while tomorrow he might kill them all in a reprisal for an attack on his headquarters.

With the fence gone, all the prisoners were kept inside for the rest of the day, the women separated from the men. Fedon sent men to see to the wounded, and before long, the door of the women's quarters opened. Many of the English women cried out, and Elizabeth did also, thinking that there were more horrors to come, but it was Poppy leading a small group of Grenadian women bearing buckets of water, sponges, and bandages for the prisoners.

Poppy ran straight to Elizabeth and took both her hands. "Did they hurt you much, Miss 'Lizbet'?" she asked. Elizabeth had no idea how to answer her. Her clothes were in shreds, she was bruised and brutalized. Her virtue was in shreds. She was a tainted woman, dirtied. She merely looked up at Poppy blankly, and Poppy began to help restore her physical well-being, if she could do nothing for her otherwise.

"I went for Fedon," Poppy said. "I wouldn' leave you, Miss 'Lizbet," she continued as she sponged some of the dirt and blood from Elizabeth's battered body. "It all right now."

Elizabeth leaned against the wall and stared at the ceiling of the boucan. Poppy was speaking to her, but all her vigor had left her. Occasionally, she would look at Poppy and wonder how she bore it. How did she keep on living after Edward went to her night after night?

Later that evening, Elizabeth sat alone against a wall and wished for death. What was to become of her now? She hoped that the English forces would attack soon, and she would be put out of her misery.

***

The boat unloaded Foster and Darcy at a small landing in a clearing. Armed only with horses, a compass, provisions for two days, and a pistol, ammunition, and a cutlass each, they were left to make their way to Fedon's camp.

"We'll make us a camp, 'ere, Squire," said Foster. "It's almost dark."

"Let us move as far as we can from the river," Darcy said, slapping his neck where the buzzing insects were already feasting. "Perhaps we can escape some of these midges."

Foster agreed, as Darcy observed that the mosquitoes were buzzing relentlessly around his companion as well. Mounting their horses, they made their way through the trees until they came to what Darcy reckoned was Concord Falls. Struggling through the thickets up the side of the mountain, they came to a meadow just as the sun was setting. There was no possibility of a fire, but the horses found feed readily, and there was a stream that provided water for both man and beast. They pitched their small tent in the waning light and settled in.

"I'll take first watch," Foster volunteered.

"Let me," Darcy said. "I do not think I could sleep now."

"All right, then," Foster acquiesced. "I will sleep but wake me at two bells. You'll need your rest for tomorrow, Squire. Make no mistake." Foster lay down and closed his eyes, and Darcy crawled out of the tent and sat beneath the tropical sky.

"Foster," he said.

"Squire?" Foster answered.

"You did not have to come with me. You could have been out to sea by now, going home," Darcy said. "Why did you come?"

"You and me is friends, ain't we?" he asked.

Darcy was much moved by this simple reply. He had few friends in his life of whom he was so sure, who did not consider his position or his fortune or his title. Charles Bingley was such a friend. Now, so was Foster.

"Yes," Darcy said. "Of course we are."

"Well, then," Foster said, and yawned. Darcy knew that the conversation was over. His thoughts returned to his life in England. In his mind's eye, he put Charles Bingley and Foster side by side. It occurred to him that only in his mind could they stand side by side as equals. Six months ago, such inequality made perfect sense to him. Now, he was not sure of anything.

As he sat in the gathering darkness, he recounted each step that had brought him to this place. Life at Pemberley had seemed to him so circumscribed, so predictable, and now... Now he was camped near a rushing waterfall, dressed as a vagabond, a man of greatly inferior station but highly admirable character by his side. The woman he loved, and one he had sacrificed everything for, just out of his reach. His dark thoughts returned. What if he found her dead? What if she had been sullied by a rebel, or by many? What if he never found her? No, he would not give in to pessimism and gloom. He had not traveled halfway round the world on this mission just to be defeated, not by an enemy, but by his own mind and character. It was time to keep his head clear and finish what he had started.

Darcy had no trouble keeping his watch but was grateful for Foster's relief when the time came. He slept fitfully and awoke before dawn. They saddled the horses and started out at first light.

The trek up the mountainside was arduous, but not so much as it could have been on foot. They stayed away from any signs of paths or roads because undoubtedly, they would be patrolled or at least watched. According to the map Darcy carried, they were due north from their camp, which was in sight of Concord Falls. By Darcy's reckoning, if they kept their present course, they should ride directly into Fedon's camp at Belvidere. Their plan was to hide the horses at least five hundred yards down the mountain and finish the scouting on foot to remain undetected. He tried to prepare himself for what, undoubtedly, was to come.

Darcy had never killed a man before and did not relish the thought. He had not asked Foster if he had ever seen battle, but there was little, it seemed, that Foster had not seen. When Darcy and Foster were to reach the camp, Darcy would stay and assess the feasibility of rescuing the prisoners while Foster was to report back to Wickham and the troops who would just be arriving at the falls and moving north.

Darcy and Foster reached a rise about a mile from Belvidere. When they reached the top of the ridge, they dismounted and concealed themselves as best they could. From their hiding place, Darcy could see the main house and much movement of people. Retrieving his glass, he carefully set about assessing the strength of the forces to which he would soon have to reckon.

He began with the house, which was somewhat obscured by the trees. There were hundreds of men camped in its environs, mostly black and mulatto.

"What'cha see there, Squire?" Foster asked, peering through the rocks and vegetation that concealed him.

"Our opponent has many men. I cannot count them all, but I would say numbering in the hundreds," Darcy rejoined.

"The best we can do, then, is see where they all are and report back," Foster said.

"That is exactly what you will do," Darcy said. "Now, let me concentrate." He moved his glass slowly and methodically from the house to the perimeters of the camp. There were barricades everywhere, and men on watch. Many did not seem well-armed, machetes and pikes, but he knew there were more he could not see who were armed with muskets and pistols. They may even have captured a cannon, but he dismissed the thought as unlikely. How would they even get it up these steep slopes through this impenetrable undergrowth? As he swept his glass over the south ridge, he could see a building with a foundation and two stories. Unlike the other buildings, there was little activity nearby. On closer inspection, he could see bare-chested black men standing every few feet in front of those buildings. To Darcy's mind, that could mean only one thing. Those men were standing guard on prisoners. If Elizabeth was still alive, that was where she would be.

"Well, Squire, what do you see?" Foster asked again. Darcy's heart was pounding in his chest. He was within a hair's breadth of the end of his quest. He quickly collapsed the glass to keep it from shaking in his hands. He handed the glass to Foster and had him look for himself.

"There's where the prisoners are, eh, Squire?" he asked, scanning the outbuildings surrounded by guards. "That's where yer headed, am I right?" he asked.

Darcy did not answer. "I am going to draw a simple map of what we saw from here. You can take it back down the mountain to the general."

"Are ye sure, then?" he asked, and looked hard at Darcy.

"Do not worry about me, Foster," said Darcy, reading his expression. "I did not come all this way to get myself killed. I have too much to live for," he continued, and smiled. Foster clapped him on the shoulder and climbed back down to where his horse was tethered. In a few minutes, he was gone.

"Now what?" Darcy asked himself. He estimated that he was a half mile from the camp, and from his perch, he plotted a course for himself that would take him primarily through trees and underbrush. He would walk his horse, since a man on horseback would be spotted more easily and the terrain was very steep.

For the better part of an hour, he struggled through the forest, plagued by insects and virtually blind as to his location in regard to Fedon's outpost. He might have been completely off course or walking straight into a band of rebels on patrol. From his vantage point at the bottom of the forest, he had no way of telling. He was ascending now and would soon be close upon the rebels. He was so close, in fact, that he could hear activity above him, and many voices speaking in French. He stopped to gather his thoughts, and then, suddenly, heard a noise behind him. He turned and not ten feet from him, were a band of men. They were not English.

Chapter 15

As Darcy turned in the wood, one of them called out to him, "*Salut, frère.*"

"*Salut,*" he replied, and realized, after a moment of panic, that they had mistaken him for a French rebel.

He had studied French as a boy and excelled in it at Eton. Latin was another matter. He was grateful that he had not been set upon by Roman gladiators. They would have seen through him in an instant.

Incredible. He could have just walked into camp any time he had a mind to. After a brief conversation with one of them, he discovered that the white men were all planters that had been dispossessed by the English. This was their chance to regain what they had lost. The darker members of the group were also planters, free men, who believed that the French would honour the ideals established by the revolution despite their African heritage. Darcy was thinking as quickly as he could. He could not set himself up as a planter; they would want to know what the name of his estate was. Instead, he kept as close to the truth as he could. He had come to Grenville to work for a merchant only a few weeks ago. The rebellion started almost as soon as he arrived. He had taken his master's horse and fled. The rest of the men seemed to accept that story. He had become an adept liar. Perhaps he had always been a liar. The small talk he made at those endless gatherings were primarily lies and flattery. Such social skills stood him in good stead at the moment.

They had reached the outer path near the prisoners' quarters and came upon a short native woman in a red scarf making her way toward the main house. One of them called to her, "*Sœur, nous sommes arrivés à joindre à la cause.*"

They had come to join the cause. The young Grenadian woman motioned for them to follow her and as they emerged into the sunlit camp, several men armed with machetes approached them. To Darcy's relief, the planter who had spoken to him spoke for all of them. The men in the camp did not seem to think anything was amiss. They offered them food and drink.

There were hundreds of men, and even some women and children in the camp. They had makeshift shelters and plenty of food and drink. There seemed to be some training of fighting men going on in the clearing behind the main house. Darcy walked about freely, and no one restricted his movements. He had to find the prisoners and Elizabeth without drawing attention to himself. He kept his horse within his gaze, as that animal was to be his vehicle of escape. His and Elizabeth's.

***

Guards were doubled around the prisoners now, and Elizabeth assumed that Fedon made a special effort to ensure their safety. She could not fathom why. He said he would kill them all soon enough. Perhaps he had another use for them. She shuddered to think.

Fedon arrived after the attack and inspected the women prisoners in their quarters and seemed satisfied that they were unmolested. Elizabeth actually heard him use that word. Unmolested. He took a special interest in the governor's wife. Elizabeth heard them talking. Mrs. Home assured him that she was not even in the courtyard when the men rushed in. He turned to leave the boucan when he looked directly at Elizabeth, but did not speak. He looked at her so quizzically that she nearly addressed him, but what would she say? What was there to say? Did he remember chatting with her on a social occasion, with Edward by her side? Did he remember her hanging on his every word and admiring his high ideals? Did he know that he personally rescued her only an hour ago? Only a little while ago, a month, two months, a lifetime ago, they were in a drawing room, making small talk. Now, he was her enemy. Her life was in his hands. He left without speaking to her.

Poppy had been ministering to her and she had been able to secure some modicum of privacy to wash and restore herself somewhat. Thoughts returned to her that were so painful that she deliberately shut them out. She shut everyone out, including Poppy, whose worried face was constantly near.

"Miss 'Lizbet'," she said softly. "Can I get sometin' for you?" She peered into Elizabeth's face, but received no reply. "You res' now. I'll go and see if I can get you sometin' to eat." She got up from Elizabeth's side and knocked on the door. The guard let her leave and peered inside to satisfy himself that all was restored to calm again.

***

After a while, the men Darcy came in with had scattered, and he wandered about, near the main building. There were guards posted there. No doubt this was Fedon's home and now his headquarters. He wondered if the women prisoners might be kept there. If Fedon was a gentleman, then that is where they would be. Darcy shook his head at his own foolishness. How ridiculous to assume that anything was as he believed it should be. Nothing in the past few weeks was remotely in his ken, and he needed to think, and think quickly. It was then he espied that small Grenadian woman who had spoken to them as they entered the camp. She was avoiding the main areas of habitation by the path leading behind the outbuildings. In her arms was a basket that had a cloth over it. Having no other plan, Darcy decided to follow her. Before she entered the shelter of the forest path, a man spoke to her.

"What are you carrying there, my little cabbage?" he asked her in French. He was very dark-skinned and better dressed than most he had seen thus far.

"Some food," she replied curtly.

"Do not waste food on those English prisoners. They will not live long anyway," he said snidely. "Come and share your basket with me," he continued, teasing. She did not reply and stuck her nose in the air, to which he reacted with laughter.

Darcy was determined to follow her. This was his chance to find out about Elizabeth and, perhaps, even to get her out of here. He waited until the man's attention was diverted elsewhere, and then followed the Grenadian woman discreetly down the forest path. Her basket was heavy, so she was not making very quick headway. He soon caught up with her.

"May I carry that basket?" he asked. "It looks too heavy for you." She stopped short and looked at him in astonishment. She suddenly looked at him suspiciously.

"There is food near de house. You don't have to take mine," she said. Her French had this odd, lilting tone to it that Darcy found pleasant.

"Really, I do not want your food. I will help you, though." He held out his hand for the basket. Still eyeing him guardedly, she put the basket in his hands. "Tell me," he said as they walked along, "what is your name?"

She eyed him suspiciously, yet answered, "Poppy."

"Poppy," he asked warily, "do you know what they did with the governor and his party?"

"I worked for the gov'nor," she said proudly.

"Really?" he asked. He tried to deliberately control his breathing and his expression. "Do you know what became of him?" It was not what he wanted to ask, but that would come soon enough.

"He is in dere, upstairs in the boucan," she said, pointing, "with all de other men."

"And," he was about to say, "and the women?" but stopped himself. It might sound as though he had rather ignoble intentions. They were getting dangerously close to buildings that were surrounded by guards. He stopped abruptly.

"What is it?" she asked. "Give me de basket back if you don' wan' to carry it."

"No, it is not that," he said. How much could he trust her? He had no other choice. He would have to ask.

"Do you know a young woman called Elizabeth Bennet?" he asked. She looked at him, her eyes narrowing.

"What do you want wid her?" Poppy asked angrily. "She already suffer enough." She made a move to take the basket back, but Darcy held fast.

"Listen," he suddenly said in English. "I have come for her." She let out a cry of surprise, which attracted the attention of the guards.

"What is the matter?" the guard shouted in French.

"Not'ing," she called back, forcing herself to sound jovial. Poppy looked back and forth from Darcy to the guard. "This man want some bread and actually he offer to pay me for it." The guard laughed, and she did too. She then took Darcy by the arm and led him off the path. They stopped in a shady spot under the cover of the fan-like leaves of a Chusan palm, and Poppy sat down and motioned for Darcy to sit beside her.

"You are English," she spoke in English, keeping her voice barely above a whisper.

"I am," he stated.

"You must take her away from here. Dere is much talk of killin' de prisoners," she said, looking directly at him.

"How do you know Elizabeth?" Darcy asked.

"I was her lady's maid at the gov'nor house," she replied. "Before de trouble start." She unexpectedly caught Darcy's arm and looked at him intently. "She teach me to read," she said, and smiled.

Darcy returned her smile. He had found his key to Elizabeth. It was someone she had been kind to. It now remained for him to separate Elizabeth from the others and get her safely away. To his mind, he had only a day before the British forces would be leading a charge up this mountain.

"Can you get her out here to me?" Darcy asked.

"Yusta be, dey let de prisoners out. Not now, 'specially de women," she said cryptically. "You see de building dere. Dat's where she is. I t'ink we wait 'til night. Be better."

He had to agree with her. They laid out a plan that Darcy would wait in this very spot with his horse. As soon as the sun went down, Poppy would ask to take Elizabeth to the privy. It would get them outside and away from the guards for a moment. In the darkness, she would bring Elizabeth to him.

"You will come with us, Poppy," he offered before they resumed their walk.

"No, sir," she said. "Wit de English, I am a slave. Wid Fedon, I can be free." He had no reply, for there was none. Wondering again if he could trust her, he watched her disappear down the path and turned to gather supplies for his escape.

Darcy waited nearly half a mile of what he assumed was directly east of the British army's position. His horse had been fed and watered and he had enough provisions for at least two days for both himself and Elizabeth. He dared not think that his mission would be unsuccessful. They would both be alive at the end of this day, and they would both be safe. Luckily, he was sure that the British army was at least twelve hours behind him and he would have the advantage of time.

He created a small, makeshift camp in his hiding place in the off chance that he would be discovered there. He could make the excuse that the upper camp was too crowded, and he enjoyed his solitude.

Early in the afternoon, he was dozing when he heard the report of a cannon, shots firing, and screams from above him. Leaping to his feet, he could see the flash of red coats as they crashed through the forest just to the west of him. The army was there already, and they were attacking in broad daylight. Many of the men were sliding backward down the mountain. Darcy realized what he was seeing. Fedon had pulled up much of the vegetation on the mountainside so that if he was attacked from below, the British would grab hold of unstable bushes and slide backward down the mountain. That was exactly what was happening. He realized also that he had been wrong about the cannon. Fedon had prepared well. General Lindsay's men drove straight into Fedon's barricades and, while a few of the troops made it over the top, the English were trapped in hand-to-hand combat on the mountainside with more rebel reinforcements coming every minute.

Darcy swiftly tucked his pistol in his waistband and mounted his horse. With one hand he held the reins, with the other, a cutlass. He made straight for the boucan.

When he arrived a few moments later, all was chaos. The few English soldiers who made it over the top were already fighting in the clearing in front of the boucan, but they were vastly outnumbered. Before Darcy could decide what to do, another wave of British marines flooded the courtyard in front of the boucan. The rebels guarding the prisoners were soon engaged by them, but Darcy, through the chaos, could see no sign of the prisoners. He could hear screaming and shouting from inside the building. Amidst the hubbub, he could hear women's panicked voices.

Darcy's horse was skittish in the ensuing tumult, so he was constantly turning as his mount reared. To his amazement, he caught sight of Wickham, who had just succeeded in dropping one of the guards. As he turned Darcy shouted, "The English prisoners are here," and pointed to the boucan with his cutlass. Wickham looked up and smiled maddeningly, as if he were enjoying himself. Wickham shouted to his men, and they ran to the doors, and in short order, the prisoners were liberated. They began running in all directions, both men and women.

Darcy called out, "Elizabeth," several times, and then hearing a roar, spun his mount around only to see hundreds of the revolutionaries streaming into the courtyard. Some were armed with pistols, but most with machetes and other knives. Most were on foot. Above the fray, a coffee-skinned man dressed in a French officer's uniform galloped into the courtyard and was shouting, "Kill the prisoners. Kill the prisoners." Darcy knew then it was Julien Fedon himself.

In all the chaos, Darcy had to try to find his beloved Elizabeth. The carnage was astonishing. All around him, unarmed prisoners were being cut to pieces, and yet he remained unscathed. He realized after a few minutes that he wasn't wearing the uniform of the enemy, so the rebels had no idea whose side he was on. He spun his horse round and round until he saw her. Elizabeth. It was Poppy's red headscarf that led his eye in that direction. Poppy had Elizabeth by the hand and the two were running toward the shelter of the foliage. He galloped after her, calling her name. Suddenly, Elizabeth tripped and was on the ground. He and his steed were upon her then, and his horse reared again. She looked up at him, terrified.

"Take my hand, Elizabeth," he shouted. "It is I, Darcy. Take my hand, for God's sake," he screamed again.

"Go," Poppy screamed, and Elizabeth's head snapped in her direction. She looked up wide-eyed at Darcy's imploring face, and scrambled to her feet, extending her hand to him. He clutched her hand and in one movement pulled her up behind him on his horse and, kicking the poor creature in the flanks, galloped off, leaving a stunned Poppy alone. He glanced back for a moment and saw her running for what shelter could be found on the mountainside. The pandemonium reigned behind them, but Darcy never again looked back.

Darcy, once they had travelled a quarter mile down into valley, slowed his horse and led him into the shade of the jungle canopy. His senses were on the alert for any movement in the underbrush. He had exchanged his cutlass for a pistol, which remained in his hand. The sounds of the battle were fading now, and he finally had time to think. He and Elizabeth had not said one word to each other, but he felt her nearly unclothed body pressed against him, her arms entwined around his waist.

The British army and marines were evacuating swiftly now, and he could hear them crashing down the mountain, the sound of their bugle blowing retreat. They would be upon them soon and be bringing the battle and the chaos with them. He edged his way through the underbrush, looking for the path he had cut when he came up the mountain. Finding it, they followed it down the mountain until they came upon a stream. His horse needed water and so did the two exhausted people on his back. Looking around for any signs of hostility, he finally let the poor animal drink in the brook and dismounted. Without a word, he extended his arms to Elizabeth, and she eased herself into them. She was dressed only in her shift, and that was nearly torn to shreds. She had no stockings or shoes. Her face was glistening with sweat, and her arms and legs showed evidence of bruises. Her chestnut hair was tangled and dusty. As he eased her out of the saddle into his arms, he thought that he had never seen anyone look as beautiful as she did at that moment.

As soon as her feet touched the ground, she pushed him away. "Who are you?" she asked, glaring at him.

He was taken aback momentarily. "Do you not recognize me, Elizabeth? It is I, Fitzwilliam Darcy."

"Darcy is dead," she said, and turned away from him. Kneeling by the stream, she splashed water on her face and began to drink thirstily from her cupped hands. He knelt beside her. She refused to look at him. Slowly, he extended his hand and lightly touched her arm. She did not recoil. He did not move his hand.

"You are very like him, you know." She sighed. "But I saw him in his coffin. He is dead and it is all my fault." When she looked up at him, tears were in her eyes.

She turned back to drink from the stream. Darcy bent to touch her and then he noticed it. The water filling the pool at their feet was being fed by a stream that came from Fedon's camp. It was swirling with an inky red substance that was nearing Elizabeth. He grabbed her by the arm and pulled her from the pool. Soon, it was running with blood.

He expected her to scream, but she merely gazed at it unmoved. They both stood quietly for a moment and still clutching her arm, he spoke.

"You saved my life, Elizabeth. It was my aunt who nearly killed me." She turned to look into his face mutely, unbelieving. "I am Darcy. I suppose I have to prove it to you, then," he stated. Standing, he opened his shirt to reveal a large, rippled scar on his left side. Then, removing his shirt, he draped it over her shoulders.

She stood to face him, and gingerly touched the wound in his side. She withdrew her hand suddenly and clutched at his shirt, wrapping it tightly around her. Staring at the ground, she did not speak.

The sounds of the retreating British were growing stronger now, and Darcy had no wish to deal with any of them. "Please," he entreated. "Let us travel on to Concord Falls and perhaps we can reach Halifax Harbour by nightfall and St. George's by morning. I will tell you the tale of how I came to be here as we ride."

She nodded mutely and let him help her onto the back of his horse. He wanted to take her in his arms and cover her with kisses, but he dared not. Her aspect was so strange. He had heard people talk of shock, and he believed now that he was witnessing it. It made no sense to press her. She was alive, and he was alive and that was enough for now. If they were to remain that way, however, they had best start upon their journey.

It was easier for him to speak about the duplicity of his aunt, and his long convalescence, while he was riding. He did not have to look at her and judge her reaction. The path down the mountain was narrow and steep, and many times he stopped speaking to negotiate their passage and steady himself and her. Several times as he looked down, he could see her arms tight around his naked waist, her flesh pressed against his. He felt her move against him as they thudded through the undergrowth. He felt intoxicated by her touch, and yet…and yet he could see plainly the bruising on her arms and feel the crush of her silence.

They stopped once, to water his horse, and again she fell into his arms as he helped her dismount. He bent down to the stream to fill the wooden cask that contained their water. She stood nearby and when he looked up, found her staring at him.

"How ever did you find me?" she asked.

He was relieved. At least now, she recognized him. "I was about to tell you," he said. "When I got to Portsmouth, the ship upon which I thought to sail had already left. I was stranded."

"Then how?"

"I found a ship that needed crew members and became as you see me now, a common sailor."

She began to breathe heavily and shake her head. "That is impossible. Impossible. No. It cannot be. It cannot." She turned from him and grasped a palm tree and leaned heavily against it.

At first, he could not fathom her reaction. Did she despise him, then, for casting off his nobility in such a manner? Surely not. He had done it for her, for his love for her. He had done everything for her.

She then seemed to collapse under the weight of what she had heard, and he rushed to her. "Elizabeth," he cried. As he reached her, he turned her face toward him and saw that it was covered in tears.

"I am so sorry," she kept muttering over and over. "I am so sorry."

Before he could speak again, he heard the report of muskets. "We need to be going, and quickly," he said. Again they mounted their steed and rode on in silence.

By the time they reached the Concord Falls, the British army had caught up with them. Foster was there waiting. He greeted Darcy with a wide smile and a slap on the back. "So, Squire, I see ye rescued your lady-love, then," he said.

"I did indeed," replied Darcy. He smiled in spite of himself. After Elizabeth extricated herself from her saddle, she was properly introduced. "Elizabeth, this is my friend, Mr. Foster," he said formally.

"Mr. Foster, indeed," Foster said, shifting from one foot to the other. "Just Foster, miss. Just Foster," he continued awkwardly.

"Pleased to meet you," she said, hugging Darcy's shirt closer to her. Foster tipped his hat to her and slipped away. Elizabeth caught Darcy's arm.

"Help me," she said.

"Of course," he said, "with what, exactly?"

She indicated her clothing. "I...my clothes," she began and stopped short when he nodded.

"Of course. How stupid of me."

Within the hour, she was dressed as a British infantryman, minus coat and hat. He noticed that she had stopped hugging her garments about her person. *The worst is over now. We are both alive and well.*

Darcy arranged for horses to take them to the coast. He was informed that the rebels were concentrated in the interior and had abandoned Gouyave. The area along the coast from St. George's northward was not British occupied yet, but at least not in rebel hands. They were offered an escort, and although Darcy was of a mind to refuse, the army had their own reasons for wanting to secure the coast, and so the offer was accepted.

"You are coming with us, of course," Darcy said to Foster as he saddled Elizabeth's horse. "Get your horse ready."

"I don't think so, Squire," Foster replied simply.

Darcy turned to him with a surprised look.

"Why ever not, man?" he asked, perhaps a little too loudly.

"Yer don't need the likes of me anymore, Squire," he said, smiling. Before Darcy could argue, he continued. "This lot will pay me to be a scout for 'em. I think it suits me."

"You know, Foster, there is always a place for you with me at—" but Foster cut him off before he could finish.

"I think I'd rather finish what we started 'ere," he said. At that, someone called "Foster" from the camp, and he was off with a wave. "We will meet again," Foster called over his shoulder, and left his friend standing there speechless. Darcy felt oddly emotional with this news but shook himself out of it immediately and the silent Elizabeth joined him.

There was not much time or privacy for talk on their way to the coast. Darcy stayed as close as he dared to Elizabeth, but she seemed lost in her own thoughts. What was she sorry for? That he had debased himself for her sake? For his being wounded in that stupid duel? As soon as he was able, he would set her mind at rest. Everything he did, he did of his own free will and was glad of it. At first opportunity, he would tell her so. Finally, on board ship, Darcy found a pallet for her to lie on, and she drifted off from what he imagined was sheer exhaustion. He was also mightily fatigued but determined to keep watch over her. They reached St. George's by evening. It was firmly in the hands of the British.

As they docked, Darcy awakened her. She awoke with a start, looking wild-eyed. "Are you all right?" he asked. She nodded. "We are here," he said simply. As they moved down the dock, a thought suddenly occurred to him. "I have no idea what we will do now," he said. "I have no money. I suppose the army could shelter us for a while."

For the first time in a long while, Elizabeth looked directly at him. "Barbara" was all she said.

Before the sun set, Darcy and Elizabeth were entering the gate of Barbara and Gerard Ellsworth's fine house. When Elizabeth walked into the drawing room, Barbara gasped in surprise. "Elizabeth?" she cried and ran to embrace her. "I hardly recognized you." Elizabeth was still dressed as a marine. Barbara held both of Elizabeth's hands and stepped back to look at her. "How much you must have been through. I am so glad to see you." Elizabeth smiled, but soon the expression on her face changed. "You have suffered much," she said.

"It is not only me who has suffered. I have news of your family," she said. Barbara closed her eyes for a moment, then opened them, "You must tell me everything, as soon as we see to you and..." She looked at Darcy. "I am forgetting my manners. I see you brought someone with you."

Elizabeth smiled at her and turned to Darcy. "Barbara, may I introduce Mr. Fitzwilliam Darcy."

Many tears followed that night. Elizabeth and Darcy met the baby, Edward Ninian, called after Barbara's brother and her father. Haltingly, Elizabeth told her friend and Darcy all that happened since their capture, and of the attack on Belvidere by the British army. There was still no word as to the fate of the prisoners at Fedon's camp. Darcy could guess but said nothing. It was beginning to dawn on Darcy what sort of horrors Elizabeth had witnessed and, no doubt, been subject to. Part of him wanted to know all that she had suffered, and part of him...part of him dreaded knowing. Part of him did not know how he would accept all that had transpired.

Darcy was provided with bath and clean clothes, and much needed sustenance. Gerard invited him for a brandy, but he was so fatigued that he could barely converse. Observing his weariness, Gerard arranged for their rooms for the night and they retreated upstairs. Darcy passed the drawing room door and could hear women's voices and weeping. He did not enter.

Chapter 16

When Elizabeth awoke in the morning, at first, she could not remember where she was. Then, all at once, the events of the past few days came flooding back to her. She clutched the sheet to swaddle herself despite the heat. How would she tell Darcy what had befallen her only hours before he arrived like a knight in shining armour? What would he think of her? To have come all this way, to have debased himself and lived like a common sailor, to have risked life and limb only to find that she was a fallen woman? She now knew why women went mad.

Surprisingly, there were a few servants who stayed with their British masters despite the rebellion. Whether it was out of fear or loyalty, no one knew. As Barbara's lady's maid helped her dress, Elizabeth's thoughts turned to Poppy. Dear Poppy. What had become of her? She had been Elizabeth's fast and true friend, and yet was left to her fate among the revolutionaries. She was so panicked during the British attack on Belvidere, that she did not hold fast to Poppy and insist she go with them. Now that Poppy had been left behind, how would they treat her? Perhaps she would be considered disloyal to the cause, a collaborator with the enemy. It was frightening to imagine what fate awaited her.

Once Elizabeth was dressed, she sat down in front of the mirror to arrange her hair, and it was then that she saw the physical evidence of her ordeal. Her neck was covered in bruises as were her arms and, she knew also, her legs. She had an abrasion over her left eye where she had fallen in the courtyard when set upon by the mad dogs who pawed her mercilessly. She shivered in spite of the warmth in the room.

"Don' ye feel well, den, miss?" the young Grenadian servant asked her kindly.

"Oh, I am all right. All right now," Elizabeth said absently, her fingers tracing the bruises on her neck. Perhaps Darcy would guess at her ordeal. How could they speak of it? A knock at the door and Barbara's voice roused her from her reverie.

"Elizabeth, may I come in?" The servant padded to the door and opened it. "Shall I have your breakfast sent up, or are you feeling well enough to join us?" Barbara continued. "Oh, and with all the excitement, I forgot to give you these. They arrived at St. George's just the day after you left for Paraclete."

Elizabeth looked down at what Barbara deposited into her waiting hands. It was several letters. The first one was from a place called Pemberley.

When they descended the stairs, the Darcy she remembered from so long ago was waiting for her there.

***

"Really, my dear," Gerard said after his breakfast coffee, as they were gathered in the sitting room. "I do think it wise to at least consider a short voyage to St. Lucia or Martinique until this rebellion is quelled. Little Edward is strong enough now. It might be best if you think you are ready to travel."

"I am ready enough," Barbara stated. "But I should not like to quit this place until I know what has become of Edward and my mother and father."

Elizabeth averted her eyes. Darcy noticed immediately. He looked at her, but she did not return his gaze. He knew, and suspected that Elizabeth did also, that the chances for survival for either of Barbara's parents or her brother were miniscule. They were saved any grimmer speculation by a knock at the door. The servants admitted a tall, dark-haired, handsome officer with a rather spectacular bandage on the left side of his face.

"A Captain Wickham here to see you, sir," said the butler. Elizabeth sent Darcy an astonished, inquiring look. He smiled serenely back at her.

"Show him in," said Gerard. In no time, there stood Wickham, hat tucked neatly under his arm. He raised his eyebrows in surprise at both Darcy's and Elizabeth's presence there. When he acknowledged them both, a conversation ensued explaining, in the most Spartan of terms, what the relationship was between them.

"So, this is a social call then, Captain Wickham," said Barbara.

"No, madam, I am afraid it is not," replied Wickham formally. "I had no idea that Miss Bennet and Mr. Darcy were here. I have come from President McKenzie and the British forces with news of your family."

"Are they alive, Mr. Wickham?" Barbara asked tremulously. Gerard rose from his seat and stood behind her, his hands upon her shoulders.

"I am afraid it is bad news," he said. "There were only three survivors of the massacre at Fedon's camp. Your parents and brother were not among them."

Barbara's face contorted, and she tried vainly to contain her emotions. She covered her face with her hands and wept openly. All in the room were at a loss until Darcy spoke.

"I will see you out, Wickham," he said and escorted Wickham from the room. Elizabeth ran to Barbara's side.

When they reached the door, Wickham grasped Darcy by the shoulder. "I am glad to see you, Darcy. I really am," he said.

Darcy smiled in spite of himself. "I am glad that you survived as well. What is this?" he asked, pointing to the bandage of Wickham's face. Wickham undid it and showed Darcy the wound.

"Great heavens, man, you will look like some duelling German," Darcy said.

"I may have many vices, Darcy, but you have put me off duelling," was Wickham's retort. Darcy looked at him to see if he was joking and laughed in spite of himself.

"You will never change," Darcy said.

"And you have changed so much as to be unrecognizable," Wickham said. He opened the door and stood upon the stair.

"Convince your friends to leave the island," Wickham said. He motioned Darcy to step over the threshold and with the door closed, began. "We were soundly routed in our raid on Fedon's Camp."

"I surmised as much from what I witnessed," Darcy interposed.

"We sent word to President McKenzie of our defeat. I do not know if you heard of what befell General Lindsay."

"Yours is our first news," said Darcy.

"He killed himself after the battle. No one knows why."

"Good Lord."

"I, personally," continued Wickham, "cannot understand it. Battles are won, and battles are lost. There is no need to be overly emotional." Wickham shrugged his shoulders. Darcy nearly smiled at Wickham's reaction.

"I do believe you are becoming quite the seasoned soldier," said Darcy.

"I think it suits me," Wickham continued. "Really, though, convince your friends to leave the island as soon as possible. St. George's is filling up with refugees from the plantations in the north. All the plantations have been raided by the rebels. Fedon's forces are gaining strength in arms, supplies, and men, but food is becoming scarce here."

"I do believe this family is well supplied," said Darcy.

"Perhaps," Wickham continued, "but soon they may be quarantined if they do not go now. There is Bulam fever about. I have heard them speak of it at headquarters. "

"And you? Are you staying in St. George's?" Darcy asked.

"I go where they tell me," Whickham said with a smile.

Darcy extended his hand. "Do be careful, George." Wickham took Darcy's hand and shoot it warmly.

"I will do that, you can be sure…Squire," he said mischievously, then mounted his horse and was gone.

Yellow fever. Yes, we must all go at once.

***

The next few days were a blur of activity. Elizabeth rarely saw Darcy and never did see him alone. She could see by his glances in her direction, the burning way his eyes met hers, that he longed to see her alone. They needed to talk of so many things, not the least of which, their future together. But did they have a future together?

Elizabeth was grateful for the activity and the respite from thinking too much. On the rare occasions when she saw Darcy, she vacillated between a desire to fling herself into his arms or run as fast as she could out of his sight. Nothing was resolved.

Also, alarmingly, Edward and his fate intruded upon her thoughts. His sister mourned him unreservedly, and Elizabeth did her best to outwardly sympathize. She had to admit to herself, however, that although she could wish death on no one, she was mightily relieved that Edward was no longer part and parcel of her life. In any case, they all had more immediate concerns.

Gerard told them all that they would be safer in Martinique, and now, knowing the fate of Barbara's family, there was no reason to remain in St. George's. The Spanish Governor of Trinidad, Don Jose Maria Chacon, had sent reinforcements to the British, and the combined armies were preparing for a protracted fight. Gerard procured passage for all of them and within two days they embarked on a small ship for safer waters.

Barbara pressed Elizabeth for details on her Mr. Darcy. Elizabeth explained what she could about his miraculous resurrection, what had happened in England, and what she knew of Darcy's remarkable voyage. Barbara was suitably impressed.

"He must love you a great deal," she said to Elizabeth on the deck of their sloop. "A man of his stature and breeding, to hire himself on as a deck hand of all things. It is quite extraordinary."

"I can scarcely believe it myself," said Elizabeth. "If you could only have seen him as I first knew him. I thought he was quite supercilious. I did misjudge him so."

"So, has he asked you to marry him yet?" Barbara asked. Even though she had been through unspeakable trials and had her dignity ripped from her, Elizabeth still could not adjust her sensibilities to the directness of those residing in the New World. Still, she supposed that directness was the correct way to respond to such a query.

"No, Barbara, he has not. But then, we have not had much time alone together since we arrived."

"You will marry him, though. Will you not?" Barbara asked. How could Elizabeth answer her? She did not want to tell her of the crimes committed against her person, and of her fall from grace. She wished Jane were making these inquiries. She would have told Jane all. When Elizabeth did not answer immediately, Barbara persisted.

"You do love him?" she asked incredulously. Elizabeth turned and the look on her face told Barbara all. Of course, she loved him.

"Barbara," she said before they parted. "You have made no mention of Edward to me."

Barbara looked down at her hands and did not speak for several moments. "I loved my brother, Elizabeth, but I knew he was not perfect. I thought a good woman might…"

Elizabeth said nothing but laid her hand upon Barbara's. She knew they would never speak of it again.

That evening, when dinner was finished, Elizabeth, not able to bear the stuffiness of her quarters below, walked up on deck and gazed into the glistening blue-black water as it slid nearly noiselessly beneath them. Just as silently, Darcy approached the rail, surprising her.

"I am sorry to startle you so," he said.

"I suppose I am still on my guard. The last month has not been easy," she replied, but did not look at him, still gazing on the water. He lay his hand on hers, and then curled his fingers beneath, holding it gently in his. She looked at him then.

Before he could speak she said, "So much has happened." This was meant to convey to him her unease and her doubts but missed their mark. They were quite alone at the prow of the ship, and he looked all about them and then took Elizabeth in his arms. She lay her head on his shoulder but felt like pulling away.

"Elizabeth, how I have longed for this moment," he said as he pulled away slightly and lifted her chin so that she had to look into his eyes. She wondered if he could see pain there. Her face must have revealed something because he asked, "Do you not feel the same as before?"

Tears sprang to her eyes. How could she tell him? "It is not that," she said, and turned away from him, breaking their embrace.

The cool night air rushed by. "What is it then?" he asked. She looked up sharply at his words, and her eyes softened. She could feel the tears sliding down her cheeks.

"Do not press me for answers, please," she said, and turned from him and nearly ran for the hatchway.

***

He stood in the tropical night, bewildered. His first thought was to pursue her and demand an explanation, but he immediately thought better of it. She was not one to be forced into anything…and then it dawned on him. Perhaps someone had forced her. Scenario after scenario flooded his mind. He tried to shake them off. *She hasn't said anything*, he thought to himself. *Do not jump to conclusions. She is just tired and still in mourning for her friends*, but the thoughts would not leave him. Then, thoughts of her captivity faded, and a new thought emerged. *Perhaps something had happened with Edward. No, that is impossible. She would not allow it and he was a gentleman, was he not?* He stood for a long time, looking out over the water, a myriad of convoluted thoughts squirming about in his brain.

Thus, the next two tortuous days passed, each not speaking more than a few words to the other. Because of their infant son, Barbara and Gerard were present only when meals were served. Their son took up the lion's share of their attention. An uneasy silence grew between Darcy and Elizabeth. Finally, they were informed by their captain that the voyage would take perhaps another day, and the last night aboard ship had yet to be endured. Another silent dinner ensued, and Elizabeth excused herself and retired to her cabin.

Darcy's patience was at an end. Things needed to be settled one way or another, at least in his mind, so at eight bells, he clattered down the gangway, resolving to demand an explanation from Elizabeth. He was even prepared to make a scene by banging on the door of her cabin until she admitted him, although that was not his fondest wish. As he approached her door, she miraculously emerged, not yet dressed for bed. He did not speak to her but walked directly in front of her, and with his determined stance, caused her to retreat from whence she came.

"Talk to me, Elizabeth. I can bear it no longer," he said. The ship was in constant motion and the cabin was small. They could not stand conversing for long. There was nowhere to sit but the bed.

"You should not be here," she said.

"Damnation," he spat, raising his voice. "I will not be put off."

"Keep your voice down, for your own sake, if not mine," she said. Gazing into his face, she seemed to be searching his eyes for something. What did she want of him? Finally, relenting, she sat down on the cabin bunk and motioned for him to join her.

The cabin was small, and their knees were touching as they sat together. Her hands were twisting her handkerchief and she would not meet his gaze. Neither spoke for a time. Finally, Darcy said, "I want you to be my wife, Elizabeth." He laid his hand on hers and she stopped fidgeting momentarily. She still would not look at him. A moment passed, and then another.

"I know," she said simply. "And if all was as it was before, I would not hesitate, but many things have changed." She stopped and took a laboured breath. "I have changed. You don't know."

He saw a tear fall from her lash onto his hand. Perhaps all was as he had feared. He realized then he had not prepared himself for this eventuality. He was keeping alive a hope that all could be as it was before. After a time, he asked, "Do you trust me, Elizabeth?"

She looked up at him and hurriedly wiped her eyes with her handkerchief. She breathed deeply again. "Of course, I trust you. I believe now that you would ruin yourself for me, and that is just what I am trying to prevent." She turned away from him then and closed her eyes.

"After all that we have been through together and apart, how can you worry over something as trivial as my social position?" he asked with almost an amusement in his voice.

She turned to him now, her eyes blazing. "That was your greatest concern from the day we first met, and now it means nothing to you?" She was nearly shouting.

He opened his mouth to speak, but she continued. "Right now, at this moment, all the social restraints we have both lived by seem far away and unimportant, but you know you must return to Pemberley and assume the responsibilities of your position and your family, and when you sit in your drawing room on an evening such as this, all that will matter is your rank and your position and your duty, and everything that has happened here will be a distant memory. You will return to it someday, fondly, and think yourself lucky to have escaped Elizabeth Bennet."

She tried to stand, but he gently, yet firmly, pulled her down beside him. He would hear her out, no matter the outcome. He had come this far and needed to know all.

"Do not tell me what I think or what is important to me," he said sternly. "I am the best judge of my own circumstances and my duty." He realized by the look on her face that he had shocked her somewhat and pressed his advantage. "If I am to 'escape,' as you have so bluntly put it, you must tell me what I am escaping from, Elizabeth." And as he said her name, his tone softened, and her eyes filled with tears again. She wiped them away hastily.

She looked at him a long while, her expression changing. He waited patiently. "I will tell you," she said finally. "But I will turn my back to you, because I cannot bear to see the revulsion on your face," she said, her last few words dissolving into sobs.

He knew then, there would be things he did not want to hear, that he dreaded to hear. He took a deep breath and released her.

She stood and groped her way to the porthole, holding fast to the rail that ran the length of the cabin. Darcy wanted to go to her and take her in his arms, but he did not dare. With her eyes fixed on the black sea glistening with moonlight, she began her tale.

She spared him nothing. Without flinching, she told him of Edward's courtship, and of his fall from grace. She told of her captivity, and the attempted rape by Viel, of her escape from him. Finally, she told him that, merely a day before he reached her, she had experienced the touch of her captors who fell upon her and the other women of the camp.

When she finished, she said to him, "So you see, I have been sullied. Not by one man, but by many men." She remained with her back toward him, and he sat quietly listening, not daring to stop her and ask her anything. None of the thoughts that had assailed him in the last few days had prepared him for what she told him. What should he do now? He loved her still, in fact, all the more for her courage in enduring all that she had endured for his sake back in England and then as a captive here in the islands. As a man, he could weather anything for her sake and blamed her for nothing. But she was right. He was not only a man, but the master of Pemberley. He had his family and position to think of. Was this to be the end of a long, excruciating road? Would it lead to nothing?

"Elizabeth," he said, his voice breaking. He stood and took a step toward her. Should he take her in his arms and reassure her that he loved her still and all that came before mattered not?

"Go, now," she said, still not facing him. He said nothing. She did not turn and look at him. He had to think. So, he left the cabin empty save for her, the door rocking open and closed with the motion of the sea.

***

Their arrival in Martinique was greeted with little fanfare. Many escaping planters and English residents of Grenada were arriving daily to escape revolution and yellow fever. Darcy and Elizabeth had little time alone together. Darcy was still wracked with conflict between what he felt to be right and what was expected of him. Above all, he loved Elizabeth. That feeling had only grown stronger with each passing day, yet, until he resolved what path to take, he could not speak to her. *What would she think of his silence?*

Every waking moment, when he was not engaged in preparations for their voyage home, he pondered Elizabeth's words. The words she used, "the men touched her, many men touched her in the most intimate of places." Obviously, she had been raped, and raped many times. She could be carrying a child, the child of one of the Grenadian slaves. Likely, she was. Although she was blameless, and the child also, it complicated matters considerably. Life, at times, was filled with cruelty. He thought again of his duty and his position. *What could be done?*

Nevertheless, he booked passage for himself and Elizabeth back to England. In small increments, everyone was again taking his or her place in society.

***

Elizabeth sat in her room in a small hotel in Fort-de-France, awaiting their departure the next day for England. She brooded on her own fate, her leaving Barbara, and the loss of Poppy, whose fate was unknown. So much had changed in such a short time, she did not know how she should ever reinsert herself at Meryton and carry on as before. Perhaps she would not, if the truth of her captivity and molestation ever reached the good people of the village. What would someone like Caroline Bingley think of her now? As she sat brooding alone, there was knock at the door. It was Darcy.

"May I come in?" he asked.

"Of course," she replied, her heart beating wildly. She must stop reacting to him in such a manner.

"There is something I wish to say," he began. She looked at him inquisitively. Dare she hope that he would throw over everything for her sake? "I love you, Elizabeth," he said, but in a tone of voice of one who was reading an interesting article out of the newspaper. "I love you with all my heart, and if I did not carry Pemberley on my back, I would marry you tonight, if you would have me."

She closed her eyes and let the balm of his words wash over her. *He did not despise her.* "You have forgiven me then?" she asked.

"Forgiven you?" he asked quite roughly. "Whatever for? Nothing that ensued from the time we left England was of your doing. Nothing. I cannot blame you for anything and I do not. However..."

At this, Elizabeth's heart sank. *However.* There it was. *Could it be any other way?* As she listened, he confirmed what she already knew. He was no more the master of his fate than she was the mistress of hers. His duties to the life he left behind must come first. Many people depended upon him and the Pemberley estate. He was held captive by his position in society even more than she. It was odd that she found this argument so insulting when she was first proposed to by Mr. Darcy, and now she found it not only reasonable but compelling.

He did not touch her in any way and remained at a distance as he spoke. She did not approach him either, since that would be unfair to both of them, but she longed for him to sweep her into his arms. He was trying mightily to maintain his previously aloof manner, but it seemed to Elizabeth that each time he looked directly into her eyes, he lost his train of thought. Perhaps he had not prepared himself sufficiently for what he intended to say. Perhaps he did not want to say these things at all. Their lives, through all their striving, had come to nothing.

"Do not despair, Elizabeth," he said at last. "You know that I cannot hide things from you and must tell you all that is in my mind and heart."

"I know that well," Elizabeth replied, recalling how, the first time he proposed to her, he made quite clear that all manner of disguising his true feeling was an abhorrence, even if those feelings may be hurtful to others.

"Do not despair, for we have come this far together, and I will reconcile all—" He stopped for a moment, pressing his fist to his lips as if to ponder, "I will reconcile my duty to my family with my deepest feelings for you. It is only that now, at this moment, I cannot see how it can be done."

He stood for a moment looking at her, and she at him. Then, looking down at the floor, he bounced upon his heels, turned, and left.

Elizabeth awoke the morning of her departure, dressed quickly, and made her way down the stairs. After Darcy's declarations the previous night, she had bid farewell to Barbara and implored her to take her leave that evening and allow Elizabeth to start afresh in the morning. Saying good-bye to her again would be too difficult. By the time she reached the doorway of the hotel, however, she saw Gerard, little Edward, and Barbara standing there waiting for her. She embraced her friend and they both promised through tears to write often. With that, Darcy gave her his hand and they stepped into the carriage that would take them to the port.

***

The return voyage to England should have been the happiest of days. Darcy had imagined them over and over again while lying in his hammock aboard the *Marlin*. He could not have foreseen this frustrating and unjust scenario. The ship was, fortunately, built for passengers. Darcy was able to secure private accommodations for Elizabeth and himself.

The moments when Elizabeth came on deck were more strained, although they still conversed with one another, the topics were mundane and stayed away from painful subjects. The seven weeks they would need to make the crossing would be unbearable if this state of affairs continued, but he could see no alternative. At least, he could see no alternative as yet.

***

They were five weeks at sea when Elizabeth was awakened in the middle of the night by the ship's evident pitching through heavy seas. She dressed quickly and exited her cabin, only to find many of the passengers running for the top deck in various states of panic or seasickness. Her first thought was of Darcy. She made her way to his cabin, but the door was open and he was not there. With many other passengers, she tried to make her way on deck. As she emerged from the hatchway, she was hit by a squall of nearly horizontal rain and the force of the wind nearly knocked her back. The lightning and thunder were fearful. Undeterred, she climbed on deck, only to see in a flash of light, Darcy clinging to the capstan as the ship pitched and fell.

He saw her and shouted at her, but she could not hear him. With great effort, he made his way over to her and grasped her by the arm.

"Get below," he bellowed through the wind.

"Come with me," she shouted back.

"No. Some of the crew were washed overboard when the gale hit. They are short-handed. I am going to help them get in the rigging," he shouted and pulled her toward the hatchway. Other passengers were trying to get on deck, but Darcy pushed them all back with enough authority that they obeyed him. She watched them scatter as they went below. When they reached the lower deck out of the rain, Darcy removed his coat, his waistcoat, his shoes, and stockings, much to Elizabeth's astonishment. He wrapped them in a neat parcel and handed them to her.

"Keep these for me," he said, his eyes sparkling. "I cannot climb the rigging in this hurricane dressed as a gentleman." He took hold of the ladder to climb through the hatchway again and the ship gave a terrible lurch, launching Elizabeth into him. He caught her and held her to him.

"You will be killed. Please, stay here," she cried.

"We will all be killed if we cannot get that sail in," he said and then, hesitating as if he were weighing his next action, he kissed her. She dropped all that she was to carry and threw her arms around him. He kissed her again. The ship lurched again, and he pulled himself from her embrace and turned to climb the stairs.

"Marry me, Elizabeth. If there is a child, even one that is half slave, we will raise him properly. I can promise you that," he said, and ran up the hatchway stairs. She followed up to the point of peering into the squalling wind and saw him grab hold of the rigging and dash upward as sure-footed as some jungle primate. The pounding rain forced her below and she lost sight of him. She gathered his things and made her way back to her cabin. Pinning herself in the bunk, she considered his words, *if there is a child, half-slave...* Whatever was he talking about? These thoughts perplexed her, but she abandoned them to her fear for Darcy's safety. What if she lost him now? To have endured all they had endured, only to have everything end in a shipwreck, all lost. She had not told him again that she loved him. What if she would never be able to again? It seemed to her that her joy would always be coloured with pain or fear. She must see him again and speak to him. There was so much unresolved between them. Still, he said that loved her. He asked her to marry him.

After what seemed like hours, the ship stopped trying to shake itself to pieces. Perhaps it was just wishful thinking on her part, but it did not seem ready to crack itself apart and spill them all into the roiling ocean. The sails must be in, or whatever it was that Darcy said they had to be. He did not return at once, so she assumed he remained on deck. The storm came upon them with such suddenness and ferocity that it had put them in mortal danger. The ship, although still surging, did not swing so precariously from side to side nor make those frightening cracking sounds that so alarmed her and the other passengers. Elizabeth, although trying to buttress her body against the violent movement, slid about as the ship climbed one mountainous wave after another, lurching and pitching. Thankfully, it did not capsize. It was madness to try to move about, so Elizabeth stayed below, bracing herself and praying for deliverance.

Finally, the howling of the wind decreased, and Elizabeth was able to stand and cross her cabin without being flung from one side to the other. Still, Darcy did not return. When he finally made his way to her cabin, he knocked at her door and she threw it open. He was again dressed and seemed in high spirits.

"I have come for my clothing," he said with a twinkle in his eye. He had barely said the words when she pulled him into her cabin and threw her arms around his neck. Darcy responded immediately, kissing her first on the mouth and then down her cheekbone and onto her neck. She wished he would never stop. Suddenly recovering himself, he turned and closed the door.

"We do not want to create a scandal," he said. She kissed him again.

"You taste of salt," she said. He laughed. She held him tight around the waist and nestled her head against his chest.

"I was so afraid for you," she said. She looked into his face again, and then recalling his words as he climbed out of the hatchway, said, "What did you mean, 'if the child was half-slave'?"

He looked at her incredulously. "You told me that..." He hesitated, and his eyes searched her face. "Let us sit down here and speak frankly with one another."

"Yes, of course," she replied. They sat on the edge of her bed, and she was sorely aware of the potential intimacy of the moment.

"Forgive me, Elizabeth, but I must bring up a painful subject," he said. She nodded mutely, and he went on. "You said that these men in the camp...that they..." He stopped again. He looked up, away from her face, and stared past her. She could see the agony in his expression. In that moment, she suddenly realized what he was thinking. He did not think of her in any way unworthy of him, but he was only concerned that a child might have resulted from the violence of that last day of her captivity.

"Oh," she cried. "Oh no."

"Elizabeth, I know this is difficult to talk about—" he continued.

"Oh, no, you do not understand. When I said that they touched me, I meant exactly that. They..." She motioned indistinctly with her hands, and it was he who now looked perplexed. She had nothing whatever to lose if she were to be completely frank with him.

"Let me show you," she said. This must have shocked him greatly for he jumped up from the bunk and hit his head on the bulwark. This broke the tension for her completely, and she began to giggle. He stood there, gaping at her, rubbing his head, and she took pity on him.

"I will show you on myself, fully dressed," she said, clarifying. He had to smile then, but his expression became abruptly serious.

"Perhaps it is too dreadful for you," he said.

"No, there must be absolute honesty between us. Absolute."

When she looked again into his face, she realized that perhaps what she was about to tell him would be as painful for him as it was for her. Perhaps more so. He undoubtedly had plans for the two of them, for his life at home, for the sort of mistress of Pemberley he had always been seeking. And she knew that he loved her. She remembered how much she suffered when he was so terribly wounded. He would have to suffer again for her. Still, some things must be endured for life to go on. These months of adventure and horror had taught her that much.

Not waiting for him to say anything that might discourage her, she stood and began. "They knocked me to the ground. There were many of them. I kicked and screamed and beat at them with my fists, but there were too many. When they had me on the ground, their hands were on me, all over my body. Some were here," she said, placing her hands on her inner thighs, "and some travelled up even farther..." She stopped for a moment, then went on. "They touched me. Their fingers probing...but only their fingers" She stopped and looked away.

He stepped toward her and touched her cheek, and she looked straight into his eyes. He pulled her forward and laid her head on his chest, putting his arm around her shoulder. She could hear his heart beating. He did not recoil from her, but held her very close, very tenderly.

"You must have a very low opinion of men," he said at last. She pulled back and looked up at him.

"Not all men," she said. "So now you know the whole truth. I will release you from your promise of marriage earlier. After all, it was in the heat of the moment."

"You will not release me, but you will consent to be my wife," he said decidedly.

"Can you live with what happened?" she asked.

"Can you?" he asked.

"I do not know yet," she said. "I will try to fulfil my wifely duties."

"Your duties," he said, a little too loudly, and detached himself from their embrace, holding her at arm's length. "I do not want a dutiful wife, but one who returns the love I am offering." His eyes were blazing.

"I do love you, Fitzwilliam," she said, using his given name for the first time. "I do not know yet how I will feel when—" and she stopped again. She thought of her wedding night, which might bring as much revulsion and nightmarish memories as joy.

His gaze at her was steady. "Life is filled with uncertainties," he said at last. "Together, I believe, we can conquer anything. Do you believe that?"

She answered him by embracing him again.

***

They arrived in Portsmouth in a little over a week. Darcy had suggested that the captain marry them at sea, but Elizabeth wanted her family to be in attendance, so she prevailed upon Darcy to wait. He could barely contain himself now and waiting even a week was agony for him. Once in Portsmouth, he arranged for them to leave the next day for Hertfordshire. Elizabeth suggested that they send word ahead of them, but the likelihood that they would arrive before the messenger was so great that they both resolved to surprise her family.

On the morning of their departure, Darcy sent by post a letter to his sister Georgiana at Pemberley, telling her that he was indeed alive and that soon he would bring his wife and her new sister home with him. He also sent a short and obligatory letter to his Aunt Catherine, also informing her of his impending marriage and his residence here on earth among the mortals.

They set their sights on Netherfield, and with three days' hard travelling, arrived the night of the third. For hours, Elizabeth had been deadly quiet, and Darcy became concerned. As they jostled their way through Meryton, she became suddenly serious. "I would like to tell my sister Jane all that befell me since our last meeting. Is that all right?" she asked. He liked that she deferred to him as if he were already her husband.

"You do not need my permission for that," he said. "What have you been thinking of this evening? I have not heard two words from you for hours."

"I was thinking that the only people who know about my captivity and...what happened there are myself, you, Poppy, and Julien Fedon and his rabble. All the others are dead. Perhaps even Poppy is dead." She stopped short and turned from him. He touched her hand. "For all the world that we know, it never happened," he said.

"But for me, it did happen, William," she said, calling him by the name he had requested she use. "I do not wish to disgrace you, but I do so want to confide in my sister."

He leaned across the carriage and took both her hands. "You may tell whomever you like, if it helps you to do so. I will soon be your husband and I will deal with all and sundry on your behalf."

She smiled at him. "My sister, only," she said. "Tongues will wag enough when we announce our marriage."

"So they will," he said. "Let them."

As they approached Netherfield, Darcy said, "I had not thought of it, but I wonder if Jane and Charles might be in town."

"Oh, I had not thought of that either," she said. "If they are in London, we will retreat to Longbourn. I am sure that my mother would love to see you." He knew she was teasing him, and he welcomed it.

They had spent the long journey concocting the "truth" that they would tell their families and all and sundry. Darcy had found passage on a ship after all. Yes, Elizabeth had been captured and held prisoner, but treated humanely. Society would be led to believe what it wanted to believe.

***

From the moment they reached England, Elizabeth could feel a shift in her perception. All the extraordinary events of the past few months began to become surreal as the familiarity of home washed over her. She could see it in Darcy's demeanour as well. He was more reserved and less candid with her with every passing mile. The constraints of their social positions became more and more acute.

Jane and Bingley were not in town; they were in the drawing room reading when the butler announced their visitors from the new world. Jane was large with child and nearly fainted at the sight of her sister. The two embraced as best they could under the circumstances and all began to talk at once.

"My, my, Jane, I seem to have returned just in time," Elizabeth shouted above the fray at last. Bingley smiled shyly, and Darcy squeezed his shoulder.

"We are to be married," Darcy said during the ensuing silence.

"I wanted you to be there," Elizabeth said to Jane, who began weeping copiously.

"This is how it has been for weeks," Bingley said to Darcy as he drew him aside. "Women who are with child are emotional, I think. Worse than usual."

"Come, Charles, pour us a glass of port, and let the women talk."

Elizabeth could see that her sister was in a delicate state all round, so she did not go into any detail as to her captivity and the brutality of all she had endured and witnessed. There was a lifetime to speak of such things. It was decided that they would go to Longbourn the following day and surprise the family. Also, a visit to Meryton was in order to announce the banns. Darcy could not wait the extra days it would require in order to be married at Pemberley. Sometimes when Elizabeth would look at him, she could see the hunger in his eyes.

The return to Longbourn was much as Elizabeth had expected. Her mother was swooning, Mary barely pulled her nose out of a book to say hello, and Kitty was all a-flutter. She took Elizabeth aside almost immediately to inform her that she was to make a better marriage to an even finer officer than her sister, Lydia.

Lydia, however, was most surprising. She was more subdued than Elizabeth had ever seen her. Elizabeth resolved to tell her of her Wickham's courage and his part in rescuing her. It was for Lydia's sake that she would inflate his virtues, the few he did possess. After all, without his irresponsible behaviour, she might have been mistress of Pemberley months ago with her dignity and virtue intact. Still, Lydia was a silly and ignorant girl, and what happened to her was not really her fault. It looked to Elizabeth as if she was paying enough of a price for her folly as it was, for here she was, home again, with a husband posted far away.

After luncheon, Darcy returned to Netherfield and Elizabeth had a moment to be alone with her father. She longed to confide in him, but his sensibilities would be overwhelmed with her disclosures; she was sure of that. Nevertheless, she found herself in his study. He was anxious to speak with her.

"Lizzy," he said finally as they settled into overstuffed chairs opposite one another, "are you sure that you want to marry this man?"

It was not the question Elizabeth had anticipated. "Of course, Papa. After all that has happened, how can you ask?"

"Much water has flowed under the bridge, Lizzy, and I do not want you to give up your whole life to a man you merely feel grateful to, although, I must admit, we have much to be grateful to him for." He looked confused, mostly by his grammar, she thought. She loved him very much at that moment, feeling, and rightly so, that of all the people in her family, he thought first of her welfare and secondly of everything else, even himself.

"I love him very much, Papa," she said. "I think that we can be happy together."

"Happiness," her father repeated. "It's an elusive thing, Lizzy, but everyone should have the opportunity to reach for it, I suppose." He sounded resigned.

She thought of her mother. "I am reaching for it, Papa," she said, and took his hands in hers.

The next few days went by in a flurry of activity. Wedding arrangements had to be made as well as travel plans for the newly married couple's return to Pemberley. Darcy and Elizabeth saw very little of each other, and she wondered if that would create doubts in his mind as to the suitability of their marriage. After all that had happened, she gave way to gloomy contingencies more often than before.

Elizabeth so wanted her sister to stand up with her, but alas, she was so big with child that she was confined at home. Lady Catherine sent word that Darcy should be married by license in his own home, but he confided to Elizabeth that he would ignore her. He was not about to wait another day, and that was that.

And so, with Bingley and her mother and father in attendance, and Mary, Kitty, and Lydia standing as bridesmaids, Mr. Fitzwilliam Darcy and Miss Elizabeth Bennet plighted their troth. There were flowers, and a blue bridal gown that had been fashioned in haste in town. The newspaper had an article that took nearly half a column. All was as it should be. The young couple left the church, had a lovely wedding breakfast at Netherfield, and departed for Pemberley.

It was not until they were face-to-face in the carriage that the import of what had happened descended on them both. Elizabeth could feel Darcy's gaze upon her but dared not interrupt his thoughts. Perhaps she should have said something, as he looked as though he was considering the possibility of exercising his husbandly prerogative right there in the carriage.

"Elizabeth," he said at last. "We will be stopping overnight soon. I have arranged for a private room at the top of the house," he continued. She looked at him and tried to smile. There was a war going on inside her. She loved him, and desired him, and at the same time, did not want any man to touch her again.

Before long, they were settled in a small but airy room in a roadside inn. It was set back from the road and quieter than the taverns and public houses than were its neighbours. The innkeeper's wife had made the bed with fresh linens and there were flowers in the room.

After they enjoyed a modest repast of cold beef and boiled turnips, Elizabeth and her husband were left alone for the night. Really, she thought, they should be at Pemberley where she could make herself ready in a separate room, and...

She could feel Darcy's eyes burning into her. She knew from experience that men's desires were overpowering, and she could see that fire in her husband's eyes. Darcy, for his part, pulled off his jacket and waistcoat and sat down on a stool in the corner and began to remove his boots. As he stood in his stocking feet and began to undo his shirt buttons, he looked up at Elizabeth, who was standing stock still watching him. He stopped. Then he crossed the room and took her in his arms.

"Are you all right?" he asked. She looked up at him with a faraway look in her eyes, as if she was not quite present. She was trembling.

"Of course," she said, shaking herself free of thoughts that conjured themselves up from her memory. "Of course," she repeated, and turned her back to him. "Could you help me undo the clasps?" she asked, and then turned her head to look over her shoulder at him. She tried to smile.

He said nothing and began undoing the back of her gown. Using both his hands, he pushed open the back and let the gown fall over her shoulders and puddle on the floor. Gently laying his hands on her shoulders, he turned her around to him. She was standing only in a chemise that fastened at the front. He said nothing to her, but Elizabeth could see the desire in his expression.

"My mother packed a nightdress for my wedding night," she said softly. At first, he smiled and then, to her surprise, he began to laugh.

"I doubt it will even be unpacked tonight, my love," he said. In spite of herself, she began to laugh too. Then suddenly, his face became quite serious and he touched her cheek. She looked up at him and noticed that her trembling had stopped. He leaned in and tenderly kissed her on the mouth. He did it again, and again, and then began to trace the curve of her throat with his lips. She was suddenly a vessel of desire. A warm, throbbing sensation began in her nether regions and her heart poured out so much heat that she thought perhaps he could feel it through his clothing.

The clothing covering his chest was not to be there for long. When his lips reached her mouth again, he stepped back and undid his breeches. As they fell to the floor, Elizabeth could see his rampant member waving about under his shirt like a triumphant flag bearer. She didn't know if she was amused, alarmed, or embarrassed. Before she could react, he had tipped her onto the bed, and felt his hand undoing the bows that held the straps of her chemise. With both his hands, he pulled the straps forward, pulling the chemise down towards her hips, exposing her breasts. Then he stopped and gazed at her for a long moment.

In spite of her desire and her love for him, she began to cry. She turned her head first one way and then another in a vain attempt to hide her tears. He touched her cheek and then kissed first one eye and then the other.

"I am sorry," she croaked out, and then slid out from under him. Elizabeth sat up in the bed, her knees pulled to her chest. She was trembling.

He said nothing, but sat next to her, his arm around her shoulder. Her first thought was to pull away and bury her head in a pillow, but she knew he would misinterpret her actions and think that she did not want him. The odd thing was, she did want him, but something inside of her was at war with her desire. Flashes of Viel's attempted ravishment and of her attack in the Fedon compound came reeling back. She leaned her head against his chest and tried to regain control of herself.

"I am sorry," she said again.

"It does not matter, my love," he said gently, kissing her forehead. "We have our whole lives together."

She suspected that he really did not feel that way. He had waited so long, that now, at the very moment when his desires were to be fulfilled, she had stopped him in mid-leap, as it were.

His words, however, made her realize that he would do anything for her, even deny himself their wedding night. She looked up at him and decided; she tore away the rest of her bodice and pulled away her shift so that she was naked in the candlelight. She could hear his breathing coming rapidly as he devoured her with his eyes.

"Come to me, my love," she whispered as she pulled him toward her. He tore away his shirt, and for the first time, there was nothing between the communion of their bodies. He kissed her earnestly and she opened her mouth to him. She remembered that embrace in her Uncle Gardiner's parlour, the first glimpse of what there would be between them.

He kissed his way down her neck and then pulled away from her, leaning on his elbow. With his other hand he took hers and kissed the inside of her palm and then guiding her, took her hand and placed it upon his turgid member. She touched it gingerly at first, and then ran her hand up and down its length. She was surprised at the softness of his skin.

He moaned, and she saw the ecstasy on his face. She touched him again, caressing him. At last he could stand it no longer.

"I must have you now, Elizabeth," he whispered as he rolled on top of her. She let go of him then, but he guided her hand back.

"Show me," he said to her, and gently eased himself between her legs.

She could feel the tears starting again but placed her other hand at the back of his neck and pulled his face into the crook of her neck, so he would not see her eyes filling again.

She opened her body to him and guided him to her most intimate spot. Memories of the violation she endured sprang up in her mind, but she fought to suppress them. She could feel him moving slowly, very slowly. She knew he was trying to be tender with her.

"I will try not to hurt you," he rasped into her ear, and then entered her.

It was not what she expected. Her body was receptive to him, and all was liquid within her. Still, she had never experienced a man and his fullness before and felt almost like he was too much to bear, but bear it she must.

He began to rock back and forth, and, recalling what she had clandestinely witnessed between Edward and Poppy that night she had come upon them together, she wrapped her legs around Darcy's and rocked with him. The unpleasant tightness began to ease, and she felt physical sensations that she never dreamed possible. She began to meet every one of his thrusts and felt herself moaning and crying out with him.

The rocking became an earnest pumping and he grasped her hard, his breathing rapid and shallow, reminding her of a galloping horse. He shuddered suddenly and held her in a tight embrace. She rocked into him twice more and a spasm rocked her entire body. It surprised and exhilarated her. She did not want him to leave her.

He moved slightly, and she whispered to him, surprising herself, "Do not withdraw, please. I want to feel you inside of me."

He kissed her neck once more and then looked into her face. This time, his eyes were moist and so open to her that she felt she could see down into his soul.

"I love you so much, Elizabeth," he said, and his head rested again in the crook of her neck.

"I love you too," she murmured.

They awoke the next day entwined.

Chapter 17

Wickham sat in the dripping rain forest, wondering how the tropics could be so intolerably hot and sweltering one minute and so cold and uncomfortable another. The rebellion was entering its fourth month, and it seemed to Wickham that Fedon would never run short of supplies or ammunition. The results of the British blockade were not evident as yet. Even the French, who had been rumoured initially of aiding Fedon when they really had not, began sending troops from Guadeloupe to aide Fedon. No doubt, they were hoping that the British forces were enough weakened that they could retake the island for themselves. Wickham never considered that they would have committed themselves to Fedon because of French revolutionary principles. He knew enough about life to recognise that there was precious little altruism to be had. Still, he commanded his own unit of men, and had been decorated in battle, so if he could survive the next few months, he would quit the army and return to his wife in England. Lydia had become much more desirable to him now that he was fighting a ground war in the bush.

"Captain Wickham, sir," Foster's voice interrupted Wickham's thoughts.

"Yes, Foster, what it is it?" he asked, swatting at the midges that were harassing him.

"Message for you, sir, from Sir Abercromby," he said curtly.

"Sit down, Foster," Wickham said as he took the tiny folded paper from Foster's hand.

"Can't sir," he replied. "'Ave to return quickly. Orders, ye know."

"Yes, I know," Wickham said ruefully. "Here, Foster, before you go, could you take this letter with you? It is to my wife."

Foster looked at him, surprised. "Din know ye had a wife," he said, then added, "Sir."

"Just in case, Foster, you know," Wickham continued. "Hand deliver it." And with that he put two coins in Foster's hand along with the letter. Foster handed the money back.

"I will do it for you just the same, sir," he said, then looking at the letter. "Meryton... sounds like a nice place."

"It is," Wickham said wistfully. "I never realized it before." Foster took his leave.

Wickham liked Foster. He had proved an able and agile scout and the men liked him. Although he was not expected to fight at their side, he had on occasion, when there was no alternative, distinguished himself in hand-to-hand combat. He confided to Wickham on more than one occasion that he had no taste for it and told him he began to regret not following "Squire" back to the bosom of his native land.

As it was, they were playing a cat-and-mouse game with Fedon, his rebels, and the French, to which there was no end in sight. The governor and the rest of the prisoners who were slaughtered on the day of Elizabeth's escape lay in shallow graves on the mountaintop. *At least,* thought Wickham, *I am still alive. When the rain stops, perhaps I could entice a few of my fellow officers into a game of cards.* He needed to win back next month's pay.

***

The homecoming to Pemberley was greeted with much fanfare. Georgiana ran out to greet her brother and new sister almost before their carriage reached the entry. The newly married couple had little time to themselves, however, as Lady Catherine arrived the next day.

Upon seeing Darcy for the first time she exclaimed, "Upon my word, Darcy, you have the complexion of a red Indian." This caused Elizabeth to turn suddenly to look at her husband and observe him closely. She had grown used to seeing him with his brown face, and it no longer looked odd to her. Lady Catherine brought both of them completely back into the reality of their life here at home.

As Lady Catherine began her inquisition, Elizabeth's mind drifted to their wedding bed, where she could see her fingers running through the hair on Darcy's bronzed chest and then moving down to touch all below his waist that remained milky white. She visibly shivered.

"Are you catching cold, Miss B—" Lady Catherine began, but then checked herself,

"Mrs. Darcy?"

"No, Aunt," Elizabeth replied boldly. She could simultaneously see Lady Catherine visibly start at the word "aunt" and observed her husband's amusement.

"So, tell me, Darcy, however did you book passage to Grenada?" Lady Catherine asked, looking at the two of them suspiciously.

"There is little that money will not buy," Darcy said vaguely. His aunt opened her mouth to speak, then closed it once again. Elizabeth waited for a more thorough inquisition, but none came. It was then she was grateful for the social niceties that governed their lives. She knew his aunt would not speak of it again.

"Really, Mrs. Darcy, you should have advised your husband to spend less time outdoors during your voyage. He looks positively...native," she admonished.

"At the time, he was not yet my husband," Elizabeth said demurely, which caused Lady Catherine's eyes to narrow. The sparring continued until after luncheon.

Elizabeth knew that Darcy was desperate to dive into his duties as lord of the manor that had been so long neglected. He excused himself the minute his aunt retreated to rest in the afternoon and adjourned to his study, where his desk was piled with documents and ledger books. She would look in on him occasionally, and he was so immersed, he did not even hear her enter. She left him undisturbed.

Elizabeth had her own duties to perform as the new lady of the house. Luckily, she had the aid of Georgiana, who knew every nook and cranny of Pemberley and introduced Elizabeth to everything a young hostess and mistress of a house would need to know. There was some resentment on behalf of the old housekeeper, who had had free rein to run the great house as she had seen fit these many years, but change was upon all of them, and Elizabeth was learning to be firm without being confrontational, most of the time. It would not do for the staff to run roughshod over her, so she stood her ground. Sometimes she would surprise herself at how adept she was becoming at giving orders.

And so, many days passed until one day a message arrived from Netherfield. Elizabeth and Darcy were now aunt and uncle to a fine boy born to Jane and Charles Bingley. They decided to call him Simon, after Charles's cousin. They had been considering Edward, after their friend who had been killed in the slave rebellion in Grenada. Elizabeth was none too pleased but said nothing to her sister. In fact, upon arriving at Netherfield two weeks after the birth, Elizabeth had no desire to tell Jane anything that had befallen her in Grenada, save what she and Darcy had agreed upon during that carriage ride from Portsmouth to Meryton. She had confided in her husband, and that was enough. It was odd, but she felt as though she could tell him anything and he would accept it. He had become her friend and confidant as well as her lover and husband.

She travelled alone to Netherfield as Darcy's long absence from his duties necessitated his remaining at home. It was a warm and wonderful feeling holding her new nephew in her arms for the first time. He was so small and delicate that she felt anxious at first holding him. When she put her finger near his tiny hand and he clasped it so strongly, she began to relax. Jane was filled with motherly love, and exhausted as well. After a brief visit of only a week, Elizabeth made the journey home. She had already received three letters from Darcy in that time and thought perhaps she needed to go home and resume her wifely duties in their entirety.

The first evening after she arrived, she felt oddly apprehensive. Darcy did not know that she had to steel herself somewhat to accept his lovemaking as the trauma of recent months was still very much alive within her. They had finished dinner and he was again in his study examining the farm ledgers and grumbling to himself.

"Is something wrong, dearest?" she asked him absently, still engrossed in a book she was reading.

"No. Yes. Not really," he said. He put down his pen and sat, staring at her. She sensed his gaze and turned in his direction. This time, it was she who closed the book and walked over to him.

He did not move but gazed unblinking at her. Her desire for him was welling up inside of her so strongly that it frightened her a little. These desires seemed to her to have strengthened during her absence from him. From her mother's pre-wedding talk and even the talk of women around her, such desires were unseemly, yet she had them. She ran her fingers through his black hair and bent down over him and kissed his waiting mouth. He pulled her to him and she fell into his lap, where he wrapped her in his arms.

He kissed her over and over again, and his lips travelled down her neck to her breasts.

"I missed you," he murmured.

"Wait," she said, pulling away slightly. "The servants." He closed his eyes and sighed. "Let us go to bed," she said and pushed herself to her feet.

He did not get up immediately to follow her. "Give me a moment," he said, his face colouring. She smiled and smoothed her hair. Their embrace was not broken a moment too soon as there was a knock at the door.

"Come in," Darcy said without hesitation.

"I do beg your pardon, sir," said John. "Will there be anything else?" Darcy looked deferentially at Elizabeth. She answered.

"No, John, thank you," she said with a smile. "We will be retiring shortly."

Darcy was already in bed when Elizabeth entered their room. The only light was the fire in the grate. The spring evenings were cold and damp, and it was such a luxury for Elizabeth to have a fire whenever she desired.

When she emerged from her dressing room, she was adorned with a white, embroidered nightdress that gathered beneath her shoulders. They were bare. She could see the intoxicating desire in her husband's eyes.

"My god, you do look beautiful," he said to her.

"This is the nightdress that was not invited to our wedding night," she said teasingly. It was odd, but with every night she spent with him, the ordeal she endured on Grenada seemed to fade just a little. Now she felt as though she was initiating this intimacy between them, and it gave her a feeling that was a mixture of guilt and power.

"Come here," he said, and she came to the bed and climbed in beside him. Darcy kissed her first on the mouth and then his lips and tongue slowly worked their way down her neck to her collarbone. She softly touched his face.

"William," she said.

"What?" he said distractedly.

"Is it wrong for me to desire this physical union with you?" He stopped kissing her, looked into her face and then smiled.

"I surely hope not," he said, laughing.

"Please, do not laugh at me," she said petulantly.

"I am not," he said, still amused. "Really. Why do you ask such a thing?"

She had pulled away from him now and sat up in bed. He was looking in her face, and she could see he was trying desperately to be patient.

"I was always told that the man was the one who had strong needs that must be fulfilled, and that women were there to fulfil them. No one ever has mentioned a woman's needs," she said.

"So, you feel that you have these needs, similar to a man?" he asked.

"I wish you would not express it that way," she said. "But yes, right now, I feel quite alarmed by my desires."

He smiled widely. "I am your husband, Elizabeth, and I am willing to do whatever you need me to do to make you happy."

"I fear that I may be quite insatiable," she said, her eyes becoming moist.

"Do with me what you will," he said, and lay back in the bed, his arms and legs spread apart, stretching his nightshirt.

"You are teasing me," she said.

"I am not," he said quite seriously. "I am giving myself over to your will." With that, he closed his eyes. She was surprised by his acquiescence as well as her own boldness. Perhaps he thought she was teasing him, but she most assuredly was not. For the first time, she felt that she had power over him. No, that was not quite right. No, she had power over the situation. That was it. For the first time, she felt that she was in control of what was happening with her own body. And soon, with his.

Elizabeth's hands lifted his nightshirt up over his thighs, past his chest and then yanked it up off his arms and over his head. He gazed at her and she was devouring him with her eyes as he had done her on their wedding night. He did not say a word.

She began at his feet, rubbing her thumbs into the balls of his feet and then running her hands softly over the hair on his legs until she reached his thighs. She then began kissing her way up the inside of his thighs, first one and then the other.

His breath was coming in short bursts by now, and perhaps it was that signal that made her stop her ministrations short of their mark.

Elizabeth, for her part, was lost in her desire. She wanted to touch him all over, to kiss every hollow of his body, to take him into her mouth. She could hear his breathing and thought it was time for him to touch her.

Rather than removing her nightdress, she took his right hand and guided it up under the skirt to her breasts. She did the same with his left hand. Still clothed, he caressed her budding nipples. After a time, she guided his hand between her legs, and with his thumb he began to massage that tiny nub that they had both discovered on their first night together.

She grasped his hand and began to rock herself against his fingers. She pulled his hand away, and bent over him and then, to his utter surprise, began kissing his standing member. She heard him cry out and felt him buck his hips upward. Still caressing him in her hand, she took him into her mouth. He continued rocking into her waiting mouth.

She released him and, swaying back on her heels, pulled her gown over her head and threw it on the floor. At that point, she did not know what possessed her. Swinging her leg over his body, she lowered herself over him until she had engulfed his manhood into her throbbing opening.

His expression was priceless. She could see in his face, what? Desire? Surely. But astonishment too. He was astonished at her. As soon as he was firmly seated inside of her, she stopped moving her hips and began to run her hands over his chest, lightly touching the copious hair that covered it and running her fingers in circles around his nipples. She was enraptured as she traced her fingers along the sculpted curve that ran from his hips to his groin.

His hips began to buck, first withdrawing himself nearly to the tip and then driving back into her. She toppled over, and he threw himself on top of her, grasping her shoulders and driving himself in and out of her, matching her rhythm with his. She entwined her legs about his lower back, and with urgency she met every one of his thrusts.

Suddenly, he exploded inside of her and collapsed on top of her, his body and hers slick with sweat. She noticed then that she had demanded so much of his member that it had retreated considerably, and yet she was still burning bright with desire.

To Elizabeth's amazement, without speaking, he slid down the length of her body, and caressing her thighs, moved them wide apart. This was not what she expected. Her breath came in short bursts. Were the thoughts of her capture and abuse to ruin this moment for her now? No, she trusted this man. She trusted him completely.

Elizabeth relaxed in anticipation. Her Darcy had given himself over to her and now she would do the same. Whatever was he doing? She saw his face disappear between her legs and then felt the most amazing physical sensation she had ever felt in her life. His tongue and mouth were in her nether regions, kissing, exploring, caressing until she rolled herself up and took his head in her hands, nearly engulfing him in her repeated waves of ecstasy. When her tremors had stopped, he kissed her again, and then rose to face her.

"My God, Elizabeth," was all he could say. She smiled.

The next day she awoke before him, and in a wave of pleasure mixed with scandal she remembered all that had happened the night before. She went immediately to the basin and sponged herself off, being careful not to make a sound so as not to wake her sleeping husband. What had she done? Was she some sort of oddity that enjoyed the pleasures of the flesh as much as a man, or was she just a common strumpet? What must he think of her? Perhaps she was thinking too much. She would dress and see what the day would bring.

***

When Darcy finally opened his eyes, the sun was streaming through the window and Elizabeth was gone. He rolled on his back and closed his eyes for a moment more, remembering what had occurred between them the night before. She was all that he had hoped for, no, more than he had hoped for. She was all to him: his helpmeet, his wife, his lover. They had begun so badly, due most assuredly to his pride and arrogance, and now? Now he knew she was the love of his life. Then his thoughts turned toward darkness again as they were wont to do. He chastised himself for putting his pride, his duty, his estate before her. Still, he was the master of Pemberley, and with that office came great responsibility. Knowing that his thoughts could turn round and round in his head if he let them, he rose from bed to wash. Then he would go find his wife.

***

Elizabeth was at breakfast when Darcy arrived. She looked up at him anxiously for a moment, and he smiled at her. He walked straight over to her and kissed her right in front of the servants. She smiled at him.

"You awoke early," he commented, taking his seat. His breakfast appeared before him.

"Yes," she said coyly. "I slept uncommonly well."

His smile broadened. "As did I," he said and reached for her hand. She gave it to him. When his coffee arrived, he let go and attacked his breakfast with great gusto. When the last of the servants had left the room, he turned to her.

"I am so happy that I married you," he said. She let out a sigh of relief. Perhaps she had misjudged what men think is important.

***

The young couple then really began their life together. The days were filled with managing the estate, visits to the tenants, and small, infrequent social gatherings. Elizabeth's uncle and aunt, who first brought her to the Pemberley estate as a tourist, visited now as family.

Darcy was congratulating himself that no one, not even his family, knew the true nature of what had transpired in his quest for Elizabeth. He had told her many times that he did not give a fig who knew, but the truth was, he did care. He cared very much for his name, his reputation, his position, and his family heritage. It was not as if he would put any of that before his beloved and her welfare, but he felt a certain peace settle over his soul knowing that there were no whispers about them in his social circle.

There were, however, vestiges of Elizabeth's ordeal that he hoped time would eventually alleviate. When his wife was particularly tired or something during the day brought her mind back to Grenada, she would sleep fitfully, and sometimes awaken screaming in the night. Her eyes would be wide open, and yet she would not recognize him when he spoke to her. There was nothing to do but wait out the episode and then awaken her gently. She would open her eyes again and, this time, see his worried face above hers.

"Have I been dreaming again?" she would ask. She felt cold and clammy to the touch and looked thoroughly exhausted. He would nod and gently stroke her cheek.

After one such restless night, he left her sleeping. He dressed and went about his duties. There was still much to unravel from his long absence. After a light breakfast, she arrived in his study, while he was working on his correspondence.

"There you are," she said, smiling. He immediately rose and took her hands in his. "You look tired, my dear," she said. "And I am afraid it is all my fault."

"Nonsense," he said, and kissed her cheek.

"I have been thinking about Poppy lately, and feeling quite guilty," she said, taking her place on the settee. Darcy joined her there.

"There was nothing we could do," he said soothingly. "I asked her to come with us, but she refused. Surely it was her decision."

She looked at him, her face all concern. "I should never have left her there. What has become of her? I also had another friend, in the camp. Her name was Sally. Her fate..." She trailed off. He said nothing. *What was there to say?* Momentarily, he thought of his friend Foster, whose fate was also unknown. They had both left people behind. Darcy took her hand but was at a loss as to how to comfort her. After a few minutes she stood up.

"Well, my dear, I am wasting your time," she said in an attempt at cheer. "I will find Georgiana and insist that she give me a piano lesson."

Darcy stood and helplessly watched her go. There was so much of her still in Grenada, still in that ordeal. For that, he could do nothing. With all his wealth and all his social position, he could do nothing.

As the leaves began their transformation, Darcy began to notice a change in Elizabeth. Her aspect became pale and her eyes began to have a dark and haunted look. Many times, she would not join him for breakfast, and if she did, she would have only tea. It worried him, but she reassured him that she was fine. By afternoons, she seemed to regain her appetite, but nevertheless seemed moody and unpredictable. He attributed all to the adjustment to married life, and to having time now to reflect at length on the events of the past year.

As the wind grew stronger, and the leaves had all but left the trees, November arrived and so did a letter from Grenada. It was addressed to Darcy. John brought it in, and until Darcy knew its contents, he swore John to secrecy. There was no point in upsetting Elizabeth further, considering the likelihood of bad news.

The hand on the envelope seemed familiar, and when Darcy opened it, he clenched his teeth. He supposed he should have expected its contents.

Dear Brother,

My wife has written me on several occasions and mentioned your marriage to her sister, Elizabeth. I hope that you are well and that your lovely wife has begun to forget her unfortunate experiences here in Grenada.

Since your departure, we have steadily chipped away at the insurgents and our victory seems assured, if somewhat protracted. Your man, Foster, has proved invaluable to us. He is a clever fellow and loyal but cannot be persuaded to join the army. For that, I cannot blame him. Still, he is adept at jungle warfare and brought us much intelligence of the enemy.

That brings me to the purpose of this letter. During the time I have had the privilege of defending His Majesty's holdings in the West Indies, I have incurred some rather troublesome debt that has put me in an awkward position with my superiors. It has not escaped me that you have provided me with a generous allowance and that I also receive a salary from the army, but my dear wife has insisted on renting a house in town for us in the hopes that I will soon be home. This, in itself, is...

And so, the letter continued on in this vein until Darcy crushed it in his hand and got up from his desk to throw it into the fire. A thought, however, stopped him in mid-stride. He took the letter to his desk again and straightened it out. Wickham was a spendthrift and a rascal, but he made no mention of holding knowledge that could ruin both his and Elizabeth's reputation. For Darcy's part, if scandal broke, he could conceivably retreat to Pemberley and never visit London again in his life, but he would not want that for Elizabeth or for his sister, Georgiana. Also, there would eventually be children, and their future depended on being received in society.

Darcy finished reading the letter and sat back in his chair to think. There was a knock at the door and Elizabeth entered. She did not look well. He rose from his seat to greet her.

"How are you feeling, my love?" he asked.

"I am quite well; do I not look so?" she asked.

She decidedly did not, but he would not say so.

"I have been thinking of Poppy again," she admitted. He thought to mention the letter from Wickham, but then, it contained no news of Poppy, so what would be the point? He did not want to encourage her brooding.

He looked into her unhappy face and could think of nothing else but to take her into his arms. She rested her head on his shoulder for a moment.

"Would you like to spend Christmas with your family?" he asked, apropos of nothing.

"You are trying to distract me," she said with a smile. "I do love you for it, and all the more for putting yourself in the same house as my dear mother." This made her laugh and him as well.

"I believe I have a visit to make to the Taylors' today. Their little one is ill with croup and Martha has made some sort of concoction in the kitchen that she swears will cure it." She smiled again at him. "I will be home for tea," she continued, kissed him, and withdrew. He resolved then to invite all her family for Christmas.

He sat again at his desk and looked at Wickham's letter. It then occurred to him that he had a willing and able agent in Grenada who could be the answer to his prayers.

It was nearly Christmas when they finally received news from Grenada. A letter from Wickham to Lydia intimated that finally, the reinforcements commanded by Sir Ralph Abercromby were making headway against the insurgents. Wickham had no idea when he might be home, but he gave the impression that the tide was turning in favor of the British. Wickham did not mention Foster again, which was not necessarily a cause for concern, but worried Darcy nonetheless. He did not share his anxiety over Foster with Elizabeth.

This news of the failing rebellion did not cheer Elizabeth. She told Darcy she feared that the reprisal for those supporting the insurrection and aiding Fedon would be hanging and was not at all convinced that the English would spare the women. During wartime, there was nothing anyone could do. He knew she was beside herself with worry for Poppy. *This damned helplessness.*

***

By the fifteenth of December, Darcy and Elizabeth were already ensconced at Netherfield for the holidays. Jane had invited them there soon after Elizabeth suggested that they meet at Pemberley. The baby did not travel well, and it was easier for Elizabeth's parents to meet at Netherfield as well, though a disappointment for her mother and Lydia especially that they would not be guests at Pemberley. The two of them mentioned this disappointment to Elizabeth often.

Little Simon was babbling and pulling himself up on the furniture only to sit down roundly as he lost his balance. Elizabeth watched Darcy surreptitiously as Simon grasped his uncle's fingers and took halting steps, squealing with delight. As yet, there was no sign of a son and heir in their future, which added to Elizabeth's anxiety.

The entire family were met for Christmas dinner and Jane proved to be a gracious and efficient hostess. As all the gifts were opened and admired, Elizabeth excused herself from the jollity and walked over to the window to watch the falling snow and gathering gloom. She was assured of her solitude and her thoughts for a moment, as Darcy was the complete prisoner of Mrs. Bennet, who was demanding his attention, and he was fixed to the spot. It was Jane, however, who left the family group and joined her sister.

"Thank you for this lovely Christmas," Elizabeth said, putting her arm around her sister's waist. "I am so happy to be here."

Jane was silent for a moment, and looked as if she wanted to say something, but did not. Elizabeth noticed immediately. "Jane, what is it?" she asked. Jane then did something absolutely extraordinary. She took her hand and put it on Elizabeth's lower abdomen. Elizabeth looked at her quizzically, and then Jane spoke. "Are you expecting a child, Elizabeth?" she asked.

Elizabeth gave a visible start. She turned immediately to look at Darcy. His gaze must have followed her, for she could see he was looking at her with concern. He remained, however, in the clutches of her mother. Mrs. Bennet would brook no distractions. She was going on and on about the gift she'd received from the Gardiners. Elizabeth could hear her across the room. She turned her attention back to Jane.

Elizabeth smiled. "I have no idea. How does one tell?" With that Jane began to ask her questions about her appetite, fatigue, and then more intimate questions. Elizabeth told her all. Jane was smiling.

"I am not a doctor, dear sister, but I can tell you that I believe you are carrying a child," she said. Elizabeth gave a small shriek, and Darcy came running.

***

As Elizabeth entered her confinement, she received a long-anticipated letter from Barbara. When Darcy put the letter into her hands, all he said was, "I hope it is good news." His expression betrayed other thoughts. Both of them had experienced warfare firsthand and knew the quixotic nature of events that unfolded when all law was suspended. *Would Barbara have news of Poppy? How would she? Would she even think to mention her?* For all her kindness toward Elizabeth, she knew Barbara entertained the same opinions as her brother Edward. She accepted slavery as a way of life and therefore accepted the demeaning belief that somehow slaves were less human than their masters. Elizabeth knew that was not only untrue, but terribly destructive.

As she held the letter in her hand, her thoughts returned to Edward. From time to time, when she was alone and given to reverie, she would think of him. How different her life would have been if she had married him in ignorance. If Fedon had planned his rebellion to start in a month's time, if she had not sought out Poppy that fateful night, she might have been his wife. She might now be bearing his child. How close she had come to a sudden turn in her fate where all would have been different.

Her husband was still standing over her as all these thoughts churned in her head. He had become very attuned to her, and she to him. It was as if they could read each other's thoughts. How upset would he now be if he knew she was thinking of Edward? Perhaps it was not her thoughts he read, but her moods. That was it. She looked up at him and smiled.

"I will leave you in peace," he said and kissed the top of her head. She watched him leave and tore open the envelope.

Dearest Elizabeth,

The rebellion is finally over. Gerard is already making plans for all of us to return to St. George's. He says we'll plant cocoa by next year at Paraclete. I suspect it is in shambles, perhaps burnt to the ground. In a way, I know I should not say this, but I hope that it is destroyed and that we need to build anew. I do not want to walk through that house and meet all my ghosts.

The rebellion ended in June. The British eventually beat back both the rebels and the French, who came to Fedon's aid at the last moment. I suspect they did it to spite us, but finally realized their eventual defeat at our hands and gave up. We heard some German colonel joined forces with us and attacked Fedon from two sides. Many of Fedon's men, facing defeat, actually took their own lives by jumping from Mt. Qua Qau to their deaths. I am only sorry they were not captured and hanged as they deserved. I know that sounds harsh, dear Elizabeth, but I have lost all my family to them. They never did find Fedon. Some say he was killed. Some say he escaped on a small boat and was drowned. No one really knows his fate.

Please write to me in Paraclete. Gerard is determined that we will restore all that we have lost. For myself, I do not believe that is possible. I think it is better to build something new, for our little Edward and all who have survived this great tragedy.

By the time your letter reaches us, we will undoubtedly have news of all our friends on the island. I do hope you are well and that all is settled between you and Mr. Darcy. We were nearly sisters, and you know that I hold you very dear in my heart. I will always remain

Your loving friend,
Barbara

As Elizabeth expected, of Poppy, she heard nothing. Perhaps Barbara was right. The only thing now was to plan for tomorrow. Barbara had her future in her son Edward. In her own household, a new life was about to begin…and hope for the future.

***

By August, Elizabeth delivered a daughter, and Emma Cordelia joined the long line of Darcys.

"I do hope you are not disappointed that it is a girl," Elizabeth said as she watched her husband cradle their infant in his arms.

"She is the loveliest child I have ever seen," he said.

"I suppose you are not disappointed then." Elizabeth laughed.

"What?" he asked absently. He tore his gaze away from his child and looked at her quizzically.

"Nothing, dearest."

It was then that there was a knock at the door.

"Come in," Darcy called distractedly.

***

Nothing could have surprised Darcy more than the sight he beheld. There, standing at the door, was George Wickham. At first, Darcy seemed at a loss, and gently handing the baby back to Elizabeth, he did something he supposed was even more of a shock to his wife. He crossed the room and shook Wickham's hand.

"I am glad I am welcome," Wickham said, smiling rakishly.

"Of course, you are," said Elizabeth. Darcy knew her well enough now to recognize when she was making an effort at being cordial. Wickham crossed the room to peer at the baby.

"My new nephew?" he asked.

"Niece," Elizabeth corrected him.

"Ah."

For a moment, all was silent, then Wickham turned to Darcy.

"Might I have a word, Darcy?" he asked. Then, looking at Elizabeth and then back to Darcy, "In private."

Darcy acquiesced immediately. He had expected a letter from Wickham, not the man himself. In several letters the two exchanged,

Darcy made it clear that Wickham could rely on him to purge all debts he had accrued provided Wickham brought some news of Poppy. Reliable, provable news.

They were soon seated in the morning room, tea set before them. Darcy, by this time, was quite agitated. "Well, man, speak up," he said the moment they were alone.

"It was like searching for a needle in a haystack," Wickham said, the scar on his cheek twitching. "There were over seven thousand of them in that mountain stronghold. They scattered to the four winds once it was over. I had men searching for a slave woman in a red kerchief with three mulatto children, an older boy about eight years of age, and two younger sisters, four and two. I saw many, many women and children. How was I to judge their ages? None of them could answer any of the questions you sent me, nor could they or would they tell me anything. Many of the rebels were being hanged for treason. All the captives were frightened. Many escaped into the jungle, and who knows if we will ever find any of them. Fedon escaped as well and was rumored to have drowned at sea, but no one knows. You do not know the chaos of it all, Darcy. Really." He stopped talking and looked up.

Darcy had known, perhaps from the beginning, that it was hopeless. At first, he felt, after all that he had overcome, that nothing was beyond the power of his will, and yet, there were always things that one could not control. He looked down at Wickham. It was particularly difficult if one had to rely on others, especially others who were notoriously unreliable.

Wickham saw the expression on his face. "I really did try, Darcy. Honestly," he said, reading Darcy's skeptical countenance. Oddly enough, Darcy believed him.

"I thank you for trying, George," Darcy said wistfully. Before Wickham could speak again, Darcy asked, "And Foster? Was he with you? How did he fare?"

"I cannot tell you that either, I am afraid. He was assigned to another regiment, and I have no idea what happened to him. In fact, I entrusted him with a letter to Lydia from me that he was to deliver to Meryton, if he reached these shores before me."

"And was the letter delivered?"

"I have no idea. I came to you first before going home."

This was a Wickham whom Darcy had never encountered before. A Wickham who put duty before his own desires.

"About those debts…" Wickham began.

"I will consider it." Ah, yes, there he was. The old Wickham lurking just below the surface.

Wickham sighed, stood, and offered his hand. Darcy took it. "Go home to your wife," he said, and left the room.

***

Darcy, at Elizabeth's urging, paid most of Wickham's debts, at least the ones that held the most promise of violence. The rest, he made clear, were Wickham's own responsibility. Elizabeth could expect no more than that, even for her sister's sake. Shortly afterward, she received a letter from Lydia. Wickham, for his part, returned to Longbourn, retrieved his wife, promptly impregnated her, and then left for France with his regiment.

Elizabeth took the news of Darcy's attempts to find Poppy amid the chaos of the failed rebellion with gratitude and with sorrow. It deepened her already all-consuming love for Darcy, that he had made such an effort to find her friend, and yet all had come to naught. She felt helpless and grief-stricken. *Poor Poppy.* What had become of her and her unfortunate children? Her dream of freedom ended in blood and chaos. Did she even survive? And if she did, what life was there for her?

October was again upon them, and Georgiana was in the music room practicing the piano. Elizabeth marveled at her dedication and remarked upon it after Georgiana finished a particularly difficult piece. Little Emma was in her arms. Elizabeth noticed early how much the baby seemed to enjoy hearing her aunt play.

"Well done, Auntie," Elizabeth said. "See, your niece is quite ecstatic."

Her sister-in-law turned on the piano bench and opened her mouth to say something, and then closed it again. She turned back the keyboard but did not respond.

"Georgiana, what is it?" Elizabeth asked.

"It is nothing, really," she said.

It was something, to be sure, so Elizabeth pressed on. "Please, you can tell me," Elizabeth continued, putting her hand on Georgiana's arm.

"I am afraid you will think me selfish. After all, Emma is still small and perhaps she should not travel," Georgiana said in a rush.

Now, Elizabeth was really confused. "Travel? Travel where? Perhaps you should start from the beginning," she said, smiling.

It was then that Georgiana told her that she had missed the last two seasons in town and how cooped up and isolated she felt here at Pemberley. It was especially trying for her during Darcy's long absence.

"Have you spoken to your brother about this matter?" Elizabeth asked. Georgiana's eyes grew wide.

"I dare not," she said. "He always seems to have much on his mind."

This, in fact, was true. Darcy did have a tendency to brood, and as the winter approached and the light grew short and grey, he drew further and further into himself.

"I do think that your brother might be persuaded to take you to London for a time," Elizabeth suggested, "and perhaps my sister Jane and Charles could join you as well." She was thinking aloud and saw Georgiana's face grow bright. Obviously, she should interject a note of caution.

"I am not saying that he will approve, and I am not saying that you may enjoy the entire season, but I do think that some arrangements can be made," she said. "I do not think I will accompany you, however. Emma is still very small, and I should not want to make such a long journey with her."

Georgiana's face fell. "He would never leave you, even for a while," she said dejectedly.

"He might be persuaded," was all that Elizabeth said.

***

Darcy could never refuse his wife anything, and so it was decided that he would take his sister to their house in town. Jane, Charles, and Simon would join them there for the season. Jane, who was always all kindness, asked Kitty to join them for a time as well. Lydia, however, who would have given one of her limbs to go, and in such exalted company, remained at home, since she was expecting. *At least,* Darcy thought, *I have Charles for company amongst all these women.*

Their first engagement was a grand ball given by a friend of Darcy's, Edmund Chauncey, and his wife, Wilhelmina. There were to be quite a few eligible young men about, and Georgiana was simultaneously excited and anxious and talked about it incessantly. Darcy was quite relieved when Jane took her sister's place in advising and preparing, and soon all were entering the magnificent house of Edmund Chauncey.

Charles was his usually affable self and, after some dances with his wife, approached Darcy, who was standing alone.

"Will you not dance?" he asked.

"As you can see for yourself, my partner is absent," he retorted.

Darcy, not one to make small talk, spent the rest of the evening either skulking about the host's art collection, or quietly observing Georgiana as she made her way among the eligible young men who flocked around her. She had changed much in the past few years. He had not noticed until this moment. She had become a woman.

When Charles found him again, he was engaged in conversation with his host on the sugar trade. The discussion was becoming quite heated when Darcy noticed his approach. Knowing his friend, undoubtedly, he would try to smooth over the feathers Darcy was deliberately ruffling.

"Surely, Darcy, you are not suggesting that the colonies in the Caribbean could function without slavery," Chauncey was saying. "After all, you put sugar in your tea the same as all the rest of us." He continued. "Can you imagine Englishmen toiling in the cane fields? Absurd." Chauncey began chuckling at Darcy's expense, and his sycophants followed his lead.

Darcy, for a moment, said nothing. Emboldened by his apparent success, Chauncey pushed his point further. "And that shirt you are wearing, made with American cotton, perhaps? Also produced by slave labour." The acolytes continued their chuckling. This gave Darcy his opening.

"Silk, actually," he said, and cocked his eyebrow. This time the chuckling was at Chauncey's expense. "Cheap sugar in our tea does not justify holding people in bondage." The amusement stopped.

Chauncey eyed him carefully. "You say this, even after you witnessed with your own eyes the atrocities of the rebellion in Grenada," Chauncey said prudently.

There was a momentary pause, and Darcy then chose his words carefully. "Can I not oppose slavery without supporting the violence of revolution?" he asked.

Chauncey was at a loss to respond. Bingley took the opportunity to insert himself into the conversation. "Jane would like to dance with you, brother," he said, smiling genially.

Darcy met Chauncey's eye once more. "If you will excuse me, gentlemen," he said solemnly, and with a slight bow of the head, withdrew with Bingley.

As he took his leave he could hear Chauncey say to the gentlemen in his company, "That was most extraordinary." *Yes, it was extraordinary. My entire life has become extraordinary.*

***

Darcy did return home in less than a month, and he left his sister in the capable hands of the Bingleys. Upon his arrival home, Elizabeth ran down the stairs into the entry hall and kissed him. He told her that Georgiana had several suitable young men pursuing her, but none who, by the time he left, really seemed to strike her fancy. To Elizabeth, it seemed just as well. If Georgiana was really interested in one of them, Darcy would be obliged to stay and keep a close watch. As it was, he could return to his estate, to her, and to his little daughter.

It seemed to Elizabeth that he was genuinely delighted to be home, but his ebullient mood did not last for long. As the weather became ever greyer, so did Darcy's humor. As soon as they finished breakfast, he would go on long rides through the estate, and John told her that it was even commented on by the servants that he would stand observing their toils for great lengths of time. He had also taken to reading a great many books on government, politics, and philosophy. Although he was an attentive husband and father, a certain pall had fallen over his spirit. Whenever his wife broached the subject, he assured her that there was nothing amiss. Elizabeth knew better, but she would bide her time.

It was late November. Darcy and Elizabeth were seated in the drawing room, the fire was lit, Emma was upstairs asleep, and a quiet evening was drowsily settling around them. Elizabeth was trying in vain to interest herself in a novel, but she really wanted to broach a subject with her husband. He had not been very approachable today, or any day since he returned from London. Her mother had warned her that husbands change from attentive and doting suitors to…how did she put it…husbands. Furtively, she glanced up from time to time, but he was trying to balance the books from the estate and seemed completely engrossed. She stared at him, willing him to look up.

When he did not, she spoke to him. "William," she called.

Still not looking up, he replied rather distractedly, "Yes?"

"I would like to talk to you about starting a school for the children of the village." He did not offer comment, so she continued. "I think the children living here at Pemberley could also attend. After all, during the winter season much of the farm work stops and…"

Before she could continue, he finally raised his head from his accounting books, and she could see quite clearly that his eyes were filled with tears. Immediately, she dropped her book and crossed the room to him. Before she reached him, he dabbed his eyes with the back of his hand. Elizabeth knelt down next to him and took his hand.

"Dearest, what is it?" she asked, her voice all concern.

"I feel quite the fool," he said, turning his head so that she would not see his face.

"You are anything but a fool. Tell me what is troubling you," she said. He got up and walked over to the fireplace, his face still turned away from her. He took some moments to gather himself.

Finally, he said, "I do not know what my place is in this world anymore. Everything that I believed about blood and breeding and social class has been…set on its head." He finally turned to look at her. "First, by you, Lizzy, and then by Foster, and then your dear Poppy, and even Wickham."

She should have realized his torment before. He had been so solicitous of her, so understanding of all that she had suffered. It had never occurred to her before this moment that all he endured for her sake had left scars upon him as well. Scars not just on his body, but upon his mind and spirit.

"You have been thinking a great deal about this."

"It has been preying on my mind."

At first, she said nothing. She wanted so to comfort him as he had comforted her. She began to think; the long rides, the mountains of books—he was seeking some way to reconcile the life he led here and that which he had experienced not so long ago. It was then that all became clear to her.

"I find that when something preys on one's mind, the best thing to do is do something," she said.

He paused for a moment, pondering. Then turned to look at her. "The school, perhaps?"

"It would be a start," she offered.

"You have been waiting to ask me this question for some time, have you not?" he asked, and smiled at her.

Her eyes danced. "Perhaps," she said and laughed.

"Yes, that is a good beginning, a very good beginning," he said. Still, his somber aspect returned. He sighed.

"But you are not satisfied," she stated, almost as a question.

"No, I suppose not," he said with a sigh. "It does not seem to be enough. There is such a wide world out there, outside of Pemberley. To think, not very long ago I would have been content to live out my life here, isolated, self-satisfied…"

"You do not feel that way now?" she asked, knowing the answer, but hoping to draw him out more. He finally looked at her.

"I suppose you heard all about my tirade at the Chaunceys' in London."

She stood and approached him. Taking his hands in hers, she looked into his face. "Jane wrote to me nearly every day that you were away, telling me all that you were not telling me."

"Of course." He looked away again.

"Is it not clear to you what needs to be done?"

He looked at her quizzically.

She continued. "There are many who are trying to change things in this country and abroad." She stopped for a moment to gather her thoughts. "For example, there are many who are working for the abolition of slavery throughout the empire. Perhaps—" She stopped short and looked at him expectantly. His eyes flashed.

"Good God, woman. Perhaps what?" He was nearly shouting.

She smiled at him and she could see his impatience. "Perhaps," she said, "you should stand for Parliament."

He said nothing, but looked at her, astonished. "I could not imagine myself speaking in Parliament."

She merely looked at him, smiling. She knew full well that if he could speak to that well-heeled rabble at a London ball, he could speak in Parliament.

"You can be the most infuriating woman," he said affectionately. "Parliament," he said again. He did not reject the idea outright, and it gave her hope.

"It may be quite easy for you to get an appointment to the House of Lords," she continued, warming to the subject.

"Or I could actually stand for the House of Commons," he said. Now it was her turn to be astonished.

"The House of Commons? Whatever would your dear Aunt Catherine say?" she teased. They both laughed.

"You know, we would have to spend every season in town—" she began but was cut short by a knock at the door.

"Yes, what is it?" he asked gruffly. John entered.

"I am sorry to intrude, sir, but this letter arrived for Mrs. Darcy."

"A letter? At this hour?" Darcy said crossly.

"It was brought by special messenger from Meryton," said John.

"Meryton?" Elizabeth took the letter from John's hands.

"Yes, madame, he arrived to deliver a letter from Mr. Wickham, and this message was waiting there for you. Your father sent it on."

"Thank you, John," she said and sat down on the settee to examine it. Elizabeth was mystified. It was too early for Lydia's baby to arrive, so what could it be?

"A messenger, you say," said Darcy.

"Yes, sir," he said. "And he made the extraordinary request to have a word with you. I told him that was impossible, but he insisted."

Darcy opened his mouth to speak. Elizabeth gave him one of her wifely looks. The old Darcy would tell John to send that upstart off without a word.

"I will be there directly," Darcy said, looking only at her. "Where is this fellow?"

"Waiting outside the kitchen door, sir," John answered.

"See that he is fed, and I will come and speak with him." John looked at his master as if he had taken leave of his senses.

"In the kitchen, sir?" he asked incredulously.

"Yes, yes, I will come to the kitchen. Tell him to wait," Darcy said, a little too gruffly. Elizabeth caught her husband's eye. "Thank you, John. That will be all," he continued in a more subdued tone.

As John left, Darcy sat down next to Elizabeth. She had, as yet, not opened the letter. Her hands were trembling.

"It is from a place called New Orleans," she said, "and it is addressed to Miss Elizabeth Bennet." She looked at Darcy. "I am afraid of what it contains. Could you open it and read it aloud to me, please?"

Darcy took her hand. "Of course," he said, and took the envelope. Opening it, he turned it toward her. She could see that it was written by someone who was still mastering the art of writing. Her heart leapt.

Dear Miss Lizbet,

It is Poppy, writing to you from my new home in New Orleans.

With that Elizabeth gave a cry and covered her mouth with her hands. Tears filled her eyes. "She is alive, William. Alive." She took the letter from her husband's hands and continued reading.

O, it is very gran here, and I am with my new husban, Francois Peschier. He was a planter in St. John's Parish. He was wit me at Belvidere and was helping Fedon. His wife give birth 'bout the same time as me. Yes, Miss Lizbet, I had one more chile of Edward Home. Francois wife gave birth at almos the same time, but she die. I took to nursing both chilren. That is how Francois and me, we begin togeder. Wen the war was ending, we escape wit Fedon. He go one way, we go anoder. We go to Sant Doming and then here to New Orleans. Francois is a good man, Miss Lizbet. He accep my chilren. We are helping wid building the city after the fire. We are going to plant rice, I tink. I wan to tank you for teching me reding and riting. I am lerning reding french now too. My chilren learning reding too. I hope we meet agin

some day. You can sen me letter here. Plese send a letter and let me no you alive.
    Your,
    Poppy

"Can they live freely in New Orleans?" Elizabeth asked when she could actually speak again.

"I do believe so," said Darcy. "I do believe so." She squeezed his hand and he kissed her forehead.

"Read your letter again, and I will go down and see what this fellow from Meryton wants."

She went immediately to Darcy's desk. "I will write her straight away," she said, beaming.

***

As Darcy walked through the hallway, he realized how fortunate he was, and how capricious life could be. He inadvertently touched his side. His near-death had brought him an entirely new life. Where once he had been so proud of his birth and rank, he found those things were no longer at the center of his existence. He had to admit to himself, he did retain a certain amount of pride, but it was in his accomplishments rather than his inheritance.

When Darcy entered the kitchen, the servants parted as if he were Moses at the Red Sea. There was a burly man with his back to him seated at the table. Darcy knew him at once. When he heard the commotion, he rose and turned toward Darcy.

"'Allo, Squire," said Foster, and extended his hand.

"Hello, my friend," said Darcy, and embraced him.

ABOUT THE AUTHOR

Maggie has always been a romantic at heart. She has spent most of her life teaching music in public schools. Her travels have taken her all over Europe, and she has lived in Africa and Asia. She refined her writing penning screenplays. *Elizabeth in the New World* her first novel.

Get in touch with Maggie:

Facebook: https://www.facebook.com/maggie.mooha

Twitter : https://twitter.com/mmooha

LinkedIn: https://www.linkedin.com/in/maggie-mooha-120a6624

Did you enjoy this book? Drop us a line and say so. We love to hear from readers, and so do our authors. To connect, visit www.boroughspublishinggroup.com online, send comments directly to info@boroughspublishinggroup.com. Friend us on Facebook and follow us on Twitter and Instagram. And be sure to sign up for our newsletter for surprises and new releases in your favorite subgenres of romance.

Are you an aspiring writer? Check out www.boroughspublishinggroup.com/submit and see if we can help you make your dreams come true.

Made in the USA
San Bernardino, CA
17 November 2018